Everyone is talking about Maxym M. Ma~~~

KINGDOM OF ~~~

"Keep an eye on Maxym M. Ma~ ~~~ ~~~ken, we have a bona fide genius in our mids~

—**Darynda Jones,** *New ~~~ ~~~ Times* bestselling author

"Original, breathtaking, absolutely fabulous."
—**C. L. Wilson,** *New York Times* & *USA Today* bestselling author

"A fresh new fantasy. Left me with a happy sigh and a fervent wish for a beast of my own. Highly recommend!"

—**Jeffe Kennedy,** RITA award-winning author

"Maxym Martineau weaves an irresistible blend of adventure, magic, and romance. A unique world full of danger and intrigue and a delightful ensemble of characters will leave fans...breathlessly awaiting more. Prepare to be charmed!"

—**Amanda Bouchet,** *USA Today* bestselling author of The Kingmaker Chronicles

"*Kingdom of Exiles* captivated me with its distinctive fantasy world of exiled Charmers, enchanted beasts, and alluring assassins. A fantastic tale of magic, romance, and adventure—I can't wait to read more."

—**L. Penelope,** award-winning author of *Song of Blood & Stone*

"A strong female lead and a band of lovable assassins? Count me in! I cannot wait to see what more Maxym has to offer."

—**Alexa Martin,** author of *Intercepted*

THE FROZEN PRINCE

MAXYM M. MARTINEAU

Published by Sourcebooks Fire, an imprint of Sourcebooks
P.O. Box 4410, Naperville, Illinois 60567-4410
(630) 961-3900
sourcebooks.com

Printed and bound in Canada.
MBP 10 9 8 7 6 5 4 3 2 1

For my husband, who would go to any and all lengths to help me achieve my dreams.

OSLO'S RUINS

LENDRIA

HIREATH

MIDNIGHT
JESTER

DEVIL'S HOLLOW   Kitska Forest

CRUOR

Penumbra Glades

NEPHESTE'S
RUINS

SILVIS'S RUINS

Glacial
Springs

Luma Lake

WILHEIM

The Gaping Wound

TYRUS'S RUINS

EASTREND

Lightwood Forest

ORTEGA KEY

Kings Isle

YUNA'S RUINS

Queens Isle

ONE

THE FROZEN PRINCE
50 YEARS AGO

The heavy beat of the approaching army's drums echoed through my rib cage. My horse shifted beneath me with a nicker, and my grip on the reins tightened. Not for the first time, Rhyne's forces had crossed the sea between our countries and landed on the flat edge of Penumbra Glades. Our armada had lost, and now the small town of Moeras was counting on me and my men to protect them. The people might have fled for safety, but their homes were here. Their *lives* were here.

And if I couldn't save them, I didn't deserve to call myself their prince.

"Ready yourselves!" I urged my mare forward, and her hooves churned through the soft muck of the marshy battlefield. Thick cattails battered her legs, and the harsh breeze carried the swampy stench of salt and earth. Flat and treeless, the expanse stretched before us, giving my troops full view of the amassing army. Glinting in the morning sun, their severe jade armor sent a chill running down my spine.

For years, that color had haunted my dreams. But no matter how many times I tried, no matter how many letters I sent in hopes of negotiating peace, the royal house of Rhyne would not listen.

All they wanted was my head on a pike: a life for a life, a prince for a princess.

Amira. I pushed away the memory of her golden hair and gentle smile. War was no place to get lost in the past. I had other lives depending on me.

With a sharp click of my tongue, my horse leapt into a canter and made for the front line. Thousands of men and women clad in steel armor stared back at me, the griffin crest of Wilheim etched across their hearts. They stood at the ready, their backs ramrod straight and gazes locked forward, the white banners with their purple emblems snapping in the wind. We had no drums. We had no horns. We had no need to declare our presence. This was our home, and the quiet town at our backs was the only reminder we needed.

We would not lose.

As I came to a halt, one man broke rank and guided his stallion to my side. A scraggly beard crawled down his neck, and when he tipped his head in my direction, umber eyes locked with mine. He gripped my shoulder with a smile.

"Let's get this over with. There's an ale with my name on it waiting back at camp." A laugh rumbled through his chest, cut short by a wet cough.

Dread stirred in my gut. "Thaleus?"

My general waved me off. "It's nothing a little ale won't fix. Best get on with this so I can wet my whistle." Straightening, he pounded a closed fist to his chest a few times, seemingly loosening whatever had caught in his throat. The coughing died, but my unease didn't.

This plague—or whatever it was—was just as skilled at killing my troops as Rhyne had proven to be, and if we didn't get out of this gods-forsaken marsh soon, I wouldn't have a kingdom left to defend.

Before I could say anything more, a low horn sounded from across the marsh. It picked up an octave right at the end before dying completely, signaling Rhyne's attack. The ground rumbled from the sudden quake of hooves and feet, and thousands of jade soldiers crashed through the muddy banks toward our ranks.

Beside me, Thaleus took charge. "Archers!" His voice rang out loud and clear, and the tiniest sliver of relief settled my fear. We'd live to fight another battle together. We had to.

Archers raised their bows to the skies at his command, and Thaleus unsheathed his sword. "Nock!" His bellow was followed by the stretching of string and arrows clacking against wood. Shoulders tense, the archers held position without wavering. I turned my back to them and faced the oncoming threat. Tightened my grip on my sword.

"Steady," Thaleus called. Blood rushed to my ears, carrying with it the frenzied beat of my heart. I took in a slow breath. Let it out. Repeated the action. Sounds dimmed, and all I could feel was the vibration of pounding feet. The time was here.

"Loose!" Thaleus's order preceded a volley of arrows that blackened the sky. The sun winked out, and our world was cast into temporary shadow. The low whistle of wood and feathers sang through the air…until metal-tipped heads clanked against armor or sank into flesh, and the definitive sound of bodies hitting the earth interrupted the steady cadence of Rhyne's war drums. Angered bellows answered our attack, and they broke formation to charge.

Thaleus signaled for another round of arrows before yanking his own sword out of its sheath. Turning to the men at our backs, he raised his weapon high. "Infantry with me. Riders with Prince Aleksander. We will not fall!"

The company of horsemen to my left waited with bated breath, their mounts pawing anxiously at the ground. Among them were three imposing figures clad in mercury armor. Sentinels. Wilheim's elite force of soldiers tasked with protecting the city and the royal family. An army of them would have destroyed Rhyne's men in a matter of days. Instead, thousands of men and women, soldiers I'd grown to love over the years, were forced to give up their lives so that my home could be protected.

Despite the war, despite my arguments with Father, the Sentinels of Wilheim remained stationed atop the gleaming diamond and marble walls—save these three. My royal guard.

Frustration brewed in my chest, but I bottled the anger tight and focused on Rhyne's forces. Father might be able to deny our troops the aid of Sentinels, but he'd never stop me from leading the charge.

"For Lendria!" My war cry burned my throat at the same moment I dug my heels into my mare's sides. She rocketed forward, and my riders followed. Spears and swords glinted in the sun as we charged toward the thick of the enemy ranks. With every pounding beat of my horse's hooves, my pulse jumped higher. We rode without fear. We rode without hesitation. We rode without thinking of anything except what lay before us. Our horses crashed into the first wave of men, and soldiers crumpled to the ground as we effortlessly broke the line.

Spears shook and splintered against shields, swords clashed against armor and men. Blood sprayed all around us, and the earthy scent of the marsh was soon coated with an iron tang. And still we rode. I arced my sword high and crashed it against a soldier, meeting the soft spot between neck and shoulder. He fell to the earth only to be replaced by another, and another. Swinging to my left, I caught sight of the morning sky aglow with something other than pale sunlight. Enemy arrows soaked in oil and licking flames careened toward my brigade.

"Shields!" With my free hand, I stripped a shield from my

horse's side and flung it over my head. Arrows thumped into the soft wood, cooking the iron holds and heating my skin. I winced with every hit as each vibration shook through my bones. Once the rain of arrows died, I lowered my arm and continued to push my mare forward. The jarring clatter of armor meeting metal filled the air, and I swiped my blade at an advancing jade-clad soldier. His head hit the ground.

Part of me felt sick. The spray of blood against my horse's legs turned her snowy-white coat a speckled red, and the sound of death was everywhere. But war was never pretty, and I'd be damned if I left my men to fight a battle I'd started, intentionally or not.

Beside me, the Sentinels were making easy work of our enemies. They'd dismounted and were cleaving through the ranks. Bodies fell in heaps around them, but they did not flinch.

Stomach churning, I stared out over the blood-soaked expanse. The muddy banks and shallow pools of water had turned a murky reddish brown, and the lifeless eyes of many, so many, stared up at me as I passed. It didn't matter if their armor was jade or steel, their expressions were the same: lost. I hated it. This was a useless war with no end, but one side had to win eventually. One side had to cave.

No, *we* would persevere. *We* would win.

An enemy rider bolted toward me, and our swords met with a harsh clang. The scrape of metal rang through my ears as I thrust my blade against his thigh, knocking him off-balance. He slid in his saddle, and his horse veered. I was about to lunge after him when a brilliant orb of sparking magic careened between us. It singed the air with electricity and cooked everything it passed until it crashed into the ground. My gaze snapped to the enemy forces and the singular woman standing clear in their midst. She'd opted for leather armor that mirrored the drab browns and sage greens of our surroundings, keeping her position camouflaged until she struck. But now, with a burnt path of grass and cattails leading directly to her feet, she was all too visible.

Mage.

Flexing her fingers, she brought her hands before her chest and summoned another crackling ball of energy. It raged and sparked between her palms, and she looked up with a ferocious grin.

Thaleus galloped toward me like an arrow loosed from a bow. "How did Rhyne manage to get their hands on a mage?"

My gaze dropped to the ashy earth before us. "Explains how they tore through our ships so easily." Mages didn't trifle with the wars of Lendria. And yet there she was, summoning another sphere of lightning that could annihilate our forces with ease. She had to be stopped.

Leaning into my mare's neck, I nudged her sides and called over my shoulder as we galloped forward. "You take command of the riders. I'll deal with her."

"Aleksander!" Thaleus shouted at my back. Enemy forces surged toward me, and I cut them down, ignoring the rising bile in my throat as more blood spilled. Blessed by magic of their own, the Sentinels chased after me with breakneck speed. For the first time since they'd been assigned to my guard, panic flickered through their barely visible gazes. Their movements were jerky, their kills sloppy. Just how dangerous was this mage?

As if in answer, the glowing orb between her fingers finally reached its pinnacle. She thrust it from her hands directly toward me. Her cry rose above the trumpeting horns and beating drums, and I swerved my horse to the side. The snarling mass of energy streaked by, searing the left side of my armor. Heat cooked my skin, and I cried out even as my mare gave a frightened squeal and reared onto her hind legs. Fumbling to grip the reins in time, I lost my balance and smacked into the earth, reddish muck squelching through the slits in my armor and coating my skin. Black dots danced across my vision as the cattails swam in and out of focus. A dull ringing reverberated in my skull.

Somewhere behind me, the Sentinels shouted. We'd separated ourselves from the majority of our forces, and a barrage of enemy foot soldiers converged to take advantage. Rolling to the side, I avoided the deadly arc of a sword and swept the feet out from under a jade warrior. He responded with a swift punch to my jaw. Pinning me beneath his weight, he brought his sword down fast. I countered with my blade and grimaced as the lingering burn of magic transformed into a bone-deep blaze of pain down my arm. Grunting, I forced all my strength into my hands and pushed. He fell onto his back, and my blade met his jugular. A wet gurgle spewed from his lips, and then he went limp. Dead. I scrambled to my feet and stumbled forward a short distance until a familiar swell of static electricity clouded the air.

From a few feet away, the mage smiled. "And now this war will finally end."

I had no time to dodge her attack. My strength was already waning, and while her first attempt had missed, this one wouldn't. The last thing I'd see was the slash of her grin across bloodstained skin. Gritting my teeth, I crossed my arms in front of me in a futile, last-ditch attempt to protect my heart.

And then a blade so black it must have been carved from the night itself exploded through her ribs. Her magic died in an instant, and she sputtered, wild hands flailing against an attack neither of us saw coming. She took one look at me, blood trickling from her mouth, and crashed to her knees, then to the ground.

Gone.

With a slow blink, I focused on the space behind her. A

man clad in sable clothes stood without moving, his gloved hand holding a black blade dipped in red. Confusion dulled the threat of battle, and I took a careful step forward. He wore the attire of a Wilheimian noble, with filigree patterns and brocades etched in fine stitching along his vest. His shoes were somehow remarkably clean, his clothes only showing the faintest signs of dirt and blood. Helmetless, his styled pompadour was on display, and not a single hair dared to jut out of place, despite the wind.

With a belabored sigh, he righted his silver-rimmed spectacles. "Thank you for distracting her, Prince Aleksander."

"It's you I should be thanking." I did a quick glance behind me and saw my guard had taken care of our nearby enemies and were waiting, gauging the distance between me and this mystery assassin. Threat or no? He wore no affiliating emblem. No colors from either army. Still, he had saved my life. As a show of faith, I sheathed my sword. "Why kill the mage? Are you Lendrian?"

"Lendrian?" The man raised a careful brow. "I suppose by geographical terms, the answer is yes."

Geographical terms? My brow furrowed. "I see. Then you should return to camp with me. I'd like to reward you for your courage."

"There's no need." With a flourish of his hand, the blade disappeared. Into a hidden sheath? I couldn't tell. It was as black as his clothing, so perhaps. The man ran his hands over his vest until they came across a stray piece of dirt. He flicked it away. "It seems as though this victory is yours."

He gestured to the fields. Sometime during my standoff with the mage, the drums and horns had been silenced. There were still cries of agony rising and falling with the wind, but the anxiety of battle had diminished. The roar, gone. Penumbra Glades was a wasteland of blood and bone. We'd held the line and protected the town of Moeras, but not without casualty. As the last bit of adrenaline fled my body, fatigue settled deep in my bones, and I let out a quiet sigh.

Slowly, I turned back to the man. "So it seems."

He nodded once, a curt jut of his chin. "I must be going. Stay vigilant, Prince Aleksander."

My gaze dropped as he stepped back into something dark as an oil slick. Rhyne must have been in a rush to douse their arrows. Taking a few quick strides, I closed the distance between us. "Wait. I insist you return to camp so I can properly thank you."

Something flickered through his ice-green gaze. "As I said, that's not necessary. I am a member of Cruor. The mage was a job. I can procure proof if necessary."

Cruor?

My father had once mentioned a guild of elite assassins living on the fringe of our country, but I'd never paid him much mind. The rumors surrounding their abilities were exactly that—rumors. No one could move with the shadows. No one could form weapons out of night.

And yet...

I stared at the dark patch beneath his feet. Shiny like ink and yet wispy as mist, it curled up in small billows. And the blade, had that been one of their famed weapons? Something truly crafted from death itself? Curiosity burned deep in my chest, and I removed my helmet. Shock-white hair spilled over my eyes, and I brushed it to the side. "Proof won't be necessary. But I'd still like you to return to camp with us. Both as thanks, and so I can learn more about you and your work." I waited for a beat to see if he'd answer, but he only stared at me with a look of disbelief. "What's your name?"

The man's gaze faltered. "Kostya, my prince."

I grinned, extending my hand. "Call me Aleksander. There are enough people around to call me *prince*."

He pressed his lips together in a fine line, as if contemplating the request. Finally, he shook my hand. "I couldn't possibly deny a request from the royal family. Shall we?"

"No, you couldn't," I joked. I gripped his shoulder, and he stiffened beneath me. I instantly let my hand fall away, but stayed by his side as we strode across the marsh, casting him the occasional curious glance.

A man born of shadows. A man born of death. The gods only knew what kind of life he led—but I was eager to discover that for myself.

Two

NOC
PRESENT DAY

Thin, grasping clouds stretched across the darkening sky outside Cruor. With the descent of the sun over the spired treetops, the bone-scraping calls of monsters began to erupt in earnest. Yet even they weren't as unsettling as the lifeless bodies lying before me. Raising the dead wasn't something I enjoyed, but it had to be done. Beside me, Calem, Kost, and Ozias stood at attention, their faces stoic.

Letting loose a breath, I gripped the back of my neck. "This it?" I couldn't help but feel reluctant to see this grim task through.

Kost gave a tight nod. "We could certainly find more, but—"

"No. It's fine."

He shifted weight from his left foot to his right. "Darrien's renouncement has everyone on edge—not to mention the number of people who left with him. Our remaining members are scared. We should consider searching for more."

I shot him an icy glare. "There are rules, Kost. And I refuse to break those rules simply to bolster our ranks."

"We'll be fine." Ozias placed a thick hand on my shoulder, chasing away the frustration building in me. "Even if they don't want to take on bounties, we can teach our new family how to use the shadows for protection."

"He's right." Calem offered a lax smile. "We've got this."

Nodding once, I brought my gaze back to the dead at my feet. Mouths agape, eyes wild and lost. The stench of iron and rotting flesh hit my nostrils, and I clenched my jaw. We had three days' time to raise a corpse before our magic would no longer work. These bodies were pushing their final hours.

Kneeling beside the first man, I willed the power of Zane, the first of our kind, to flow from my core and streak to my fingertips. The nails along my right hand honed to fine points, fashioning blades sharper than swords. I sliced open the man's chest straight through to the bone. His unmoving heart dominated my vision.

I carved open my palm and poured blood over the wound. My power, Zane's power, to restore life seeped into the man. The heart pumped once. One achingly slow and shuddering beat.

Then the heart beat again, this time with more fervor and less strain. Once the cadence was steady, I placed my palm flat against the man's open chest and willed the wound to reseal. When I pulled my hand away, nothing but smeared blood and smooth skin remained. Fatigue hit hard and fast, and my shoulders rolled forward.

Three more to go.

Kost, Calem, and Ozias waited in silence until I finished. Until the four bodies before me were breathing on their own. With their closed eyes, they could've been sleeping. But I remembered what this moment had been like for me. How the darkness of death had started to shift to something unfamiliar and gray, until Talmage had woken me from it all.

Just as the moon crested over the dark wood of Kitska Forest, I cleared my throat. "Rise."

It was such a quiet, simple command, and yet it rolled through us, over us, with an electric wave of energy. Behind us, Calem sucked in a sharp breath, and I jerked my chin in his direction. The line of silver threading around his muted-red irises flared, and his body tensed. Kost and Ozias shifted closer, worry clearly visible in the subtle tensing of their muscles.

"Calem?" My gaze darted between him and the new assassins waking at my feet.

A full-body tremor raced through him, and then he shook his head as if chasing away a bad memory. The mercury hue of his gaze vanished with the abrupt coughing and sputtering of our newly raised brothers and sisters.

Shoulders tight, I dragged my gaze back to them. For now, Calem could wait. "Welcome back."

The people before us were all so vastly different, and yet I'd just handed them the same fate: life as an assassin of Cruor. The first man was a Wilheimian trader who'd gained the reputation of a swindler. He'd cheated the wrong person out of a valuable rug woven by a particularly skilled mage, and so his bounty had been handed to us.

He pushed himself off the ground, straightening his now-ripped midnight-blue tunic. Shaky fingers attempted to fasten the silver toggles in a bizarre show of modesty. He gave up halfway through and instead let his fingers tremble by his sides.

The woman beside him followed suit, standing with wary eyes. Short, spiked hair stood perfectly on end, and she folded her arms to her chest, hiding the exposed skin with a look of sheer defiance. In tattered tunics and bland breeches, the remaining two were dressed for function, not appearance. They clung to each other, too scared to move or do anything more than seek comfort in each other's touch.

Slipping my hands into the pockets of my loose trousers, I gave them a nod. "You've been given a second chance at life as a member of Cruor."

The older man coughed. "Cruor? The assassins' guild?"

"Yes."

"I see…" He scratched his jaw. "Is Darrien around?"

My back stiffened. "How do you know Darrien?"

"He was a client of mine. Sold him a rare tapestry a couple years back."

He fidgeted, deep-blue eyes darting from the manor to me and back again. It wasn't unusual for newly raised brethren to be on edge. Being thrust back into our reality was jarring. And yet…

"What's your name?"

"Quintus," he responded.

His name didn't ring any bells, but I'd never seen him at any reputable vendor stand. It wasn't overly surprising that Darrien had seedy connections outside of Cruor. What he did with his bits was on him, but if this dealer thought selling wares to Darrien would put him in good graces with me, he was sorely mistaken.

"Darrien is no longer with us."

"Ah." Weighted silence stretched between us, then he frowned. "I'm…sad to hear that." If he held any warmer emotions for Darrien, I couldn't tell. And I wasn't eager to correct his misunderstanding. He shook his head once, and his expression cleared. "So, assassins, yes? I'm not sure I'm cut out for that kind of work."

"You don't have to kill if you don't want to." I shifted my weight onto my heels and stared at each one of them pointedly. "I won't force that on any of you. There are other methods for earning your keep."

"Do we have to stay?" The woman's voice was surprisingly low.

"No, but I'd highly recommend it. No one else can teach you how to command the shadows like we can. And no one else will understand your predicament like we do. Here, you're accepted. Out there"—I gestured in the direction of Wilheim—"you're exiled."

"Seems to me like we were better off dead," Quintus scoffed.

I lifted a shoulder. "That can be arranged. If you'd rather return to death than lead this life, I'd understand. It would be quick. Painless."

The couple gasped together, and the young man tucked the woman's head into his chest. With a flicker of boldness, he met my gaze. "We never got the chance to live. Not together."

"I know. That's why you're here—your families paid to have you raised. To give you that chance." For a moment, my mind slipped away to the woman waiting for me in our room. Leena. I'd found her because of Cruor, and now this couple could find joy in each other too. As long as they never returned home. I cleared my throat. "That said, you won't be welcome in your old town. They made it clear that your kinsmen wouldn't know how to accept your new...life."

The young man suppressed a shiver. With a tight grimace, he nodded once. "We'll stay, then. But no killing." He glanced down at the woman, and her watery brown eyes mirrored his sentiment. With an almost imperceptible nod, she agreed.

The spiky-haired woman shrugged. "I'll kill if I have to. But I know for a fact no one paid to have me raised. So, what the hell am I doing alive?"

Her teakwood gaze burned with a fire I'd learned to recognize: resilience. She was a survivor. A fighter. And judging by her wiry frame and the pop of muscles along her arms, she wasn't against throwing a punch or two.

The tension knotting in my shoulders faded, and I raised a brow. "Two guild members heard of your death and requested I raise you. Practically threatened murder if I didn't. Iov and Emelia tend to get what they want."

Her mouth fell open. "Iov and Emelia are assassins? Sign me the fuck up. Where are they?"

Chuckling, I shook my head. "In due time."

"I'm still not convinced." Quintus glared at me and then my brothers, and my smile turned to a grimace. "Why am I here?"

"You were a by-product of a job. Someone wanted you dead and then raised so you could live with the knowledge of your demise."

He paused for a brief moment, as if contemplating my response, and then angled his chin high. "And what, you're our *leader*? I don't even know you."

Calem hissed and took an agitated step forward. "Watch your tone." His nostrils flared wide, and the loose bun of blond hair threatened to topple over with the jolt of his movements. The mercury thread around his irises flared. Always ready for a fight. Ozias gripped his shoulder and held him in place while Kost subtly edged closer.

Maybe it was Calem's sudden outburst, or Quintus's obvious disdain, or perhaps even the reminder that Darrien could be working against us even in this. But whatever its cause, a dark impulse flooded me, and I extended my arm forward. My fingers itched to form a fist. To clench tight and command my blood in the trader's system to come to a screeching halt. A phantom burn spasmed on my inner wrist.

Kost's gaze riveted to me, wide and full of shock. That look sent a wave of panic and uncertainty through me, and I dropped my hand to my side.

Using my blood to rob him of his free will, his ability to *breathe*, shouldn't have even been a thought in my mind. And yet, for a moment... Dropping my gaze, I spied the ink-black scythe on my wrist. The oath. Was its magic the culprit?

Clearing his throat, Kost took over. "If this life displeases you, Noc can swiftly and *painlessly* end your life. That said, such blatant disrespect will not be tolerated at Cruor."

"This is our home," I said, regaining control of my shaky

emotions and clenching my jaw tight. "If you cause a disturbance in it, we will have problems. Understood?"

Paling, Quintus managed a shaky nod.

"Good." With our new members safely raised and somewhat agreeable to their new fates, adrenaline left me in a rush. A deep ache settled in my bones, and my eyes grew heavy.

Ozias took charge, clapping his hands together and moving to stand before the new recruits. "All right, let's get you all cleaned up and assigned to rooms." Calem joined him, an easy smile on his lips and no trace of the strangeness from earlier lingering in his gaze. Kost gave me a gentle push toward the porch, and the two of us headed back together.

"What was that?" he asked, voice low.

"It's nothing." I rotated my wrist. There was still a faint warmth around the mark that I couldn't shake.

"It's not nothing. It's the oath, isn't it?" He pinned the damned mark with a knowing glare.

"Maybe." No one had denied Cruor's Oath before. Whenever we accepted a bounty, the mark simply appeared and would remain inked onto our skin until the job was done. If we tried to renege on our promise, our life would be sacrificed in exchange. No one had ever risked such a fate. We had no idea how long it would take for my life to end...or what would happen to me in the days leading up to my inescapable fate.

"Noc..."

"I don't want anyone to worry." I paused before the back doors to Cruor. I didn't want anyone inside overhearing our conversation. "There's no reason for alarm just yet. I'm still me. I'm still in control. I just... I just need some rest." My mind wandered to Leena. To her comforting touch and soft reassurances.

Kost hesitated, but eventually nodded. "We'll talk about

assignments in the morning, then." Even the thought of doling out more bounties added to my weariness, and I ran a weak hand over my face. We had too many jobs and not enough willing applicants. But I'd never force someone to accept Cruor's Oath, especially when I was still searching for a way to escape from the weight of mine.

"Prepare me a list of those who are willing. I'll review it first thing tomorrow."

"Of course." With that, he stepped into a plume of shadows and disappeared. Which left me to return to my room, body fatigued and desperately in need of rest, but heart warming at the thought of seeing Leena again.

———◆———

I'd never get used to the sight of Leena.

For a moment, all I could do was stare. Her mouth was barely parted as she slept, her cheeks lightly flushed. Wearing nothing more than one of my white work shirts, she looked like a goddess—mussed hair and all. She'd kicked off the silk sheets down to her ankles, but her toes remained covered. She couldn't stand to have them exposed while she slept. My lips quirked at this small revelation. We were still learning so much about each other. Understanding. Growing. It'd only been three days since we'd returned to Cruor from Hireath, and if the guild hadn't demanded my constant attention, I would've spent every moment, waking and sleeping, with her.

A dwindling candle on the verge of burning through its wick flickered on the oak nightstand beside her. The faint orange light played against the shimmering silver font of a book, splayed open with the pages against the wood. *The Magic of Words*. I still remembered the way she'd tried to sneak through the library to catch me reading what felt like an age ago, back when we were strangers.

She wasn't a puzzle anymore—I knew where she fit. Where we both fit. I'd never felt more whole.

The candle gave a sudden flicker as the flame devoured more of its wick, and her face fell briefly into shadows. *She wears them well.*

No. I couldn't think like that, but... She was so painfully *mortal.* I'd almost lost her to Wynn's charm. She could've *died.* And I'd only just learned what it was like to hold someone in my arms again. What it meant, how it *felt,* to express love and devotion without deadly ramifications.

I'd never lose her again.

A soft hum escaped Leena's parted lips. "Noc." She shifted, turning on her side and extending her arm out across the space where I should've been. Her fingers curled toward her palm. A silent beckon. I stripped out of my clothes, dropping them to the snowy rug stretching across the hardwood floor. Slowly, I eased myself into bed. The mattress shifted with my added weight, bringing her closer to the middle.

Stifling a yawn, Leena brought her hand to her mouth and opened her eyes. And damn if her gaze didn't light up at the sight of me. The barest hint of a smile touched her lips, and she tilted her chin my direction. "Hey, there."

"*Anam-cara.*" The ancient term used by Charmers, signifying they'd chosen a pair bond. Leena had *picked* me. After so many years of locking my emotions away, just the thought of that brought warmth to my heart. I pressed a kiss to the crown of her head.

She snuggled contentedly against my chest. "I love you."

"I love you too."

Leaning back to give me the full weight of her stare, she pulled her brows into a slight frown at whatever she read on my face. "Long day?"

"The longest." Securing the dead had taken some time, not to mention the physical strain of actually raising them. I wrapped my arms around her, allowing the weight of my troubles to melt away. For a moment, we simply held each other and took comfort in the silence that stretched between us. The sheets rustled as Leena pressed deeper into my side, resting her head on my chest. Her breath was warm against my skin, and she trailed a light finger down my sternum. I could tell she wanted to ask more, to unearth why my day had been so stressful. But she waited, busying herself with a slow exploration of my body.

Minutes dragged by until she sighed, resting her palm flat against me. "Did something happen?"

I placed my hand over hers. "No, nothing like that."

She slipped out of my embrace and pushed herself into a sitting position. The movement caused the collar of her shirt to slip down her shoulder, exposing smooth skin. "Then what is it?"

I traced the curve of her neck with a brush of my thumb. "There's just a lot on my mind right now."

"Like what you mentioned back in Hireath? About your past?"

I stilled. "No. Not that."

"You can trust me, you know. I want to know everything about you." She cupped the side of my face, sweeping delicate fingers across the faint crescent-moon scar on my cheekbone. "Like this—where did this come from?"

She always circled back to my past, the part of me I didn't want her to know. Former lives were better left in the dirt—that was the rule of becoming a Cruor assassin. And aside from Kost, no one knew anything about who I'd been. It was safer to keep my identity buried. Safer, especially, for my incredibly mortal *anam-cara*.

Back at Hireath, I'd promised her everything, secrets and all. But I'd underestimated how difficult it would be to find the words— the courage—to risk so much.

She leaned in close, her breath soft against the faint mark on my cheek. "Give me this, at least."

Chills raked my body, and I sat up so I could press my lips to the hollow of her throat. "There's not much to tell. I was just a boy, sparring with my father." I nipped at her skin, and she shivered. "He nicked me with the tip of his sword. Mother nearly castrated him on sight." At the thought of my parents, long dead, a sudden pang tightened my chest. If they were still living, what would they think of their son now?

Leena must not have felt the monstrous weight suddenly caving in the room. "What were they like? Your parents?"

Tensing, I paused with my lips poised just above her collarbone. "They were great." I dragged my fingers down the soft curve of her hips. When I skirted them closer to her thighs, she arced into my hand.

"Tell me about them."

"Now?"

She nodded. "I want to know about your past."

My past. The heavy silver ring on my finger winked up at me in the candlelight, the squared emerald a perfect cage of magic that needed to remain intact at all costs. I pulled my hand away and looked to the ceiling. "I'm happy with the life I have now. The one before Cruor was full of heartache. A lot of people I loved died."

"I still want to know about it." She snared my chin and forced me to meet her unyielding gaze. *So much fire.* My heart stilled as she ripped away my defenses and left me raw. "Why is it so hard to talk about?"

I let out a heavy sigh. "Because I don't like who I was."

Her answering smile was so unbelievably tender. "Noc, this life I have, here…" She gestured to the walls of Cruor before wrapping her hands in mine. "I wouldn't have it unless *you* ended up here. Unless you went through everything you did. I love you now because of who you are, and you couldn't be that person without your past."

"But the damage I've done—"

"I will always see you, Noc. You, not the monster you think you are."

I cupped her face in my hands as warmth bloomed in my chest. "I love you."

Even so, I'd been selfish before. I'd tossed logic to the wayside to allow myself to feel, and it had nearly killed her. The curse might be gone, but Cruor's Oath wasn't. The bold etching of an onyx scythe taunted me from my inner wrist. One day, when this bounty was gone, when we had one less issue to deal with, then maybe I'd risk another challenge for us to face.

"I love you too." Leena's tired gaze slipped from my face to my wrist. She glared at the oath, but placed a gentle kiss on it just the same. "We'll get rid of this."

"We will." I wanted to believe it. I *needed* to believe it.

Not a single member of my guild had ever denied the oath's magic. We had no idea how long it would be until the ax came down. But if my past had taught me anything, it was that the blow *would* come. It was only a matter of when.

"Hey. Let's get some sleep. We can talk later, but we *will* talk. Okay?"

Sighing, I slumped into the mattress and pulled her with me, tucking her to my chest. "I promise."

Her answering hum purred against my heart. "Good."

Peaceful silence stretched between us, and I stroked her hair as I stared at the dying candle flame. Lazy fingers dipped low to the space where the hem of her shirt met her waist, and my eyes grew heavy. Her steady breath was a lullaby that dulled my senses, and awareness trickled away. I almost didn't hear the high-pitched screech of a monster calling from the forest, but it cut through Leena's quiet breathing and drew me back from the shores of sleep. Slowly, I peeled open my eyes to find the balcony doors propped open, a faint breeze toying with the thick pleated curtains.

A disgruntled, sleep-filled mumble escaped from Leena's lips. She must have heard the cry as well. Chuckling, I untangled myself and strolled across the bedroom to the parted curtains. The moon sat low over Kitska Forest, desperately trying to shed its cool ivory light on the undergrowth, but the dense branches of twisting trees stitched together to form an impenetrable barrier of gnarled extremities and fluttering leaves. A low howl broke through the reverie and chased a flock of birds high into the night.

"Noc?"

"Coming." I shut the door and drew the curtains tight, sealing away the chilly air and the errant calls of monsters. As I turned my back to the balcony, my feet rooted to the floor in horror. Leena was standing at the foot of our bed, wild hair splayed about her shoulders. Her accusatory stare—wide and bloodshot—pinned me to the spot. Mouth ajar, she worked her lips as if to speak but came up empty.

She looked like death itself.

Panic lit a fire in my muscles, and I rushed toward her. "Leena? *Leena!*"

A wet gasp sputtered from her lips, and her hands shot to her paling neck. Blue fingers scratched and dug at paper-thin skin, creating a bloody necklace that dripped over her collarbones.

I pried her hands away, terrified for her. "Gods, stop it. Leena, what's wrong?"

Fingerprint bruises formed in ghostly impressions along her neck of their own accord, and suddenly I was viscerally reminded of the first time we met. The feel of her weight suspended by my grip as she clawed for air. The way her eyes glassed over and her vocal cords flared against the palm of my hand. The way it felt to almost kill the woman I would come to love more than anything. I could've destroyed her then.

You could still destroy her now.

"Noc." Her raspy call barely registered. An unfamiliar red film descended over my vision, and the dark shadows turned to bloody blades. Waiting. Eager. They were toxic in their allure, and my breathing hitched.

What is this feeling? It wasn't wholly mine, and yet it felt so *right*. The red seeping into my vision deepened. A burning pain blossomed in the base of my skull and fractured outward like broken glass. The searing heat branded my mind and promised it would all be over if I'd just do what I was hired to do. *Kill.*

I wrapped my hand delicately around her throat, matching my fingers up with the blueprint of death already laid out before me. She didn't shy away, only stared back at me with parted, bluing lips. The feel of her smooth skin against my callused fingers jolted something deep inside me, and I stared in horror at what my hand was doing.

What *I* was doing.

Something shattered in my brain and the red film dissipated. The room upended in a tornado of swirling black with a single flickering light in the eye of the storm. Shrill whistling pierced my ears, and the surrounding darkness was beyond my reach. It didn't respond like my shadows, instead burying me under a swell of shocked guilt.

A sudden sharpness, like nails biting into skin, pricked my shoulders.

"Noc, wake up. I'm here. I'm right here." Leena's strained

voice broke through the horror, and the welcome pressure of her hands on my body yanked me from the turbulent storm.

I bolted upright and jerked away from her, terrified that I had hurt her. My gaze flew immediately to her neck. No blood. No purple bruises. Nothing but blissfully unmarred skin. Leena stared back at me, eyes wide and beautifully alive. Slowly, she raised her hand to cup my cheek, and I recoiled from her outstretched fingers.

Her hand froze midair. "Noc?"

Confusion and hurt played through her gaze. But only moments ago I'd been strangling her. My hands, my touch had stolen her life. A chill raced down my spine, and I studied my hands. It had felt so *real*.

"What happened?" I croaked. Our bedroom lazily swung back into view, just the hint of dawn light peeking beneath the bottom of the velvet curtains. A slight breeze toyed with the edges, thanks to the still-open balcony door. Closing it must have been the beginning of the nightmare.

"Nothing happened." The lines mapping her forehead deepened. "Are you okay?" She tried again to inch her hand closer. I tensed, but forced myself to remain still, to let her fingers graze the side of my cheek. Warmth spurred to life beneath her gentle touch. It wasn't her fault that my mind had conjured something so awful.

My shoulders slumped. *A dream. It was just a dream. Right?* "Yes. I'm sorry I woke you."

"It's all right. Did you have a nightmare?" She fell back into bed and reached for me. I hesitated, wanting desperately to seek comfort in her embrace, but the memory of her caught beneath my grip was still so vivid. My hands trembled. Gently, she coaxed me down with her, fingers sliding soothingly through my hair. "Want to talk about it?"

Her steady breathing calmed my frayed nerves. "No."

She sighed. "I get them too, you know." Delicate fingers

worked peaceful circles against my scalp, swirling and massaging in indecipherable patterns. "Wynn plagues my dreams."

Every muscle tensed. I wrapped my arms around her waist and held her tight. The velvet feel of her warm skin was so smooth here, but I knew if I allowed my fingers to travel south, to dance along the expanse of her legs, I'd find a map of raised scars. Slowly, I exhaled and let the unease my dream had brought slip away with it. My hell had only been a nightmare, but hers had been all too real.

"Get some rest." I brushed a soft kiss against her collarbone.

"Mmm." Her mumbled response was answer enough, and slowly the pressure of her fingers in my hair faded as sleep reclaimed her thoughts. But the tantalizing draw of peaceful slumber eluded me, and the barest shade of fiery red clung to the edges of my vision. Haunting. Beckoning. Whispering.

The oath was making itself known.

THREE

LEENA

Pulling the throw blanket I'd snagged higher about my waist, I reclined into the cushioned seat of the library bay window. Morning light filtered through the panes, casting the labyrinth of bookshelves and tables in a peaceful light. The room was quiet, save the occasional crackle of fire in the hearth. While the library was hardly ever packed, the total absence of people today reminded me of just how many we'd lost. Sighing, I gripped the blanket tighter.

When early morning light had sliced through the curtains and woken us both, I'd expected Noc to pull me closer to his chest. We'd had little time to simple *be*. But he'd been quick to dress, back ramrod straight and shoulders tense, leaving me with nothing more than a chaste kiss and a claim that he had bounties to review. I believed him, but I couldn't miss the haunted edge to his stare, the way his hands shook as they loosely brushed back my hair so he could skim his fingers down my neck. He'd disappeared after that without a word, leaving me with a sinking feeling of unease.

And so I'd escaped to the library, *The Magic of Words* in hand, and stolen the first blanket I could find. While he worked, I could too. Since we'd returned to Cruor, he'd go about his day returning the guild to something like normal, and I'd end up here, looking for clues that could help us eradicate the magic of his oath in case my fellow Charmers didn't come through.

Yesterday, I'd finished a chapter on blood oaths and found myself furiously turning the pages, hoping the answer would leap out at me. The conditions were so similar to Cruor's Oath: binding and near-unbreakable. And yet, nothing. There was no documented way to break a blood pact. If Cruor's Oath held any of the same limitations, we were screwed.

Time slipped by as I skimmed passages about prophecies, curses, and powerful spells. Despite the wealth of information, there weren't any answers to be unearthed concerning Noc's oath. The magic of Cruor was one of a kind.

Pressing the book to my chest, I leaned against the cool panes of the window and glanced out over the open lawns behind Cruor. A sea of grass starting to brown at the tips stretched out before me, ending in an abrupt and riotous wall of gnarled trees and snarling, purple vines. The Kitska Forest never changed, no matter the season. The cursed wood had been that way ever since the First War between Charmers and Wilheimians. One myth suggested that the monsters who called the festering wood home were actually the souls of beasts reborn, trapped in our realm after they fell defending their Charmers during the First War.

Lightly, I stroked the bestiary puckered beneath the fabric of my shirt. A spark of warmth answered in response, and guilt sank low in my heart. Onyx, my beloved Myad, hadn't been right since we returned. He'd seen—and inevitably experienced, due to our strong bond—my grief over Calem's death and subsequent return. Onyx had been slinking through the woods of the beast realm yowling ever since. Begging for forgiveness.

Snapping my book shut, I stood and stretched my hands to

the ceiling. Research could wait. Today, I needed to take care of my beast. He had nothing to apologize for, and it was high time he found the solace I'd been unable to attain for myself.

———◆———

Cruor's backyard was mostly quiet. With winter hinting at an early arrival, the morning chill was just plain cold, and the light breeze tickling my cheeks sent a shiver racing through my limbs. I was dressed in leather breeches, knee-high boots, and a long-sleeved tunic, with only my face and hands exposed. And even that was, apparently, too much.

I'd expected to find the lawns empty, but Emelia, Iov, and a woman I didn't recognize lounged on the grass a few yards away. Laughter billowed up around them in a breath of mist, and I paused. I'd come out here with the intention of spending time with my beasts, but the last thing I wanted was to remind anyone of the horrors of Hireath. In the heat of battle there, Onyx had killed their brethren. Would the assassins of Cruor be able to forgive that deep a loss?

I ran my hands over my arms to chase away the sudden chill and turned to head back inside, but Iov spotted me and shouted a hello, his enthusiastic wave brooking no room for argument. Wearing similar getups of sleeveless tunics and loose-fitting black trousers, the trio looked entirely at ease.

Death must make the cold bearable. Suppressing a full-body shiver, I walked toward them. "Hey there."

Emelia and Iov smiled in unison, the sun heating their sepia skin and giving it a warm glow. Twins to their core, they even shared similar widows' peaks and full lips.

As one, the group stood to greet me, and Emelia brushed

her braided ponytail off her shoulder. "Hey, Leena. We wanted you to meet Astrid. She's one of the new recruits Noc raised last night."

Iov nodded. "We grew up in the same town. She's the younger sister I never needed, but somehow got anyway."

Astrid cut him a glare. "I'm not your sister."

"And yet you pester me just the same." His eyes warmed despite the teasing words, and he reached to muss Astrid's spiked locks. "You're saying you didn't miss us when we died?"

She batted him away. "Of course I missed you."

I frowned. "I'm confused. Little sister? You all look the same age to me."

"We died at the glorious age of nineteen," Emelia said. She offered Astrid a gentle smile. "Astrid was sixteen at the time."

"And now I've finally found you again. Except, now I'm technically older. Wouldn't that make you *my* younger siblings?" She gave Iov a devilish grin.

"Not on your life."

My smile died at her words. Astrid had aged years before being raised, and in that time she'd grown, matured. That would happen to me too. Charmers aged slower than humans, but Noc would still outlive me. He'd stay frozen in time, and I'd eventually die and leave him alone. We'd never talked about what that meant for us. What that would mean for *him*.

I could ask him to raise me.

My gut churned, and I pushed that errant thought far away. I couldn't imagine a life without Noc, but the shadows of Cruor... They permeated everything. No Charmer had ever been changed before, and the risk was too great. I had no idea what death would do to my beasts, to their realm.

Their lives were more important than my happiness.

"Anyway," Astrid said, pulling me out of my thoughts, "it's nice to meet you, Leena."

I offered her my hand. "Nice to meet you, Astrid."

She shook it with a force that threated to shatter my bones. "Pleasure is all mine." Two impossibly deep dimples accompanied her crooked grin. A smattering of freckles, a shade darker than the golden-brown of her skin, danced across the bridge of her long nose. She placed her hands on narrow hips. "These two told me you're a Charmer. Can you show us some beasts? I'd love to see what you've got."

Iov rolled his eyes. "You couldn't handle all she's got."

A fire glinted in Astrid's eyes. "I could probably handle more than she's used to."

Iov knocked his shoulder into her, and she winced. "Trust me, you couldn't. She's shacked up with our guild master." He lifted a shoulder in weak apology as he snuck a suddenly sheepish look my way, unable to hide his unabashed grin.

I laughed—a real laugh—the sound surprising me in its warmth. I'd spent little time with the guild members since returning. Between my hours of research and the guilt I felt for the battle I'd caused, I hadn't managed the courage to face them. Not when I'd robbed them of so much.

My grin faded as I shifted, and the scars on my legs caught against the seams of my pants. The battle of Hireath had changed us all. Running my hands over my thighs, I took a steadying breath. "Don't worry. I won't tell Noc."

"I don't care if you do," Astrid said with a brazen wink. "But I still want to see what you've got."

Emelia groaned. "It's your second funeral. Leena?" Her eyes slid to my bestiary, the chain just visible at the hollow of my neck, thanks to the open cut of my jacket.

Without thinking, I stroked the small, book-shaped bump beneath the layers of clothing. If Emelia was asking, maybe she wouldn't blame my beasts for the orders I had given after all. I felt myself begin to relax. "All right."

Splaying out my right hand, I focused on the well of dormant power brewing in my core, relishing in the sudden flare of eager warmth. My precious beasts were only a call away, and their unconditional love filled me to the brim. Power surged through my fingers, bleeding out through the Charmer's symbol on my hand. The once-barren tree sprouted leaves and flowers as it grew, showering us with a rosewood glow.

A low rumbling filled the quiet air, and the invisible door to the beast realm creaked open. Flipping through the pages of my bestiary in my mind, I sought a familiar, low-level beast to introduce to my new family.

At our feet, my Groober, Poof, appeared. He was round and covered in soft, white fluff with stubby arms and legs that ended in padded hooves. Saucer-shaped eyes dominated most of his face, and he let out a happy croon from the back of his throat.

"Oh. My. Gods." Emelia fell to her knees. "This is the cutest thing I've ever seen."

I chuckled. "Go ahead, pet him. Just avoid the backs of his ears unless you want to trigger his scent glands. Otherwise, you'll find yourself hankering for a nap."

Astrid crouched and tickled his belly with a cautious finger. Her eyes widened, and she stared up at me with a slack jaw. "He feels like a cloud."

Iov folded his arms across his chest. "Cute. But you don't have to start small for our sakes. We've seen you fight. Why not bring out Onyx?"

My heart stilled. Emelia and Iov had witnessed the power behind my beast. Had seen firsthand as his claws shredded Calem's chest and ended his life, only to have him brought back again *changed*. Flexing my hand, I stared at the ground. I could feel Onyx waiting. Lingering on the edge of the realm between his world and mine.

"We trust you." Iov looked at me without an ounce of fear. No judgment. No worry. "What happened in Hireath... It was war, Leena. This is different."

My fingers trembled. "Okay," I whispered.

Coaxing more power into my veins, I channeled my thoughts to Onyx. To the black legendary feline beast that had changed everything for me. The rush of power that preceded his entrance raised the hairs on my arms and ushered in an eerie calm. Rosewood light exploded in a brilliant sunburst, and the assassins shielded their eyes.

When the glow faded, Onyx stood before us. Lithe muscles rippled beneath thick fur, and the iridescent peacock feathers lining his spine and tail shimmered in the sun. Extending his wings, he beat them once, and a rush of air staggered us, forcing us to fight to keep our feet. He was so magnificent. So stunning. And yet... Wet fur lined the corners of his eyes. A fist wrenched my heart. I should've summoned him sooner.

He sighed and knocked his head into my chest with a heady purr. I planted a gentle kiss on the raised ring embedded in his crown. On my ring. "Hey, Onyx."

"Holy mother of gods." Astrid scooped up Poof in one arm and inched closer. "Can I touch him?"

The assassin's lack of fear soothed the last of my worry. "Sure. Just go slow. He's very protective of me." I guided her palm to the thick of his neck. Gooseflesh rippled over her forearms, and she worked tiny circles with her fingers into his fur. Onyx groaned, turning his head away from me to sneak his nose between her fingers.

"Traitor." I grinned at my beast, and he huffed before closing his eyes. Taking Poof from Astrid, I nodded for her to use both hands. "Guess he likes you more than me."

Wide-eyed and cautious, Iov and Emelia followed Astrid's lead. Slowly, the tension in Emelia's shoulders disappeared, and she buried her nose in Onyx's fur. Iov stuck to kneading circles behind Onyx's ears, grinning like a giddy kid and whispering endearments better served for newborn children.

And Onyx ate it up. After a while, he crashed to the ground and sprawled out, rolling around on his back and kicking up grass with his massive paws. One of his feathers came loose, and Iov used it to tickle Onyx's nose. Pupils wide, the Myad batted at the shimmery toy and let out a series of playful yowls.

Astrid laughed. "He acts like a giant kitten."

My heart soared. He needed this. Needed love and attention. The guilt I'd been carrying for the past few days had kept me from summoning him, and the pain I'd inflicted... I had failed him. I'd promised to be as devoted to him as he was to me, and I hadn't been able to face what I'd done to Calem. But that wasn't Onyx's fault. It was mine. Bending down, I rubbed the side of his maw. He paused his playful batting to nudge my hand. *Forgiven.*

Everyone else was so quick to forgive, yet I couldn't seem to offer that same reprieve for myself.

Without warning, Onyx's head turned and he leapt to his feet. His body went taut, and he peeled his lips back to reveal rows of sword-sharp teeth. Dark scruff stood sky high. Feathers quivered as he crouched low into his haunches. Gaze focused on the edge of the Kitska Forest, he waited to pounce.

"Onyx?" Fear doused the warmth my beast had summoned, and I handed off a softly keening Poof to Astrid. "What is it? What do you see?"

A low, menacing growl ripped through his throat. As I followed his stare to the edge of the snarling wood, a flash of blue winked at me from the thick overgrowth of trees. An influx of power hummed from the dark, accompanied by another unexpected glimmer of aqua.

"Get behind me." I stepped in front of my family. "Onyx can handle this."

"You're out of your mind." Emelia submerged her hands in shadows until a glittering halberd solidified in her grip. "Noc would have our heads if something happened to you."

"Astrid, fall back." Iov followed Emelia and fashioned an ax.

"Wait, I—"

But the signature groan of the beast-realm door rushed over the clearing before I could speak, and a blanket of rosewood light cast us into temporary blindness. The force of the energy smacked into my body and rattled my bones. I flexed my hand, and power sparked from my symbol. One of my beasts had forced its way out without my calling. *But, how? Why?* I touched my bestiary as a flush of adrenaline surged through me. Time seemed to stretch endlessly as the rosewood hue dispersed. A blur of white fur streaked away from us toward the wood.

"What is that?" Astrid squeezed Poof tight to her chest, and a hint of lavender and valerian perfumed the air.

"That's..." My stomach revolted, and for one blinding moment, I was back in that prison again, Wynn's blades hot against my skin. "Dominus." Powerful claws churned the earth as he ran, a mass of sheer force and otherworldly strength. Vibrant emerald and violet wings sprouted like jagged glass from his ankles, and the glinting chest plate of crystal protecting his heart flashed in the sun. The Mistari. Wynn's beast. Or rather, *my* beast now. How did he manage to escape the realm without my call?

I didn't have time to figure that out. In that moment, a liquid-blue monster in the shape of a feline exploded from the forest and rushed into the open to meet Dominus head-on. They came together in a clash of snarls and yowls that rattled windows along the rooms overlooking the field. Shadows rushed from the manor, carrying a flurry of assassins ready to protect their home.

"Onyx, go," I said, and my beast launched into the sky. Electric-blue wisps trailed from his legs and eyes. Wings beating fervently, he barreled toward the blue-and-white ball of fury and gnashing fangs. The two great cats were locked in desperate battle. But despite all their might, neither beast landed a blow. For a split second they broke apart, and the shimmery blue feline rolled onto his back. Sapphire paws smacked against Dominus's maw, and the Mistari growled before pouncing.

It was almost...playful.

"They're not hurting each other." Straightening, I studied the way they circled before bounding together in a tangled mess of limbs—claws completely retracted. Relief, followed quickly by a wave of anxiety, stirred in me. Riveting my eyes to the sky, I found Onyx circling the pair. "Onyx, wait!"

His head snapped to me...and then he descended, landing a few feet from the yowling beasts. He cocked his head before settling into his haunches to watch their play. I loosed a heavy sigh. "Thank the gods."

Beside me, a rush of shadows darker than the rest appeared. Inky tendrils flared outward, cocooning me in a world of black on black. And then Noc stepped out, hands shaking and eyes wild as he stared at the threat on the edge of his land. Calem, Kost, and Oz flanked his side, each one already gripping blades. Calem spotted Onyx and his face paled, but he held rank and settled low into his heels.

Noc turned to me with barely capped fury—and concern. "What's going on?"

"Just a man who likes to make an entrance." Placing a hand

on Noc's forearm, I nodded to the legendary beast with its watery scales and finned tail. A Zystream. I'd been under Wynn's charm the first time I'd seen Gaige's prized feline. The fog that still clung to those memories had slowed my recognition, but it was clear as day now. "That's Gaige's beast. Dominus must have recognized him and came out to play."

Noc gave me an incredulous stare. "Play?"

I shrugged. "They lived together for how long?" My gut twisted, and my fingers traced one of the scars on my outer thigh. "He came without me calling."

The angry shadows swirling about Noc's frame receded, and he gently stroked the back of my hand. My fingers stopped their wandering. "Without you calling? Is that normal?"

I chewed on the inside of my cheek. "No. I don't know. It's something that usually happens with non-Charmers who've only had their beasts for a short while. It's never happened to me before."

My throat tightened, and Noc leaned in closer, words barely a whisper. "Are you okay?"

There were too many answers to that question. "I don't know."

The beasts broke apart, tired from their romping, and flopped on the ground. Heavy pants fell from Dominus's open maw, and he looked back at me with the first glimmer of happiness I'd seen since welcoming him into my world. Jade eyes alight, Dominus nudged Onyx with his nose until he complied and ran a scratchy tongue over his face.

The blue feline turned toward the forest line and let out a content yowl. Stepping out from the shadows of the trees, Gaige—one of the members of the Charmers Council—strolled over to his beast and placed a loving hand on his head.

"See?" I broke away from the army we'd amassed and crossed the clearing with Noc, Kost, Calem and Oz on my heels. "Always making an entrance."

Gaige flipped up the collar of his glossy wine-red coat and grinned. He wore tailored black trousers with silver studs along the seams neatly tucked into polished leather boots. Steel-blue eyes glinted with obvious mischief beneath angular brows.

"Hello, hello."

Noc's words were pure ice. "Next time, try the front door. How did you manage to get here, anyway? The portal to our estate isn't accessible without the help of an assassin."

Gaige smirked. "Beasts are wonderful creatures." He reached into the pocket of his coat and extracted a small, pale-blue beast that sat snugly in the palm of his hand. It had a jelly-like body and four stubby tentacles that moved slowly, curling toward the center where a circular aquamarine gem glistened like the ocean.

My eyes widened. "That's a Kaiku. I've never actually seen one before in real life." I itched to move closer, to skate my fingers over its radiant stone. "Where did you get it?"

"Not on Lendria." His smile deepened, and then his emblem glowed as the beast-realm door groaned open. The Kaiku disappeared. "A Kaiku acts like a compass, pointing its Charmer in the direction they seek without fault. I didn't need assistance getting here because my beast simply read my desires and showed me the way."

"I see." Noc bristled, clearly unhappy that there was a creature out there that could bypass Cruor's defenses.

"Regardless, I apologize for any alarm I may have caused." He offered a polite nod before returning his gaze to me. "By the way, Leena, I do appreciate you allowing Dominus to stretch his legs. Okean has missed him."

Upon hearing his name, the liquid-blue beast rammed his massive skull into Gaige's side and nipped at one of the silver studs. Gaige batted him away with a loving shush, and Okean sauntered toward Dominus and Onyx before dropping to his haunches. With the back of one of his paws, he rubbed the finned whiskers lining his jaw and throat.

I fisted my hands behind my back. "Of course." My lack of control over Dominus was not something I wanted to share publicly, let alone with a Council member. We still didn't know who to trust in Hireath. Yet.

Kost spoke my thoughts aloud. "Do you bring word of the bounty?"

"Unfortunately, no." Gaige held Kost's stare. "I went straight to Wilheim after escorting you home from Hireath. I'm on the return journey now. Kaori asked that I check in on Calem."

Calem's spine straightened. With a wicked smirk, he laced his fingers behind his head. "Oh, I'm fine. But if she's not convinced, you can tell her I'm always open for a personal checkup." Oz elbowed him in the side, and Calem shot him a slitted glare.

"Don't get your hopes up," Gaige said, a slight grin tugging at his lips.

Noc's hand found my waist. "We won't keep you, then."

"Oh, I'd rather you did." His playful gaze pinned Kost for a half second longer than needed before sliding back to Noc. "You see, you're not the only one who finds it mildly unsettling that my people haven't turned up information on the person who contracted Leena's bounty."

My pulse jumped. Gaige folded his arms across his chest, and the jeweled citrine glow of his Charmer's symbol glimmered in the morning sun. He met Noc's hard stare head on.

Noc remained impassive. "Oh?"

"I make it my business to deal in information. Someone is holding their cards very close to the chest. So, I took the liberty of sussing out a mage and setting up a meeting for tomorrow."

"A mage? Here?" Calem's eyes went wide. Oz's hands

slackened by his sides, and his brows crept toward his hairline. But Noc and Kost... An electric current surged between them. It was so minute that, if I weren't connected by Noc's grip on my waist, I'm not sure I would've felt the jolt in his fingers. A tendon feathered along his jaw, but he kept his gaze steady.

Unease settled low in my gut. Sure, Kost and Noc had had decades together. A life and secrets and experiences I couldn't begin to hold a candle to. It bothered me to no end that we still hadn't openly discussed his past, and their unspoken words only fueled my frustration.

Kost removed his spectacles and began to polish them with a cloth from his breast pocket. "There are very few mages on our small island continent. They have enough discord to keep them focused on their own lands. How did you manage to find one?"

Gaige narrowed his eyes, seemingly tracking the invisible thread of tension between Kost and Noc. "I have my sources." After a beat of silence, he cleared his throat. "My point is, I secured the meeting for you. The mage wants something of me, and in return, he's offered his magic to secure what *I* want...within reason. Perhaps the mage can sever the oath, and we can put this whole mess behind us."

"What does the mage want from you?" Noc asked.

Gaige lifted a shoulder. "That is between me and him. I try to form relationships with a number of powerful players. You never know when their skills might come in handy."

"You did this on your own? Why?" Kost got to the heart of my concern before I could voice it.

"Because it seemed like the right thing to do." Gaige paused, running a hand along his jaw. "Though I could always keep the meeting for myself if you're not interested. Mages are powerful. There's no telling what I could gain from his favor."

"So much for *the right thing to do*." The low note in Noc's voice hinted at danger and unexpected anger. He was usually more collected than this. "What do you want from me in exchange?"

Gaige hummed. "As I said, I trade in information. Because I'd be giving up the chance to secure rare and valuable insight, I'd be remiss if I didn't take the opportunity to gather precious secrets elsewhere."

Kost's fingers were bone-white against the metal frame of his spectacles. "We have nothing to give you."

Noc placed a firm hand on his shoulder. After a moment, he turned his gaze to Gaige. Obsidian eyes as hard as metal betrayed nothing. "If you take us to see the mage, then I will give you full access to our library."

"I've been to many libraries in my lifetime." Gaige ran an errant hand down his sleeve, feigning indifference. But there was an unmistakable glint of intrigue in his stare. "I'm not sure your tomes will yield anything of interest to me."

Noc lifted a shoulder, but the tension in his body remained. "You'd be surprised. Tell me, what kind of secrets are you looking for?"

"They wouldn't be secrets if I told you." A grin tugged at his lips. "I'm merely a collector of information. You never know what could be useful in the long run. One day, I hope to find myself in the royal library in Wilheim."

Noc offered a cool smile. "I see. My guess is that whenever you visit Wilheim, you're escorted every step by Sentinels and not permitted to linger. But some of my assassins were nobles before they turned. Historians, poets, philosophers—they brought their knowledge with them. If you really want to learn about Wilheimians, we've got plenty of books to get you started. Information like that seems like it would be valuable to the Charmers' emissary."

Gaige grinned. "You've got yourself a deal."

"Good." Noc slipped his hands into the pockets of his trousers, and the inky scythe on his wrist disappeared from view. Maybe this was our chance. Mages were powerful beings with unparalleled magic. They rarely crossed the sea to deal with anyone outside their realm. Rumors suggested they were as disgusted with the outcome of the First War as Charmers were, and rather than succumb to the ruling of the First King, they'd left.

To be granted an audience with one now…

"I don't know how you managed this, but thank you," I said, voice unfailingly polite in order to hide my mistrust. Gaige's inscrutable gaze drifted to me. What were his motives? Why had he gone to such lengths? There was no way of knowing how many people Wynn had won over. And judging by Dominus and Okean's relationship, it was safe to say that Wynn and Gaige had spent a decent amount of time together. Maybe Gaige knew more about our enemy than he let on.

Maybe he was even on her side.

Regardless, this wasn't an option we could pass up. Perhaps he was an ally on the Council. Or maybe he was just using his wits to further his own agenda. It was so hard to tell. After everything I'd been through, between my exile and this bounty, trust wasn't something I had in great supply.

Noc gestured toward the manor. "You can stay with us until tomorrow."

Gaige channeled the god of mischief himself with his crooked grin. "Excellent."

I wasn't sure if *excellent* was the word I'd use, but risking another debt to the Council was a small price to pay if it meant saving Noc.

FOUR

LEENA

We took the familiar path to Midnight Jester just after breakfast the following morning. Snarled, plum-colored vines covered in thorns threaded through decaying branches, creating a thicket of swirling darkness along the dirt path. Kitska Forest never slumbered, and the shimmering pods of pinesco trees winked like eyes in the faint breeze. Pulling my leather coat tight, I quickened my pace to keep up with Noc, Kost, Calem and Gaige. Dressed entirely in black with a trench coat that fell to his calves, Noc walked like a predator. Darkness oozed from his fingers and curled around his legs, mingling with the shadows of the forest and blending with the onyx shade of his hair. It was hard to tell where one nightmare ended and the other began.

No. Not a nightmare. At least not to me. I could decipher all the shades of slate and ebony and charcoal intermingling to form a world of beautiful depth. But to an outsider? Noc wore danger like a garment. And it's the exact thing he wanted this mage to know; that he, and invariably us, wouldn't be easy marks.

Kost and Gaige flanked him, twin threats in their own right. Kost because he wore his own sharp expression, coupled with a similar arrangement of black-on-black attire. Gaige, because I couldn't bring myself to trust that brain of his. Why grant us this meeting with the mage? What was his plan? If only I had a Nezbit at my disposal. Then I could ask Gaige point-blank if he was involved with Wynn, with the mystery woman behind the bounty, and know truth from lie.

Flexing my fingers, I studied the tree inked into my skin, as if the rosewood color would suddenly spring to life and wash away my concern.

"Cold?" Calem knocked into me with his shoulder and nodded toward my hand. "It might be time for gloves."

I shoved my hands into my pockets and forced a smile. "That's what pockets are for."

Calem grinned back, and my stomach knotted. That boyish expression haunted my dreams. It was the last thing I had seen before his face contorted in pain. Before the red coated my hands and the stink of iron rooted in my nose. Before the life in his eyes died as his head lolled in my lap. Last night's nightmare had been no different.

The multigrain toast I'd managed to eat this morning tried in vain to crawl up my throat. I swallowed. Hard.

Calem watched me with cautious eyes. With a gentle finger, he poked my forehead. "Everything okay in there?"

"Just peachy." Dried-up twigs snapped beneath my boots as we walked. Midnight Jester was visible on the horizon, and a new chill joined the winter air nipping against my skin. "We should've brought Oz too."

Calem tossed a cursory glance behind us in the direction of Cruor. "Someone needed to stay behind. Everyone's on edge since Darrien left."

The bloodbath of Hireath was always at the forefront in my mind. "Are you sure that's it?"

He stopped and clasped my shoulders. "Would you cut it out?"

Ahead of us, Noc, Kost, and Gaige halted. "Listen, Leena. I'm okay. Stop blaming yourself."

I let out a brittle laugh. "I'm trying." But as much as he wanted me to believe he was fine, nothing could dim the subtle glow of mercury around his irises. Whatever Kaori's beast, Stella, had done to save Calem's life was still evident in his eyes. And we had no idea exactly what ramifications he'd face because of it. "Why does it feel like we're all on the edge of an explosion?"

Calem sighed and wrapped me in a one-armed hug before leading us down the path again. "We'll figure it out."

Noc searched my face as we approached. But as much as he wanted to help, there really *wasn't* anything he could do. I offered him a reassuring smile and inclined my head. Some of the tension roiling across Noc's face faded, and he started again toward Midnight Jester, the local black-market tavern, with Kost and Gaige.

"How's Noc holding up?" Calem's hands swung by his sides, long hair bouncing along his shoulders in time with his gait.

"I'm not sure." I hadn't been the only one battling through the night. "Probably worse than he's letting on. You know him."

Calem sighed. "We don't know much about what happens when an oath is ignored. Hopefully, this mage will help." He slowed as we hit freshly laid stone pavers marking the entrance to the tavern. My brows drew together as I toed the first slab and was met with a solid thump instead of the rolling squish of dirt.

How long had it been since I'd been back? Enough time for pavers to be laid. What else was new? A shiny iron doorknob glinted in the sun, no longer dented and barely hinged to the door. My gaze flitted to the stone masonry and shuttered windows. Weathered, sure, but was that fresh paint? Ivy shrubs clambered against the walls, and I searched for any other signs of change. It wasn't like Dez was lazy, but—

Dez. A different flavor of unease hit me as Noc wrenched open the heavy oak door and disappeared inside with Gaige and Kost. Spinning to Calem, I gripped his hands in mine.

"I need a favor."

Calem raised a brow. "Okay?"

"The bartender is going to cause a scene when he sees me."

"What kind of scene?" His body went rigid, and his lips peeled back in a perilous show of teeth.

"Not that kind. I'm safe. It's just…" Meeting Calem's muted-red eyes, I willed him to catch my drift. It's not like I'd talked about my previous relationships with any of them. But if anyone would understand, it'd be Calem. He studied me for a moment before realization hit him, and the angry growl brewing on his lips turned into a full-blown laugh.

"Does Noc know?"

I shook my head. "He's on edge lately, thanks to the oath. We can't have him going off when we desperately need the information this mage can give us."

Calem sighed, dropping my hands and gripping the iron doorknob. "You're asking a lot of me, you know that? Just try to keep this bartender in line. I'll do my best with our new hothead." With a subtle smirk still lingering on his lips, he opened the door and walked into the dim lighting of my old stomping grounds. As I followed in his steps, a man with cropped red hair rushed out. He knocked into me, took one look at my annoyed expression, and bolted toward the Kitska Forest.

Manners didn't apply to those who dealt in black-market information, apparently. Suppressing a scowl, I shut the door behind me. The rush of stale booze and dirty dealings welcomed me, and I hid behind Calem for a moment longer to avoid the inevitable and savor the familiarity of what had once been my home. A few patrons near the door glanced up at our entrance, but they seemed otherwise unmoved. No one asked questions in a place like this.

Iron wall mounts with flickering candles clung to the shiplap, and heavy plank tables with murmuring patrons were scattered across the creaking floorboards. But aside from the errant cobweb here and there clinging to out-of-reach rafters, the place felt remarkably clean. The signature filigree pattern of mold on the windows had been scraped; the pilings of wax on tables were gone; even a few of the booths' black cushions had been patched. They didn't match, more of a graphite shade than a true raven's black, but clothing would be safe from snags.

Our troupe had taken refuge at a small table toward the rear with mismatched chairs, and Noc sat with his back to the wall. With the seat beside him empty, he waited with careful eyes for me to join him. Calem glanced back at me with a wicked smirk and stepped away, effectively jettisoning me from his shadow and leaving me alone to face the music. Calem was fast, but not fast enough to plop himself in Noc's sight line before Dez turned from his place at the bar and dropped the mug he'd been polishing.

The shattering of glass cut through the murmuring conversations and ushered in a curious silence. Dez rushed around the bar, unconcerned with the way his boots ground shards into the soft wood, and wrapped me in an embrace that threatened to splinter my bones.

"Leena, thank the gods." His lips skirted across the crown of my head, and I swear I felt Noc's stare embedding into my skull.

"Hi, Dez." I gave him a quick hug before disentangling myself from his limbs. "You've been busy. This place actually feels clean for once." The backdrop of muted discussions resumed as patrons returned to their business. Calem's voice carried above the rest as he tried to engage Noc in conversation, but he never responded.

A goofy grin captured Dez's lips, revealing too many teeth and hinting at the rugged charm I'd fallen prey to before. "I had some free time on my hands without you around." A callused thumb brushed the length of my jaw. "You took your sweet time coming home."

"Dez—"

"I left your room the way it was. No need to thank me." Voice low, he placed a hand on my waist and squeezed. The jagged scar running from his earlobe to his jaw twisted as he smirked. "I take that back. I'd very much like you to thank me."

I didn't even get a chance to warn him. Shadows exploded in a plume of inky black, and suddenly Noc was beside me. Hands tucked into the pockets of his trousers, he ignored me entirely and instead twisted invisible knives into Dez's hide with his stare. His sudden display of power sent everyone into a frozen state of silence, each one balancing on a tightrope of alarm.

Dez, for all his worth, took one look at Noc and pulled me behind him. "Can I help you?"

Somewhere, Calem cursed.

Eerie calm swept through Noc's hard expression. "You can take your hands off her."

"Back off, or I'll throw you out. This is my establishment."

"Dez." I gripped his forearm, and his brown gaze softened as his eyes landed on me. "It's okay. I know him."

"I'm not sure you do." He turned back to Noc. He may have been unaware of the danger lying in wait before him, but I couldn't miss Noc's telltale signs. The balled fists in his pockets. The wild muscle ticking in his jaw. Dez only settled further into his heels and folded his arms across his chest. "I remember you. You came in here before to barter with someone over a Charmer's life. Considering there's only one of those around, my guess is that's you, Leena. This man is trying to kill you."

Noc growled. "That was a private conversation."

Dez cracked his knuckles. "Nothing's private in my house. Now, get the hell out."

"Enough." Slipping away from Dez, I placed myself between them. Noc's lack of control was wildly apparent to me. I knew it was all thanks to the oath leaking poison into his veins, but of course, that meant nothing to Dez. "I know about that."

"Leena, he tried to kill you."

"There's a lot going on here you don't understand." Touching my chin to my shoulder, I held out my hand to Noc. His fingers twined with mine in an instant, and he gave them a gentle tug. "He's with me, Dez."

"He's with you?" He took a quick step back and looked at our threaded fingers with new meaning. "He's your partner?"

I let the heavy silence linger just long enough that Dez knew my answer before I voiced it. "Yes."

Beside me, Noc flinched. His fingers went lax in my hold, but he held his gaze steady. Behind us, the door to Midnight Jester groaned open and thudded closed, but nothing could break the tension simmering to a boiling point between the three of us.

Except for Gaige. Somewhere in the middle of our standoff, he'd come to stand beside us. He cleared his throat. "Not to interrupt this stunning display of machismo, but we've got company."

He nodded toward the entrance where a newcomer loitered, hammered-nickel eyes alight with curiosity and deadly intelligence. Glossy, blue-black hair kissed the tops of his ears, with a few locks on either side stretching down to his jaw. The lazy way he reclined against the doorframe reminded me of Noc's ability to lull offenders into a false sense of security, and panic flared in my core.

Mage. Unbridled power rolled off him in waves, and he straightened himself when Gaige offered his hand. "Interesting start to the day."

"Indeed." Gaige gestured toward the table still occupied by Kost and Calem. "Shall we?"

As Gaige and the mage passed us, he spared Noc a glance with a raised brow and an arrogant smirk. He dragged his fingers along the backs of chairs, seemingly claiming the space as his own without uttering a word. Noc bit back a growl and relinquished my hand before following them through the maze of chairs and tables. *Great. Another person likely to spark Noc's oath-induced irritability.* Turning back to Dez, I opened my mouth to speak, but he cut me off.

"You can grab your stuff later." Hurt lanced his words, and he picked up a rag and began polishing mugs. The broken shards of glass at his feet went unnoticed.

"Dez—"

"You couldn't trust me with your life, but him?" He scoffed and tossed the rag into the metal basin. "Better join your group." Stalking through the hidden back door where the ale and liquor was stored, he disappeared and effectively ended our conversation.

Guilt threatened to send me running after him, but the mage wouldn't wait, and I had a sneaking suspicion neither would Noc. Retreating to our table, I slid into the seat next to him and placed a hand on his thigh. Aside from the slight twitch of a muscle, he didn't acknowledge it.

"Thank you for meeting with us," he said to the mage sitting across from him. "I'm Noc. This is Calem and Kost, and you already know Gaige." Noc gestured around before tilting his chin in my direction. "And this is my pair bond, Leena."

I swallowed the hefty rock lodged in my throat. Acknowledging him as my *partner* in front of Dez instead of my *anam-cara*, or pair bond, had been a mistake. "Partner" could be anyone—a fling, an early romance, a friend. The unintentional burn must have left him reeling. Angry was not the way we wanted to enter this negotiation. Noc leaned his forearms against the heavy planks of the table. The silver ring clinging to his hand caught in the flickering light of the candle.

The man's eyes went straight to the winking emerald. Slowly, he returned Noc's gaze. "I arranged a meeting with Gaige. Not you."

Gaige tossed an arm over the back of his chair, angling his body in the direction of the mage. "My apologies, Eryx. I should have given you notice, but I only happened across this opportunity yesterday."

Opportunity? My nails bit into Noc's leg, but he didn't flinch. Corded tension knotted tight at the base of his neck. "We need your help."

Eryx was unfazed. "I'm here to help Gaige. That was the deal."

"I'll still hold up my end of the bargain, as promised. I'm just passing off the benefits of your expertise to my friends here. Satisfactory?"

Eryx's sharp gaze flitted from assassin to assassin. "That's your call, I suppose." Knitting his fingers together behind his head, Eryx leaned back in his chair. The muscles across his chest flexed with the motion, visible thanks to the plain white-collared tunic that opened to his sternum. His cuffs were folded up over the black sleeves of his jacket, revealing foreign magic ciphers inked in glimmering black on his inner wrists.

Gaige straightened and extended his hand. "Whenever you're ready."

Eryx shot him a warning look. "I'm not a forgiving man, Gaige. If anything should happen—"

"Then I will incur your wrath, along with the entirety of your clan. I can assure you, your prize will be hidden and bound. No one will discover them, let alone read them. We have secrets here too, that need protecting." Gaige waited with his hand outstretched.

"As long as you understand." Slipping one hand inside his jacket, Eryx extracted a delicate roll of parchment tinged brown with age, a twine knot holding it in place. "These pages must remain hidden. I cannot stress this enough."

"Of course." Gaige gingerly took the parcel from Eryx and tucked it in his own jacket pocket.

"And if you try to undo that twine, your eyes will burn to ash long before you can even attempt to decipher the first word. No one is to look upon them until I come calling again." He stared at the spot where the parchment was concealed. On Gaige's other side, Kost flinched and tried to hide the action with a sudden clearing of his throat.

A mischievous glint flickered in Gaige's steel-blue eyes. "Noted. Now that we've got that out of the way, you owe me a boon for hiding your secrets. Which I'm granting to Noc."

"Fine." Peeling his eyes away from Gaige, Eryx pinned Noc with a languid raise of his eyebrow. "Your request wouldn't have anything to do with that fancy ring, now would it?"

Noc's jaw twitched at the same time Kost clasped his hands together, knuckles turning bone-white. Noc reined in his emotions first. "No. It's this we need your assistance with." Rotating his wrist face up, he bathed Cruor's Oath in the buttery-warm light of the candle. Eryx frowned and leaned in closer to inspect the inked scythe that had already brought us so much pain.

"A blood oath?"

Noc shook his head. "Not quite. Its magic is unique to our guild. When we accept a contract, we're bound to fulfill it. If we don't, we sacrifice our life in exchange for the failed bounty."

Eryx scrunched his nose. "Who on earth would accept something like that?"

Noc ground his teeth together. "It's not an option. Part of our curse."

"I can't remove it." Eryx pulled away from Noc's wrist and folded his arms across his chest. "You're better off killing your mark."

Noc glowered, and I placed my hand over his to keep him from lunging across the table. "It's safe to say that won't be happening."

Eryx rounded on me with a knowing look. "Forced to kill your own pair bond? Cruel." He drummed his fingers along the planks from thumb to pinkie and back again. "Still, it can't be done."

"Can another mage do it?" Calem moved a fraction closer to Noc. It was unsettling to see Noc—who had always been so calm, so controlled—this openly frazzled. On the verge of rupturing without so much as a second thought for the consequences. My heart squirmed, and I ran a light hand down the length of his spine.

Eryx snorted. "There aren't a lot of us running around in your country. As soon as we're done here, I'll be heading back to my lands. And while our talents might differ, I don't think any mage I know could eradicate this curse."

Noc leaned into my touch. "Can you tell us who placed the bounty?"

My world narrowed to Eryx and the sparkling intellect clear in his stare. I hadn't forgotten about Raven, the newest Council member whose symbol shared the same hue as the Charmer who placed the bounty. While I suspected her, to have proof by way of a mage, especially with Gaige as witness... Eryx just needed to say yes. To tell us her name. Then we could act. Force her to remove the oath or suffer the consequences. Exile for her actions. It only seemed fitting.

Eryx pursed his lips. "No. That's not written in the magic."

Noc cursed. "Is there anything you *can* offer us? Any information about the nature of this magic?"

"You don't have long." He said it so nonchalantly that he could've been commenting on the weather. But when he cradled his chin in his hands and targeted the mark with a somber stare, the weight of his declaration sent my heart crashing to the floor. "You've already denied the call of the magic, and it knows."

"What's that supposed to mean?" White-faced and still as stone, Kost studied Noc. To lose him... My own stomach curdled at the thought, and I tore my gaze away.

"Magic is a living thing. Unless you have years of practice and an innate ability to control it, it will swallow you whole. With your bounty so close and you constantly fighting against the oath, I can only assume you'll start to deteriorate. Quickly."

Calem banged a fist against the table before standing. Muscles popped along his forearms, and the mercury thread around his irises flared. Maybe Noc wasn't the only one we needed to keep our eyes on. "Gaige, you're not getting your bargain's worth. Or rather, *we're* not. If he can't fix it, then tell him to use his magic some other way. Force him to find the culprit."

Eryx tilted his head, his bluish-black hair skating against his jawline. "Sit down and be silent, Calem. Adults are talking." His words were syrupy and thick, full of unseen magic that weighed down the surrounding air.

Calem's muscles flared as he fought in vain against the obvious command. Eyes bulging and a low groan rumbling from his chest, he finally caved, nearly splintering the chair with his need to obey. He did not say a word.

My mouth fell open. Were all mages this powerful? Did they all harbor such compulsory talents? Either way, it was clear we couldn't force Eryx to do *anything*. And with the magic he wielded, we were puppets just waiting to be toyed with.

Noc seemed to know it. He clenched his jaw tight and spoke through barely parted lips. "It's clear you can't be swayed to help further." He struggled to find words. I could only imagine what he was thinking, the threats dying to be spoken. What was it that he'd once told me? Assassins don't fight fair, and they only strike when they know they're going to win. Noc *could* win, if he waited for the right moment. But what good would that do us?

Gaige cleared his throat. "Point taken, Eryx."

Standing, Eryx reached his palms toward the rafters in an unhurried stretch. Glamour gone from his stare, he offered a smile that was all too easy and hid far too much. "Glad we're on the same page. Parting advice, Noc: Kill the person who ordered the contract, or complete the bounty. Quickly. The rules are written cleanly in the magic."

Noc didn't move. Everything about him was sharp and ready to strike.

Standing, Gaige offered his hand. "Thank you for your insight."

Eryx lifted his shoulders in a lazy shrug. "Of course. Keep the parchment safe, Gaige, or you'll be hearing from me." Turning on his heels, he strolled out of Midnight Jester. Gaige slumped back into his chair, offering an apologetic glance in Noc's direction.

"Fat lot of good that did us," Calem mumbled the moment he was released from his compulsion, kicking his boots up on the table and jostling the tarnished candleholder.

Noc batted Calem's feet away, and his ring once again snared my attention. The mark was a terrifying prospect, and the curiosities that ring held—the way it had sparked tension between him and Kost—was a welcomed distraction. Catching his hand, I brought my lips to his knuckles. "Why would he ask about this?"

Noc only hesitated for a breath, but it was enough to raise the hackles on the back of my neck. "No idea."

No idea? Lie. That much I could tell. Noc dipped his head, and I caught the hint of a plea in his gaze. Did he not want the others to know? He'd promised to tell me everything after our battle in Hireath, but we hadn't gotten the chance to discuss much. Sure, the guild had kept him busy, but there was a distance between us that hadn't previously been there. A haunted look that would occasionally cloud his expression. I didn't know when to push for answers and when to simply be there for him.

Gaige eyed the ring before running his fingers through his hair. "Interesting."

"Let's get back, shall we? I believe we have research to do." Kost stood, shooting me a death glare. I bit my lip and angled my chin high, battling silently against his frustration. He wasn't the only one privy to Noc's world.

Gaige's eyes lit up. "To the library, then?"

Noc sighed. "Though this proved futile, I'll hold up my end of the deal." As one, we stood and navigated around tables and chairs in pursuit of the exit. Pausing at the bar, I placed a tentative hand on Noc's arm.

I couldn't stand the intensity of his stare. The lingering thread of hurt for not openly claiming him as my *anam-cara*. The worry of what we'd just unearthed, thanks to the mage. So much uncertainty and frustration. It battled with longing and love as he tried to soften his expression for my sake. Releasing a heavy breath, he tucked loose strands of hair behind my ear.

Leaning into his touch, I placed a gentle kiss on his palm. "Wait for me outside? I'm going to grab my things."

"Do you need any help?"

"It will only take a minute."

He looked past me, taking in the bar and invariably Dez. He'd returned from the storeroom sometime during our meeting with Eryx to wipe down the countertops with concentrated fervor. Noc stiffened, but nodded once before placing a chaste kiss on my forehead and slipping out of the establishment.

Before he could sneak away to the storeroom again, I turned to Dez. "Hey."

He stiffened, but didn't leave. "Your things are upstairs."

"Dez..." I sighed and slid onto an open barstool. It creaked beneath my weight, and I leaned against the damp countertop he'd just finished scrubbing. "I'm sorry."

"Leena, I..." Finally, he dragged his gaze upward and met my stare. The tension in his neck softened a hair. "We enjoyed each other's company. That's it."

"No, it's not." I reached out and placed my hand over his. "You were, are, my *friend*. I should've treated you as such. I didn't have much opportunity to get word back to you while I was... working with Noc, but the moment things died down, I should've come back. I should've *told* you."

Dez's fingers twitched beneath mine. "Yeah, you should have. I was worried about you."

"I know."

He let out a long breath. "I always knew you were too good for this place. That you'd end up somewhere else. I just hoped..." He shook his head. "Nah. Look, just promise me you're all right. You're not in any danger?"

"I promise." I gave his hand a squeeze. "And this is still my favorite tavern. You can count on me to bother you from time to time."

He rolled his eyes and pulled his hand away, but offered a small, sad smile. "Yeah, yeah. You'll still need to get your things, though. I've got renters interested in your room."

Standing, I gave him a nod. "On it. And Dez?"

"Yeah?"

"I really am sorry."

"I know. Now, go on. Get your stuff." He turned his back on me and busied himself with rearranging glassware along the shelves. I wished I'd handled things differently all around, but at least he wouldn't worry anymore. I turned away and headed up the rickety stairs to the few rooms tucked away for wayward souls like me. The only difference was, Dez had rented them out by the week to others, while mine had never come with an eviction notice.

Until now. And while my new life didn't require me to keep a room above a black-market tavern, I knew a piece of me would always call Midnight Jester home.

FIVE

NOC

artner. The word tasted like bile on my tongue, and I curled my hands into fists. I knew she didn't mean it, but... My nails bit into my palms. Not enough to draw blood, but enough for me to feel the swell of power. To make me consider summoning a blade and... Irrational anger came easily on the breath of red shadows sneaking beneath the familiar onyx tendrils.

"You'll start to deteriorate. Quickly."

Eryx was right. Slowly, I let my hands relax by my sides. We needed answers, and we needed them fast. I hated the lack of control, the swell of emotions that didn't feel wholly mine. The *dreams.* As if the person who'd placed the bounty was somehow contorting my mind and stirring up feelings like a grand puppeteer.

I wasn't a toy to be fucked with.

Pinching the bridge of my nose, I let out a heavy breath. "Calem, go check on her."

Monstrous willow trees marked either side of Midnight Jester, and their dangling leaves tangled in Calem's hair. He brushed them aside with an annoyed look. "Give her a minute. She's fine."

Kost adjusted his glasses. "I should have arranged for her stuff to be moved long ago. An oversight on my part."

I waved off his apology. "There was hardly time for that."

"Yeah, besides, you somehow pulled off shopping on her behalf before we went to Ortega Key. Does she even know?" Calem smirked. "Careful, she might find out you like her."

Kost went straight into defensive mode. "It was the most prudent course at the time. I would gladly offer my assistance to *you*, but why waste the effort on someone who can't tell the difference between amaranth and magenta?"

Calem blinked. "Wait, are you referring to this?" He pointed to the pop of color lining his neck from beneath his black, fitted tunic. "It's red."

"Not even close."

"What are you, master of the color wheel?"

Kost pursed his lips. "Details matter."

Calem shook his head. "They only matter if they're relevant. Telling me my collar is amaranth instead of magenta means nothing to me. Especially when it's really just red."

Kost ground his teeth. "Pointless."

Gaige chuckled, but otherwise kept his thoughts to himself. He stared at the weak light casting sunspots at the base of a few trees lucky enough to soak up the rays. The jeweled-yellow Charmer's symbol snagged my attention.

"Gaige." I nodded at his hand. "Is there a beast that can fix this?"

Calem and Kost stilled, gazes riveted to the Charmer. Gaige grimaced. "There's always a Gyss, but that's a dangerous bargain."

A Gyss. Winnow, my beast, would be unable to grant any wishes for nearly six months, but Leena also had one. Wishes weren't granted freely, though, and the price was always high. My Gyss wish had made it possible for Leena and me to be together, but it'd also resulted in her being taken prisoner by her own people. And the damage Wynn did to her... My mind traveled back to that day we'd stormed the clearing in Hireath. To the moment I'd laid eyes on Leena's weakened frame, thanks to Wynn's charm. To her cloudy eyes and hollow cheeks. I hadn't known about the scars on her legs then, but I did now.

I'd never risk something like that again.

"Too dangerous," I agreed.

"I'll grant Leena permission to read my bestiary with fresh eyes. If she were on the Council, the others might be inclined to share their knowledge too." His fingers snuck beneath his collar to extract a book-shaped locket the same size and shape as Leena's. It was hard to imagine someone else's bestiary could hold more knowledge than hers.

But I knew why she'd hesitated when she was first offered a seat on the Council. She didn't know who to trust. Leena suspected a Council member—most likely Raven—had placed the bounty, based off Wynn's murmurings while she was under his control. Not to mention that Raven's marking had a similar shade to that of the culprit. I didn't have the opportunity to dissect every color variation on the battlefield or get close enough to examine Raven's hand in the throne room after. Perhaps if Kost had gone with us, what with his eye for detail, he would have known for sure.

Still, I was inclined to believe Leena. Her conviction was strong. And yet, if she could play along and join the Council, either find a beast or find proof of Raven's treachery, we'd have a chance at removing this oath once and for all.

"I'll talk with her about it. For now, let's—"

The sunspots loitering by Gaige's feet were thrown into abrupt darkness, and a flurry of shadow-clad bodies exploded from the edge of the forest. Gaige instantly dropped to the ground, barely dodging a glittering blade to the jugular, but a second set of hands swiped at him. He screamed as knives tore flesh.

Kost reacted in an instant. Leaving my side, he dove into darkness to reappear in front of Gaige. With a strong upward swipe, he rooted a shadow blade in the skull of a slender man. His hooded chestnut gaze and scarred neck were hauntingly familiar. *Viktor.* One of the assassins who'd left with Darrien.

Calem and I joined Kost, encircling Gaige with our backs to each other. Shadows ripped through the daylight, and six assassins bled into existence. I catalogued their faces, recalled their positions within our home, and cursed. All warriors before their death, all capable of wielding a blade with unearthly precision. Darrien was nowhere to be found.

My hand quivered, and Zane's blood screamed to be released. The blood of the first assassin and guild master, ready and waiting to exact punishment. "I gave you free passage, and this is how you repay me." Rage scraped my throat, and a surge of red infiltrated the shadows in my vision.

"You sent us away without a means for survival." One of them stepped forward. Kira. A skilled knife-thrower who rarely missed her mark. She dared to challenge me with a reckless snarl. "No ability to replenish our numbers since *you're* the only one who can raise our brethren. No jobs to speak of since the capital only knows of *your* existence. Forcing us to leave was just a different kind of death sentence."

"I didn't force you to do anything." I'd given them a *choice*.

Her laugh was brittle. "You call it a choice, but I call it an ultimatum. You spit in the face of our predecessors with your bullshit, and we wanted no part of it."

"An ultimatum?" Sharpening my nails to fine points, I slit my palm open and let the blood trickle down my fingers. "If that's what you want, I'll gladly give it to you. I can still command you to follow my will." Something inside me screamed at the wrongness of what I'd just threatened, and yet... The red haze claiming my vision seemed to blanket my other senses, so all that mattered was making Kira pay for her transgression, for abandoning Cruor.

No. My fingers quaked, and blood shone against my nails. *I gave them a choice. Keep it together.*

"You wouldn't dare." She smirked and flicked her wrist.

An agonizing shriek ruptured Gaige's lungs, and he white-knuckled his thigh as a wisp of shadow oozed from somewhere deep in the wound. Kost's face blanched, and he submerged his hand in darkness to forge a deadly rapier.

With harsh, ice-green eyes, he glared at Kira. "Remove the blade at once."

"Such a tiny thing." Her fingers twitched, and Gaige screamed again, his cry ratcheting up several notches. Blood dripped between his clasped hands, and he fell to the forest floor. His symbol glowed for a moment, as if he were trying to determine what beast could help him, when Kira formed a tight fist. His body shuddered in response, eyes rolling to the back of his head, and he passed out. "Just a shard making mincemeat of his veins. How long before it destroys the main blood line to his body? Only I know."

Beside me, Calem let out a dark, guttural chuckle. "I never did like you much." His body tremored, and he tilted his head to the side. Gone were his muted-red irises, and instead, the entirety of his eyes from corner to corner had turned a shining mercury. He targeted her with an animalistic ferocity that shone in the reflective surface of his stare.

"What the hell is wrong with him?" Kira faltered, taking an involuntary step back.

Calem lunged without fear for Gaige or use of his battle wits. His usually fluid movements had gone jerky, as if the muscles straining against his skin had been electrified. Despite that, he found his mark with ease. Twin blades manifested in his hands, and he sank them deep into Kira's chest. But when the spray of blood coated his arms and the smell of death hit the air, something in him snapped.

It happened so fast, I barely had time to process what I saw. His skin shifted to thick gray hide, and he fell on all fours, spine cracking and legs elongating. Stone-tough scales formed along his lithe body. His clothes shredded to pieces as he outgrew them, falling around heavy paws that used to be hands and feet. Sharpened claws gouged the soft earth. Lifting his head to the heavens and pinning his ears back, he let out a bone-splitting howl. Then the hound that was once one of my closest friends targeted his next victim and pounced.

He tore into his target, separating flesh from bone, and the sickening rip of skin drowned out all other sounds. Save his pleased growl, which shook the very marrow of my bones and spurred everyone into motion. The remaining assassins dove into the shadows to avoid Calem's fury and manifested before us. Ink-black blades flew from their hands, aimed squarely at our hearts. Kost jumped before them and parried with his rapier. They clattered to the ground before disappearing in a puff of smoke. Hot and angry, the blood in my hands begged to be used. And I had no sense to deny it. I eyed my first victim.

The door to Midnight Jester flew open and crashed against the masonry. Leena bolted from the tavern with panic in her eyes as she took in the scene. She dropped a duffel at her feet and gaped at Calem. Behind her, Dez and a handful of patrons stood at the threshold with slack jaws.

"Stay back!" I shouted. But she didn't listen and instead rushed into the clearing. Leaving Kost to handle the assassins, I joined her side just as she thrust out her hand and showered the air in a vast rosewood glow. The groan of the beast door sounded, shaking nearby pinesco pods into a frenzy. A mass of black rage tore through the air, and Onyx snarled as he raced toward Kost and took down the nearest assassin. Leena slowed and brought her hand back to her side when another creaking groan escaped from the invisible realm.

"Again?" Her gaze riveted on the white legendary beast now flanking Onyx. Dominus growled, and the plates along his chest rumbled. He shot one cursory look toward Leena for direction before following Onyx's lead and sinking his fangs into the neck of an assassin. Blood surged from ruptured veins and coated the ground in a sickly red.

Calem's ears stood on end, and he abandoned the man he'd been tossing around like a rag doll to target Dominus and Onyx. Hackles shot upward in his mindless rage, and he crouched low to the ground. He leapt into the air and snared Onyx's wings with his teeth, smacking him to the ground and dragging him through the dirt.

"Onyx!" Leena made a move to run to him, but I anchored her to my side before she could put herself in danger. Wild eyes pinned me with fear and rage. "Let me go!"

"You'll get yourself killed if you get in the middle of that." I hated the way she damned me with her stare, but I couldn't put her at risk. Between Calem and the assassins, there was no telling who would strike first—or when.

Dominus yowled and rammed into Calem's side, dislodging his jaw and setting Onyx free. Both legendary beasts hissed and spit, circling Calem with quivering muscles and otherworldly fury.

"Noc, on your left!" Kost moved to join us, but a red-haired assassin appeared and kicked him to the ground.

Shadows detonated in my peripheral vision. A blade pierced Leena's shoulder from behind, and the sharpened point broke free just beneath her collarbone. Her pained cry echoed through the air and stoked the fire building in my core. Pure rivers of red chased away the shadows in my mind, leaving me with nothing more than the desire to kill.

Heat flooded my fingertips, and I willed my blood to form into a deadly serrated blade. And then I struck. Hard. The weapon sawed through flesh and bone, coating the ground in a spray of tantalizing red. Sick happiness flooded my senses, and I fought against the urge to smile.

But then Leena's soft whimper grabbed my attention. Clutching her wound, she stumbled but remained standing. A clean strike and not life-ending. *Why not go for the kill?* She pulled her bloody fingers away from the hole in her shoulder, and fresh anger swelled in my veins. Drowned my thoughts. Carried me on a swift current to a place of sheer chaos, and in that moment I didn't give a damn if I ever found my way back. Slipping into the shadows, I manifested by Kost's side where he was still locked in combat with one of our former brothers.

The traitor froze when he saw me. I stuck him right through the gut and lifted him in the air until his feet skated above the ground.

"Wait." Leena followed, her focus divided between the clashing of beasts and the red-haired assassin in my grasp. "He ran into me on the way out. He must have told someone we were here."

Kill. The feminine drawl in my mind shook the very essence of my reality. My body went stock-still. My gaze raced over the clearing as I tried to find the source of the sound, to find the woman who was begging me to end this man's life. Who was she? Why? A dull ache formed at the base of my skull, and my panic deepened. No one was here.

Kill. Just a whisper, and yet so powerfully tantalizing that my fingers twitched on their own. The man squirmed. With a shaky breath, I tried to ignore the allure of her command. To focus and find control.

"It's Brody, right?" I managed to rasp.

His hands fluttered around the space where my blade entrenched in his gut. "Y-yes."

Wrapping one hand around his neck, I kept him suspended and allowed the blade in his belly to disintegrate into a pool of blood. As it rushed into him, I felt the connection snap into place. An invisible line between us that granted me the power to command him at will. I poked at it with my mind, and he winced. Again, a small part of me cringed for using this power I had always told myself would be the last resort. Objections started to surface in my mind as guilt threaded my gut, but the suffocating red haze was faster. It weighed down those concerns, dragged them somewhere far away, and the only thing that mattered was exacting punishment. A strange sense of surety settled deep in me, and I felt myself smile.

"Good." I dropped him to the ground. "Don't move."

He barely mustered the effort to breathe as my command took hold and gripped him tight.

"Noc." Kost didn't bother to smother the fear threading through his voice. He stared at the space where my blade had been before swallowing twice, dragging his gaze back to the snarling mess of beasts where Calem battled Onyx and Dominus. After a moment, he cleared his throat. "What do we do about Calem?"

Leena glanced between me and Brody, her eyes wide. She opened her mouth as if to speak and then pressed her lips together. Shook her head once. Finally, she turned toward Calem. "I'll subdue him. You call Felicks and tend to Gaige's wound before he bleeds out." Leena stepped out of reach as she walked toward the storm of fury.

Kill.

My mind revolted. "Leena, stay away!"

"I've got this." Wincing as she extended her arm, she doused the area in rosewood light and closed her eyes. The beast realm opened again, but instead of the powerhouse I expected, a tiny, shimmering bird appeared. No bigger than a finch, its iridescent rainbow wings beat continuously, and its tail feathers fluctuated like the rudder of a boat. A sharp, needle-shaped beak longer than its body ended in a fine point.

Leena pointed at Calem, and the bird took off. It hummed above his head, pivoting left and right, until suddenly it dove just behind Calem's ears. Its beak pricked beneath one of the raised scales, and it flew back before he even knew he'd been stung. Calem growled, snapping his head feverishly, until his steps became sluggish. He blinked several times and shook his head from side to side as if to fight off sleep. Dominus and Onyx backed off as he took a few lumbering steps forward. Then he tripped over his own paws and fell to the earth with a heavy thud. His eyes slipped closed.

With Calem subdued, Onyx, Dominus, and the bird returned to their master. Leena crouched before Onyx, inspecting his mauled wing with delicate fingers. He hissed as she assessed the damage, but her soft coos and whispered endearments kept him from pulling back. After a moment, she sighed.

"You'll be all right. Go on, return to the realm." Leena flexed her hand, and the beast realm called her creatures back to the safety of their hidden world. Sweat dampened the collar of her tunic, and she shrugged off her jacket. Blood stained the soft blue of her blouse, and she cupped her hand over the wound as she walked back to us.

The red flares of anger battling against my shadows pulsed. I fought to ignore them. "Is Calem okay?"

Her body trembled, and she sank to her knees. "Yes. Kels is a Naughtbird. She produces a powerful sleeping draft with her beak. Calem won't wake for a while."

"Is he going to stay like that?" I eyed the scaled hound, unsure if I'd ever see my friend return to normal.

"I don't know. I've never—" The sound of the beast realm door opening cut her off, and her gaze dropped to her hand. Yet, no rosewood glow pulsed from her emblem. Instead, a soft light had bloomed from a pile of shredded clothes a few feet away. A bronze key was just visible beneath Calem's torn tunic, and suddenly a shrieking streak of mint green was flying through the air toward his slumbering form.

"Effie!" Leena leapt to her feet, wincing slightly as she cupped her shoulder, and took off after Calem's Effreft. His beast didn't acknowledge her. Instead, she circled her master and let out a series of concerned birdcalls that tugged at my heart. It was all too reminiscent of her sudden appearance at the battle of Hireath. And while I knew Calem was still alive—albeit not entirely himself—I could only hope Effie wouldn't wake him. If she did and he hurt her, he'd never forgive himself. Sparing a quick glance at Kost, who was focused on tearing Gaige's trousers to better assess his wounds, I followed after Leena and Calem's beast.

Tossing her head to the sun, Effie beat her wings feverishly. Small particles of glistening magic fell from her wings, coating Calem's tough hide. When she was pleased with her work, she landed beside him and nudged her beak against his snout, soft coos full of worry.

"Effie." Leena kneeled beside her. "It'll be all right. He'll be okay."

The Effreft rounded her worried pink gaze on Leena for a moment before turning back to Calem.

"Come on, why don't you stay with me where it's safe?" She held out her hands just as Calem snarled. Still asleep, but visibility agitated, he shuddered as the magic settled deep into his hide. Effie startled at the sound and took several hops back, a heartbreakingly soft call slipping from her beak. She flapped her wings a few times before settling them against her back and scooting closer to Leena. Her eyes never left her master.

Gently, Leena scooped Effie up and held her close to her chest, ignoring whatever pain may have sparked from her wound. "Shhh. You did fine."

"Will that help him return to normal?" I asked. I prayed that it would. He *had* to come back to us. For Effie's sake. For Leena's. For all of us.

"Maybe? We're in uncharted territory here. Kaori would know. Possibly Gaige." Her head pivoted back to the man lying still before Kost. Problems from every direction, it seemed. I placed a gentle hand on her back, and she rolled her lower lip into her mouth. Squeezed Effie a little tighter.

"He'll be okay too. Let's see if Kost needs any help." I led her back to Kost, my hand steady on her back. Would she blame herself for this? How could she? We never could've predicted the attack, and yet the way she'd stared at Calem… His predicament wasn't her fault, either, but guilt had a funny way of ignoring logic when the heart was involved.

We came to a stop before Kost, and Leena sat Effie on the ground by her feet. He had summoned his Poi, Felicks, while we'd inspected Calem, and his fox-like beast was waiting with rapt attention.

"How's he doing?" Leena asked, voice strained.

Kost never looked up from his work. With Gaige's pant leg torn clean off, the jagged gash along his thigh was clearly visible. Blood flowed in a slow but steady trickle, and Kost sighed. "The blade should've dissipated with Kira's death, but something is still in there." With unparalleled precision, he dove two fingers into the wound and extracted a tiny silver needle. Then snapped it in half. "She must have propelled it in with her shadows."

I scowled at the weapon. "But he'll be fine?"

"Yes. Felicks, come here." He never tore his gaze away from Gaige's leg. Felicks moved instantly to his master's side. Settling into his haunches, he angled his head down and began licking the length of the wound. Slowly, Gaige's skin resealed. When the work was done, Felicks glanced around and let out a soft bark. Kost finally relaxed a fraction and turned to meet our gazes, pausing when he noticed Leena's wound. "Let Felicks patch that up for you."

She slumped to the ground beside Effie, nodding wordlessly. Felicks bounded toward her without needing a command and stood on his hind legs, licking her exposed wound. Magic saliva dripped from his chops and sewed her skin together.

Leena shivered. An iron fist wrenched my heart, and I sank to the ground beside her. No doubt the scratchy feel of this beast's tongue was calling up memories she'd rather forget. Right on cue, her shaking fingers went to her legs. I caught her hands between my own and placed a kiss on her knuckles. After a moment, Felicks stopped and Leena rolled her shoulder, wincing slightly. The skin may have resealed, but the knife had gone clean through. Muscles would take longer to heal, even if Felicks's saliva had dripped through to the bone.

Effie paced beside her, continuously tossing glances back to the open clearing where Calem slumbered. Felicks cocked his head to the side, tracking Effie's movements, and then offered a soft nudge into her side as she passed. She practically wilted into him. Felicks didn't seem to mind her added weight, and instead began licking the length of her neck, preening her feathers.

A soft smile touched Kost's lips before he looked past them to the red-haired assassin, Brody, lying frozen on the ground. He glowered. "What are we going to do about him?"

Pulling Leena up with me, we towered over him. "Stand."

Without hesitation, Brody stood, compelled by my blood. Wide eyes shifted between us. "Are you going to kill me?"

Kill. Gods, I wanted to. The languid red sheen threatened to close over my thoughts, but I steeled my ire and reached for Leena's waist. The feel of her warmth and steady beat of her heart grounded my senses. I'd need to tell her—tell all of them—about the voice I swore I heard...but now wasn't the time.

"That depends entirely on you." I glanced at the decimated bodies of the fallen assassins. They had once been my brethren. I'd never wanted to kill them. But if it meant protecting my own... "You will answer all my questions. What was your mission?"

He shifted uncomfortably, but couldn't resist the command of my blood. "After I saw you enter Midnight Jester with minimal forces, I reported to Darrien." Swallowing hard, he ground his teeth together. Muscles jumped along his neckline.

Anger flared deep. "Fight it all you want, but you won't succeed. Why did you attack us?"

Brody's eyes bugged. "To capture Leena."

"Me? Why?" Leena frowned. "For the bounty? Even if you killed me, you wouldn't know who to present my body to. Not to mention the Crown of the Charmers Council has pardoned me, even if they haven't found the Charmer responsible. It would be futile."

No. That's not it. Her wound wasn't fatal. If they'd wanted to collect on the bits, no matter how futile she insinuated it'd be, they would have killed her first instead of distracting us with Gaige. This wasn't an attack on her life, but a kidnapping in the making. "You wanted her as collateral."

Brody nodded. "So you'd relinquish Zane's power to Darrien."

As if I'd ever do such a thing. And yet... My gaze drifted to Leena. My greatest weakness. I would do anything to keep her safe. I'd been willing to give up Cruor before if it meant being with her.

And after commanding Darrien and my men to aid in her rescue after the Gyss wish went south... He knew exactly what he was doing. And he'd continue to exploit my love for Leena until he got what he wanted.

Kill. My fingers quivered. "Count yourself lucky that you were the last one alive. Run back to Darrien and tell him this: Come near me, Leena, or Cruor again, and I won't stop at eliminating his forces. I'll come for him. I'll come for him, and I won't stop until every last drop of blood has been drained from his body. Understood?"

Brody paled. "Understood."

I jerked my chin over my shoulder. "Go. And don't ever come back."

Falling into a world of shadows, he bolted north along the Kitska Forest. Kost watched the whole thing silently, but his damning green stare said more than enough. The weight of his gaze sat heavy on my shoulders, and I rolled my neck from side to side. I'd never used my blood command so freely before, and he knew it. Forcing Brody to obey had been so *easy*. As if the red haze claiming my senses had somehow lessened my inhibitions. It was *necessary*. I had to protect Cruor. My family. Leena.

With a thick swallow, I met Kost's hard gaze. He could reprimand me later. Leena looked back and forth between us, her brows pinching together. She opened her mouth as if to speak, but was interrupted by a groan from Gaige. His eyes fluttered open. Pushing himself up into a sitting position, he stared uneasily first at the mangled remains of assassins and then at his leg, where Kost's hand still rested right above his healing wound.

A sly, if weak grin claimed his lips, and he cleared his throat. "Looks like I've been in...*capable* hands."

Kost furrowed his brown in confusion, until he followed Gaige's probing stare. I bit back a chuckle as he immediately jerked his hand away and stood. "Felicks attended to your wounds." At the use of his name, Felicks sauntered over and plopped before the men, a happy tongue lolling out the side of his mouth.

Gaige worked tufts of fur behind the creature's ears, but his eyes never left Kost. "Thanks, Felicks."

Footsteps sounded behind us, and Dez came to a halt a few feet away. He'd smartly stayed out of the battle and had just now moved away from the safety of Midnight Jester. He set Leena's duffel gently on the ground. The jagged scar on his cheek twisted as he grimaced and studied her shoulder. "You all right?"

"Yeah." Leena graced him with a genuine smile.

I tried to be nice, but my voice came out sounding curt. "We'll take care of the bodies. You can go back to your business."

Dez flattened his lips. "And what about him?" He yanked his thumb in the direction of Calem. During my interrogation, he'd apparently shifted back to human form and was sleeping in all his naked glory. Effie perked up and took off toward her master, flying in excited circles around his head.

Relief washed through me at the sight, and the last, lingering threads of red in my peripheral vision seemed to fade entirely. Calem. He was human again, but for how long? What kind of triggers would we have to watch for? He'd always launched into battle without hesitation, but this time, it was different. He was immediately unreachable, unable to discern friend from foe. And that was a dangerous thing.

Leena jerked her gaze upward and away. "We'll take care of him too. Sorry about the commotion."

Dez ran a hand over his scalp and gripped the back of his neck. "Yeah, okay. Take care, all right?"

She nodded. "Of course. Take care."

"Dez." I tried to push aside the simmering, reckless anger

inside me. Logically, I knew he'd done nothing wrong. Leena had an entire life before she met me. But the oath made it all too easy to succumb to dark impulses, and I'd nearly attacked him for simply trying to protect Leena. "Sorry about earlier."

He raised an incredulous brow. "Sure."

Gait stiff, Dez retreated to Midnight Jester and closed the door, leaving us with a mess of bodies, two injured Charmers, and a drugged-out assassin-beast. I ran a heavy hand through my hair and sighed. The problems were mounting quicker than we had time to assess them.

As if sensing my heavy thoughts, Leena pressed close. Standing on her toes, she whispered into my ear, "One thing at a time."

My chest hitched. With gentle fingers, I brushed the hair back from her face. It wasn't just Calem I was worried about—it was me. *Her.* Because these deadly visions, coupled with the strange new voice, had to be the oath's call getting stronger. Once we got Calem settled back at Cruor, I'd have to tell her, if only so she could protect herself from me.

Heart heavy, I sighed. "One thing at a time."

SIX

LEENA

After returning to Cruor and bathing to get rid of the muck of blood and battle, I found myself in the library with Gaige and Kost. The familiar welcome of the room I'd grown to love was missing, replaced by a sense of foreboding I didn't want to acknowledge. And while it was impossible not to feel small in a space that took up more than a quarter of the manor, I somehow felt microscopic. Defeated. Uncertain. I would've given all my bits to the mage for answers, and yet we were still here. Still searching.

Vaulted ceilings with curved walnut rafters and an endless maze of bookshelves stretched before Kost, Gaige, and me. The room was dry and warm, thanks to the crackling fire in its massive hearth, and smelled of cedarwood and books.

"This is impressive." Gaige stepped around me to survey the space. Large oak tables with high-back chairs were nestled between the shelves. Tiered candlelight fixtures acted as centerpieces, and inkwells with blank scrolls of parchment and quills were neatly organized for use.

"I've read just about everything in here. I can point you in the right direction if you're looking for something specific." Kost wandered over to the first shelf, trailing his hand along dusty spines of varying colors. "Though I haven't gotten around to this one."

He extracted a tome nearly as thick as his waist and set it with a definitive thud on the table. *A Brief History of Wilheim* in archaic, bold font caught the light.

Gaige raised a brow. "So much for brief."

Kost hummed. "My thoughts exactly."

"What are we looking for, again?" I followed behind them and acted as a cart while they loaded tome after tome into my open arms. Kost paused and snared a handful of tied-off parchment bundles. He neatly added them to our growing pile before hooking a right down an offshoot aisle with even more books.

"Gaige traded for access to these texts, so I suppose whatever he wants." He glanced over his shoulder at Gaige, who was debating between two texts. After a shrug, he tucked both beneath his arm and rejoined us. "As for you and me, we're looking for information that might pertain to Noc's oath."

"I haven't been able to find anything yet." I shifted the weight of the books against my chest.

"Me neither." Kost started to layer even more tomes into his own arms. "I'm hoping there's something I've missed over the years."

Gaige peered over the thick binding of a book etched with green lettering. "This might prove interesting." He ran a light finger over the title: *Zane and the Fallen Leaders*. A flare of magic sparked beneath his touch, sending a green ember into the air.

Kost smiled. "That's a special book. More alive than not. It changes to keep record of Cruors' doings. We couldn't alter it if we tried."

Gaige's eyes went wide. "Fascinating."

Kost nodded before refocusing on our overflowing arms. "I think we have enough to start with." Leading us back to a table, he organized the texts by year and relevancy, mumbling quietly to himself as he pondered which tome to study first. Gaige followed Kost's lead and took the chair at the head of the table, fingers snagging *Zane and the Fallen Leaders.*

Silence, save the occasional whisper of parchment scraping together, dominated the room. Even the low-burning fire hardly popped. I sank into a nearby chair with tufted arms and an ottoman, but I couldn't bring myself to read the tome before me. Not with Calem slumbering on a medical cot upstairs.

Noc and Oz had taken him there upon our return, and they still hadn't shown their faces. I could've gone to the medical wing. Pushed open the heavy double doors and taken a seat by Calem's side. But the sight of my friend as a raging monster burned in my mind, and I couldn't help but feel guilty. *Responsible.* And so I avoided the wing altogether, first taking a long bath, then simply standing in my bedroom with the hope that Noc would come and find me. But he didn't, and an idle mind only made things worse. So, I'd changed and found Kost and Gaige, insisting we follow through with Noc's request.

But now that I was here, with too much knowledge and no idea where to start, the whole damned thing felt pointless. A wave of cold rushed over me, and I brought my fingers to my lips as the walls of the library threatened to close in.

"Leena."

I startled, nearly falling out of the chair, and looked up to see Gaige crouching before me. Kost tore his gaze away from his text to watch.

My voice cracked. "Yes?"

Angling his chin down, Gaige reached behind his neck and unclasped a simple silver chain. "Why don't you start with this?" The book-shaped pendant dangled before me, and he reached for my hand. Forcing my palm open, he pressed his bestiary into my grasp. "I give you permission to read its contents."

Sparkling citrine light exploded from where our fingers met, and the projection of a large book floated to life before us. The branded tree on the worn leather cover matched our marks, and I stroked the inscription of Gaige's name written in our ancient language across the binding. The bestiary purred and flipped open, waiting for me to browse its pages.

I gave him a relieved smile. "Thank you."

Gaige's chuckle warmed my soul. "You're welcome. I'm not certain there will be a beast in there that can help, but it's a start." As Gaige stood, Kost ducked his head and returned to his book, but not before I could catch a faint spark of interest in his gaze. Perhaps the Charmer's lure was starting to work on Kost, making him more amiable toward Gaige, but I strongly suspected it had more to do with these subtle hints of kindness tucked away behind Gaige's flirtatious demeanor.

Hours ticked by as I worked my way through Gaige's massive bestiary. At some point, Kost had left and returned with three coffees and brown sugar cubes. The sweet richness of vanilla rolled over my tongue, and I settled further into my chair. It was easy to get lost in the world of beasts. In my mind, I imagined taming them all. Learning from them. Watching them find peace in the realm. But the closer I got to the final page, the less the warmth from the coffee or the subtle murmurings of the men could chase away the doubt and fear. Those emotions were monsters, not beasts, and I didn't have the wherewithal to tame them.

I flipped another page. The mirage of an inky-black horse with turquoise, fuchsia, and emerald-green auroras dancing across her hide bled to life. She tossed her endless mane, and powerful, feathered wings unfurled from her back. A curved horn more like a blade glowed a painful white, and light streamed about her on a hidden current of air.

"Gaige." I reached for her, but my fingers met formless magic. She rippled out of existence only to reappear once I dropped my hand. "How did you get a Zavalluna?"

He looked up from his coffee and offered me a crooked grin. "She was gifted to me."

"Who would part with such an amazing beast?" Awe filled my words. Zavallunas weren't found anywhere on Lendria, and were extremely selective when it came to their masters. I'd never met, or even heard, of another Charmer who had one. It was entirely possible that Gaige was the only one.

"It's a long story for another time." His smile turned sad.

Kost set his book down and peered at the floating text surrounding the image of the mare. "An A-Class beast?"

"Yes, but not because they're dangerous." I suppose Kost would be surprised that something so docile would be ranked so high. But rankings took several factors into consideration: power, rarity, magical ability, limitations, danger. The Council was responsible for assigning ranks as a means of keeping untrained Charmers from attempting to tame a creature beyond their capabilities. If a new beast were to appear, the Council would debate for weeks, maybe even months, before announcing a rank. Once it was announced, they'd hold a ritual before the statue of Celeste in Hireath, relying on the goddess's magic to alter all Charmers' bestiaries. That way, if anyone ever encountered the new creature and tamed it, the information would appear without fault.

But a new beast hadn't appeared in decades. There was no way we'd discovered them all—the world was too vast. We were just too reclusive. Only a handful of Charmers ever left Lendria for fear of being too far from Hireath.

Gaige nodded as he studied Kost's profile. "Zavallunas are incredibly rare, supposedly residing somewhere in the mages' lands. They're not exactly a welcoming bunch, as you experienced earlier."

Kost pressed his glasses up the bridge of his nose. "What can she do?"

"She amplifies the powers of other beasts. Her horn emits magical energy that flows in a small radius around her. If another beast is nearby, they'll be able to do incredible things." Gaige studied the mirage of his creature. "Though it's an exhaustive talent. If she uses it for too long or too frequently, it can do irreparable damage to her horn."

"Some say the first Crown rode one into battle against the Wilheimians and the First King. Her power would've been otherworldly." I closed his bestiary and stood, stretching my hands to the ceiling.

"Indeed." Gaige leaned across the table and snatched *A Brief History of Wilheim*.

I returned the bestiary to him. "Unfortunately, she has little to offer in the ways of removing a curse."

Gaige grimaced. "I know." Something told me he'd known all along I wouldn't find what I needed, but the gesture wasn't lost on me. Maybe I could trust that brain of his. Maybe he really *was* here to help. It was hard to know who to put my faith in when so many had turned on me before, but everything about this latest kindness seemed genuine.

And yet, as kind as that gesture had been, I was still without answers.

As if hearing my thoughts, he cleared his throat. "You might consider joining the Council. The others might be inclined to share their bestiaries or know of a solution."

And just like that, my body stiffened. Learning to trust Gaige would be hard enough. And while it was easy to believe Yazmin, Crown of the Council, was on my side—given she'd pardoned my past offenses—there was no telling who Wynn had won over. Accepting Yazmin's offer would put me in close proximity with the very person who was trying to kill me.

But there's no telling what I could learn, either.

"If we can't find answers…" I swept my gaze over the endless stacks of books. "Maybe. But for now, I'm going to stretch my legs." Waving over my shoulder, I hid my frustration by slipping into the maze of shelves. The soft snap of a burning log was the only sound, and I let my fingers wander along bindings as I walked. Night peeked through the bay window, and thousands of stars winked against the dark expanse.

The dawn of the next full moon would mark the Winter Crest. As a Charmer, we never participated in Wilheimian traditions, but I'd learned of this one during my time living above Midnight Jester. Even black-market workers would put aside their jobs for the occasion, celebrating in their own way with too many ales and stories about balls and dancing.

Climbing the rungs of a ladder propped against a shelf, I peered out into the vast darkness. It was impossible to see Wilheim with Cruor tucked safely in the thicket of Kitska Forest, but I didn't need a glittering castle of marble and diamond. I'd rather a celebration with family who refused to turn their backs on me. Noc to hold me when the first frost dusted the grass beneath our feet—something Charmers did celebrate.

"What are you doing up there?" Noc leaned against a bookshelf, an amused smile toying at his lips. Shadows clung to his ankles, reminding me that he could have been observing me for gods only knew how long. His gaze lazily trailed to my backside. "Not that I'm complaining about the view."

I wiggled my hips for effect. "Glad to be of service." I descended the rungs and he reached out his hand, helping me down the last few steps before pulling me into a hug. His honey-tinged scent teased my senses, and I buried my face in the collar of his shirt.

"How goes the research?" His voice was steady. Low. Warm. My heart squirmed, and I leaned back to take stock of his expression. He'd been on the verge of exploding so many times lately, thanks to the oath—had seemed both so dangerous and so fragile— that I'd almost forgotten about the slight curve of his lips when he relaxed into a smile.

I hooked my hands behind his neck. "Not good. Someone is distracting me."

His grin deepened. "Breaks are allowed."

"Good, because my brain can't handle much more of this." I gestured to the rows of books cocooning us in silence.

"Oh?" His fingers teased the hem of my cashmere sweater, finding bare skin along my midriff. "I suppose I can provide you with a more physical activity. That is, if you're willing to spend some time with your pair bond."

Pair bond. The Wilheimian term for *anam-cara*, and the very thing I should have called him in front of Dez. Pulling out of Noc's embrace, I wrapped my arms around my stomach. "Noc, I'm sorry."

He dropped his hands to his sides. "For?"

"You're not my partner. You're my *anam-cara*. My pair bond. I wasn't prepared for today, and I didn't react well." Thickness swelled in my throat, and I swallowed. Raising my eyes to meet his, I prayed he could read every ounce of love I had for him in my gaze. "I love you. I'm not afraid to say it or ashamed to be with you. No one understands me like you do. No one can look at all my broken pieces and see how they're supposed to fit back together. No one would even dare to try. But you do. Every day. And I—"

Noc closed the distance between us and cupped his hands on either side of my face. He slanted his lips across mine and captured my words, pouring nothing but love and devotion back into me.

"Enough." He spoke softly against my lips. "I should be apologizing, not you. This oath... The way I have been behaving..."

I gripped his waist and held him close. "What's it like?"

"Bad. Lately, I've been having—" His words died on a strangled grunt. After a moment, he cleared his throat. "Sorry."

"That's all right. You were saying?"

"I've been having—"

Again, he abruptly cut off, words stifled by a garbled noise at the back of his throat. He swallowed thickly. Tried again to speak, but was met with the same strange reaction. The veins along his neck bulged beneath reddening skin.

"Noc? What's going on?" I moved toward him and placed my hands on his chest.

For a moment, all he did was stare right through me, as if I weren't even there. Eyes tight. Lips parting for a fraction of a moment only to seal again. He shook his head once, then let out a long, shuddering breath.

"It's the oath."

A dull ringing sounded in my ears. We were running out of time. "What's happening?"

He hesitated, as if weighing every word before deciding to speak it. "The words won't come. It's as if I can't..." His voice trailed off, going raspy, and then he rubbed his throat. "I don't feel like I'm in control. Not always."

"How can I help?" With the removal of his decades-old curse, cast on him by a priestess from his old life, he was able to let loose. Feel freely. Love wholly. But he would never forget what it was like to hold himself in check. Control was a skill he'd perfected over decades. If he was losing it now...

"I can handle it." He tilted my chin up and sighed. Light fingers danced across my collarbone, and he offered me a soft smile.

"You don't have to face this alone." His touch was soothing, but not enough to chase away the uncertainty brewing in my gut.

He placed a kiss on my cheek. "I'm not alone. I have Cruor. I have my family. And most importantly, I have you." His hands trailed along my back and teased the waistline of my loose-fitting breeches.

Clearly, he wasn't as concerned with his inability to speak as I was. "Are you sure you're okay?"

He raised a playful brow. "For a moment, let me think about something other than the problems we're facing. Please." With ease, he slipped beneath the fabric to cup my ass.

A shiver of pleasure raced through me. "Fine. Just remember, I'm here for you. You'll always have me." And he would. I'd never stop fighting for him, helping him. Loving him. I needed him to believe that with every fiber of my being, because if his control really was slipping, then I would be his rock.

He groaned and hoisted me up, knocking over a few books in the process. I giggled, and he pressed a long finger against my lips. Which I promptly sucked into my mouth. Dark eyes flashing, he devoured me with a single glance. He carried me across the room, pressing me hard against yet another bookshelf.

Nicking the soft skin of my neck with his teeth, he covered me in passionate kisses as he fumbled through random books. Tome after tome fell to the floor until his fingers snagged a muted-yellow binding, and the book partially gave way with a heavy click. The bookshelf at my back swung inward, and he carried me into his private study.

The door groaned to a close behind him. Gravelly and thick, his whispered words wreaked delicious havoc on my senses. "Never has there been a better use for that door."

"Agreed."

He kept my body flush to his chest. Freeing one arm, he knocked books and scattered parchment across his desk in an attempt to clear it. Inkwells toppled over, covering the pristinely carved wood with dark splatters as he set me amidst the glorious mess.

"You'll ruin the varnish." I couldn't care less what it did to the desk, let alone my clothes and skin. I sounded breathless. Hungry. I hoped to the gods he didn't stop to clean it up.

They answered in favor, and Noc growled, "I don't care." His hands dove under my sweater, yanking it off in one easy motion. The soft, white bralette was next, and he had no qualms utterly destroying that, either. Lace drifted to the floor, and he brought a tender hand to my body. An aching moan slipped from the back of my throat.

Voice thick with want, he stared openly at my exposed skin. "You are my everything."

"As you are mine." With a gentle caress, I traced the scar on his cheek. He turned, planting a kiss on my palm, and then nipped at my fingers. A devilish smirk claimed his lips and stoked a fire in my core. Laying me across the desk, against the ink and parchment and now broken feathered quills, he moved to my trousers. They were gone along with my undergarments before I could even register the spark of his fingers at my waist. For a moment, my mind jumped to the nightstand beside our bed where a vial of imperit was waiting. I'd been taking it regularly since our first time to prevent pregnancy. Had I taken a dose this week? *Yes*, I remembered, relaxing. We were safe for several more days.

"Gods," he murmured, pulling my focus back to him. His

glittering black gaze roved the entire length of my body. Left no inch of skin unappreciated. Placing his palms on either side of my head, he leaned down and captured my mouth in a kiss. "You're beautiful."

"And you're entirely too clothed."

"That can be fixed."

Sitting up, I tore at his clothes until he was as naked as me. I traced the dips and grooves of his torso, and then I dropped my hands farther until he let out a graveled moan.

His long fingers danced down my spine, and a pleasant shiver rushed over my skin. I would never grow tired of his touch. Never shy away from the feel of his fingers on my body. He gripped my waist and pulled me to the edge of the desk. Slowly, our limbs intertwined, and we began moving as one. My entire world narrowed to his existence, to the feel of us. Pulse thudding in my ears, I let out a heady moan.

He palmed the expanse of my legs, and when his fingers grazed those scars, I swallowed a gasp. Not because of Wynn. Not because of the damage he'd done to my body and soul. But because Noc hadn't even noticed them. Hadn't skipped over them for fear of what they'd feel like. He'd smoothed over them entirely. Etched a tale of love and devotion with his gentle touch, completely indifferent toward scarred ridges or velvet skin. Because in his eyes, I *was* beautiful. Every gods-damned inch of me.

Leaning back, he tilted my face up, and worry lined the creases around his eyes. So soft. So concerned. "Leena?" A thumb brushed along my cheeks.

A weak sob broke through my chest. "I love you. You make me feel..." The word caught in my throat, and I shook my head. *Whole.*

His own eyes glimmered with return emotion. "I've loved you for a long time. Long before I was willing to admit it to myself." He pulled me closer, heat radiating from his body. "I just wasn't willing to risk your safety. But gods, Leena. You're such a warrior. You hooked me, and I was gone."

I kissed him so hard our teeth clashed, but I didn't care. Noc had given me so much. A home. Family. Love. Being with him was the very thing I never knew I needed. And everything I'd die to protect. A wondrous exhale rushed through my lungs, and I dragged my nails along his back.

"Noc." The breathy exclamation elicited a purely animalistic growl from his throat, and delicious heat surged through me. This slow-building eruption would be my undoing, and gods did I want to come undone. Completely. Entirely. For him. We fell apart together, lips locked and bodies wracked.

For a moment after, we didn't move. We simply stayed connected, breathing together. I didn't know what this oath would do to him, but I knew I'd continue to be here for him. Show him how much I loved him. If I could provide that, if he never forgot about our connection, then we'd make it through this somehow.

With heartbreaking tenderness, Noc placed a kiss on my forehead. "I love you, Leena Edenfrell."

"I love you, Noc..." I let it trail off into a question. How was it possible that I still didn't know the last name of the man I loved?

A familiar uneasy flicker smothered the brightness of his eyes, but instead of dissembling again, he said, "Noc Feyreigner. But please don't go parading that knowledge around. I like the life I have now. Not the one I had before." For effect, he gave my butt a squeeze. "I especially like the company I have now."

I rolled my eyes. "You don't have to keep your past under lock and key. Not with me. Remember? You promised." I couldn't even fathom why he was so concerned about sharing his secrets with me. My knowledge of Wilheim was beyond slim, thanks to my upbringing in Hireath. And my years on the run as an outlaw weren't exactly filled with days of leisurely reading or courtly activities. He could've been a baker's son or a traitor to the king, and I wouldn't have known the difference.

"I remember. When we're not naked with the possibility of someone busting in," he nodded toward the door leading out to the main halls of Cruor, "we can chat all you want."

"Let's get dressed, then. We can talk in our room."

He sighed, pulling away a fraction. "Leena…"

"You don't have to be afraid, Noc." How long had he spent guarding himself from emotions? Connections? I knew it wouldn't be easy for him to fully let go. Not so soon after the curse had been lifted. It would take time. Reassurance. "I just want to know more about you. You don't have to worry about what I might think or say."

He pressed his eyes shut. "I'm not afraid of that."

"Then what?"

Slowly, as if it pained him, he met my stare. "My past is… dangerous. If anyone here found out…"

I frowned. "You're worried about your brothers? I thought you trusted them."

"It's not a matter of trust." His voice strained. "One thing I've learned about working as an assassin is that information is *everything*. It's the most powerful resource, and if my brethren learned of my past, that would be problematic. They'd become a target. I doubt they'd willingly betray me, but," he paused, and with deadly calm pressed a light finger to my temple, "apply the right type of pressure to anyone, and they'll crack. If information about me gets out, then all of Cruor will be jeopardized."

Cold swept through the room and chilled my bones. I couldn't suppress a shiver. Noc pulled me close in a tight embrace, running his hands down my back to spark warmth again. Could it really be that bad? That dangerous?

I chewed on my lip. "I don't want to make things harder for anyone here, but…" I couldn't help myself. I wanted to know more about the man I loved.

Noc relented with a tired smile. "I promised I would tell you. But even in Cruor, the walls have ears. When there's no one else around to listen in, we can talk. Okay?"

"Okay." I pressed my nose to his sternum and breathed deeply. Curiosity burned in my chest, but something far warmer trickled through my limbs. Noc *trusted* me. Enough to tell me about his past. Enough to give himself to me fully. I just had to wait a little longer.

Fatigue hit me hard. Depleted from our lovemaking—coupled with the lack of sleep and food—my body trembled. Leaning against Noc's chest, I let out a tired sigh.

"Bed?"

Noc's warm chuckle was a blanket on a cold night. "Believe it or not, that was my original intention before you seduced me on that ladder. Such a temptress."

I bit his shoulder, and he hissed. "I know. Now take me to bed."

"Careful, Leena. There are two ways to take that statement, and I'm more than happy to comply with both."

I winked. "Good." And with that, he slid on his drawers before sweeping me into his arms and draping my clothes across my body. I giggled, tucking my face into the crook of his neck. Within his warm embrace, it was almost possible to forget about his curse and the way it hung over us like an ax about to come down.

Almost.

SEVEN

KOST

My fingers grazed the open tome before me as I devoured paragraph after paragraph of useless information. Gaige and I had been quietly reading for hours, and the weight of the day's events was eating away at my energy. Calem, a monster. Noc, waiting for Cruor's Oath to bring the axe down. Leena...

I let out a quiet sigh. It was probably for the best that she'd taken her leave some time ago. There was only so much we could do, and just knowing that neither she nor Gaige had a beast capable of helping was hard enough. Shoulders slackening, I pushed away the book and leaned back in my chair.

"Everything all right?" Gaige glanced up at me over the top of *Zane and the Fallen Leaders*. He'd yet to put down the tome, occasionally letting out a surprised hum as he read. Warm light from a dying candle softened his expression. Or maybe he thought to offer that small smile to lull me into a false sense of security. His intentions weren't exactly crystal clear, and I'd hardly spent enough time deciphering his motivation. Something I'd have to rectify.

"Of course not." I pulled off my spectacles and extracted a cloth from my breast pocket. Methodically, I began to polish them.

Gaige set down his book with a heavy thud. "Want to talk about it?"

I raised a brow. "What's there to talk about? You're well aware of the problems we're facing."

"Sometimes, talking helps. Even if it's just to repeat what's already known." He ran his fingers along his jaw, and the citrine emblem on the back of his hand stole my attention. It truly was the most stunning shade, somehow almost as vibrant and alive as Gaige himself. Even now, with tired eyes on the verge of closing, his steel-blue stare was intriguing. And unnerving, but... I replaced my glasses and dropped my gaze to the heavy table between us.

When I didn't respond, Gaige only shook his head and stood, shrugging off his wine-colored overcoat. He draped it over the back of his chair and then stretched his hands toward the ceiling. The action pulled his tunic tight across his chest, hinting at corded muscles. I forced down a hard swallow.

Charmer's lure. What a ridiculous magic. Leena had mentioned it to me once, how all Charmers naturally produced an undetectable aura that put those around them at ease. Made them more amicable. She'd sworn up and down it had nothing to do with love or attraction—just a soothing, gentle energy of sorts. The type of magic that would always come in handy when taming beasts.

But I wasn't a beast, and I wasn't about to let someone like Gaige—someone we knew nothing about—whittle away at my defenses. Magic or not.

Clearing my throat, I nodded toward *Zane and the Fallen Leaders.* "Are you enjoying our history?"

He continued to stare directly at me for a long moment. "It's fascinating, really. I'd heard of Zane before through some of my other studies, but his history, his recount of death and the magic he brought back with him…" He waved his hand around for emphasis before offering me a grin. "Words escape me."

"How infrequent that must be."

He laughed, a deep, pleasing sound that stirred up an odd feeling in my gut. "Was that a joke? How *infrequent* are those for you?"

"Very."

"Shame." His grin was downright devilish. With deliberate slowness, he abandoned his place behind his chair and walked toward me, parking his hip on the table just a few feet away. "I bet you're actually quite funny."

With a quiet scoff, I shook my head. "Don't be absurd. In my entire *long* life, there's only been one person who ever referred to me as 'funny.' He considered himself quite droll, and thus an expert on the matter." I tilted my head, the bittersweet memory reflected in my tone. "Though to be honest, his dry wit got him in trouble more often than not. It didn't help that he made it a point to badger drunk hotheads."

He trailed his fingers along his jaw, smile still intact. "You sound fond of this mystery man. Who was he?"

Shock rendered me immobile. Had I really said that out loud? His damn Charmer's lure must have loosened my tongue. One moment I'd been in total control, and now here I was, revealing facts about a life I had no intention of sharing. Leave it to Gaige to stir up something, *someone*, I hadn't thought about in ages.

Not ages. I suppressed a shudder. There was no sense in lying to myself about Jude. There was a perpetual, phantom pang in my chest, one that stemmed from the jagged scar just above my heart. The fatal wound I'd endured to save his life. The ache was dull, but constant. A reminder of something I could never escape, no matter how hard I tried.

Gaige waited, his captivating stare doing peculiar things to my gut. My fingers itched to once again remove my glasses, to polish the lenses and busy myself while I sorted out the strange feeling. There was something about the way his words, though obviously tinged with humor, held a semblance of warmth.

"No one special." I finally caved, letting only the barest sliver of emotion tinge my words. A small lie. One to keep the conversation going, because I couldn't bring myself to shut down, not entirely. But certainly not the truth. I wasn't willing—*ready*—to share that with anyone. Not yet. Perhaps not ever.

"But you won't tell me who? Maybe I can guess, then. Your tense suggests it's someone from your past, but your description sounds an awful lot like Calem."

"Calem finds my *actions* humorous," I said, and my back relaxed into the hard wood of the chair. As if I had no choice in the matter. My own body betrayed me, painted a picture of tranquility for Gaige, when all I really wanted was to throw up sky-high walls. "But that's not the same as thinking I am funny."

He inched closer. Let his fingers dance along the grains of the table. "Something tells me it isn't Noc—"

"Definitely not." My jaw tightened, and I clasped my hands together. *Noc*. No, there'd never been that sort of ease there. He'd been distant. Cold. Unflinchingly loyal. It was the perfect combination to draw me in. Someone who could never truly love me, and therefore someone who could never hurt me. Someone who could—no, *would*—never betray me. It'd taken me years to understand why I had been so enticed by Noc, why I'd fallen for him even knowing the ramifications his curse would have if he ever returned my affection. It was a way of coping with the unimaginable pain Jude had caused. Pain that, even now, I refused to face. Falling for Noc was toxic, but it had worked. The memory of Jude had faded ever so slightly, *and* I had protected myself from suffering the same agony all over again.

A deep hum escaped the back of Gaige's throat, and he stopped trailing the whorls in the wood. As he leaned back on the palms of his hands, his broad chest stretched and the leather cord lacing up his collar loosened a fraction. The action pulled me from my reverie and chased away some of the brooding emotion—and fine, yes, it made my throat go a little dry too. I narrowed my eyes. Was he aware of his actions? Of the way his lax stance read like an open invitation? In the dim lighting of the library, surrounded by books and the low crackle and pop of a dying fire, he was picturesque. Soft brown hair curled at the ends, skating just above his shoulders. Thin lips pulled into a wry smile. He belonged in one of the oil paintings clinging to the walls. Not here before me, tangible, real, and very, very dangerous.

"Someone I don't know, then," Gaige said, voice low. Soft. He tilted his chin ever so slightly toward me. "I'm still curious. About you."

Stock-still, I barely breathed. He was close enough that every inhale brought with it the scent of cedar and pears. He swallowed, and my attention dropped to the hollow of his throat.

For the first time in years, I failed to find words. Failed to think of an appropriate response. Why couldn't I think? Or rather, why could I only think of him? All thoughts of Noc, of Jude, simply dispersed. There was only Gaige, waiting with a crooked grin. I forced myself to focus on that quirked lip. It was the perfect reminder of the threat he posed. Of the emotions he could stir up, the vulnerability. I had no use for those feelings. They would only result in pain, and I needed my mind clear in order to help Noc and my family as we dealt with Cruor's Oath. I folded my arms, and my body practically screamed with indignation. He was so *close*. And yet I'd buried my hands and scooted away, putting distance between us without leaving my chair.

"We should get back to work." Calm. Cool. Uninterested. The tone I set was far from the churning swell of emotions I refused to acknowledge within me. His lure was too strong. Too much. It was the only acceptable explanation.

Gaige's smile faltered. Slowly, he pulled back. "Of course."

There was no mistaking the disappointment in his slackened frame, but I resisted the urge to engage him further. It would've been cruel to make him think that there was a chance, that there was something here. There wasn't. There *couldn't* be. Sinking into his chair, Gaige once again reached for *Zane and the Fallen Leaders*.

"If you change your mind and want to chat, you know where to find me."

Despite how tired I was—both physically and mentally—I returned to the pile of tomes before me without giving him a response. It was easier—safer—to get lost in a world of words than in a conversation with Gaige. Especially when there was no telling what kind of story he'd attempt to dredge up.

EIGHT

NOC

When Leena and I returned to the library the next morning, we were shocked to find Kost and Gaige still manning one of the tables. Cheek pressed to a book and glasses askew, Kost slumbered with his arms folded beneath him. An unfamiliar double-breasted, wine-colored coat was tossed over his shoulders like a makeshift blanket. Gaige was passed out beside him, face planted directly into an open book, as if he'd fallen asleep while reading. A stack of parchment paper towered near his hand, cramped handwriting filling the pages from top to bottom.

The only other person in the room was Quintus. He was peering over Gaige's shoulder with a perplexed expression that immediately cleared to one of indifference when he locked eyes with me. After a curt nod, he slipped out of the library without a word.

"Who was that?" Leena asked.

"Quintus." My eyes narrowed. All assassins were permitted to use the library, but why was he here reading over their shoulders? He'd done little but complain since being raised, according to Ozias. Nothing overtly out of line, but he didn't exactly inspire trust, either. "He's new."

My voice startled Gaige, who bolted upright from his chair.

His brown locks stood on end, as if he'd dug his fingers into his scalp too many times before falling asleep. Blinking, he took in the room and paused when he saw us.

"Morning." Leena rolled her lips together, fighting a smile. "How did you sleep?"

"What?" He looked down at himself and rubbed his bare arms, his gaze momentarily flickering to Kost. "Oh. I hadn't realized I'd dozed off."

Hope sparked in me, and I asked, "Did you find something?" The call of the oath was getting worse by the minute. Not to mention my physical inability to truly explain what was happening to me. My throat still felt scorched raw from the night before when I'd tried to tell Leena of my visions. But an invisible hand had choked me tight, preventing me from revealing anything about those horrid nightmares. It seems I was meant to drown in them. To lose sight of what was real and what was fake.

And I was afraid it would work.

Gaige stared at me as if he'd never seen me before, but after a moment, he shook his head once. "No, unfortunately not. But you were right—this is a library unlike any I've seen. I got swept away in reading. Happens more often than not where I'm concerned."

A knot formed in my gut. "I see." Glancing past him to the stack of tomes and papers, I tried to get a glimpse of what he'd been reading. But our conversation roused Kost, and he sat upright in such a flurry that he knocked over a perilous stack of books and obscured the titles. A thick red mark stretched from forehead to chin where the binding had pressed into his skin. Righting his spectacles, he blinked furiously. Then he ran his fingers along the red overcoat draped over his shoulders and drew his brows together.

"Ah, sorry about that." Gaige reached over and took it from him, slipping it on. "You looked cold."

Leena snorted and Kost attempted to murder her with his stare. "Thank you. But if I'd been cold, I would have fetched a blanket." With precise hands, he began the process of smoothing his hair.

Gaige's lips thinned. "Noted."

A low, strained chuckle sounded from behind me. "Looks like I missed a slumber party." Calem sauntered into view, heavy bags beneath his bloodshot eyes. His hair was knotted in an unkempt bun atop his head, and he tugged at one of the loose strands teasing his ear. Ozias followed him in and leaned against the first bookshelf his back could find. The wood creaked with his added weight, and he dug the palms of his hands into his eyes.

"I take it none of us really got the rest we needed." Kost pushed away from the table, studying Ozias with mild concern.

He shrugged. In a rumpled, sleeveless work shirt and loose cotton pants, he was a walking picture of sleep deprivation. "Someone had to keep an eye on this guy." He jutted his chin toward Calem.

"I'm fine." Calem's gaze jumped between all of us one after the other as if it had been electrified.

"You're not fine," I said with a scowl. The mercury thread surrounding his pupils had widened, nearly dousing the entirety of his irises. His fingers twitched involuntarily as he rubbed the back of his neck.

"That bad?"

Leena shifted closer to me. "Do you remember anything?" I looped a supportive arm around her waist.

He cast his eyes to the floor. "Yes. Everything. Though I...I swear, I couldn't control it. It was like watching myself from a dream or something. Is Onyx all right?"

Leena barked out a laugh. "I can't believe you're asking me that. Onyx is fine."

"Guess that makes us even?"

"Hardly." She sighed, then paused for a moment before speaking again. "Effie was worried about you."

Calem stiffened. Remorse flickered in his eyes. "I know. I remember. I've barely spent any time with her since... Well. You know." He dragged a heavy hand down his face. "I'm just afraid of what she'll think of this *thing*. Of this monster. Or worse—I'm afraid I'll hurt her."

Leena shook her head. "You won't hurt her, Calem. You'd never hurt her. I wouldn't have gifted her to you otherwise."

"Yeah." He faked a smile. "I'll get it under control."

Stepping toward him, Leena placed the back of her hand against his forehead. His eyes slipped closed as his shoulders slumped forward. "You're burning up."

"We should take him to Hireath. Immediately." Gaige tied a few rolls of parchment together with some twine and tucked them into his jacket. A small scrap slipped free of his grasp and floated to the table, but he didn't notice. "I can escort him."

"Alone?" Ozias straightened. "I'll go with you."

"And what good would that do?" Calem shot him a weak grin. "You've played mother hen long enough. The new recruits need your guidance, and you can't do that if you're hovering over me. I doubt the Charmers would let you do much, anyway."

"He's not wrong," Gaige said. "I can take him alone—it's no trouble."

My gut tightened. As much as I wanted to trust Gaige, I couldn't bring myself to let my brother walk into Hireath alone. There was no doubt he needed help. It was obvious in the way his skin jumped with every breath. But there was also the matter of my oath. We didn't know who we could trust in Hireath, let alone how to unearth that information.

Leena shifted beneath my touch, and I slanted my gaze to her. Would it be too much to ask her to go? I didn't *want* her to leave. The idea of her being away from Cruor in dangerous territory set my teeth on edge. But we needed answers. If she accepted the Council's offer to join them, she'd have more resources than we did now. Even if they couldn't unearth the woman behind the bounty, she'd have access to more bestiaries. More chances to find an alternate solution.

I cleared my throat. "Leena, why don't you go?" Even as I said it, my fingers tightened against her hip. "Maybe it's time you take the Council up on their offer."

Silence stretched on for minutes as she turned to face me, eyes full of questions. She grazed her bestiary and twisted the chain dangling about her neck. When she finally spoke, her words were soft. "I don't know if that's the right thing to do."

Gaige frowned. "Why? It's possible one of them might know of a beast that could help. But you'd likely have to accept their invitation before they'd allow you to review their bestiaries."

Her fingers froze against her collarbone, and her voice went cold. "I don't know if I can trust the Council."

Scratching his jaw, Gaige parked a hip on the table. "I'll admit that I'm leery of the lack of information on all this. But to insinuate that someone on the Council is responsible?" He shook his head. "I can't fathom it."

"That's not what Wynn implied."

"And you're trusting the musings of a delusional man? The very person who enslaved you and used you as a weapon?"

A low hiss scraped through my teeth, red painting the edges of my vision. "Watch yourself, Gaige."

Leena didn't falter. "He may have been delusional, but he wasn't lying about that. Something changed him, Gaige. And someone was behind that." She wrapped her arms around her stomach and took a slow breath. "In the end, what happened to him is hardly any different than what happened to me."

Silence followed her declaration. I expected her hands to fall to her legs, to trace the near-invisible scars on her thighs hidden beneath tailored linen breeches. But Leena held her chin high. Anxiety I hadn't even realized I'd been holding on her behalf loosened in my chest.

"Not to mention, Raven's symbol is the same shade as the woman who placed the bounty," Leena added.

Gaige's eyes widened a fraction, then slanted to me. "Raven? This is news. Are you positive?"

"I'm the wrong person to ask. I didn't see it firsthand. All I know is that it's reddish in color—"

"Currant," Kost interjected. "It's currant."

Calem managed an eye roll. "Sure, Kost."

Gaige's brows drew together. "There are a number of Charmers with similar hues living in Hireath. It could be any one of them." He pinned Leena with his stare. "I'm sure you've realized that."

"I have." She let out a breath. "Which is why I haven't openly accused her of anything. I know what it's like to be wrongly exiled. But I don't trust her, Gaige. She's the newest member of the Council. What do you really know about her?"

Gaige gripped the edge of the table and crossed his ankles, a quiet hum escaping from somewhere deep in his chest. "Admittedly very little. But she's proved herself as a Charmer in the eyes of the people and her beasts. I'm not ready to accuse her, either. So, we'll have to be careful. If anything, this proves you should still join. You'll have the opportunity to gather information on beasts—and keep an eye on her or any other who may prove suspect."

"Can we trust Kaori?" Calem ran an absent hand down his arm. "How many other people are involved in this?"

"We don't have much of a choice when it comes to Kaori. She's the only one who knows what's going on with you." I kept my voice steady and my gaze level. If his inner beast was as volatile as the pressure of my oath, then we had to keep him calm. He needed to believe that there was a chance he'd make it through this. *I* needed to believe that.

And so did Leena. She rolled her lower lip between her teeth and nodded. "Let's hope it was just Wynn and Raven. No one else."

Ozias pushed off from his place against the bookshelf and gripped Calem's shoulder, giving him a reassuring nudge. "Just be careful."

Leena's brow furrowed. "I just don't understand *why*. Why keep the bounty active? What is Raven hoping to achieve? Everything I overheard while under Wynn's spell is like static. It's there, but I can't grasp it."

Kost pursed his lips. "There's something bigger at work here. We just have to figure out what that is."

"Maybe I should come with you." I grazed Leena's cheek with light fingers, and she smiled.

Hurried, uncareful footsteps crashed against the tile of the main hall before hitting the library's floorboards with a definitive thud. Unease ratcheted up several notches in my throat. No assassin moved that loudly. Not unless they didn't care about being heard. Or worse, if something was wrong.

Judging by Emelia's frantic, wide-eyed stare, something was definitely wrong. She'd been on sentry duty since dawn and was still a few hours shy of being relieved from her post. Only intruders would cause her to come rushing back.

Perhaps Hireath wasn't an option for me after all.

"What is it?"

Windswept hair clung to her flushed cheeks. "Darrien is coming."

A heavy pounding started in my ears. "*What?*"

Emelia flinched. "It's worse. Quintus met him at the gate. It seems he's jumped ship."

"I should've sent him back to the grave the moment he mentioned him." I clenched my hand into a tight fist. "No matter. Darrien poses a larger threat."

"I'll kill him. You don't even have to ask." Calem brushed off Ozias's grip. His nostrils flared wide, and the veins tracking his arms pushed against his skin. Mercury flooded his stare. "I swear to the gods, I'll bury his ass in the ground."

"Calem." Kost eased toward him with his hands in the air. "Calm yourself."

The whites of his eyes disappeared entirely as he rounded on Kost. "He's a traitor. I don't care if Noc gave him the option to leave. No one should abandon Cruor like that. Quintus too. Annoying prick." His muscles quivered. Stone scales began to ripple across his flesh.

I pushed Leena behind me and planted one hand against his chest, shoving him back. "Take a breath."

An animalistic growl split my eardrums as black talons shot out from his fingernail beds. Chest heaving, he backed into the nearest bookshelf and knocked it to the floor.

Emelia stared in horror. "What's happening?"

The sound of the beast realm opening cut through Calem's muffled howls, and rosewood light bloomed from Leena's symbol. She stepped around me and thrust her hand forward. "Kels. Iky."

The tiny rainbow bird from before appeared first, heading straight for Calem's jugular. With one swift dive, she buried her beak in his neck. Clear, sappy liquid dribbled across a pinprick hole, and Calem smacked his hand over the opening. Scales raced across his arms, forming and disappearing as Kels's draft once again dragged him under. Wild, confused eyes met mine for a moment before his lids slipped closed, and he crashed to the floor.

"Iky, carry him." Leena extended her finger, and Kels perched there while Iky moved forward. Translucent limbs wrapped Calem in a makeshift cradle, and Iky pressed him flush to his chest.

"We need to get him to Hireath. Now." Gaige's steely gaze flickered between Calem and the door. "A Naughtbird's draft is strong, but so is Calem's beast. He could already be building a tolerance to it—I simply don't know."

Leena commanded Kels back to the beast realm. "Then let's go."

Threats in Hireath, threats at our front door... Even though I'd suggested Leena go, every fiber of my being screamed for her to stay. Still, I kept myself calm. Controlled. "Be careful."

Turning to look at me, she cupped my face and placed a quick kiss on my lips. "I will, so long as you do too." Her hand dropped to my chest where my heart thudded madly against her fingers.

"Don't stay long."

"I won't."

A glimmering yellow halo of light poured from Gaige's hand, and a beast manifested by his feet. It was the same creature Wynn had used to take Leena. Its lizard-like head rounded on its master. Unhinging its jaw, it summoned a swirling white portal that crackled with electrical currents.

Leena hummed. "I really need to get me one of these. A Telesávra would make traveling between Hireath and Cruor a cinch."

"Next time, I'll join you," I said.

She smiled. "Next time." Offering the beast a careful pat on the head, she touched her chin to her shoulder and gave me one last parting glance. "See you soon."

And then she stepped through the portal and winked out of my life for the second time.

With her absence—*with her escape*, that horrifying voice whispered inside of me—control was suddenly much harder to come by. Red tendrils dripped across my vision and threatened to pull me under, but I focused on the sable shadows and called them to me instead. Begged them to cling to my senses and dull the hammering, intoxicating bloody mess festering in my mind. They obeyed, and the foreign anger subsided to a dull roar at the same time Iky, Calem, and Gaige slipped through the portal.

The beast disappeared.

"Holy fuck," Emelia let out in a rush. My attention snapped back to her. Fingers steeped in shadows, she remained perched on the edge of summoning a weapon. "What the hell just happened?"

Gritting my teeth, I brushed aside her inquiry. "Where's Darrien?"

"I'm right here." Stepping through the doorway with Iov, Astrid, and Quintus at his side, Darrien clasped his hands in front of him. Iov's glittering ax was flush against his chest, and Astrid had a small blade just barely holding form pressed against Quintus's jugular. She also fisted Darrien's bow at her side, keeping his corporeal weapon out of reach. Not like he'd need it. He could summon a blade faster than Astrid could blink.

I jerked my chin toward the intruders, and Emelia rushed to her brother's side, adding her own halberd to the back of Darrien's neck. Poised for the guillotine.

He didn't seem fazed. Shadows flirted with the curls of his hair and slithered over his clothing. Amber eyes full of malice glinted beneath heavy brows. Darrien let out a pitying sigh, tossing a curious glance at Astrid.

"Back to raising, I see."

"You would know," I said, voice icy. My gaze slanted to Quintus, who withered beneath my stare.

"He was a friend beforehand. Can't blame him for seeing my side of things."

"Tell me why I shouldn't execute you right here. After I explicitly told you never to come near Cruor again." Kost and Ozias flanked my sides. Shadows spired in their auras, forming endless rows of blades just waiting for my signal. Waiting to do our bidding.

Kill.

Maybe I would.

Darrien eyed the empty chair where Gaige had been working. "We should talk first."

My lips curled. "I'm not interested in talking."

"I'm not looking to fight anymore." Darrien worked his throat in a hard swallow. "May I sit?"

"You have two minutes."

Darrien stepped out of reach of Iov and Emelia and sank onto the chair. "You can dismiss them. We both know that you could kill me faster than they could."

As irritating as it was, he was right. "Then your new lackey leaves too."

He barely deigned to shoot Quintus a glance, but gestured over his shoulder with lazy fingers. The newly raised assassin looked all too pleased to disappear. He rushed from the library and headed for the main doors.

"You three, keep him outside at the gate," I said to Emelia, Iov, and Astrid, and they sank into the world of shadows, leaving Darrien alone with me, Kost, and Ozias. None of us moved.

Shadows trailed from our frames and crept along the floors toward Darrien. He'd never escape all of us.

Propping his arm on the table, he scattered a few papers and nudged a book. His gaze shifted to the tomes and inkwells. "Doing a bit of light reading?"

"What do you want?" I slipped my hands into my pockets. They itched to wrap around his neck, and I couldn't trust them not to act of their own accord.

His fingers dawdled across the open pages. "To make a deal."

My eyes narrowed. Darrien had always been calm. Self-assured. When he wanted something, he demanded it. But the way he was fidgeting now... It didn't fit. What was he really after?

"Get the hell out," Ozias snapped.

"You can't undo what you've done." Kost's nostrils flared. "Leave before it's too late."

Heat simmered beneath Darrien's words. "I was here before any of you even took your first breath." Tempering his rage, he inhaled sharply. "Talmage was a close friend. Why he named you leader...I will never know. But it's out of respect for him that I'm here now. And I'm imploring you to consider my request for our people. His people."

"What are you getting at?" My nails elongated, forming tight points and scraping against my pockets. One slit and the blood would flow. A single blade could notch his skin, and he'd be mine to command.

No. Gods. It was getting easy, too easy, to fall back on the possibility of exerting my control over someone else. When I'd done it with Brody, it'd felt *good.* Wrong, but somehow right. The contradiction ate away at my insides, and I ground my teeth together.

Darrien dropped his gaze, returning instead to the books strewn across the table. "You're the only one with the power to raise the dead. Zane's blood lives in your veins." His fingers traced what looked like a network of bloodlines and family trees across two pages. "I can't replenish my numbers when a job goes south. I'm asking for your help, and in exchange, I won't orchestrate any more ambushes."

I let out a cold, brittle laugh. "Orchestrate all you want. You won't succeed in capturing me or forcing me to relinquish my power early. And if that fails and you kill me instead, the power passes to the assassin of *my* choosing. We all know that isn't you."

My gaze slanted to Kost. My second. The man who would live or die by Cruor's code. He angled his chin high and glared at the traitor.

Darrien growled. His restless hand had moved to a new book laid open beneath the first. Yet another family tree with swirling black ink played across the pages. His nails dug against the names and crinkled the paper.

"I will keep trying if I have to."

"You came after my pair bond. I should kill you for that alone." The memory of Leena's wound burned in my mind, feeding the frenzied red haze claiming my senses. Control. I needed to stay in control.

Fingers dawdling, he picked up the scrap of parchment that Gaige had dropped. "And I'm sorry for that." He let the paper fall to the table, gaze roaming back my direction. "Talmage wouldn't want this. He'd want us to continue on. All I'm asking is that you raise an assassin for my guild every now and then. I'm not looking to amass an army. Just keep those who followed me safe."

Kost broke. "How dare you mention his name after what you did." He clenched and unclenched his trembling fists. "Talmage was my friend too. Kill him, Noc. Get this sorry excuse for a man out of our home."

I bit back the rage and settled on an icy response. "I won't raise the dead for you. You made your choice when you left Cruor. Recruit normal, human assassins and leave the shadows to us. That's my final verdict."

Voice surprisingly soft, Darrien's response was barely audible. "Are you sure?"

"You're not offering me anything in return. You're simply asking for a favor. And after all that you've done, it's hardly warranted." Slowly, I extracted my hands and flexed them, ignoring the bloody welts marring the skin of my palms. "Get out."

Something foreign raced through Darrien's expression. "If that's your final decision…"

The way his words trailed off rattled my nerves. Something was wrong. I expected him to argue, to defend his case longer. I'd known Darrien for decades, and he *never* caved. He'd stand by his beliefs, however misguided, with everything he had. The only person who was ever able to convince him to see things differently was Talmage.

Unease crept under my skin. "Ozias, get him out of here."

Darrien stood in a hurry. The slightest hint of a grin tugged at one corner of his mouth. Without so much as a single complaint, he allowed Ozias to shove him out of the library and into the main halls of Cruor. My breath froze in my lungs until the double doors leading to the outside world banged shut, and Darrien retreated from my home.

Kost broke away, muttering to himself as he stacked tomes together and arranged loose papers. I caught a glimpse of two titles from Gaige's stack, *A Brief History of Wilheim* and *Zane and the Fallen Leaders*. Kost continued to close spare books with more force than necessary and knocked over an inkwell. He cursed at the mess before fishing a cloth of his breast pocket. Ink slowly spread toward the small piece of parchment, coloring the edge, and Kost snatched it up before it could soak through entirely.

"Something is wrong. Darrien had to know I'd never agree to raise assassins for him." Running a tense hand through my hair, I replayed the conversation in my mind. Why hadn't he fought back? What was I missing?

"Noc."

I turned to find Kost still holding the stray parchment. Face pale, he looked at me over the top of his spectacles.

"What is it?"

"He knows who you are." Kost upended my world with his words.

"Who?"

Slowly, he held out the ink-soaked parchment. I snatched it from his hands, tearing apart the cramped handwriting. *Gaige.* He'd pieced my past and present together. The ceiling and walls converged in an onslaught of shadows, and my stomach hardened to solid rock.

And Darrien had read every word of it.

My vision tunneled, and I crumpled the parchment into a ball. "Darrien saw this."

Kost slumped into his chair. "Fuck."

Fuck indeed.

NINE

THE FROZEN PRINCE
50 YEARS AGO

As I walked back to camp with Kostya by my side, evidence of our battle was everywhere. People hurried about while commanders barked orders to establish a night patrol. Others still carried armor and weapons to the temporary blacksmith for repair. More were heading toward a line of campfires where pigs roasted on spits, the scent of ale and smoke already thick in the air. A smile tugged at my lips. I'd have to introduce Kostya to Thaleus.

Turning to the assassin, I was about to offer him a place by the fire when a foot soldier from Thaleus's unit rushed toward me. He came to a screeching halt and offered a haphazard bow before righting himself.

"Sir, Thaleus has been injured."

All thoughts of ale and good conversation fled in a breath. "What happened?"

The man fumbled for words. "I...I don't know. I didn't see. He just collapsed."

My world narrowed, and I barely tossed Kostya a glance before pushing past the soldier and sprinting toward the medical tent. The white canopy dominated my vision. "Where is he?" I burst through the open flaps, only to find rows and rows of bodies strewn on cots. Some were covered head to toe in sheets, a ghastly declaration of death. Others were propped up on pillows, bandaged and bleeding, with frantic attendants rushing from bed to bed. I snared the first one who hurried by and forced her to meet my gaze. "Where. Is. He?"

She paled but nodded toward the far end of the tent. I released her the moment I spotted Thaleus's scraggly beard. He laid quietly between two cots. The man on his left screamed wordlessly as healers attempted to set his broken leg. The cot on his right was silent, the outline of a body decipherable beneath a sheet. I hated how close they put him to those who'd already passed through to the realm of the gods. Crossing the tent quickly, I came to his side and gripped his clammy hands in mine.

Weak eyes stared up at me. "Aleksander."

I swallowed the rock in my throat. "What happened to that ale?"

A brittle laugh scraped through his chest. "Might have to wait on that."

"Where are you hurt?" I scoured the length of his body, searching for wounds or bandages only to come up empty-handed. And yet, the ashen tint to his skin spoke volumes, and I tightened my hold on his fingers.

"Nowhere. You think some Rhyne soldiers would get the best of me?" His words were weak, and he paused for a moment to catch his breath before continuing. "I'll be fine come morning. Just need some rest."

My heart gave a pitiful thud. Not a single soldier had survived the plague. Priests and priestesses were brought in, and still no one could get a grip on the sickness rampaging through my camp. And while I couldn't possibly be held responsible for something as uncontrollable as this, I couldn't help but blame myself. This entire war was because of me. Because I'd fallen in love with a Rhyne princess and slighted the High Priestess. Her curse had killed my love, and yet Amira's parents hadn't believed me. No one believed me. Even now, when the battles were done and men crowded around fires with ales in their hands, there were whispers. Frustrations. They had all believed my claim once. But too much death had soured their perceptions. I didn't blame them—curses were rare and hardly left proof. Whether or not I had ended Amira's life, I was responsible for her death.

"Hey, stop that." Thaleus wrenched his hand free to place it gently on my forearm. "I can see those wheels turning. This isn't your fault. I'll be fine by morning, just you wait. Now, get out of here. You don't need to see,"—he winced as a piercing shriek split the air—"or hear any of this."

"Thaleus…" Words failed to form, and my chest tightened. What would I do once he was gone? Who would I joke with or share ales with or let myself just *be* with? No one wanted to brush elbows with the prince who started it all. If I were in their shoes, fighting a war I didn't understand, I'd be hesitant to rally to my side too.

Go home. I clenched my jaw tight. Returning to Wilheim and the safety of my castle would only cause more discord. I needed to be here, fighting with them. Not commanding from afar.

I owed them all so much.

"Go on. I need to sleep." He slapped my arm with a slackening hand that lacked any semblance of strength.

I turned without another word and slipped through the tent. My heart was as heavy as the deadweight of each body I passed. When I stepped out into the camp, I gulped down air…and fled. Broke into a sprint and ran toward the fringes of our settlement, ignoring the pensive stares of my royal guard as they decided whether to follow. I prayed they didn't. I needed space. Room to breathe. And so did my men. They needed time away from *me*, time to vent their frustrations and speak their minds without fear of the royal house coming down on them. There was too much death hanging low over us all.

I didn't know how long I ran, only that I did until the sounds of camp faded in the distance. Slumping to the ground, I worked muck and grime between my fingers as I sought for a grip on reality. And then I crumbled. Because I knew. I knew Thaleus wouldn't make it. I knew this war, all this death, was on me. No matter what lies I told myself, this was *my* doing. A sob cracked my chest, and I held my head in my hands. Thaleus wasn't the first brother or sister I'd lost over the years. There was Helena. Broderick. Parvis. Amira... So many more. There was no solace to be found, but at least it was quiet out here. At least there were no whispers or false smiles. At least death was stuck in that gods-awful white tent.

Hours ticked by until the faint light of dusk claimed the sky and the first brave stars dotted the horizon. Behind me, someone cleared their throat.

I jumped to my feet and reached for the small blade I kept at my hip.

Kostya eyed my weapon. "Decent reflexes, though it would've helped had you known I was here to begin with."

My hand wavered. "I heard you approach."

Kostya sighed. "Because I alerted you to my presence. How long do you think I'd been waiting?"

Everything left me in a rush, and my shoulders slumped. I didn't care if he'd been there since the beginning. Running a hand through my hair, I gave him a weary glance. "Sorry I took off like that. You're free to leave if you'd like."

Kostya studied me for a long moment before removing his

glasses. Slowly, he pulled a cloth from his breast pocket and began polishing the lenses. "What's wrong?"

"What's wrong?" I barked out a harsh laugh. As if it wasn't glaringly obvious.

"Something is troubling you." Kostya replaced his glasses.

Giving way to absurdity, I tossed my hands to the sky in exasperation. "Of course something is troubling me. Were you not there today? Didn't you see the battlefield? How many people, on both sides, had to die for this endless fight?" I started to pace, acutely aware of the way his gaze tracked my progression. "I've tried to negotiate with Rhyne. I've tried to explain what happened to their princess. I've tried everything I can think of to bring this to an end, and nothing is working.

"And what's worse is that my men are paying the price. If they're not dying with a sword in hand, they're dying with their backs on a cot, courtesy of a plague no one can cure. It might look like Lendria is winning, but everywhere I turn, we are losing *everything*."

Kostya was silent for a long breath, as if waiting to see whether I'd continue. Only when I finally came to a stop did he fold his arms across his chest. "You said you've tried everything?"

"Yes. Everything."

"And you're sure about that?" His harsh green eyes softened before he looked away to the night sky.

The raging pulse that had been building inside me quieted. "What are you saying?"

Kostya cleared his throat. "What does Rhyne want? All wars boil down to what one side desires but isn't getting."

"Vengeance, I suppose." I went to slip my hands into the pockets of my trousers but failed. I hadn't even had time to toss aside my armor. The metal gauntlets covering my fingers scraped against my plated thighs.

With a deliberate slowness, Kostya dragged his gaze back to mine. "Specifics matter. What *exactly* do they want?"

It didn't take long for me to answer. "Me. They want me."

Kostya said nothing, but his stare was so damning I had to fight to keep my chin held high. Shadows started to fester in the space around him, and he dipped his hands into the abyss. Onyx tendrils pooled in his palms before spilling out between his fingers. "Then you haven't tried *everything*."

"What you're suggesting is out of the question." We'd lost so many soldiers over the years. Simply giving in now would mean their deaths were in vain. They'd fought for me, believed in me. To simply give my life over to the enemy...

"I'm not suggesting anything. I'm merely stating a fact." With that gut punch, his shadows darkened, and he added, "I'll be going now, Prince Aleksander. I wish you luck with your never-ending war."

Before I could clear my throat to speak, a vacuum of darkness swallowed him whole, and he was gone. If it weren't for the way his words lingered in the air, I could've convinced myself he'd never been there at all. But he had been there. He'd listened. And he wasn't wrong—all Rhyne wanted was my head on a spike. I'd been fighting against my own death for so long that the concept of giving in had always seemed foreign. Like admitting defeat. And yet... I slumped back to the ground and stared out over the darkening marsh, my world reorienting around the assassin's parting words.

Thaleus would soon be gone. Amira was gone. Nearly everyone I loved, gone. They were only blips of brightness in my life, stolen away before I was ready to say goodbye. How many other families and loved ones were suffering through the same heartache?

Maybe Amira was waiting for me in the gods' realm. Maybe a world without me truly was better. Those deathly shadows that had swallowed Kostya whole hadn't seemed so dangerous. He'd almost seemed to welcome the way they moved, the way they cocooned him in a solitary reprieve reality couldn't offer.

Think of your parents. I pictured my father's eyes, a frozen blue that mirrored my own. The stern gaze that turned soft with wrinkles when he smiled. My mother's warm embrace that always welcomed me home. Followed by a stern, yet loving smack to the back of my head when I did something she disapproved of. If I were to die, they'd be heartbroken. I was their only son. And yet...

This war would never end while I still breathed.

Rocketing to my feet, I stripped the armor from my body and cast it to the ground. In a simple tunic and light breeches, I was entirely unprotected. A gentle breeze kissed the exposed skin of my arms, and it felt like home. Like affirmation. With my armor went the blade, and I paused for a moment at the lack of its weight. But no—where I was going, weapons weren't needed. And then I started walking with more purpose than I'd felt on the battlefield that morning. This war would end tonight. I'd make sure of it.

I walked until the muddy marshland shifted to sediment-filled banks of black sand. We hadn't destroyed the entirety of Rhyne's forces, and those who'd retreated were in the midst of loading gear and bodies onto ships. Flickering fires cast the beach in an orange hue, and the quiet murmurs of soldiers created a lull that competed with the ocean waves. For a moment, I paused and focused on that sound. On the ebb and flow of the tide creeping over the sand and washing away the remnants of the war. Of the blood and horrors these people had faced.

Raising my hands above my head, I walked to the first campfire I could find. I had no delusions they'd take me alive. I'd offered my imprisonment before to end the war, and they'd spit on the letter and sent it back, sealed with the wax and emblem of the royal family.

This would be different. A strange sense of peace flowed through to my fingertips, and for the first time in years, relief relaxed my lips into a gentle smile.

TEN

LEENA
PRESENT DAY

The natural beauty of Hireath stilled my heart every time I caught sight of those glistening falls. Trees netted together against the morning sky, casting shadows across the aqua basin of water. Walkways and bridges packed with Charmers stretched from gargantuan oaks. Tree houses with large open windows were anchored to heavy branches, and larger communal spaces with wide-open archways burrowed into the trunks. But the crown jewel? The shimmering castle of ivory and stone carved into the mountain with the streaming falls cresting down its side.

I breathed deeply, and the mist-coated air, thick with the scent of minerals, hit the back of my tongue. Iky sauntered to my side, an unconscious Calem still cradled like a child in his arms. Gaige ran a hand along his jaw and eyed my friend.

"Let's find Kaori first."

"Agreed." Gently, I brushed my fingers along Calem's forehead. Sticky heat met my touch, and droplets of sweat clung to his hair. Magic was cooking him alive.

We took off toward the keep, its cobblestone courtyard packed with flowers in full bloom. With winter upon us, the normal petals of lavender, fuchsia, and teal had given way to deep mahogany, plum, and vivid sapphire. A maiden carved of the same stone as the castle poured water from a vase into a wide fountain, and Charmers lingered on benches ringing the space. Beasts twined between their ankles, and their soft calls competed with the backdrop of crashing water from the falls.

While the water would never freeze, the trees would soon be dusted with icicles, and Charmers would hang decorated snowflakes from their doors. The first frost was near, and there was a palpable hum of excitement in the air. The veil to the gods' realm, and therefore Celeste, was thinnest on crisp winter nights. Charmers would gather with loved ones to offer thanks for everything she'd offered.

Magical. Even with the horrors I'd endured, there was something special about coming back, especially during this time of year. A few curious glances targeted Calem and Iky, but no one was brave enough to ask. Passing through the open archways into the main floor of the keep, we rounded a corner and took the first set of ivory stairs.

"Kaori's quarters are on the second floor." Gaige peeled off after one flight of steps, and we paused in the foyer.

It'd been the same with Wynn. An entire floor dedicated to him. I craned my neck upward and tried to see through the ceiling. Would they offer me those quarters if I joined the Council? Bile soured my tongue. There had to be other floors, other spaces available. I hadn't thought to count the flights.

Light footsteps sounded against the smooth slabs, and Kaori appeared in the mouth of the nearest archway. Her sleek, sable hair was glossy in the morning sun, and she wore a white charmeuse gown. Gold stitching lined the V-shaped cut around her collarbone and dripped down her sternum in filigree patterns. Velvety and red, the inside of her collar curled up against her chin, and cap sleeves fit snug against her slender shoulders. She was ethereal.

Her dark eyes swept over us and snagged on Calem. With a strangled breath, she waved over her shoulder and retreated in the direction from which she came. "In here."

We followed the billowing tail of her gown into a formal seating area. Pale-blue armchairs encircled a low, walnut coffee table, and a chaise longue complete with indigo pillows was situated between two sets of double glass doors thrown open to the falls. She ushered us toward the chaise, and Iky placed Calem on the cream-colored cushions. As soon as his head met the pillow, I sent Iky back to the beast realm with a flood of rosewood light.

"When did it happen?" Kaori sank to the floor beside Calem and rested a delicate hand across his forehead.

"Yesterday." I wrapped my fingers in my bestiary and chewed on the inside of my cheek.

Gaige's heavy stare flickered between us. "He'll be okay. Right?"

"It's not too late." Kaori's fingers combed through Calem's hair, fanning it out on either side of his face. If it weren't for the glistening sheen of sweat across his bronzed skin, he'd almost seem peaceful.

"I should let Yazmin know we're here. She'll want to know about your decision, Leena." Gaige tilted his chin in goodbye and turned, retreating from the room without looking back.

Kaori pinned me with an inquisitive stare. "Decision?"

I sank to my knees, and the cool stone bit through my breeches. "About joining the Council." My hands fluttered aimlessly by Calem's calves. "I need information."

"What kind of information?"

To tell or not to tell? *Those sharp eyes.* They reminded me of the way Noc assessed people. I could trust her, right? She knew of the oath, but maybe telling her about my suspicions regarding Raven wasn't the greatest of ideas. They were probably friends.

Confidants. If I wanted to confront Raven, I needed to catch her off guard rather than give her time to prepare a story.

I braided my fingers together. "I need to find a beast that will help me remove Noc's oath. He's getting worse."

Kaori's gaze returned to Calem, as did her hand. "Is anyone well in that place?"

I let out a bitter laugh. "Physically? Sure. I think we're all mentally and emotionally a little bruised in one way or another, though."

She nodded. "It's feeding his beast. The turmoil. He should stay with me for a while. I'll teach him how to control his emotions"— something dark raced through her expression, and she arched a single brow—"and when to let them run free."

My pulse quickened. "That doesn't sound exactly...healthy."

She flashed a weak grin, and the points of her canines seemed to sharpen. "Trust me, it's healthy for people like us. I'm not suggesting he allow them to consume him—just channel the buildup in a way that keeps his mind intact."

My jaw tightened. *I did this.* "If you say so."

"Leena." Kaori gripped my hand. Her sapphire emblem caught in the light, drawing my attention to the network of mercury veins pulsing outward across her wrist.

"Yes?"

"You're partially to blame for this, you know."

Black spots burned in my peripheral vision, and a sudden burn of tears turned my world blurry. To have her say it out loud... To verbalize the guilt I already felt... "I know."

"No." She shook her head once, bringing my focus back to her. "He fought for you and his brother. He accepted this risk. What I mean is, you not being able to move on, you not forgiving yourself for what happened... How do you think it makes him feel when you can't even look at him? Not like you used to, anyway. Not like he needs. He is the beast because that's what you see."

My throat tightened. "How…"

"Because it was the same with me." She swallowed, eyes cast far away, reliving some memory I couldn't see. "Calem and me, we're different now, but we're still us. We don't need anyone reminding us of what happened or what we sacrificed to get here."

Tears fell down my cheeks, and I wiped them away with the back of my hand. "I can't look at him without reliving how he died. How I caused that."

Kaori stood and offered me her hand. "He made a choice, Leena. Respect that."

I took it, allowing her words to click into place in my mind. They settled like tiny weights, pushing down the doubt and fear and guilt. I couldn't stand around and wait for Calem to crack. Couldn't punish myself for something that had already happened. Why was it so hard to assume that Calem could forgive me for ordering Onyx to attack? He already had. Likely a thousand times over, and he would say it to my face a thousand times more if that's what it took. I just needed to forgive myself and let go.

"Thank you, Kaori." I sighed and wiped away my tears.

"You're welcome. Now, why don't you go find Yazmin and Gaige? It sounds like you have an offer to accept. When Calem wakes, I'll be here." She called for an attendant from the foyer and rattled off instructions for a pot of tea containing honey, mint, and some other herb I didn't recognize. Eyes light, she offered me a soft smile. "He'll be fine. Go."

"Take care of him." Turning on my heels, I walked out of Kaori's quarters and hit the stairs. Maybe it was simply knowing that Kaori had dealt with this before, or maybe it was finally accepting what had happened, but a lightness invaded my chest and took hold of my heart. If Calem had hope, then so did Noc. I'd find a way. I'd protect them all.

Crossing the courtyard and heading for the main portion of the keep, I hooked a right into the hall that fed into the open throne room. Dotted with droplet-shaped crystals and laden with leaves, heavy tree branches were threaded together to form a makeshift ceiling. Rays of sunlight pooled through small openings and bathed the marble slab in splotchy light.

One beam fell directly onto the statue of Ocnolog and Celeste just behind the Council's thrones. The stone glimmered in the light, and my gaze traveled from top to bottom, taking in the expert craftsmanship. Even the ancient symbols etched into the wall beside them, detailing the age-old Charmers' prophecy, seemed to throb with power.

Yazmin sat in her throne, thick platinum hair tied in a fishtail braid with wisps framing her face. She wore a flowy chiffon gown the color of eggshells, with soft-pink flowers stitched into the fabric. Face dipped toward a handful of parchment, she didn't notice my entrance.

I cleared my throat. "I hope I'm not interrupting."

She looked up, startled, then smiled. "Leena. Gaige said you were here." Her hand fell back to the pile of parchment in her lap. Inked handwriting filled the pages from top to bottom, and her fingers lightly danced across the lines.

"I can come back later if you're busy."

"What, this?" She held up the pages before smiling and rolling them into a tight cylinder. "Just Gaige's report from his recent trip to Wilheim. Our relations with the king are still new, only about a decade old. While I have no desire to mingle with them, it never hurts to know about what's happening outside our sanctuary. But enough about politics." Standing, she secured the roll by slipping it between her hip and loose rose-gold belt. "We must discuss Noc's predicament."

A trill of excitement sped through me. "You found the culprit?"

She grimaced. "Unfortunately, no. Walk with me." Taking the few steps down from the dais, she veered toward the open courtyard. "Gaige told me he's getting worse."

"He is." I fell in line beside her, and we came upon an outdoor staircase that spiraled up a monstrous oak and connected to the side of the castle. The steps were wide enough for several people to stand comfortably, and we began to ascend together.

"I'm so sorry to hear that." She reached over and placed a soft hand against my back. "We're searching night and day for the Charmer responsible."

Her expression was tight as she studied each step before her, chin tucked to her chest. I was sure it pained her to know that one of her own was out there, deliberately defying the Crown's pardon on my life. Her hand fell from my back, and she let it drop to her side.

And yet, years of distrust, of not knowing whether or not I'd ever be able to call Hireath home again, kept me from immediately grabbing her hand and offering comfort. She hadn't been involved in the trial that led to my exile, but at least for now, we were working toward the same goal—my bounty absolved so Noc could be free of the oath. "I know you're trying, and I want to help."

Yazmin tilted her head to the side, brows inching together. "How?"

A young boy rushed passed us with a Groober tucked beneath his arm. He giggled, and a hint of valerian and lavender perfumed the air from the tight squeeze he gave his beast. That scent, the boy and his beast, the Charmers going about their day throughout the city—they gave me hope. Perhaps not everyone here was bad. There was the culprit, sure, but that was just one person.

It wasn't always just one. I fought back a shiver as the memory of Wynn drew to the forefront of my mind. But he was gone. Dead. He'd never hurt me again. And right now, the only thing that mattered was protecting the man I loved. If I had a way to help Noc through this, then I'd do it. No matter the cost.

"I'd like to formally accept your offer to join the Council."

She came to a full stop on one of the stairs, forcing a few disgruntled Charmers to part around us. "Really? We'd of course be honored to have you. But I know Cruor is your home now."

Home. My home was with Noc, with my family. If that happened to be in Cruor, then that's where I belonged. But that didn't mean I had to give up the part of me that loved Hireath. I would do anything to keep this city, and its people, from harm.

We started up the stairs again as I found my words. "I want to do this. If I can help you find the Charmer responsible for my bounty, if I can save Noc, then I'm protecting my home—both this one and the one at Cruor."

"Of course. We wouldn't force you to choose between Hireath and Cruor, though you would need to spend some time here to give the public a chance to become acquainted with you as a member of the Council." More Charmers passed us on the stairs, and she offered each one a regal nod.

Unexpected excitement sped through my veins. I could do this. I *would* do this. "The honor would be mine. This place matters to me too."

We came to a halt about four flights up. A large platform stretched out across the branches, and vendor stalls with thatched-leaf roofs lined the railing. The sticky-sweet aroma of fresh fruit filled the air, and laughter swelled around us. Small beasts scampered beneath our feet and flitted through the trees.

Once upon a time, this life had been mine. Cruor *was* my home now. But there was still a part of me that longed for Hireath. I didn't know if I could ever find peace here like I had before, but I couldn't deny where I'd come from, either.

"You must know that the Council protects its own. You and your family will be safe from harm." Her voice dropped an octave as she brought her lips close to my ear. "And the person responsible for your bounty *will* be dealt with."

I nodded. Her words reverberated with promise. "So, what happens next?"

"I'll assemble the others, and we'll make it official tonight. There's a bit of a ritual involved." She gave my shoulder a squeeze, and I glimpsed the pale pink of her Charmer's symbol. It was much lighter than my own rosewood hue, but still in the same family. Perhaps that's how faint the difference could be between reddish and currant. As much as I wanted to confront Raven and end this, I'd need something more definitive than a Charmer's mark.

"Ritual?" I asked.

"You'll see." Her smile was genuine. "In the meantime, I think I can help you with Noc. We'll continue our hunt for the culprit, but in case we don't turn up answers quick enough, there might be another way."

All thoughts of Raven faded. "Another way?"

She nodded. "Give me a few hours to sort through my records. I don't own the beast myself, so it's not as simple as checking my bestiary. But there's hope yet, Leena."

Happiness welled in my chest and threatened to spill over in the form of tears. Hope. I could see it in the shining faces of the kids running rampant around us. In the smiles of vendors and happy calls of beasts.

Maybe Hireath could bring me peace again.

———◆———

The ritual to join the Council was a closed affair, attended by only Council members, and I'd never come across records or books detailing the event. Which meant I wasn't prepared when two attendants whisked me away after Yazmin left, practically appearing from thin air to usher me toward the top floor of the castle. My new housing arrangements, should everything go as planned. The room centered around a circular bed fit for giants with a graphite-colored upholstered headboard. Stacks of plum, amethyst, and violet pillows sat atop silver satin sheets, and soft organza draped from the ceiling like clouds stretching across a dark night.

Apparently, these accommodations had once belonged to Eilan, the longest-sitting member, but when he and Raven announced their courtship, he moved into her quarters several floors below.

Raven. Tonight would be the first time I'd seen her since the battle. I had to be careful. Meticulous. Noc would know what to do, what to look for. But what, exactly, was I looking for? How would I get her to confess and remove the oath? I stewed about Raven for the majority of the afternoon, making it easy for the attendants to prepare me for the ceremony.

First, an hour-long soak in a copper claw-foot tub. Then came the hair. And cosmetics. And the gown. I'd never experienced such finery. Somehow tailored to my curves, as if Yazmin had known all along I'd accept her offer, the blush chiffon dress was near see-through and backless. Silver beads and sequins were stitched in the shapes of trees and leaves, stretching from my midsection to cover my breasts. The hems of my sleeves were drenched in pewter crystals, and the fabric ghosted over the length of my arms.

If only Noc could see me. We'd never done anything together that required more formal attire. There simply hadn't been time. We'd been robbed of so much: a real courtship, peaceful outings together, even the sacred ceremony of *anam-cara*—something I'd yet to broach with him. Wilheim traditions for pair bonds were unknown to me, but when Charmers announced their *anam-cara*, customs dictated a three-night celebration. It wasn't exactly required—the bond stood regardless of public acknowledgment—but choosing an *anam-cara* was so revered that everyone felt the need to rejoice.

I rolled the lip of my sleeve between my fingers, and the crystals left an icy kiss across my skin, like Noc's shadows.

When this is over, we'll celebrate. In our own way, with Cruor and our family.

With hope once again surging in my chest, I made my way to the throne room just as dusk tinged the sky and welcomed the first glimpse of the waxing moon. The ground had been coated in a layer of pale-pink petals, and they whooshed in soft circles as my gown swished against the floor.

Rather than reclining in their thrones, each member stood in a half circle and held a flickering ivory candle. Their mercury cloaks were fastened shut, hoods pulled low over their faces and casting their expressions in shadow. The teasing candlelight would illuminate a feature here and there—a flash of steel-blue eyes from Gaige, a glimmer of pale skin from Kaori, Tristan's unruly hair flaring from beneath the lip of his cloak. Eilan's molten-gold eyes burned without the help of his candle. Which meant the woman beside him... Raven's flame wavered, and a wisp of coppery hair snaked across her forehead.

"Welcome, Leena." Yazmin stood in the center with her hands clasped together. She was the only one without a candle, and the only one with her hood pulled back.

I dipped my chin in a show of respect. "Crown."

Yazmin's smile was warm. "Shall we?"

"I'm ready."

Pressing her palms together and bringing her thumbs flush with her sternum, she closed her eyes. "By the goddess who has granted us beasts, we offer our devotion." Imbued with power, Yazmin's voice hung in the air as she slipped into the ancient tongue our people used for ceremonies. The elongated vowels rolled through me with the force of the ocean, and faint movement caught in the corner of my eye. Tilting my head up, I studied the statue of Ocnolog and Celeste. The beast's ruby eyes flared to life behind Yazmin's head. My breath caught in my chest.

What's happening? I cast a quick glance around the circle to find everyone's eyes had closed in prayer.

"By the Charmers who have made Hireath a sanctuary, we offer our protection."

Ocnolog's scales shuddered in a guttural breath, and he leveled me with a threatening stare. I pressed my hand to my chest and felt a jolt straight to my heart. *This must be part of the ritual.*

Yazmin continued without pausing. "By the beasts who have enriched our lives, we offer our love. It is in your honor that we welcome Leena Edenfrell to the Council of Charmers, protectors of Hireath and followers of Celeste."

The candle flames shot to the ceilings like torches, but their warmth couldn't touch the cooking sheen of heat glistening before Ocnolog's maw. And then came a hand, so delicate and tender. The stone carving of Celeste sighed, and her fingers trailed the length of his face, from nostrils to the crown of spikes at the base of his skull. The heat wave faltered.

"What say you, Leena?"

Yazmin's words rattled my rib cage. Or maybe that was Celeste's stare. She'd riveted her gaze on me, and the slightest of curls tugged at the corner of her lips. The perpetual wind toying with her hair and cloak sailed around her, and she gripped her harp tighter.

I sank to the floor, the sheer fabric of my gown doing nothing to fight off the stinging cold. Such a stark contrast to the heat of the candles and Ocnolog's magic. I stared right past the Council, into Celeste's waiting gaze, and opened my palms to the heavens. To the beast realm. To everything that made me, me.

"I humbly accept your offer, and pledge to follow in the footsteps of our goddess."

Nothing could have prepared me for the rush of energy vibrating through my bones. A flood of pale, soft light tinged the edges of my vision, erasing the concrete world and narrowing my focus to the stone representation of Celeste.

Gaze downcast and heavy, she shook my existence with a lyrical whisper that echoed through my mind. *She who offers devotion, protection, and love. Will she also offer her heart?*

Her heart? What do you mean? I strained to push my thoughts toward her, to understand exactly what she was asking, but the endless expanse of her power had a dizzying effect that made the room spin.

And then Yazmin clapped her hands and the magic of the ceremony rushed out in a flood, leaving the air biting cold and my skin raw. Gone were the heat of the statue and the eyes of my goddess. Her upturned face was normal, body unmoved. And Ocnolog slumbered on, completely still.

Yazmin approached me as the Council removed their hoods. Extending her hand, she offered me a warm smile and dropped the formality of our ancient language. "We're fortunate to have you."

Taking her hand, I stood before brushing dirt off the knees of my gown. "I'm fortunate to be here." Quiet murmurings sounded from the Council as they grouped together, exchanging smiles and pleasantries. Kaori gave a quick wave before mumbling something to Gaige and retreating down a corridor. Back to Calem, I hoped.

Jitters claimed my muscles, and I let out a steadying breath. "What now?"

Raven tilted her head in my direction, a wave of unruly copper hair skating along the sandy skin of her exposed neck. Muted-yellow eyes devoid of emotion. No upward curl to her lips. She seemed wholly uninterested. As she cupped the side of her face and turned her attention back to Eilan, her reddish symbol dominated my vision.

Yazmin followed my gaze to the group. "Normally, we'd ask you to remain in Hireath with us for at least a few weeks, but I know you're eager to find a cure for Noc." She slipped a hand into one of the many thick folds of her mercury robe and pulled out a folded piece of parchment. "Which, I believe, I've found."

"You did?" All thoughts of Raven fled my mind.

Yazmin's wide smile burned brighter than the gems in the trees. "Yes, but it won't be easy." Something foreign flickered through her gaze, and her grin faltered. "The beast in question resides near Silvis's Ruins, but the taming process is...complicated."

She handed me the sealed parchment, and I had to fight to keep my fingers from ripping it open. "How so?" Behind her, Eilan and Raven peeled off and disappeared down the same corridor Kaori had exited through, leaving Gaige in an animated discussion with Tristan.

A soft hum worked its way through Yazmin's lips. "You'll need a rare ingredient to lure it out. That ingredient can only be found in Oslo's Ruins just north of here."

Anxiety gripped my stomach and twisted. Oslo's Ruins to the northwest, Silvis's Ruins to the northeast. We'd need days of travel time. There weren't any easy modes of transportation between the two, and Noc was already going from bad to worse. Not to mention that powerful beasts tended to congregate around sacred locations.

Something about the gods' power called to them, fed their souls, and stoked their magic. Nepheste's Ruins had Gyss, which were powerful in their own right. Might wasn't just about physical strength. No other beast could commune with the gods like a Gyss, or alter the very fabric of the universe in exchange for the promised sacrifice.

"It will be all right. There's time if you hurry, but the beast is dangerous. You might need backup," she said.

I chewed on the inside of my cheek. "Another Charmer?" My gaze skipped past her to Gaige, who was waving goodbye to Tristan as he left. Tristan sauntered by us with a tight nod, presumably retreating to his secluded home somewhere in the woods away from people.

"No, you don't want to confuse the beast with the possibility of more than one Charmer." Yazmin touched a finger to her lips. "Perhaps Noc? His mental state may be deteriorating, but I fear it would only get worse if you two were separated."

Even with the oath weighing heavy on his mind, Noc was still the deadliest being I'd ever met. And with Kost, Ozias, and Calem—

My heart leapt to the second story where I'd left Calem slumbering in Kaori's quarters. "I'll get my things in order and leave immediately."

Yazmin's fingers dug into my shoulder with a tight squeeze. "May the goddess watch over you."

———◆———

After changing back into my travel gear, pausing only for a moment to run my fingers over the liquid mercury robe that had been brought up as a gift, I stopped by Kaori's room to check on Calem. He was still sleeping but much less fitfully, and she assured me she could handle him.

And that, under no circumstances, should he join me on my

beast hunt. It made sense, really, but the thought of leaving him here when our enemy was still hiding in plain sight... Or just the notion that he wouldn't be joining us on our hunt, meaning Noc would have one fewer trusted soul helping me keep watch over his mental state...

Too many problems. Not enough time.

Mind heavy, I left Kaori and made my way to the library where she'd indicated Gaige would be. I'd reviewed Yazmin's note the moment she'd left and nearly cried. There were four prerequisites to taming the Azad: blood of the master, which was easy enough; a handful of fire opals to catch in the light and draw the creature's eye; a full moon at its highest point, which was slightly trickier, given the rushed timeline, but we'd make do; and a ruska fruit, a prized treat for the beast, found on a singular tree somewhere near Oslo's Ruins.

Given that I hadn't the slightest idea what a ruska fruit was, or even what an Azad looked like, I needed Gaige's expertise. And a promise.

"Gaige?" I stepped through the ceiling-height double doors and into the communal library. Built into the trunk of an oak, it was just a short walk from the keep. Roots puckered through soft dirt and around large cobblestone paths dotted with clover. The air was thick with the scent of flowers and parchment, and windows formed out of gaps in the trunk were sealed shut against the chilly night breeze. Enchanted flameless lights floated in orbs—a creation we'd paid mages a great deal to make in order to protect our texts from a potential fire hazard—and cast the area in a warm yellow hue. Circular wooden shelves were packed to the brim with tomes and pressed flush with the sides of the tree. Platforms of branch and stone jutted out in lofts at every flight.

Gaige poked his head over the polished railing of the second floor. "Up here."

I took the first set of steep stairs to my left and met him at the edge. Calves screaming from the number of flights I'd forced them to climb in the past twelve hours, I let out a quiet huff. "Good thing you weren't higher up."

Gaige failed to conceal a grin. "I imagine you didn't have a problem with them when you lived here."

"I was used to it." I plopped into the first cushioned chair I could find and held out the instructions Yazmin had given me. "I need your help with something."

He took them and scanned the paper. His brows knitted together. "What's this for?"

"For taming an Azad. The actual process makes sense. But I don't know what a ruska fruit looks like. Same goes for the Azad. I was hoping you could share your insight, Council member."

The last bit was meant to be a joke, but he neither saw my wink nor even acknowledged the playful lilt to my words. Instead, his brows were furiously trying to become one. Without warning, he turned away from me and stalked down the rows of shelves.

"Gaige?" My muscles groaned, but I shot off the chair after him. "Where are you going?"

His answer was an unintelligible mumble. Hooking a sharp right, he disappeared into a hidden enclave sequestered behind two thick shelves with a gap just large enough for a person to pass through. An enchanted orb followed us, bumping along beneath thick branches to light our path.

I brushed twigs and strands of shimmering leaves aside. A small circular room with a handful of bookshelves, a tan couch, and a knee-high, cedar-planked coffee table came into view. Weak light from the moon filtered through a circular window just above a particularly knotted portion of the tree wall.

"How did I not know this existed?"

Touching his chin to his shoulder, Gaige glanced down at me with a scrunched-up face. "Only the Council is aware of this room. Actarius's magic keeps all others from finding it."

"Actarius?"

A soft and affirmative cluck drew my attention. The knotted wall at the back shifted, and three gleaming ochre eyes blinked back at me. An owl beast. Twin, branch-like horns stretched from his head, embedding themselves into the wall. Bark-colored feathers dotted with moss camouflaged him entirely, and thick talons sank deep into his perch.

My mouth fell open. "What is that?"

Gaige's focus returned to the parchment in his hands. "That's a Whet. He was one of Celeste's beasts. He was outside of the realm when she gave her life to place Ocnolog in slumber. He's been watching over Charmers ever since."

Stepping around Gaige, I approached Actarius and offered him the back of my hand. He clucked and gave a gentle nip to my index finger. "Celeste's beast. That's incredible."

"Mmmm." Gaige moved to one of the shelves. "His horns allow him to transmit thoughts into text. By connecting to the tree, and therefore these tomes, he records information that is passed through Hireath." With careful hands, Gaige selected a thick book with a dusty brown cover, and green vines pulsing with magic retreated from the binding, rushing back into the wall. Actarius shivered.

"For example, this is an accurate account of every Council meeting for the last..." He flipped open to the first page with a list of dates printed in perfectly legible text. "Fifty years. Though I haven't done more than skim the dates at the beginning—dry stuff. He can't possibly hear and transcribe everything, though he tries."

"What does he have to do with the Azad?"

Gaige's fingers danced over a few more books. "Here's the thing: I don't rightly know. I've never tamed an Azad. So if Yazmin says it's what you need to cure Noc, then I believe her. But I swear I've seen these ingredients somewhere before. I just can't put my finger on it."

My shoulders tensed. "Is that a bad thing?"

Gaige's already creased expression somehow caved in deeper. "No. More of a curious thing."

Annoyance flared deep within me. "Look, I don't have time for this. Every minute I spend pondering my next move is a minute lost in Noc's battle against this oath. Can you help me or not?"

His steely gaze slanted to me. "Of course I can. The ruska fruit is rather simple to locate. In the middle of Oslo's Ruins is a tree larger than Hireath's keep. Its branches reach upward in the shape of a bowl, allowing the leaves to grow like dense hedges and form a platform. There's a field of ruska fruit up there. They're pear-shaped and glow a vibrant pink."

"As for the Azad..." He handed the parchment back to me before folding his arms across his chest. "Most Charmers don't think to leave descriptions of their beasts for posterity, given their bestiaries automatically record details for them."

"Which means you've got nothing." I parked a hip on the arm of the couch and slumped forward.

"Not nothing. It's been close to a century since a Charmer has tamed one, so all I've got is a rough notion of what one looks like. They're tiny, mouselike, and their white hide blends perfectly with the icy landscape of Silvis's Ruins. But since Yazmin figured out that the ruska fruit is the key to luring one out into the open, I'm betting you'll have more luck than any previous Charmer."

I straightened. "Thank you, Gaige."

His knit brow returned as his fingers resumed their dance

across book bindings. "If anything else turns up about those ingredients, I'll find a way to get word to you. I swear I've read something somewhere…"

"Okay. I have another favor to ask of you." I stood just as he turned, tilting his head to the side.

"Yes?"

"Promise me you'll watch over Calem. I trust Kaori, but…"

"But there's still the matter of our unknown assailant."

My throat tightened. "Right."

Gaige nodded once. "I promise. I've grown very fond of your assassins already. I'd be lying if I said I didn't care what happened to them."

Really, now? I remembered how his red coat had found its way over Kost's sleeping shoulders. I wasn't sure if "them" meant all of those at Cruor or just one member in particular, but I'd take whatever assurances Gaige could give me.

Folding the instructions neatly into a square, I tucked the parchment away and offered him a parting wave. "I better get moving. Enjoy your research."

He waved me off, turning back to his books. Part of me wanted to question him further, to understand his sudden interest in finding out where he'd seen those ingredients before. But I needed to get to Noc and cure his oath as quickly as possible. Everything else could wait.

ELEVEN

NOC

After stripping out of my tunic and sinking into bed, I dropped my head in my hands and pressed my fingers hard against my scalp. Gaige knew. *Darrien* knew. Kost and I had deciphered Gaige's cramped notes, which carefully detailed my possible lineage. It's not like either text actually stated that Aleksander Nocsis Feyreigner, the Frozen Prince who started a war with Rhyne by killing their princess, his lover, *was* Noc, current guild master of Cruor. But both names were there in their respective tomes. Clinging to family ties and bloodlines and damning my existence entirely. Gaige was smart—too smart—and already fascinated with my "doppelgänger."

But Darrien... He'd never been one to pick up a book. For him to come into the library and purposefully dawdle over Gaige's research... The only plausible solution was that someone had given him a tip. Someone like Quintus, who had allegiances to Darrien before his death. It wouldn't have surprised me to discover that Darrien had orchestrated Quintus's death simply to have a man on the inside. To learn how to take me down. Red haze had claimed my senses at the realization, and I'd nearly destroyed the entirety of our library, even with Kost's attempts at reassurance.

And so, at his urging, I'd left the library and waited for Leena's return. But with each minute that stretched by, every hour that ate at my patience and invited anger into my veins, the sinister red film took hold. I needed her here.

Where is she? Day had long since bled to night. With the curtains drawn open, the glow of the moon beamed through the glass doors leading to the balcony. White light reflected off the floor and sharpened the shadows curling in my peripheral vision. They were familiar. Cool. But the gashes of red, like wounds slitting through an onyx sky, were becoming more frequent. Bolder. Taunting.

"*Noc?*" A female voice, so achingly familiar, broke the silence.

I jolted from the bed. This curse was diluting my senses; I hadn't heard even the slightest hint of footsteps or the ghosting of breath from parted lips. Let alone the steady cadence of a heart. But Leena was home, and I needed to hold her so bad my fingers hurt.

"Leena?" I turned toward the door, and the breath left my lungs.

A woman with wheat-colored hair and golden eyes stared back at me. Motionless, and yet a gentle, invisible air current swirled around her. A faint whisper of movement from the long locks kissing the sides of her hips. A shudder through the soft fabric of her ivory gown. Elegant fingers toyed with the golden belt around her midriff. The motion was so genuine, so lifelike.

"Amira," I murmured.

Her smile broke me. "*Aleksander.*"

Noc. That was my name. Aleksander was a dangerous memory. "You're not real."

Freckles danced across the bridge of her nose. She didn't look a day older than when I'd found her dead. Dropping her hands to her sides, she took a careful step forward. "*Aren't I though?*"

My pulse thundered in my ears. The rational part of me screamed to wake up. To acknowledge that her presence, likely brought on by the resurgence of my past, signaled a dream. But there was the chill of the tile beneath my bare feet. The electric tinge of adrenaline pumping hard and fast with every breath. She wasn't real and yet—

She reached out and cupped my face with her hand. Just like she used to. "*You've been busy.*" A flicker of red snaked through her gilded locks, but I didn't care. Agony and guilt crashed together in my chest.

"You can't be real." My words lacked the conviction I wanted them to have.

She trailed her thumb over the scar on my cheek, and that action ushered in guilt of a different kind. *Leena.* I stepped out of her reach. *Leena, I need you. Where are you?*

Amira tilted her head to the side. "*What's wrong?*"

Endless shadows, angry slices of red and brilliant waves of gold collided together, making it impossible to decipher dream from reality. "You should go."

"*Why?*" She placed her hands on her hips.

"Because you don't belong here. Because you're not real and—"

A deep bass voice, rich with the hint of something gravelly, sounded behind me. "*What about me? Am I not real enough?*"

I whipped around, and every fiber of my being solidified into ice. Leaning against the wall with his ankles crossed, wearing his signature crooked smile, stood Bowen. The man I'd met and loved after joining Cruor. Textured auburn hair tangled across his forehead, and he stared at me with eyes so clear the color resembled glass. He swallowed, and the movement drew my stunned gaze right to his throat.

"Bowen?" I didn't know how I found my voice. I didn't know how I managed to remain standing.

His grin deepened, and he ran a hand over his bare jaw, full of impish charm. "*What are you doing, love?*"

Something ripped my heart clean out of my chest. Stabbed it over and over until it was a bloody mess on the floor, eviscerated and near-unrecognizable. My control had slipped from my grasp. I couldn't cast these visages away.

I need to wake up.

Bowen sighed and pushed off the wall, closing the distance between us with three long strides. "*Do you know why we've come?*"

Control. Control. Control. I reached for it in the shadows, bathed my hands in onyx tendrils, and willed the nothingness to seep through. Darkness surged in a cloud around me, but Bowen slipped through and gripped my shoulder. Gentle pain flared beneath his fingertips and broke through it all.

"*You can't hide from us.*"

Amira dropped her gaze and joined Bowen before me. "*We're here to help, Aleksander.*"

The shadows died, leaving nothing more than haunting red lingering like a fine mist. "I don't need help."

Bowen pinned my chin between his forefinger and thumb before letting out a quiet scoff. "*Always the tough guy. Was he the same for you?*" He tossed Amira a sidelong glance.

Her bell-like laugh had always been my undoing. "*Yes.*" The entire exchange left my head swimming. She sighed and wrapped a loose strand of her hair through her fingers. The action was painfully familiar, reminding me of the way Leena toyed with her bestiary.

Bowen sighed. "*You're not well.*"

I forced a swallow. "As evidenced by your appearance."

"*Hush.*" Amira placed a gentle hand over her heart. "*Please, listen.*"

"*Please,*" Bowen echoed her a breath later.

Suffocating haze thickened around them, turning her hair a dripping strawberry blond and setting Bowen's locks aflame.

Thoughts I'd never even dared to speak, guilt for their deaths, ripped through me. The aftermath of what I'd done was within arm's reach.

I'd never been given the chance to beg for forgiveness.

My chest ached. "I didn't know. I didn't mean for any of this to happen. I'm so sorry."

Bowen ran a tender hand down my forearm. "*We know. We don't blame you.*"

"*But there is a way to make amends.*" Amira shifted closer, and the scent of honeysuckle and sunshine surrounded me. Eyes downcast and clouded, her somber words shook the room. "*If you're willing to help us find peace, that is.*"

The words were out of my mouth before I could even consider the implications. "Of course. Tell me."

"*We've been wandering since our deaths.*" Bowen's scent of cardamom and orange melded with Amira's, creating an aroma that smelled like my past. Like opportunity. Like the chance to do right by them.

"You have?" I wasn't sure what death was supposed to entail. When I'd gone under, there'd been nothing but darkness and quiet relief. But before I could follow the path to the gods' realm, I'd been brought back. Were Amira and Bowen really trapped? Caught somehow in between worlds? They couldn't be living in the underworld. That treacherous place was for wayward souls with no chance of redemption. It's where I imagined I'd go. But not them. They were both too bright. Too good. They belonged in the gods' realm, eating succulent foods and drinking rich wine, dancing without ever tiring. Smiling. Always.

But they weren't there. They were here. Stuck. Because of me.

My room slid entirely out of focus, enveloping us in a cocoon of red. Their touches were soft and sinful, damning and saving all at the same time. Amira ran her knuckles along my jawline, and for a moment, my eyes slipped closed. Their hearts beat as one in my ears. Cadences that had been silent only minutes ago surged through my world, establishing a rhythm that kept me tied to this moment. To them.

Bowen pressed a gentle hand on my low back, and my eyes fluttered open. "*Leena is your love, just like we were. First Amira, then me, now her.*"

Amira's gaze was pure red now, but her voice was gentle. "*We're so glad you've broken the curse. But…*"

"What?" My question was more of a rasp. There was an unspoken ask lingering on the tips of their tongues. Something appalling. Something they expected me to balk at. But I'd *condemned* them to this. Me. It was my fault. If I could somehow find a way to alleviate that, if I could grant them passage to the gods' realm…

It would be the first step on a long path to redemption.

Amira's fingers tensed. "*I don't want to add to your burden.*"

I placed my hand over hers. "Tell me."

"*Everyone who's been touched by your curse is forced to wander. To wait. When you broke the priestess's spell, we were supposed to be given passage. And yet, here we are.*"

Everyone. Thaleus. Countless faces. All those men and women who'd died on the battlefield during the war with Rhyne. All those deaths I mistook for a common illness associated with warfare. Friends, mentors…so they were left wandering too.

Something small and demanding begged me to remember what had happened in the clearing when Winnow had removed my curse. I had seen all those pained faces, but when the curse had been lifted, life had reentered their bodies. They'd *smiled* at me, as if somehow I'd been forgiven.

It didn't seem like there were wanderers left. But Amira,

Bowen... I glanced back and forth between the two of them. They *felt* real. Their deaths still weighed heavy on my heart. Maybe I was wrong. Maybe...

"I didn't know."

"*We know. We don't blame you.*" Bowen's nose brushed against my ear. They were both so close, surrounding me. Drowning me. "*But you can help us find peace. All you have to do is give us the last wanderer. Then we can all ascend together.*"

The last wanderer? My mind reeled. Tried and failed to connect the dots. Between their heady scents and the thick red tendrils wrapping us in our own private world, nothing made sense anymore.

"*Please, Aleksander.*" Amira leaned closer, trailing her fingers along the bare expanse of my chest. I was frozen beneath their touches, mind revolting at the thought of...of what, exactly? They deserved peace. I'd wanted that very thing for so long. If I had the power to alleviate their pain, then I would do it. Without question.

My throat was tight. "How?"

"*She needs to go.*" Amira's voice was soft. Pleading.

Kill.

Something hard crashed through my gut. "She?"

"*She is the last one. She was at death's door, and the curse feels robbed. If you give back what you stole, then we'll all find peace.*" Bowen pressed his forehead against my temple, his breath hot on my neck.

Noc. Leena's voice reverberated through my mind. Lilac and vanilla filled my senses, chasing away the tantalizing mix of Amira and Bowen.

"*You could raise her.*" Amira's words were a tempting offer I didn't even want to acknowledge, and yet how could I not? An eternal life with the woman I loved? The idea sank deeper than it should've, and the red haze thickened.

"*We've seen her thoughts. Her deepest desires,*" Bowen whispered. "*She wants to walk with the shadows.*"

"No." My voice was weak, unconvincing. She *couldn't* want that. Could she? I'd only brought it up once in passing since our return from Hireath, and she hadn't acknowledged it. Her beasts... What would happen to them?

"*Give her what she wants, and then we'll all be free,*" Amira said.

No. I can't do what they're asking. I can't kill, Leena. I could never—

"Shh. It will be all right."

I couldn't tell who had spoken. Their forms were red, their voices melded, their hearts beating as one.

"Noc."

I moaned. "I can't."

"Noc!" Two delicate hands cupped my face. A thumb worked over the trail of my scar. "What's going on? Are you okay?"

Brilliant rosewood light doused the maelstrom of red, and there she was. Leena. Wide hazel eyes stricken with fear. Rich-brown streaks of windswept hair tangled around the shape of her face. Bow-like lips parted. Her very breath battered against me.

Control. Shadows exploded outward and blanketed our room in a riot of onyx and charcoal, tendrils slithering over one another like snakes in search of the vile red that had previously claimed my mind. I grabbed Leena and pulled her close. Buried my nose in the crown of her hair and inhaled her familiar scent. She was real. Tangible. Not a ghost or a memory, but my *anam-cara.* My pulse slowly shifted back toward normal.

Quaking hands pressed firm against my back, and her voice broke. "Are you with me?"

"I'm here."

I felt her exhale, and her body slackened. "You were just standing here, staring at nothing. I couldn't reach you."

Shadows licked our bodies and kept us close. "You can always reach me. I heard you."

Tilting her chin up, she studied my face. "What happened?"

"It's these damn—" My voice cut off as if someone had wrapped their fingers tight around my throat. An ugly cough sputtered from somewhere deep in my chest, and I turned away.

If I couldn't physically tell her about the danger I posed, then she wouldn't know to leave. To keep her distance. It was up to me to keep her safe, and yet she was the only thing that seemed to stave off the madness. She grounded me, and while being near me put her in harm's way, it also made it easier for me to think. Breathe. I could rationalize in her presence.

Her presence kept me sane.

My presence put her in danger.

No matter where we turned, the oath was winning.

With a thick swallow, I chose my words carefully. "The oath. It's worse when you're gone." She needed to be protected at all costs. For both our sakes.

I'd never let anything happen to her. I'd never... A shudder passed through me. I would *never* fall prey to the delusion that she needed to be murdered in order for Amira and Bowen to find peace. Killing her would be like killing them all over again.

And yet a glimmer of red still loitered in my peripheral vision, trying to take root without care for logic.

"I know how to break it."

A dull ringing started in my ears. "What?"

Wrapping her arms loosely around my neck, she offered me a tired but hopeful smile. "There's a beast that can do it. We need to leave first thing tomorrow."

Hope, pure and radiant, spread like wildfire in my chest. I slanted my mouth across hers and tasted the relief on her lips. But the thought of Amira and Bowen still lingered in my mind, and my body stiffened as quickly as it had relaxed. A shiver raced over my skin. I *wanted* to tell her all that I'd seen. But I *couldn't* tell her of the visions, and bringing up what Kost and I had discovered earlier... What Gaige had discovered... Not while the walls had ears and eyes, though no assassin would ever admit to eavesdropping. I trusted they were loyal, but information was deadlier than any blade, and those who had it were often manipulated without choice.

Taking a step back, I let out a shaky breath. "I need to speak with Kost."

"What? You're joking." Her fingers tightened on my waist. "I just got back and told you I have a cure, and you're leaving?"

"It's urgent, Leena."

She let out a miffed snort. "Okay, if it's so urgent, then why don't I come with you to chat with Kost?"

"There's no need."

She narrowed her eyes. "There's certainly a need. *I* have a need to know what's going on."

Gently, I brushed away her hands. "Don't wait up for me. Get some rest before our journey."

Fire brewed in her stare, and she took a defiant step toward me. "No. Gods dammit, Noc, *talk to me*. What the hell is going on? Why are you pulling away?"

"Because I..." A sharp tingling burned my throat, and I swallowed. "I want to make sure we're prepared. We'll talk more tomorrow, once we're on the road. I promise."

"Another promise?" She folded her arms across her chest. "I've yet to see you follow through on one."

Her accusation burned, but I could take it. For her safety, I'd endure her anger until we had a chance to talk openly. Until I could explain myself and beg for forgiveness. I only hoped it wouldn't take too long.

"Good night, Leena." My chest tightened as I caught the hurt in her gaze, but I turned my back on my love and stormed out into the halls of Cruor. An unfamiliar feminine laugh ghosted through my mind, and the red tendrils flared.

The sooner we ended this madness, the better.

TWELVE

LEENA

On the edge of Cruor's property was an ivy-clad stable with ten stalls all housed with Zeelahs. Thick straw and wheat-grass crunched beneath our boots as we approached four saddled mounts, readied by Astrid and Emelia for our departure. The faintest glow of morning light slipped through the oblong windows above each stall, and a sleepy barn owl let out a soft hoot from the rafters. We hadn't taken Zeelahs to Wilheim on our first journey, knowing we'd catch a train, but there wasn't a more direct route to Oslo's Ruins. The remoteness of it ate away at my hope and allowed anxiety to settle deep in my bones. Time was not on our side.

Astrid passed worn leather reins to me, and a small flicker of warmth bloomed in my chest. The last time I'd gone on a journey with assassins, I'd nearly lost my life, but I'd found my love. My gaze flickered to Noc. Charcoal eyes tight and framed by bags from sleepless nights. Tense hands forming fists visible through the pockets of his black trousers. Onyx tunic and overcoat. He was the lord of the shadows, and even with the edge of fatigue clinging to his frame, there was a hint of ferocity in the angry muscles tightening his shoulders.

"Noc, are you sure about this?" Emelia handed over his reins before clasping her hands before her. With her thick hair braided away to leave her face open and clear, it was easy to decipher her uncertainty.

Noc placed a hand on her shoulder and squeezed. "You're more than capable. I trusted you to watch over the guild last time."

"You trusted Darrien—"

Noc held up his hand. "And you to keep an eye on him. Don't doubt your abilities, Emelia."

Astrid sidled close to her, gaze slanting from Noc to Oz and finally to Kost. "What if Darrien returns?"

"He won't." Noc abandoned Emelia to step into the stirrups and settle onto his stallion's back. Oz and Kost followed suit wordlessly, but there was a thread of tension between Noc and Kost riddled with unspoken words. Oz's brow furrowed.

At least I'm not the only one picking up on what's not being said.

"How do you know?" Emelia looked up at her guild master with so much steely devotion that my frustration with Noc subsided for a moment. I'd only recently become a member of the Council—my name was virtually unknown to my people. But I would protect them, help them, because that's how they looked at the Crown. With total and utter belief that she—that all of us—would guide them to safety and keep our land a haven.

Noc allowed himself a tight smile. "Because I know Darrien. He has wounds to lick and plans to devise. He won't harm Cruor. His biggest concern is bolstering his ranks. If anything, he'd try to win you over."

Kost nodded once. "If that happens, do not resist him openly. Win the war, not the battle. Keep everyone safe until we return."

A visible shiver raced through Emelia, and she dropped her chin to her chest. "I'll do my best."

"I'm not in the business of making false promises." Noc shifted, and his mount pranced in place. "I'm in the business of being prepared. I don't think he will come. He's after me, not you. But if he does, do as Kost says."

False promises? I bit my tongue. He'd certainly been good at those as of late. I could only hope last night's promise, that we'd finally *talk* once we were outside the walls of Cruor, wouldn't turn up false.

Astrid placed a firm hand on Emelia's back, wide smile steady. "We'll be fine. Emelia and Iov are strong. I'm new, and I'd still follow them anywhere."

He let out a soft chuckle. "Good." Tilting his chin in my direction, he nodded to my mare. "Ready to go?"

"Yeah." I hiked my leg over my mare's back and settled into my saddle. Yazmin's directions burned in the inner pocket of my overcoat, sending heat straight through to my heart. "Let's go."

Noc and Kost led the charge, kicking their mounts into a steady canter and heading north parallel with the Kitska Forest. On our left, swirling purple vines thick with thorns wrapped around dying brush. Trees with flaky dark bark and gnarled branches stretched in unruly patterns. Shimmering pinesco pods, with their eye-like patterns, winked in the stirring winter breeze. Such a stark contrast to the wide, open plains of dormant grass rolling toward Wilheim. A faint glimmer twinkled in the distance, just barely visible through the morning fog. Those diamond and ivory walls were a beacon in any season.

An errant screech rattled from somewhere deep in the wood. Pulling my coat tighter, I dipped my chin to my chest as we rode. Oz's mare shifted closer to mine, and he hunkered down against the chill. For the most part, the pace set by Noc and Kost kept us silent. Between the cold and the jostling from our Zeelahs, our tongues were liable to be caught by chattering teeth. It wasn't until after the late-afternoon sun dipped below the tree line, leaving behind a smearing of burnt orange across the sky, that Noc and Kost stopped. They dismounted, surveying a particularly flat portion of the wide, open plains across from Kitska Forest. The monsters deep within the festering wood likely wouldn't come this close to the edge of their territory, but I had no doubt Kost would have us sleeping in shifts. Just in case.

Oz and I joined them, and immediately set to work pitching our tents. As soon as we finished, Oz busied himself with the fire while Kost rummaged through our bags, searching for our provisions. Noc stood slightly apart from it all, arms folded across his chest and jaw tight. Flames from the fire reflected in his faraway stare.

"Everything okay?" I asked, sidling up next to him. We were finally out in the open, away from Cruor, and it was high time he told me what was going on.

"Yes." His answer was low, barely audible. My gaze flickered to Kost and Oz. Did he not want them to know? No, that couldn't be it. Kost knew *something*.

"Now that we're on the road…" I let my voice trail off, hoping he'd pick up where we left off last night.

He didn't.

"How was Gaige while you were in Hireath?"

"What?" I blinked.

Noc remained unreadable. "Did Gaige say anything that struck you as odd?"

My mind rewound to the previous day's events. "He was a little taken aback by the ingredients needed to tame an Azad, but other than that, he seemed fine. I only spoke to him after my acceptance into the Council."

"I see."

"Noc, what's going on?" I edged closer, placing a gentle hand on his forearm. "Why are you asking about Gaige? Did he do something?"

"No." Noc shook his head. "We just don't know who to trust."

"Including me?"

He frowned and finally met my gaze. "What are you talking about?"

It was so hard not to scream out of frustration. I let loose a long breath. "We're not in Cruor anymore. You said you'd tell me what's going on once we were on the road. Well"—I gestured wide to include the path near our camp—"we're officially on the road."

He tensed, then looked away. "It's not that simple."

"Isn't it? Noc, I need you to *talk* to me."

"I will. It's just…" He ran a rigid hand through his hair, then spied Kost near one of our tents. "I need to check the perimeter. The last thing we need is another surprise attack from Darrien or a monster from the woods."

"Wait, I'll—"

"Kost." He cut me off, calling to his brother. "Let's go."

And then he walked away. Again. Shadows swallowed them whole in a matter of seconds, and he was gone. My hands curled to fists by my side, and I stormed toward the tent meant for him and me.

Oz looked up from the fire. "You hungry? I can throw something together."

"Thanks, but I don't really have an appetite. I'm calling it a night." Peeling open the tent flaps, I went inside and set about the task of arranging the hides and blankets for my makeshift bed. After changing into my nightclothes, I fell into the bed in a huff and stared up at the faded-green canvas. Aside from the crackling fire and the occasional shuffle from Oz as he moved about, I heard nothing.

Time moved slowly as I waited for Noc to return. I envisioned him sweeping into the tent, the perfect picture of remorse as he apologized for leaving me high and dry, and then diving into the story of his past. Or filling me in about whatever secrets he and Kost kept. *Anything.* Anything to make these false promises ring true.

But as the hours passed, nothing changed, and I was forced to fall asleep alone and angry.

———◆———

When I awoke the next morning, the blankets beside me were cool, as if they'd never been occupied. I quickly changed and emerged from the tent to find the men had been busy. Everything, save my sleeping arrangements, had already been packed. The Zeelahs, readied. Oz greeted me with a smile and breakfast—cooling coffee, a hunk of bread, and dried fruit. Kost nodded a hello and then immediately started to break down my tent.

Noc stood by and watched it all. His gaze flicked to me for a moment, and his shoulders slumped. Just a fraction. Then he pressed a chaste kiss on the top of my head before turning away to help Kost.

Anger simmered deep in my gut. How could he not see the damage he was doing by keeping me in the dark? Brushing away the crumbs of breakfast on my breeches, I headed for my Zeelah. The next time I got Noc alone, I would force him to talk. Even if it meant summoning Iky to hold him in place so he couldn't disappear on me.

We rode hard for hours, but even the rub of the saddle against my legs didn't chafe like the tense silence that stretched between Noc and me. At one point, he nudged his mount faster so he could ride beside Kost instead of me.

"How are you feeling?" Kost murmured, his words barely audible. I leaned forward, straining to hear their muted conversation.

"I'm managing," Noc said. His rigid spine suggested otherwise. "I'm thinking...*feeling* things that aren't real." He seemed to choke out the words, then shook his head. "We can talk later. I don't want anyone to worry."

Feeling things? What did that mean? Before I could interject, he pushed his steed into a faster trot, putting distance between us. Kost rode after him, glancing in my direction before saying something I couldn't hear.

I gripped the reins until my knuckles burned. "Oz."

"Yeah?" He shifted in his saddle, angling toward me. Muscles bulged in the tight fit of his wool-lined coat, and he placed a thick hand on his thigh.

"What's going on with those two?" I jerked my chin in the direction of Kost and Noc without breaking Oz's stare.

His brows inched together. "I'm not sure. There's so much happening, I don't even know where to start."

My throat tightened. "I know. It's a lot." I let loose a sigh, and my hands relaxed a fraction. "I'm sorry, Oz. I haven't even thought to ask how you're managing through all this."

"Me?"

"Yes, you." I tangled my fingers in the chain of my bestiary. It was always Oz and Calem. Together. Bantering, joking, keeping things light. His brother was wounded and suffering. *No, two of his brothers.* My gaze skipped to Noc's back.

Oz rolled his head from side to side, stretching his neck. "I'm managing. Calem usually helps me with the new recruits. It's... quiet without him around. He's fine, though. He'll pull through." I wasn't sure if he was convincing himself or me. "It's Noc I'm most worried about."

"Me too."

Ahead of us, Kost stiffened and kicked his stallion into a

full-blown gallop, leaving an exasperated Noc in his wake. Running his fingers through his hair, he yanked his Zeelah off to the side and waited for Oz and me to catch up.

"Everything good?" I asked when my mount fell into step beside his.

"We should make camp soon." Noc gritted his teeth. "He's scouting to make sure the route is safe."

"Is that all?" Oz didn't hide his suspicion, and I sent a silent prayer of thanks that I wasn't the only one frustrated by Noc's secrecy.

"He doesn't think I should be on this expedition." Gaze level, he continued to stare ahead without turning to face us. "He worries I'm not mentally...sound."

Was that it? Kost's frustrations felt deeper, steeped in history that I couldn't dream of touching.

Noc fished a canteen from one of his saddlebags and took a quick swig before passing it to me. His fingers grazed mine for a moment, and their icy familiarity eased some of my frustration. He'd said the oath was easier controlled with my presence. Maybe that was the cause of his ever-shifting mood. Still, I craved to hear it from him rather than be left to my own assumptions. Mineral water slicked over my tongue, and I swallowed hard. Twisting the cap back in place, I returned the canteen to Noc.

"Do you think he's right?" I asked. In the distance, Kost's silhouette waited for us on a rounded hilltop. Rolling dark clouds churned and rumbled, flashes of white light streaking across indigo swells.

Noc studied the sky while letting out a low hum. "I'm not sure."

"Should we be worried?"

"No." Noc shook his head. "I should check in with Kost." With a click of his tongue, he urged his Zeelah to pick up the pace and galloped toward Kost. I gripped the reins of my mare so tightly my knuckles turned white.

"Enough of this." I dug my heels into the sides of my mount and pushed her hard, sending her racing after Noc.

"Leena!" Oz shouted from behind. He let out a grunt, and the pounding of hooves sounded as he followed suit.

I was done with Noc's caginess. Yes, the oath was affecting his mental state. Yes, he had a list a mile long of things to worry about. But my safety wasn't one of them, and if he was keeping things from me yet again to protect me, then he was about to get a piece of my mind. Or a swift kick in the ass. Possibly both.

My Zeelah thundered after him, ascending the small hill in record time. "Someone needs to tell me right now what's going on."

Kost's green eyes flared behind his glasses. "Nothing is going on."

"Don't you start with me," I seethed.

"Leena." Noc placed a firm hand on my forearm. "Look." He tilted his head down the slope of the hill to a ramshackle two-story manor. Misshapen gray stone was framed by wooden beams, and a gable roof with sunbaked tiles sagged under the weight of years of neglect. A dormer window with iron bars across the pane was dark, and the arched front door was ajar.

"So it's an abandoned house. Is that supposed to mean something?"

Noc's smile was tight. "When we come this way for jobs, we frequently stay here. We still need to make sure it's safe before we enter."

Oz steered his mount beside me and frowned at the slumped house. "Looks about the same to me."

"It appears so." Kost's voice was barely audible. Slipping out of his saddle and landing quietly on the earth, he shot Oz a quick glance. "Regardless, let's do our due diligence. Shall we?"

"Yeah." With the same grace, Oz dismounted and sat low into his heels. Shadows festered around their ankles, swimming upward in a quiet storm of darkness, until they both disappeared into the onyx abyss.

Noc tracked their invisible forms with his stare. "They're checking for people. We should be able to use it for the night." He glanced up at the darkening sky. "Better protection against the elements."

I didn't care about the damn elements. "What were you and Kost talking about?"

"I told you, he doesn't think I'm well enough to—"

"Let me stop you right there." I folded my arms across my chest just as a deep, bone-rattling rumble echoed above us. "I know you're not telling me the truth. Or maybe you are, but I know it's bigger than that. It's time to be honest with me."

Noc wrung his reins tight. "It's hard to explain."

"Is it? So hard to explain that you can talk to Kost, but not to me?"

"Leena…"

Above us, the clouds split in an onslaught of sudden rain. Neither of us moved. Numbing cold settled against my skin, and Noc's tunic went from dry to soaked, clinging to every curve and contour of his chest. I'd withstand any downpour if it meant I could finally get him to open up. His throat worked as if he wanted to speak, but no words ever left his lips. Fingers trembling, he buried his face in his hands.

He looked so…*broken*. It wrecked me entirely, and the anger that had been fueling my tirade faded. I edged my mare closer. "Noc?"

"Can I ask you something?" His words were raspy, barely audible over the crashing thunder. Slowly, he dropped his hands, and his pained expression sent a wave of dread coursing through me.

"Yes."

"What am I supposed to do if you die?"

I blinked, unable to follow his train of thought. My death wasn't something I'd thought about since I'd been pardoned by Yazmin. "Why are you asking me that? I know the oath is weighing heavy on you, but Noc, I'm not going to die. I'm okay. I'm safe."

"But what if you aren't?" He didn't blink. Didn't speak. Each moment of silence that followed was a thousand waves crashing in my ears, each more deafening than the last.

"What do you mean?"

He ran his hands through his wet hair, and his locks slicked smooth against his scalp. Trails of water trickled over the high angles of his cheekbones and darted down his face. Brow twitching, he cupped his hands in his lap and stared at his palms. "What if I can't protect you?"

"There's nothing to protect me from. Right now, we need to be focused on helping you."

Wild eyes pinned me again. "What if you need protection from me? What if I hurt you? I'd never be able to live with myself. We worked so hard to break the priestess's curse, only to be scrambling to put out another fire, then another. I couldn't live with myself if you got caught up in the flames."

"Noc." I inched my Zeelah closer, and our thighs touched. He flinched. "You'd never hurt me. I'll be safe *because* I have you."

"And if you're wrong?"

It was so quiet I barely caught his question over the clash of thunder in the sky. Shadows bled from his frame, as if he needed them to remind himself he still had the ability to control *something*.

"Don't think like that."

"And if you're wrong?" he repeated as if I'd never spoken, boring right through me with eyes that weren't wholly his anymore. "If you die?"

I swallowed twice. "Then it's my time. Is that what you want me to say?"

With a trembling hand, he reached for me. "No. I want you to say that I should raise you. That you want to live as an assassin of Cruor."

"Noc..." I wrapped my fingers in his. How long had he been contemplating this? My life was always a blip in comparison to his. Something destined to flare for a moment in time, while his embers would be stoked forever. His shadows weren't frightening to me, but never had a Charmer entertained such an existence.

We'd only discussed such an outcome once before, late at night right after we returned from the battle of Hireath. I'd chalked it up to him being afraid after seeing me under Wynn's spell, and instead of answering him, I'd only brushed the hair from his face and placed a kiss on his forehead. Told him I loved him and that he didn't need to worry about such things. That *we* didn't need to worry. But maybe I was wrong.

For a moment, I willed myself to imagine such a fate. I'd always found his shadows beautiful and soothing, but they were so starkly different from the boisterous, vibrant life of the beast realm. Would I still have access to both? Could I? What if those shadows leaked into that world and tainted my beasts?

My beasts... They were the reason for my hesitation the first time he'd asked about raising me. And they were the reason I was about to hurt him deeply with my answer.

Squeezing his hand, I implored him to understand. "It's not just my life, it's my beasts'. They're tied to the realm because of me. When I die, they're allowed to remain. There's no precedent for what would happen if I came back. If those shadows permeate every facet of your life, what would they do to the realm?"

His voice cracked. "I don't know."

"Me neither." I studied our intertwined fingers. "And I can't risk that. Risk *them*."

A loud holler snared my attention. Oz waved from the porch with both arms, beckoning us to join him. A flicker of orange warmth sparked behind the windows and promised to chase away the cold.

But not from my heart. I dragged my gaze back to Noc. "If it's my time, then you have to let me go."

Noc dropped my hand and reached for the reins of Kost's Zeelah. He nudged his mount forward a few feet before speaking over his shoulder. "And that is why I have to protect you. At all costs."

Without waiting for a response, he made a soft clicking sound and led Kost's Zeelah toward the dilapidated house. Wind and rain crashed against my senses, but nothing compared to the slow dredge of ice water in my veins. There was no right answer to his question, and yet, I couldn't help but feel guilty as I led Oz's Zeelah toward our temporary camp.

THIRTEEN

NOC

Leena huddled before the stone hearth on a threadbare love seat. Eyes lost in the hungry flames, she hadn't spoken once since entering the house. She'd nodded her thanks to Ozias when he'd dug through our provisions for some dried lamb and bread, but that was it. He'd accepted her silence without complaint and was now busying himself in the kitchen. Visible from the main room, he tinkered with a wood-burning stove and relit a stack of logs in its belly. Meanwhile, Kost had disappeared to a room on the second story to change clothes.

"There's not much, but it looks like a few wanderers have used this place since we were here last." Ozias rubbed the back of his neck and frowned. "Some old food, a few dishes." He nodded to a wire structure with ceramic plates and bowls. "There was some wood under a tarp out back that we can use to keep the fire lit and cook in the morning."

Kost and Ozias had done a quick but thorough sweep of the premises before calling us inside. Fortunately, there were no people to be found. We had a roof with beds, and we'd packed our own supplies. In the very least, we'd be dry and somewhat comfortable.

Still drenched but unwilling to drift far from Leena, I joined Ozias in the kitchen. "At least we're not pitching tents in the rain."

Ozias folded his thick arms across his chest. "True. There are enough beds for all of us, though the blankets look a little dusty. Might be best to use our own."

Leena shifted on the couch and shrugged off her coat. Rain had snuck between the layers and dampened her blouse. She toyed with the strings laced across her chest and sighed.

Ozias nudged me. "What did you do this time?"

"Nothing." It was one thing to assume she'd always shy away from the possibility of being raised, but to hear her say it out loud... I slipped my hands into the pockets of my trousers and formed neat fists. "Just a lot on her mind."

He didn't buy the shit I sold. "Sure." Thick hands snared four chipped mugs from an overhead cabinet, and he placed a teapot over a steady flame on the stove. "Listen, it's not my place to pry, but we've got enough going on. Don't keep her in the dark."

My brow furrowed. "What?"

"Whatever you and Kost aren't telling us. She deserves to know. I'd like to think I deserve to know too." His weighted stare spoke volumes, and I sighed.

The creaking stairs preceded Kost's entrance. Fatigue, frustration, disappointment—a maelstrom of emotions kept him from moving silently. Socked feet hit the uneven floorboards and he padded toward us, running his hands over a fresh cotton work shirt and black knit pants.

"There are spare candles in the cupboard upstairs if needed." He wound his way around the back of the couch and eased into one of the four chairs pushed around a small wooden table. "It's quite dark up there."

Leena leaned into the cushions. Tilting her head slightly, she tracked Kost's progression toward us. It's as if his presence reminded her I still hadn't told her all the things I kept promising to reveal. All the things Kost knew, but no one else. Her jaw hardened.

"If it's my time, then you have to let me go."

Bile soured my tongue. How could she say something like that? How did she expect me to go on without her if anything happened? A sliver of red flared to life beneath the shadows.

"There's dried lamb and bread if you're hungry." Ozias parked his hip on the lip of the counter and eyed Kost.

Kost nodded once. "Yes, we should all eat."

"I already ate." Leena's voice was quiet but firm, tinged with a hint of anger. I gripped the back of my neck. If she was on edge, then it was my fault. It seemed like lately it was always my fault. Everything I tried to do to make her life easier kept backfiring.

Kost tossed me a curious glance. "Good. There's no telling what we'll encounter tomorrow. It's best we be rested and well fed, so we can be prepared."

Leena huffed, pushing herself off the couch to turn and fold her arms across her chest. "You know what? I *would* like to be prepared."

Kost's brows furrowed. "Are you lacking something? I assure you, I packed extra provisions, so if—"

"No, Kost. Not *provisions*." She dragged the word for emphasis. Finally, her fiery gaze left him and pinned me to the wall. "I want to know what's going on. What you two"—she gestured between Kost and me—"have been talking about."

"I don't know what you're referring to."

"*Stop.*" Leena rounded on him, her words steely. "Don't think I haven't noticed. Don't think I don't know you—or better yet, *you*." She turned back to me. "Something is going on. Something you're not telling me. And don't you *dare* say I'm imagining things, because I'm not the only one who has noticed."

Ozias cleared his throat. "She's got a point."

Frame rigid, Kost fell silent. After a long beat, Leena took a few steps in our direction, her boots squeaking against the floorboards. "Well?"

Her stare was damning. Clearing my throat, I came around the table to stand before her. "Leena, there's nothing going on."

She let out a wordless noise and jammed her finger into my chest. "Don't do that, Noc! Do you not trust me?"

"No, that's not—"

"Then what is it? Tell me what it is, because this isn't how an *anam-cara* acts."

The room swam out of focus. Floorboards meshed with the wooden paneling of the walls, and the cobwebs in the rafters seemed to drift down and snare me. Her words, the honesty and truth behind them, branded me with shame.

And yet I couldn't find my voice. For so many reasons. The oath wouldn't let me reveal anything I'd been seeing. And my past... The knowledge Gaige and Darrien likely unearthed...

Hedging my words, I started with the oath. "When I said Kost didn't think I was well enough to travel, that wasn't a lie. I'm starting to think and...*feel* things that aren't real."

She studied me for a moment, weighing my words. "Like the nightmares?"

Kost straightened in his chair and threw me a wary look. With a long breath, I nodded. "Yes, like the nightmares. I can't..." My throat began to burn. The specifics of what I saw—Amira, Bowen, what they'd asked me to do—tried to force their way out, but invisible fingers gripped my vocal cords tight. "I'm worried about your safety."

"Again with this?" She shook her head. "Noc, I'm fine."

"The bounty was placed on you, Leena. What do you think the oath is trying to get me to do?"

Her brow furrowed, and she stared off without really seeing anything. After a moment, she shivered. Voice quiet, she turned her gaze back to me. "I'm not going to die."

Everything we'd just talked about outside surged into the forefront of my mind. I so badly wanted her to understand how real this was. How dangerous I was. And yet I couldn't tell her. Couldn't explain the way Amira and Bowen were urging me to end her life. Couldn't articulate the feelings they stirred in my chest.

"This is serious," I said.

"Kost and Oz are with us," she said, gesturing to my brothers. They nodded their agreement. "Nothing will happen to me." She dropped her hand and turned to them, gaze snagging on Kost for a fraction too long. He met her stare head-on, but said nothing.

Pivoting back to me, she asked, "Anything else?"

I paused. "What do you mean?"

She let out an exasperated sigh. "Noc, I *know* you. You wouldn't have waited this long just to tell me about these...*feelings* if you thought I was in danger. You would've acted." After a beat, she tilted her head. "Why did you ask me about Gaige?"

While telling her about my past didn't spark the same magical compulsion to be silent, the words were reluctant just the same. "He might know something."

"About the oath?"

I shook my head.

She pressed her palm flat against my heart. "Tell me, Noc. We're not in Cruor anymore. The people in this room—your brothers, *me*—can handle the truth."

"It's not a matter of whether or not you can handle it." The words left me in a rough exhale, and I rubbed my temples to get my thoughts in order. "Leena, this truth? It could put you in danger."

She threw up her hands. "Everything puts me in danger!"

"Not just you. Cruor. Maybe even Hireath and the Council."

Her hands fell to her sides. "Why?"

"Because of me or, rather, because of who I used to be." I pinched the bridge of my nose and caught the glint of silver on my finger. Such a hazardous truth.

"Noc, you mustn't—"

Kost barely spoke before Leena ate him alive. "Don't you dare. No more secrets. No more hidden agendas." She glared at me with the intensity of one of her beasts. "What. Is. Going. On? I've waited long enough, Noc."

Time seemed to slow. I needed to tell her. I couldn't keep pushing her away. I'd lose her entirely, and that was the exact opposite of what I was trying to do. "My name isn't Noc."

Her brow twitched. "I swear to the gods if this is some kind of joke—"

"My name," I braced myself for her rage and let out a slow breath, "is Aleksander Nocsis Feyreigner, Frozen Prince of Wilheim and rightful heir to the throne. Our royal adviser took over after my parents passed. His son, Varek, now rules over Lendria."

"For gods' sakes," Kost muttered. He removed his glasses completely, setting them on the table and staring off into nothing. Ozias's jaw hit the floor, and he slumped into a chair, nearly splintering it in half.

Leena's face was carefully blank. "Explain."

Gesturing toward the two open chairs at the table, I urged her to sit. She refused to move. "I died fifty years ago during the war with Rhyne."

Ozias's throat bobbed. "You were murdered."

"He sacrificed himself to end the war." Kost clenched and relaxed his hands, still staring at the empty chair across from him. "It was honorable."

"You killed the Golden Princess." Leena's voice was as sharp as a blade and severed my heartstrings with its edge.

Sinking into the chair across from Kost, I nodded. "The curse did, yes. But no one believed me."

Realization slowly filled her expression, and she took a step back. "The priestess."

"Amira's death was the beginning of it all." I rotated the ghastly ring around my finger. "Years and years of carnage. I couldn't stand it anymore—soldiers fighting and dying for a prince they didn't even believe. It was all my fault. So I ended it."

"Why didn't you tell me?" Her hazel stare was entirely too damning. Lies. Secrets. My reason would mean nothing to her.

"To protect you."

"I'm so sick of that excuse!" Her fist slammed into the wall, and rosewood light exploded from the back of her hand. The air throbbed with power. "When will it end? How many more secrets are there?"

Red tendrils leaked into my peripheral vision, and anger swam through my veins. "Don't you understand how dangerous this information is?"

"Just because it's dangerous doesn't mean you should keep it from me."

"He kept his lineage a secret to protect *all* of us," Kost said through clenched teeth. "He knew that if Varek learned of his existence, he'd squash Cruor and anyone Noc held close—any *allies* in, say, the Charmers Council—with the might of the capital. To him, it would look like the prince was raising an army to reclaim the throne. Never mind that Noc has no intention of ruling."

Leena glowered, and the light around her hand sharpened. "He trusted you with the truth, didn't he?" she asked Kost.

His mouth fell open as if to respond, but he gave up and pursed his lips. Ozias ran a hand over his shorn hair, fingers tense and unrelenting. His disappointed gaze cut deep, and I forced myself to look away.

After an eon of silence, Leena capped her power and rested her hands on her hips. Voice cold, she stared somewhere above my head instead of meeting my eyes. "So where does this leave us?"

I wanted to bridge this distance between us. But everything about her was jagged. Piercing. She'd cut me right now and not think twice about it. It only fueled the foreign anger brewing inside me. How could she not see the danger behind my name? How could she still be so defiant? A hint of red toyed with my vision. It was so hard to focus with the pressure of the oath. So hard to remember to breathe.

Kost sighed. "It leaves us in a predicament, seeing as Gaige is the one who put the pieces together that night in the library."

"That's why Noc asked me about him." She didn't even look at me. Didn't acknowledge my presence. She spoke around me as if I weren't there at all.

Kost tilted his chin, but I shook my head once and a strange mixture of relief and frustration tugged at his features. Slowly, I let out a breath. "Exactly. Though if he didn't mention anything to you, I'm hoping that means he didn't tell anyone else."

"But there's still the matter of Darrien," Kost said.

Ozias held his head in his hands. "Darrien? How does he play into this?"

"He knows too." My words were low. Defeated. "If I had to guess, I'd say Quintus tipped him off after spying on Gaige and Kost. When Darrien was in the library, he was way too interested in Gaige's research. Judging by the way he acted when you escorted him out, I'm betting he felt like he had an upper hand we didn't know about." My fingers twitched, nails involuntarily elongating.

My blood screamed to infiltrate Darrien's system and command him to stand down. Either that or kill him. It was hard to separate the warring desires inside me—mine and the oath's.

"But he has no physical proof." Kost finally replaced his spectacles. "We would've noticed if he'd taken something. That piece of Gaige's left-behind research."

"And you don't look like the Frozen Prince anymore." Ozias tossed a sidelong glance in my direction. "I've seen the history books and paintings. Your appearance is different enough."

"Thanks to this." I tapped the monstrous ring on my finger. "This emits a glamour that alters my looks, as well as keeping people from even questioning any similarities I might share with my former self. Well, until Gaige, that is." Sighing, I ran a heavy hand through my hair. "He asked me about a doppelgänger at the hearing. Which means the magic must be fading."

"How do we fix it?" Ozias asked.

"Find a mage. Talmage bartered with one when he raised me to keep my identity safe and give me a chance at a new life."

"Eryx?" Leena asked.

"No. A different mage with different magic. It'll take time, and that's something we don't have right now. It's strong enough to deceive most people, so we should be fine. As long as this ring remains intact, I'll always be just Noc."

Leena's scoff was an arrow straight to the heart. "Sure."

"Which is why I've been against you joining us on this endeavor. There's too much at risk," Kost said..

Leena shot him a simmering glare. "How so?"

I grimaced. "Because each one of the sacred ruins holds special significance to the royal family. There, messages from the gods, passed through powerful deceased mages, are given to an ascending prince or princess. It's required to visit each location before accepting the crown." Pushing away from the table, I stood slowly. "If I go to Oslo's Ruins and Silvis's Ruins, that will make three. It would be hard to deny who I am and have the king believe me if he were to discover I'd been visiting these sacred sites."

"He'd see it as a bid for the throne." Kost drummed his fingers against the table. "Noc would likely be executed. And Cruor and Hireath... If he thought we were rallying to his side, everyone would be in danger."

For the first time since I'd announced my bloodline, a flicker of concern darted through Leena's eyes. She smothered it in a moment and leaned against the wall, tipping her gaze to the ceiling. "So the way I understand it, Darrien has no physical proof as long as the ring's magic holds, and we keep our presence in the ruins a secret. Right?"

I took a step toward her. "Right."

She stared right through me. "Kost was right. You should've stayed home." Pushing herself away from the wall and taking the stairs two at a time, she called down to us without a second glance. "Be ready to leave at dawn."

"Leena—"

She slammed the door to one of the rooms, effectively ending the conversation.

Red haze seized control of my limbs and I continued after her, each footfall a deafening warning begging my muscles to listen. Control had gone the way of frustration. She was so close. Within reach. I couldn't let her go. If I did, I'd lose it all over again. Amira and Bowen would come back and beg me to do the thing I'd been fighting since the beginning. Hand outstretched, I reached for the railing to follow her up.

"Noc." Ozias appeared in a plume of shadows and braced a heavy hand against my chest. "Let her go."

Someone pulled the strings attached to my body, and I bared my teeth without thought. "Get out of my way."

"No." With a forceful push, he shoved me back toward the table. "You're not acting like yourself. Don't make things worse."

I steeled my anger with a slow breath. He was right, of course, but it was so damn hard to control the raging emotions inside me.

Unmoved, Kost sighed. "That could've gone better."

"You could've told us sooner." Ozias folded his arms to his chest, eyes downcast. "Calem too. We're all here for you, Noc."

The unbridled disappointment in his low tone deflated me entirely. Red receded to a pale mirage, and I swallowed hard. "I know. I didn't want to burden you. I wanted that life to stay in the ground. None of it mattered until recently."

"Then you should've told us when it mattered." Moving toward the stairs, Ozias paused at the first step. "I'm not a fan of who I used to be, either. And never once have you asked me to dredge up the past, so I get that. But when it could affect us, we deserve to know. To help. You're not the only one who wants to protect the ones they care about." He climbed the stairs without another word, leaving Kost and me alone to sift through the shattered remains of my lies.

FOURTEEN

THE FROZEN PRINCE
50 YEARS AGO

The first thing I saw was darkness. A maelstrom of shadows that varied from slate to onyx to sable, all somehow unique. They were gentle in their touch, and I realized I could feel my fingers. My limbs. My body. There wasn't any pain. There wasn't much of anything at all. The total and complete silence was deafening and yet comforting. The sounds of war and death, gone. Here there were no whispers or judgments threading low through conversations.

And then there was a pinprick of light—a pale gray that hinted at smoke. It grew until it devoured the expanse, blanketing out the darkness and bringing with it sounds. A rustling of bodies and hushed words. Voices I didn't recognize and couldn't piece together through the veil of mist. And then a fiery heat bloomed in my chest, and my heart, which had been still, beat once against my ribs. Searing pain cracked through me like a hammer battering brittle wood. Light blossomed behind my eyes. Again my heart beat, this time with less anguish but more vigor, and more flickers of light erupted in the gray.

The voices grew impossibly loud, and suddenly I could *feel*. I was flat on my back somewhere, blades of grass tickling my neck.

My clothes were damp, as if my body had been soaked at one point and was only now beginning to dry. The cool air was thick with pine, and as I took a staggered breath, the fresh scent of earth and blood skated along the back of my tongue. My eyes flew open. The world of gray traded for an indigo expanse dotted with millions of stars. Treetops towered high like jagged spears against the sky. And darkness. Thin tendrils of shadows unrelated to the night snaked through my peripheral vision, as if they'd always been there. As if they *belonged*.

Someone knelt beside me and placed a hand over my chest. A man I didn't recognize peered down, his curling hair the color of weathered bark falling about his shoulders. Framed by heavy wrinkles, his dark eyes held nothing but wisdom—and perhaps a glimmer of pity.

"Where am I? What happened?" My words were a harsh rasp, and I desperately wished for water.

The man didn't move. "You're safe. You're still in Lendria."

"Did you heal me?"

"No, I didn't heal you. You died as you intended, and I merely brought you back." His gruff voice was oddly soothing, but his words set me on edge. I shouldn't be *back*. Prince Aleksander *needed* to stay dead to end the war. It was a decision I'd made of my own volition, and apparently it had been ripped away from me without my consent.

Curling my hands into fists, I stiffened in place. "Who are you? Why did you resurrect me?"

"My name is Talmage. I'm the guild master of Cruor. You're alive because of Kostya." With a nod, he indicated a man standing to my left wreathed in shadows. Just like outside the camp, he hadn't made a sound. But this time, I could hear the subtle inhale and exhale of breath, the minute scraping of cloth on cloth as he straightened his tunic. The way his swallow seemed forced. Death had done something to my senses, and the unease in my gut ratcheted up several notches.

"I don't want to be here." Anger colored my voice. I hardly recognized it.

Talmage clasped his hands together. "That can be arranged. I won't force you to live as an assassin of Cruor if you don't want to."

I ignored him entirely and glared at Kostya. He averted his eyes, unwilling to meet my gaze.

"I felt responsible for your death. I...I fear my words may have driven you to take such extreme action." He cleared his throat and gripped the back of his neck. A beat later, he dropped his arms to his sides. "While it may have ended the war, you didn't deserve to die. I thought, if you wanted a second chance..." His low voice was clouded with guilt, and some of my anger fled. Perhaps his words had been the catalyst, but the decision was my own.

"You chose your death. Kostya found you without armor, without weapons. I can't say this life will be easier, but it will be new. You can move on. You can forget. We leave everything from our past in the ground." Talmage's words hinted at a possible new beginning, at a life outside of the wars I'd grown so used to. But that was the thing—no matter how alluring it sounded, no matter how much he promised my previous life could be left in the dirt, there was simply no way a prince of the realm would be forgotten.

There was no outrunning who I used to be. Who I was.

Pushing myself into a sitting position, I bit back a growl. "I don't get that choice. As long as I live, Rhyne will continue to fight. I died so my men could find reprieve. I died so all of this would end. You might as well kill me now, because I'll walk right back to their forces if I have to. I won't let my country suffer any longer."

"We have ways of hiding your identity." Talmage's words were so soft I barely heard them. "The only people who would know of your past would be myself and Kostya."

"And what of my body? I'm supposed to be *dead*. Rhyne won't accept my disappearance as proof, and the war will continue."

"About that." Kostya gave a curt nod to my wet clothes. "They were transporting your body to the main ship on a rowboat when I came to...extract you. During the confrontation, the boat capsized. No one was seriously injured, but your body was lost to the depths of the ocean. Or so Rhyne thinks."

"One of the men transporting your body was a high-ranking official. His word will be good enough for Rhyne." Talmage steepled his hands together, and I pursed my lips. I wanted to believe in this absurd possibility of a different life, but what if they were wrong? What if Rhyne continued to fight?

"Aleksander." Kostya crouched before me and leveled me with one look. "You've done enough. You've done more than any prince has ever done for the people of Lendria. You don't owe this world anything else. If you truly wish to die again, then I'll do it myself. But if you want a chance at living, at being someone other than the Frozen Prince of Wilheim, then take it. If at any point you change your mind, I'll end it quickly. This I promise you."

Silence stretched on for an eternity. Part of me was livid. I'd found peace in death, and they'd brought me back to a world where I'd done nothing but cause others pain. I wasn't sure I could live with that knowledge. But another smaller part of me burned with a new hunger I'd long since forgotten: hope.

Hope was a funny thing. All it took was a moment of reflection. One second of attention. And then it was blooming and burning in my chest, overtaking the fears and doubts I'd carried with me to the grave.

Kostya stood and offered me his hand, already reading the answer on my face. "Well?"

I took it after only a breath of hesitation, and he pulled me to my feet. "If I change my mind, you end it. No questions asked. Understood?"

"Understood."

Talmage straightened. "Before we take you to Cruor, we've got to see a mage about your appearance. But first, you'll be needing a new name. You're not a prince anymore, Aleksander Nocsis Feyreigner."

You're not a prince anymore. Nothing in my life had ever sounded sweeter. It would grieve my parents to no end that their son had died, and they'd probably spend weeks, maybe months, dragging the ocean for my body only to come up empty-handed. Guilt flared for a moment in my chest, but I buried it deep. A world without the man who sparked a never-ending war with Rhyne was surely better off. They'd find a suitable replacement to take the throne once they passed, and life would go on. This would be but a small note in history, and my new life was just beginning. With a tentative smile, I glanced at my newfound brethren.

"Noc," I said. "My name is Noc."

FIFTEEN

LEENA

Sleep eluded me for hours, and I tossed in a bed too large and too empty for my liking. I kept reaching for Noc, expecting to find warm, silken skin and the steady rise and fall of his chest. But cold sheets were jarring, and the lack of his body next to mine ripped apart my fitful slumber and sent me careening into awareness. The empty room only made things worse, so I tossed the blankets aside, pulled on some clothes and boots, and made my way outside to clear my head in the early morning air.

Shivering, I slumped onto the porch step and pulled my knees to my chest. Crystalized dew clung to blades of grass, and my breath hung in a white fog around my head. Pale light blossomed on the horizon, just a smearing of faint blue against an indigo night. With the Kitska Forest at our backs, there was nothing but rolling, empty plains before me. Endless. Quiet. I let out a heavy sigh.

Why didn't he trust me? I rolled my lower lip into my mouth and frowned. What else was he hiding? I'd been so open with him about my past, about everything.

At least he had given me space when I needed it. The creaking floorboards from his constant pacing were like a lullaby in the night. He was more anxious than ever, and while I wouldn't let something like this ruin what we had, I wasn't sure how to feel. I was tired of him withholding information for the sake of my protection. It's how we'd started our relationship, but it didn't have to continue that way.

The front door creaked open, chasing away the silence and startling me to my feet. Noc stood quietly with his hands tucked into the pockets of his trousers. Chest bare, every tense muscle was visible. Every ripple of unease and frustration. Dark eyes roved the length of my body, from his oversize work shirt I'd stolen to sleep in down to my booted feet. In my rush to get outside, I hadn't bothered to lace them.

He frowned at the exposed skin of my arms. "Aren't you cold?"

"A little." I wrapped my arms around my stomach.

The wood frame of the door groaned as he leaned against it. "Leena..."

"It's fine."

"No, it's not." He pushed away from the wall and walked toward me, halting just barely out of reach. "You're right. I should've told you sooner. I'm sorry."

"Do you trust me?" I held my hand out to him, hoping he'd take it. Praying that he believed he could confide in me.

Noc was silent for a beat, and then suddenly he was there, wrapping me in a hug that lifted my feet off the ground. "Leena, I trust you with my life." He buried his nose in my neck and shuddered. "This oath... It's not an excuse, but it's making it hard to focus. I'm so terrified I'll slip up. I'll lose myself and hurt you somehow. I'm doing whatever I can to protect you so that won't happen. Do you understand?"

I pulled his chin up so I could meet his faraway gaze. "I understand. But, Noc, remember you're not in this alone. The more we know, the more we can help." He pressed his eyes shut, and I placed gentle kisses over his lids. He'd lived with his curse for so long that sharing thoughts, feelings, didn't come easy. For him, it was simpler to protect. To put himself in the line of fire instead of possibly jeopardizing someone else. And while I understood that, I didn't like it. We were together. A team.

Slowly, I brought my lips to his. The ache in my chest lessened, and I melted into him.

He set me down but kept me pressed flush to his body. "I'm sorry I didn't tell you everything sooner. I just... Information like this is dangerous. If no one has it, they're less likely to be targeted. But even so, I know I shouldn't keep you in the dark."

"I'm not used to it like you are," I joked, but his answering smile was forced. "Besides, this doesn't change who you are to me."

He grimaced. "I need you to understand how dangerous this is. How dangerous I am."

I couldn't help but roll my eyes. "I remember the first time you told me that. At first, I didn't believe you, and then I did. And what do you know, I still believe you." Standing on my toes, I ran a hand down the side of his face. "But I don't believe you're dangerous for me. I believe you're dangerous to those who would hurt the ones you love."

"Leena, you could die." His gaze was so heavy I had to fall back to the flats of my feet. "Varek would do anything to keep his claim to the throne. He'd find out about you, and he'd use that against me. If something were to happen... I wouldn't be able to live with myself."

Whether it was the morning chill or his words, I didn't know. But I shivered just the same and pulled him closer. "Then we won't let him find out. Ever."

"No one can know. Do you trust Gaige? Will he tell someone about me?"

"I want to. I don't think he would do anything to intentionally hurt us. Once we're done with this beast hunt, we'll talk to him. Okay?"

Noc's jaw went taut, but he nodded.

I couldn't stand the way he slipped back into his old frozen self, so I ran an absent hand across his chest and offered him a sly grin. "Should I call you Aleksander?"

His chuckle thrummed through my fingertips. "Please, don't."

"Good. I like Noc better, anyway." I smiled up at him. "Everything is going to be fine. I promise." For effect, I channeled some of my power to my hand, allowing rosewood light to claim the space around us. "I can protect you too."

The rightness of that statement warmed me to my core. Charmers never used their beasts to outright attack humans, but if it meant defending my family, the people I loved, then I knew my beloved beasts would come to my aid. Hireath. Cruor. Noc. I would defend them all with my dying breath.

Noc sighed and trailed a light finger along my Charmer's emblem. "You don't know what I see when you're not around."

"What do you mean?" A tremor raced through my hand, and he clasped it tight.

"Just things...people...from my past. It's Cruor's oath trying to force my hand."

"Amira?"

He nodded. "And Bowen. Two people my curse claimed." He blinked, touching his throat in surprise. "I've been trying to tell you that since the beginning."

"Why couldn't you?"

"The oath wouldn't let me. I can still feel a slight burn"—his fingers trailed down his neck—"but it's bearable." Slowly, he met my gaze, then targeted the soft glow about my hand. "It's you. Your magic. Something about it is lessening the oath's control. I don't

know how long it will last. It seems to get stronger every day."
He continued to stare at the rosewood light slipping between our
fingers. "I've been trying to warn you since the beginning, but I was
so afraid my past would ruin things, that being open would just put
you in more danger…"

"But it didn't. I'm still here, and now I can help you." I
squeezed him tighter.

"It's been so hard." His voice broke just slightly, and my chest
tightened. "There's this voice in my mind. One I can't place. Every
day it gets louder. More insistent. I feel like I'm slipping away."

My body stilled. "What does it want you to do?"

His fingers dug into my hip, seeking purchase. "Kill. To follow
through with the oath. And Amira and Bowen… They're hallucinations. I can say that now, with you in my arms. But when they're
around, when *you're* not around, it's harder to differentiate truth
from lie. I rationalize doing things I never would've before."

"Like what?" I didn't want to know the answer, but Noc was
talking. Sharing. And as terrifying as his words were, I wasn't about
to stop him.

"Like using my blood to command someone." His voice was
low, painful. "Like killing you and raising you, even though I know
you don't want it."

A dull ringing started in my ears. His fear from yesterday, the
questions about my life after death… It all made sense. Killing me
would satisfy the oath. Raising me would keep his heart intact. It was
the perfect lure. And his former loves were dangling it before him,
convincing him that there was a way to satisfy everyone involved.

Everyone except for me. And he was fighting against their
wishes with all his worth because he knew that. Because he loved
me. Because he was my *anam-cara*, and sacrificing himself for my
happiness was exactly what he was trying to do.

"Noc." I breathed in deeply and settled my fear with his honeyed scent. "I love you. We'll get through this. You won't hurt me."

He studied me without any sense of belief. "Just be patient with me, okay?"

"Okay." I pressed a kiss to his chest. As much as it grieved me to do it, because it was the very thing that made it possible for him to speak, I capped my power. The rosewood glow faded, and with it Noc's demeanor hardened. What I would've given to have an endless supply of magic.

"We should get going. We've still got a few days' ride to Oslo's Ruins, and we have to make it to Silvis's Ruins by the first full moon of winter." I craned my neck over my shoulder to stare out at the horizon where the early rays of sunlight were claiming the sky with golden-pink fervor.

When we returned inside, Oz was already busy in the kitchen and Kost was digging through our saddlebags, rearranging contents to suit his liking. Noc and I dressed in our travel attire quickly, and we ate some quail eggs Oz had found in the woods. He also unearthed some roasted coffee grounds tucked away in a cupboard, and I summoned Tila, my monkey beast, to ensure they were safe for brewing. The kick of energy from the coffee, coupled with the warmth in my chest from having an honest conversation with Noc, left me feeling prepared to take on anything.

We continued to ride north for two days until the Kitska Forest tapered off, leaving nothing around us except an open expanse of endless, knee-high grass. For the most part, the travel went smoothly. It was as if opening up about his past allowed Noc to gain some control over his oath, even without my powers, and there was an easiness to his breath that had been missing before. I'd still find him staring off into the distance sometimes, jaw clenched and eyes unseeing, but when I intertwined my fingers with his, he always came back to me.

By the time the sun reached the middle of the sky the next day, a lone tree had sprung into view.

"It's huge." Ozias craned his neck upward as our Zeelahs slowed to a walk. Fading wheatgrass had transitioned to a thick blanket of lime-green moss and lush clover. Roots bigger than people crested through the soft earth, creating bark-covered hurdles that reached up to our chests. They radiated outward from the thick trunk of the tree in a circle that seemed larger than the city of Hireath. Dilapidated stone walls with loose masonry formed feeble archways and pillars around the tree's base, and a tiered landing draped in thick vines held what appeared to be a sealed sarcophagus made of marble.

Noc pulled his Zeelah to a halt. "Oslo."

I glanced past him to the ruins. "Is he really buried there?"

"A mage is buried at every site." He dismounted but didn't move any closer. "Nepheste too. We just didn't cross the lake to the altar."

"Are you all right?" Kost slid out of his saddle and pinned Noc with a hard stare.

"Yes." His eyes remained glued on the ruins.

Slipping to the ground, I tilted my head upward. The tree reached toward the sky and formed a bowl, the leaves trapped between the endless blue stretch and the thick patchwork of branches. Splaying my hand out, I called on my power and was met with the groaning of the beast realm door. Onyx appeared with a happy yowl, and he rammed his head into my chest.

"I know this isn't your favorite, but can you take me up there?" I scratched behind his ears and jutted my chin to the platform above. Onyx huffed and shook out his mane, teal feathers shooting out in a display of discontent. "C'mon, please? You flew me home from Hireath."

"Does he not like that?" Oz scratched the back of his head.

"Not particularly. It's not that he can't carry me; he's just finicky. He's the only beast I have who can, though. Dominus's wings can only propel his own body weight." I reached down and scratched the expanse of his chest. Onyx sighed and tilted his head to the side. Permission granted.

I trailed my hand over his back and gripped the fur at the base of his neck, hoisting myself up. His lithe muscles rippled beneath my legs, and I gave him a tight squeeze. A purr that bordered on a hiss dripped from his maw.

Noc finally dragged his gaze away from the ruins. "You shouldn't go alone."

I tried in vain to subdue my frustration and pointed to the tree. "Can you climb that? Onyx can only carry me safely. He's not used to transporting people. I'd have to train him to do so, and as you can see, he's not a fan of that."

"It'll be fine, Noc." Oz placed a hand on his shoulder. "Really."

"She's picking a piece of fruit. There's no danger involved." Kost glanced between the two of us. "Just be quick, Leena."

Noc caved. "Better yet, be safe."

"I will." The tension in my shoulders faded. He was trying, that much I could see. "I'll be right back."

I nudged Onyx's side, and he crouched low into his haunches before leaping into the air. Wings beat hard, and his body propelled us toward the cloudless sky. Rippling muscles raced beneath his skin and pulsed against my forearms. Sharp and cool, wind whipped my hair and battered my face, but it couldn't chase away the inevitable grin that claimed my lips. With each beat of his wings, we soared upward and away. Away from the unease and anxiety. Away from the problems we were fighting to solve. Dazzling sunshine doused the world in a soft radiance. When we climbed high enough to see over the lip of the branches, my mouth went slack. A field of pear-shaped fruit just barely visible beneath a thicket of rubbery leaves and thorns glowed a vibrant pink. Hope. Tangible and real.

Leaning against Onyx's neck, I spoke into his ear. "All right, Onyx. Find us a place to land."

He circled three times before descending, finding a particularly thick tree limb that supported his body. Sliding off his back, I kept my weight in the balls of my feet and straddled between two netlike patches of leaves and branches. Onyx let out a soft yowl. Slumping to his stomach, he steadied himself with his legs draped on either side of the limb. Lazy eyes slid closed.

"Take a nap, why don't you?" My gaze flickered between him and the high sun. He huffed, taking in the warmth and ignoring me entirely.

Gingerly, I took a step forward. The rubbery leaves were springy and bounced back against my boots, giving lift to my step. The dense packing of greenery was remarkably sturdy, but I didn't trust it to hold my mass for too long. Peering beneath the pool of green, I spied a nearby ruska fruit glowing like a beacon. It was caged by thorns and elbow-deep beneath the branches, ensuring it wouldn't be snared without enduring a considerable number of scratches.

Tightrope-walking along the branch, I sidled up beside it and left Onyx slumbering behind me. I dropped to a crouch and rolled back the sleeve of my coat. My shadow pooled beside me, and a slow-moving vine receded with the sudden lack of direct sunlight. I frowned at the retreating, thorn-covered trap, but brushed away my concern. A few less scratches—no complaints from me. Diving my fingers beneath the thicket, I let out a soft grunt as the first series of thorns dug into my hand and wrist.

"C'mon." I pushed farther and winced when the jagged barbs nicked my forearm. The ruska fruit glowed with expectation. One final cage of thorns barred my path. Fashioned like rows of teeth, they held firm until my fingers just barely grazed their glistening skin. A quiet exhale trembled through the leaves, and the thorns parted.

Was that a sigh? I glanced back at Onyx. Still sleeping, his paws twitched against the leaves. Vines started to move of their own accord and reached up with deadly quiet, sneaking around his limbs.

An agonizing pain radiated from my hand, and I shrieked. Yanking my attention to the fruit beneath me, I paled. The thorns had come crashing down, snapping around my hand and embedding themselves in the soft muscles of my arm. Vines lashed out in a frenzy and crawled up toward my shoulder.

Onyx roared, but the moment I'd screamed, the tree had come to life. Snarling vines covered in glistening barbs wrapped around him, keeping him ensnared. I tried to run to him, but the trap held strong. Barbed thorns bit into his fur and locked him in place.

"Onyx!" I jerked and sent a wave of power to my symbol, contemplating which beast to summon. A flash of rosewood light erupted from my hand, and the trap released with a high-pitched whine. From the center of the tree, a creature emerged. Endless streams of vines shot outward from its center mass. The beast was no bigger than a toddler, and two spheres made up its body. The larger sphere was hollow with branch-like bars displaying an empty cage. The smaller, bulbous sphere was its head. Another shrill whine escaped from a jagged rip masquerading as a mouth beneath glowing yellow eyes.

Behind me, Onyx howled. Still trapped in a net of vines, he couldn't fend off the continued barrage of attacks.

"Let go of him!" I sprinted toward the beast, tossing sure footing aside and charging instead toward its center mass. Vines reacted in an instant, creating a wall of needles that ripped into my clothes and flesh and stopped me in my tracks.

I needed fire, but summoning Lola would be a mistake. Her weight would cause her to go crashing to the ground. My mind worked on overtime. If I couldn't save Onyx by force, I'd have to send him back to the beast realm and pray he'd agree to fly me down when I was through. Channeling power through to my hand, I opened the realm door.

"Go!" I begged him to take the invitation. The thorns had done more damage than I'd realized, growing slowly to form spikes the size of my arm and digging through his flesh. He needed to heal. But he only looked at me with worried eyes as he ignored the promise of safety.

"It's okay. Please, just go home."

He refused to move, each moment costing his silky hide more and more gashes. A vine lashed out and scraped the side of my face. I'd never encountered or heard of a beast like this, but unexpected creatures were bound to appear from time to time. It was what made filling the pages of our bestiaries so exhilarating.

A sudden flux of power raised the hairs on my arms as one of my beasts approached the open door and barreled their way through. Lustrous white fur and plated scales caught in the high sun, and Dominus roared to life beside me. Onyx took one look at him and seemed to decide that I was safe. Finally, he disappeared into the realm, leaving an empty cage of vines behind.

I closed the door on him before he could dart back out. Then, I turned my attention to Dominus. Once again, he'd come without prompting. He hadn't even been on my mind. I'd glossed right over him as I ran through a list of my available beasts. I tangled my fingers in my bestiary as I pushed away my shock and instead focused on the beast before us.

"Stop those vines," I said.

With a menacing yowl, Dominus charged. The wings about his ankles flared outward, and he leapt over the vine wall before us. The beast's endless limbs re-formed and lashed out, but Dominus's agility made him a moving target with unpredictable patterns. In a matter of moments, he'd scaled the wall. Through the trembling vines, I was just able to catch a glimpse of him crashing into the beast with deadly accuracy. Everything went still.

Dominus snarled and waited, teeth poised above the beast's head. The creature shivered, and my heart ached. We'd disrupted his home. All he was doing was guarding his precious bounty, and I'd tried to steal one. And even though Dominus was just protecting me, as any of my beasts would've done, it wasn't right for this creature to suffer. Onyx would heal, thanks to the realm, but if Dominus struck? This beast would be left to recover on its own. And I couldn't live with that.

Mind set, I raced around the barrier. "Hold on, Dominus."

His answer was a simmering growl, but he didn't sink his teeth into the beast. A garbled whimper rushed outward from the pinned creature, and his circular yellow eyes held nothing but terror.

Crouching beside his head, I placed one hand on Dominus's snout and the other just above the beast's eyes. "Dominus won't hurt you unless I tell him to. Now, may I please have a ruska fruit? We'll leave you alone after that." He'd likely spent his entire existence in this tree, watching over his prizes. I'd only take what was needed and leave the rest.

A series of clicks and a soft scraping, like kindling coming together to start a fire, slipped through its mouth. A lone vine dove into the pool of leaves and emerged with a fresh fruit. Taking my hand off Dominus, I gently cupped the fruit and smiled.

"Thank you."

Channeling my power to my symbol, I opened the beast realm door and glanced at Dominus. "And thank you. Will you check on Onyx for me?"

His gaze darted from me to the beast as if deciding whether or not it was safe for him to leave. I nodded my encouragement, and he lifted his paw, allowing the beast to squirm a short distance away. Finally, Dominus huffed and disappeared.

Adrenaline fled in a cool rush, and I slumped to a thick branch. "Now I just have to get down."

Slowly, the beast crawled toward me. More clicks and scraping. The thorns along its limbs pressed flat to its body. A tentative vine, now devoid of dangerous barbs, slid forward and touched my mark. Rosewood light bloomed in the space between us, and a connection solidified into place. Charmed. I hadn't even been trying.

Why? I stared at my hands and the fruit captured between them. The rosewood hue hung about my fingers, defying everything I knew about charming. Taming shouldn't have been this...*easy.* Sure, there was a handful of lower-level beasts that didn't require more than basic charm, but this? Blinking, I stared at the beast. Its jagged gash of a mouth pulled up in a smile.

A slow-moving tingle crept over my skin. *What did this mean?* Maybe it was a benefit of being named a Council member. Maybe we were blessed by the goddess in a way that made taming easier... Maybe...

My brow furrowed. No, I would've known about that. This felt different. I'd have to ask about it later, but for now...I extended my hand outward and felt a rush of warmth as the creature's vines wrapped around my fingers in a gentle squeeze.

"Can you get me down from here?"

The second, cagelike sphere splintered open as if on a hinge, and a handful of vines urged me toward it.

I raised a brow. "I'm not going to fit in that."

But the vines kept pushing until I stumbled toward it. With its body pried open, I barely fit cross-legged in the bottom sphere. A low groaning sound drifted from its wood-like frame, and slowly, the creature's body enlarged until it could enclose around me. The bars elongated to match my height and bowed outward, giving me enough room to sit without grazing my head.

With a smile, I touched my bestiary. "I'm definitely going to have to read up on you."

And with that, more vines rushed from his core and we were off, crawling toward the edge of the tree with a ruska fruit safely resting in my lap.

SIXTEEN

NOC

Oslo's Ruins called to me. Unadulterated power vibrated from the raised tomb, rippling outward and washing against my skin. Poking and prodding, as if trying to understand my purpose in the ruins. Electricity surged through my muscles, and I took a few steps forward.

"Noc." Kost's hand snared my shoulder. "Don't."

"I'm already here." The tomb dominated my vision, and a foreign heartbeat throbbed in my ears. "Distance doesn't matter. From the moment that tree came into sight, I was caught."

Caught. It didn't feel right to put it that way, but I wasn't sure how else to explain it. The pull of the magic was undeniable, an invisible current tied to me by the royal blood coursing through my body. Whether or not I intended to take the throne didn't matter. The gods recognized my existence, and they weren't going to let me escape without the ritual.

Letting out a long breath, I closed my eyes. Just like before, Leena had delivered a part of my past right into my hands. Five hidden ruins strewn about Lendria. All five necessary to visit before ascending to the throne. Nepheste's welcome had been silent, just a recognition in my soul, but it had been enough to start the process.

"The first welcomes," I mumbled as I opened my eyes.

Ozias shot me a concerned look. "What?"

"The second questions." I moved toward the tomb. The steady thrum ratcheted up a few notches, a heady beat so low and deep that all other sounds faded save that cadence. Kost and Ozias followed me, their worried calls muffled and indecipherable. All that mattered was Oslo and what he had to say.

I passed under the last archway before the tomb, pushing aside dripping vines and standing before the slab of marble. Hungry shadows lurched around me, but a glowing white sphere held strong like a star above the sealed sarcophagus.

I was far from prepared. Many royals visited the first grave site alone, but every location thereafter garnered more attention, more witnesses to the claim. Other heirs. Siblings and parents. Priests and priestesses. My gut tightened.

Even so, Oslo came. His white light throbbed over me, illuminating my usual black-on-black ensemble of tailored trousers and fitted tunic, complete with overcoat. I lacked a crown, the Wilheimian crest, or the royal white cloth embroidered with sapphire stitching. Out of habit, I slipped my hands into my pant pockets and leaned into the heels of my boots.

"*Aleksander Nocsis Feyreigner. I've waited a long time for the Frozen Prince's arrival.*" Oslo's voice crashed with the ferocity of falling water against stone in my mind. It shook my bones and set my heart racing. The Frozen Prince. A title coined by the people for my looks and further hammered into place by my father. "*Too aloof and detached,*" he'd said. "*How will you ever connect with your people?*"

I'd connected with my people after all—it just took dying for me to find them.

"*To be honest, I never had the intention of coming,*" I thought back to what I assumed was Oslo's spirit.

The orb wavered. *"We know."* There was a collective sigh, a scraping of wind from multiple voices, and the hairs on the back of my neck stood on end. The gods? Perhaps. *"And yet we waited. Your questions have been prepared. Answer to be deemed worthy of the crown."*

"I don't want the crown."

A tittering of voices squawked in contrasting octaves before Oslo's rumbling chased them all away. *"Why?"*

"Because I don't find myself worthy."

Silence stretched in the endless abyss. Finally, a chuckle that sounded more like two stones scraping together. *"Why?"*

"Is that your only question?" I glanced around, wondering where Kost and Ozias had gone. No other form was visible in the swirling mess of shadows. Not even a flicker of red. Sweet relief doused my senses, and for a moment I wished I could stay. Forever caught in Oslo's web and strangely free from the oath. While I was trapped, Leena would be safe.

Leena.

My heart pounded loud, and the orb drifted close. *"I ask the questions. Why are you not worthy?"*

"I murdered the one who deserved to rule. She was kind and just. My blood doesn't afford me those same traits."

A clap of thunder ricocheted from the darkness, and the orb inched closer. *"You make interesting assumptions."* Without warning, the orb floated through me and seated itself in my heart. Gentle warmth, followed by an unbearable sense of knowing, flooded my mind and shot outward to my fingertips. Countless pairs of eyes studied me from the dark. They blinked like stars and weighed what they saw. I itched for the shadows. This kind of darkness didn't offer the same reprieve I'd grown used to. Instead, I was entirely too exposed.

The orb left my body. Unfathomable emptiness stretched through the cavity of my chest, and Oslo sighed. *"You worry you'll do the same to your pair bond. Tell me, is she kind and just?"*

"Yes." Warmth gathered in the palms of my hands and chased away the chill left by his words.

"Does she deserve to rule?"

I frowned. *"She governs her own people. I doubt she has any interest in leading those who condemned Charmers to exile after the First War."*

Frenzied excitement exploded from the orb, and dust particles of pure crystalized light began to fall from above. Streams of trailing, sparkling dust followed their descent. Oslo's voice seemed lighter.

"Do you think Zane deserved to rule?"

Zane. At the sound of his name, something deep stirred in the pit of my belly. His blood resided within me, and it was as if the mage acknowledging his name woke a slumbering part of me, of him. History had named him the Viper of Wilheim for his battle prowess and agility, and suddenly I was seeing the image of a snake with inky-black scales. It uncoiled before me, hood flaring wide. He never got the chance to ascend to the throne, but now, through my blood, he could.

"I can't say."

"Why?"

"He died for his father's cause. But to say he deserved the throne would be like admitting he made the right decision to slaughter the Charmers." I ran an errant hand through my hair and tipped my chin upward. *"Some say the king's command was the first bounty, and Cruor's Oath was born. Magic would have willed Zane to abide, not to mention loyalty to his family. He had his sister to think of. Perhaps some other fealty beside that. By blood, the answer is yes. By conscience, I cannot say."*

The snake seemed pleased. So did Oslo. *"You and your pair bond can rewrite history."*

His statement hung between us, begging to be acknowledged. *Rewrite history?* Charmers wanted nothing to do with Wilheimians, and I couldn't blame them. I could no sooner ask them to fall under Lendria's rule than I could tame a beast in the Kitska Forest. Especially when I wanted nothing to do with the throne.

My gaze snapped to the orb. *"I don't want to rule."*

"And that's why you must. You've been questioned and found worthy. Go forth and have your claim realized."

A resounding clap chased the shadows away, and the orb of light disappeared in a blink. Vibrant green life surged into view in the form of moss and leaves and vines. All magic from the marble tomb was gone. The sticky scent of pears hung heavy in the air, and I turned to find Ozias and Kost walking toward me.

"You all right?" Ozias asked.

"Yes." No. I didn't know. Physically, I was unharmed. But... Oslo's words reverberated in my mind.

"Let's get back to the Zeelahs before something happens." Kost pivoted his hips in the direction of our mounts, but kept his gaze locked on me.

"It already did." In the time it took for me to take a single breath, Oslo had assessed me. A communion with a mage backed by the gods, meant for royals' eyes only. I'd been welcomed and questioned, but there were still three more ruins to go, and no chance in hell I'd follow through with the gods' plans. At that indignant thought, though, a glimmer of inky scales flashed through my mind. Zane. I could practically feel his disappointment, his longing for redemption. Oslo had brought his memory to life, only for me to deny his blood, *my* blood, and its place on the throne.

Gritting my teeth, I stalked past Ozias and Kost in the direction of our Zeelahs. "Let's go."

A sudden burst of heat flared from the ring on my finger.

Go forth and have your claim realized. I was already a prince in name, but without completing the ritual, it meant nothing. If the gods acknowledged my claim, though... Would the glamour of the ring hold up? It grew heavier with each passing breath, and I itched to rip it off and allow my true self to be free.

No. Shaking my head, I slipped my hand into my pocket to remove the thing from sight. Thinking like that was dangerous.

Right as we reached the Zeelahs, a strange beast lowered from the tree on a series of vines. Leena peered at us from a cage in its belly, and I froze.

She took one look at me and immediately thrust her hands through the bars. "Wait! I'm fine. I swear." Just as she said that, the cage splintered in half and she stepped out. Scratches marred her skin, but she seemed otherwise unharmed. She cradled a glowing fruit in her hands, and she rushed toward us.

"I got it." Her smile was so genuine it chased away the frustration coiling inside of me. "I also tamed a beast. This is Tok."

"Tok?" Ozias inched closer. A bold vine shot out and touched his nose. "What kind of beast is it?"

"I'm not sure. Never seen one before. When I send him back to the realm, my bestiary will update. For now, though, let's make sure this stays safe." She held the ruska fruit as if it were breakable.

The anxiety of seeing her caged ebbed with her smile. Running a hand through my hair, I studied her prize. "Will it keep long enough for us to get to Silvis's Ruins?"

She shrugged. "I think it will be fine. Yazmin didn't mention any need for it to be freshly picked. I don't see how anyone could get it from here to there that quickly, anyway."

"I'll take it." Ozias secured the fruit from her and gently carried it over to his Zeelah. With deft hands, he unfastened a side pocket of his saddlebag, wrapped the ruska fruit in cloth, and nestled it securely between what appeared to be a spare change of clothes. "That should do it."

"Thanks." Leena extended her hand, and the beast realm welcomed Tok home. Her fingers immediately went to her bestiary, and she stroked the pendant. No doubt eager to read about her newest addition.

Kost swung his leg over his Zeelah and righted himself in the saddle. "There's a small trading town a few days to the east of here. Let's travel quickly. The nights are getting colder, and we've got to think about what it will take to get to Silvis's Ruins."

Leena's fingers paused. "I'm not sure I follow."

A ghostly chill raced over my skin. "It means we'll have to pass through Wilheim."

Three pairs of eyes rounded on me. There was no other way to get to the ruins. We were close to the ocean here, and the trading town would provide temporary lodging, but there were no docks or easy places to land along the mountainous coast of Glacial Springs. Perpetually lost in snow, the freezing range would be devastating to try to pass during the winter months, which left one point of entry: Wilheim. Through the dangerous walls under constant watch of Sentinels. Through the back alleys of the city with a thousand lights. Our shadows didn't stand a chance.

Kost grimaced. "Exactly. We've ventured through the city once before undetected, but now..." His gaze pointedly slid to my ring. "Your glamour isn't exactly holding up like it used to."

"I know." I flexed my hand. "But it's the only way."

He adjusted his glasses and gave a tight nod. "We'll keep a low profile and blend in with the locals. Draw as little attention as possible."

"Agreed." Swallowing the rock in my throat, I hoisted myself onto my Zeelah and steeled my churning gut. One way or another, we'd get to Silvis's Ruins. We'd remove this oath. And then we'd be on with our lives away from the people of Wilheim.

But as we rode away from Oslo's Ruins, disappointment not entirely my own threaded through my gut, and the vision of a hissing snake flooded my mind. Zane was far from pleased with my desire to cast away the crown. Regardless, his blood would never have the chance of returning to the throne if we didn't make it out of Wilheim alive.

SEVENTEEN

CALEM

The ceiling in Kaori's quarters was the lightest shade of blue. I suppose it was painted that way to inspire a sort of tranquility, but considering I'd gotten overly familiar with it after having my ass handed to me time and time again, it didn't really have that effect on me. Wincing, I sat up on the cool tile and rubbed my lower back. Pain flared beneath my fingertips. Kaori had stiff-armed me, and she still held her pose as she determined whether I'd retaliate. In her flowy pants and loose camisole, she looked liable to be carried away by a strong breeze. But I knew just how sturdy that stance was. How she grounded herself and made it nearly impossible to take her down. Ozias would be impressed. Hell, I certainly was.

"Good," she said as her arms relaxed and fell to her sides. "It seems losing no longer triggers your anger like it used to."

"I didn't lose," I said. Heat simmered just beneath the surface of my skin at her insinuation, threatening to spill over and drown my senses. With a steadying breath, I pushed it away and met her cool gaze. I still hadn't figured out how to read her. How to decipher exactly what was going on in those dark eyes. Ever since I'd woken up in Hireath, I'd spent nearly every moment training with her. Still, nothing.

"You're the one on the ground. Not me."

"We both know that if I'd used the shadows, that wouldn't be the case."

"Using the shadows teaches you nothing." She turned to the creamy chaise longue behind her. The previous one was a deep blue, but I'd destroyed that by accident during our first session. She scooped up an off-white sweater that fell to her knees and slipped her arms through it. "You already know how to control those. Your temper, on the other hand... Not so much."

My bones creaked as I stood. We'd been at this for days. When she'd first recommended sparring as a way to subdue the beast within me, I couldn't have been more excited. And a bit reserved, if truth be told. I never was any good at holding back, and I didn't want to hurt her. But none of that mattered. She'd put me in my place within five minutes and had been doing so ever since.

The first few times, I'd snapped immediately, shifting into the monster I still didn't fully understand. And I was never in control. The transition was violent—immediate—and it was as if I were suspended above my body, watching the horror unfold. I couldn't calm myself down. Couldn't keep myself from gouging the tile with my swordlike claws. I screamed at myself to stop, but my voice was always silent. Just...gone. Kaori never flinched. She'd simply wait for me to strike. And I always did. *Always.* I'd lunge at her without thought or care, and she'd deftly avoid my attack. Again and again she'd dodge until I'd burned through my anger and my body changed back in a trembling heap.

She crossed the room to stand before me and gently touched my chin, tilting my head left and right. She frowned as she studied whatever it was she saw in my gaze. "An hour of meditation, and then we'll start again."

"What?" I moaned, pulling away from her grip. "That doesn't help me at all."

"One hour." She made her way for the door, then paused as she gripped the smooth, silver handle. "All forms of training are equally important. We can't always let our beasts out, so we must also learn how to calm them." There was a faint hint of a smile there as she added, "You can do this, Calem."

With that, she exited her quarters and locked the door behind her with a definitive click.

"For gods' sake." I dragged my hand over my face. Grumbling, I snagged an oversize, indigo pillow from the ornate bed on the far side of the room and dropped it on the floor. A quiet chuckle escaped my lips. Strange to think I'd spent all this time in her quarters and the only thought I had when looking at her bed was for sleep. With her constant drills and mental training, I'd barely had time to think of anything else.

For a moment, I ignored the pillow and instead glanced around. Kaori was just as organized as Kost. There wasn't a single item out of place. No clutter or trinkets taking up space on her open shelving. Minimalist furniture, not a speck of dust anywhere. Part of me wondered if it was yet another tactic to keep her beast controlled. If that were the case, I'd be in trouble. I edged toward the tall windows, damning pillow still visible in my peripheral vision. I wanted to *go outside*. To explore. Meditation was...boring.

But necessary. I scoffed and tipped my head back to the ceiling. My voice or hers? These days, I couldn't be sure. When had my conscience been so loud? I couldn't help but sulk as I returned to the pillow.

Sitting, I crossed my legs and placed my hands palms up on my knees. Closed my eyes and slowed my breathing.

Okay, so there's this ball of energy. No, that's not right. My fingers twitched. During my previous meditation sessions, Kaori had remained with me and guided me through the process with a soothing, peaceful message. But without her watchful eye, it was nearly impossible to focus.

Oh, yeah. A mist! It was a mist. I'm surrounding by this gentle mist, and every time I breathe it in, I... I shifted in place. Peeled one eye open. *Keep your eyes shut, dammit.* Forcing back a growl, I pressed my eyes closed as hard as I could. Focused only on my breath as it moved through my body. Listened to the steady, rhythmic sound of the waterfall crashing outside her windows.

Mist. Back to the mist. With every inhale, I invite this... healing? My fingers twitched. *Not healing. Pacifying? Whatever. I invite this calming mist into my being. It starts at the top of my head and flows down through to my limbs.* Time stretched by, and my muscles grew heavy. My breathing deepened.

And with every exhale, I expel... My mind whirred, and I felt my muscles tense all over again. A trickle of heat, of frustration that would give way to anger if I weren't careful, started to form in my palms.

"It's not about the words. Don't focus on them so much as the process of pushing out that violent energy."

Kaori's advice bloomed in my mind. One of her many lessons I'd yet to grasp, apparently. But if it worked and made this meditation go by faster, then I was all for it. I stopped thinking about the exact words she'd chosen and instead homed in on my breathing. On the rise and fall of my chest. On welcoming gentle thoughts and eliminating my anger.

There we go. This isn't so bad. I bet we're already at least halfway there. Before I could stop myself, I opened my eyes and glanced at the weathered, standing clock beside the hearth.

"You've got to be kidding me." Three lousy minutes. That was it. That was all I'd managed. Throwing my hands up, I abandoned my pose and started to pace. I eyed the door each time I passed it. I was in control now, right? I could handle some free time. Some fresh air. My feet slowed to a stop, and I shoved my hands into the pockets of my leather coat. My fingers grazed something cool, and my heart dropped.

Effie. Gently, I rolled the copper key between my forefinger and thumb. Ever since I'd been raised by Kaori's legendary feline that fateful day, I hadn't summoned my beast. I could *feel* the amplified anger, as if someone had set fire to my veins. I didn't want to hurt Effie. Ever. But she'd come of her own accord outside Midnight Jester when Darrien's men attacked, and she'd seen exactly what I'd become.

I extracted the key and held it out before me. Effie hadn't fled at the sight of me. Rather, she'd rushed to my side despite it all. If she didn't fear me, then… Thinking only of my beast and the bond between us, I focused on the key and opened the beast realm door. Effie came flying out without hesitation, her joyful birdcalls echoing throughout the room. She perched on my shoulder and rammed her head into my cheek. Then, playfully nipped at my ear.

"Hey, girl." I craned my neck toward her and scratched beneath her chin. "We good?"

A happy chirp slipped through her beak. Relief chased away the tension lingering between my shoulder blades. For days I'd been working to control the monster within me. Right now, all I wanted was to simply be me. And I didn't want to stay cooped up in this room for a moment longer.

With a wry grin, I gestured toward the door. "C'mon. We've got a little time before Kaori gets back. Let's explore." In a matter of seconds, I'd fashioned a small, slender pick out of shadows and opened the door. The corridors of the castle were quiet, but I moved quickly and kept close to the walls. With the help of my shadows, I suppressed the sound of my footfalls, descended the marble stairs and crept toward the exit. Effie remained perched on my shoulder, somehow aware of the need to be both still and silent. Once we hit the lawns, though, she stretched her wings and took to the skies, erupting in giddy chirps that mingled with the already-present litany of beast calls.

I tracked her erratic flight pattern and grinned. One Effreft enjoying the afternoon sun wouldn't draw that much attention. Not when every Charmer in sight had a beast of their own by their side. Hooking a right, I made a beeline for a spiraling staircase wide enough for several people to stand side by side on the steps. It wrapped around a gargantuan tree and climbed upward to a network of buildings high in the leaves.

I'd never explored Hireath before. And as I strolled about—careful not to directly interact with anyone in case Kaori caught wind of my whereabouts—I was fascinated by their way of life. Vendor stalls with fresh fruits and baubles and flowy clothing so unlike the restrictive garb in Wilheim. Charmers everywhere, bright smiles on their faces and beasts weaving between their ankles. They didn't exchange bits either. The more I watched, the clearer it became that their society was exchange based. Dried fruits for silken thread. Promises for future wares when they didn't have anything immediately on hand to offer. It was…bizarre.

It also explained why Leena had resorted to other means of work outside of Hireath in order to survive in our world.

Before long, my gaze traveled where it always did when I found myself in a town—to the kids. They rushed around me playing a game I didn't know, shouting at the top of their lungs and racing across wooden bridges. They were boisterous and full of life. They had friends, beasts, families. There were no alleys housing malnourished street kids, no traces of displacement at all. They were all… loved. My chest tightened. If only I had been so lucky.

Stop griping. I shook my head just as Effie landed on my shoulder, a soft, almost-worried coo accompanying a nudge to my cheek.

"I'm okay." Forcing a smile, I scratched the back of her head. She narrowed her eyes as if in disbelief but caved once my fingers started in earnest. Appeased, at least for now.

"Whoa, you have an Effreft? How did you manage that?" A nearby boy screeched to a halt before me, pausing in the middle of whatever game he was playing with his friends to stare at Effie. The rest of his group rushed over, each one displaying a similar look of awe. Toothy smiles beamed up at me.

Grinning, I crouched before them so they could get a closer look. "I have a really good friend who was kind enough to give her to me. Want to pet her?"

"Yes!" It was hard to tell exactly which child had answered, given they all squealed and inched closer. Small fingers delicately trailed the length of Effie's mint-green body, and she eyed them with a mixture of delight and caution. After a few moments, she deemed them safe and hopped off my shoulder to roll on the ground before them.

"Go ahead, scratch her belly," I said, indicating to her soft underside. "She loves that."

"I wonder if she loves being as reckless as her owner."

My entire body stiffened, and I bit back a groan as I slowly turned in place. Looking up at Kaori, I offered her a sheepish grin. "Hey, there."

She folded her arms. "This doesn't look like meditation."

"Maybe not in the traditional sense." I glanced back at the kids. Completely absorbed by Effie's antics—she was now flapping her wings and chasing her tail, fully aware of the giggles she was eliciting from her new fan club—they didn't notice Kaori. Or maybe they didn't care.

"Not in any sense."

"I was on my way back, I promise. I just needed—"

She turned on her heels, the end of her long coat smacking me in the face. "If you're not back in that room before I arrive—and I'm on my way now—you'll regret it." Then, thrusting her hand outward, she summoned her legendary feline and slid onto her back. She stroked her silver hide and then bent her head low so her lips just barely ghosted the beast's ear. "Run, Stella."

Right before her feline bolted, I swore I saw the smallest of smiles.

"That's not fair!" I shouted after her retreating form. Yet I couldn't help but grin. I turned to my beast and signaled for her to land on my shoulder. "C'mon, Effie. We've got work to do."

EIGHTEEN

LEENA

I don't like this." Standing at the train station just outside of Wilheim's borders, we left our Zeelahs in a nearby stable and stared at the throng of people. The vendor stalls brimming with twinkling wares hinted at luxury, and the rich scents of vanilla and baked goods hung heavy in the air. For the moment, we drew little attention. Those living on the outskirts of the capital didn't live as lavishly as those within the walls, and their simplistic yet functional attire meshed with our own traveling gear. But if we were to make it through those walls? We'd stick out like a Laharock among butterflies. Which was the exact problem Kost assured us we had to fix.

"Me neither." Oz shifted from foot to foot, casting his glance upward at the monstrous white wall a short distance away. Crammed cobblestone houses and colorful vendor stalls ran right up to the edge, growing more luxurious in style the closer they got to the walls. As if the splendor of the city was something that could be captured by proximity and enough bits.

"We'll be fine." Noc placed a hand on my shoulder and gave me a gentle squeeze. I glanced up at him and tried to hide the sudden rush of anxiety that chomped on my insides. He hadn't slept a wink in the days it'd taken us to get here. Dark veins tracked the under-side of his eyes, and there was a perpetual tremor tugging at the corner of his brow. One he didn't even seem fully aware of.

Interlocking my fingers with his, I placed a shaky kiss on his knuckles. "Of course."

"Come on." Adjusting his messenger bag across his chest, Kost led the way against the sea of people. "My tailor lives right up here. She'll have what we need."

"You have a personal tailor?" I tried to hide my smile by press-ing my lips together. Of *course* he had his own tailor. I'd always thought his fashion sense belonged to someone of Wilheim, not an assassin thriving on black-market work.

Kost frowned. "I don't trust anyone else to make my garments, though I'm hardly the only one she designs for."

I gave up on fighting my grin. "Right, because the fashion outside of Wilheim is so blasé."

"Quite." He brushed his hands along his traveling tunic, understated but still embellished with brocades just a shade lighter than the black fabric. "To be fair, I saw some beautiful pieces during my short time in Hireath. I'd be interested to see what your tailors could do."

My brows shot to my hairline, but Noc jumped in before I could tease further about who exactly he'd seen wearing something he admired. "Let's go, Kost."

"Right." Kost turned. "This way."

We followed close behind with no belongings in sight. As it turned out, Tok was a beast known as a Drevtrok, and his specialty was his cage. Able to reshape and re-form to adjust to what needed protecting, he could store belongings or people in his lower sphere. Furthermore, while items from our world would disappear without us in the realm, they stayed intact within Tok's body. Which meant our travel supplies were neatly resting in his cage, safe and unassuming in the beast realm. One less thing to draw the Sentinels' gazes. Kost only held on to his bag so he could use bits if we so needed.

Our plan was simple: sneak through Wilheim, cross Luma Lake using the pre-established path set up for nobles—apparently it was a "spiritual" trek many took during the summer months—and visit Glacial Springs where Silvis's Ruins were located. All in all, we figured it would take two days' time to make it happen. Wilheim was deceptively large, and we'd likely have to stop at least once after making it across Luma Lake. Timing was tight—with the first full moon of the winter exactly two nights away, we couldn't afford any disruptions.

So Kost suggested we walk through the front door with the authority of someone who belonged there. If we tried to sneak along the outside wall, we'd be met by patrolling Sentinels and pass guard towers. It would look far less suspicious if we merely adopted Wilheimian garb and passed through the gates like the rest of its citizens.

We moved between vendor stalls, pausing only for a moment when we reached a gem dealer about halfway to Wilheim's gates. I selected twenty or so fire opals and gestured to Kost so he could pay the man with the bits from his satchel. After money was exchanged, the dealer handed over a small leather pouch holding one of the necessary ingredients for taming the Azad, and my chest lightened. We were getting closer.

We waved goodbye and carried on. Peeling off the main road, Kost veered right and headed toward a quaint cottage with faded wooden shutters, redbrick masonry, and a periwinkle-blue roof. Lively flower beds with spire-like purple blooms shot upward around an arched teal door with gold trim. Wispy curls of smoke streamed from the chimney, and a buttery glow oozed from the windows.

Kost rapped on the door three times. "Fiora? It's Kost."

"Kostya?" A woman's animated voice bellowed from somewhere deep in the house.

"Kostya?" I raised both brows.

The tips of his ears burned red. "It's my full name. Only Noc and Fiora use it."

I whirled on Noc. "Since when?"

He shrugged and bit back a smile. "Usually when I'm angry, though that's rare. I think I've only called him that once in front of you." I racked my brain to remember, but Kost's rapidly reddening jawline and neck were distracting.

He cleared his throat. "That's enough, I think—"

With more force than necessary, the door flung open to reveal a curvy woman with coiled brown hair piled high atop her head. Round eyes the color of autumn and just as warm raked over us. Her flowy gown was protected by an apron brimming with loose thread, and her small hands were covered in scars and faint-pink scratches.

She wrapped Kost in a hug that made him sputter. "It's so good to see you, dear. Two visits in such a short time! I think it was a couple weeks or so back when you said you needed women's clothes for a visiting—"

Kost cut her off just as more heat flooded his face. "Fiora." He removed himself from her embrace and jerked his chin in our direction. "I've brought guests."

"Ah!" She beamed at us with a smile wide enough to reveal all her teeth. "Please, please, come in." She hurried inside, the hem of her gown sweeping the wooden floors beneath her feet.

Kost sighed and followed with the rest of us right on his tail. Fiora's home was cozy. Paneled walls with floating shelves were packed with bolts of cloth and vibrant threads. A black sewing machine with antique gold patterns foiled right onto the base sat beside the bay window. The foot pedal was raised, and a garment vaguely resembling a blouse was draped off the side. Fiora kept moving through the main room, passing a desk and armchair laden with pincushions and scraps.

"You're in luck. I just made a fresh pot of tea." She ducked into the kitchen with a little sashay of her hips.

My gaze immediately went to the wall of vibrant fabrics. She'd taken a rainbow and magnified it, somehow finding colors I hadn't even known existed. Lightly, so as not to soil them, I ran my fingers along the bolts. "These are beautiful."

"Oh, hon." Fiora returned with a tray holding five cups and a bowl of sugar cubes. "You haven't seen anything yet." She did a quick once-over of my body before quirking her brow high and turning to Kost. "She's the one you had me tailor for, right?"

"What?" I glanced at Kost.

He took a teacup and ignored me entirely. "It was the most prudent thing to do before we left for Ortega Key."

"I can tell by your build." Fiora nodded to my cup, urging me to take it. I didn't know whether to be impressed or embarrassed that she read my figure so easily. "I wanted to go bolder, grander, but Kostya insisted I stick with the bare minimum. Not to mention he gave me the slimmest of turnaround times. It was rude of him to stifle such creative genius." Ozias snickered into his tea. Noc leaned against the only open wall space he could find and chuckled.

Kost still refused to look in my direction. "This time, Fiora, we need all the flair you can give."

Her eyes lit like a fire. "I thought you'd never ask."

"But, like last time, we don't have time for custom pieces," he cut in before the wheels could go too far off the rails. Though judging by the way Fiora bounced, I'd bet a handful of gold aurics she already had.

She waved him off without the slightest pout. "Winter Crest is two days away. I have so many leftover creations that I'm sure something's bound to fit." She rolled her eyes and set the tray down on a low coffee table. "You know how nobles are. If one bead is off, the whole thing needs to be remade. And I'll be damned if they spout nonsense about my craft at one of their galas."

"Fiora is the best tailor in Wilheim. She's even made clothes for the king." Kost took a delicate sip of his tea.

"Then why do you live out here?" My gaze flickered to the looming castle that housed King Varek and his court.

She shrugged. "I have a shop in the city too. But I do my best work out here. There's more room to breathe and less pretension in the air."

I couldn't help but laugh. Noc smirked and reached for me, looping his fingers through mine. It's as if the sound calmed him. Some of the veins tracking the space beneath his eyes faded, and his own smile chased away the sallowness of his cheeks. I'd laugh for him. Every damn time if it meant keeping him sane.

Kost set his now-empty teacup on the tray. "We can't tarry, Fiora. I appreciate the hospitality, but let's talk garments."

The spark in her eyes glimmered bright. "My favorite kind of talk." With a twirl that had her skirts swirling about her, she moved to a rack of outfits and began thrusting garments into our open arms with fervor.

———◆———

We left Fiora's after changing, with a spare set of Wilheimian attire and our old rags handed off to Tok. One set for venturing in, one set for leaving. And gods help me, I could not stop staring at my assassins. They walked with a sense of purpose, their heads carefully trained forward but their eyes darting every which way, scouting for potential threats as the gleaming gates came into view.

Fiora had somehow captured each one of their personalities without fault, highlighting their preferred traits and giving them a polished glow. A shimmery bronze overcoat with gold flecks tapered into Oz's midsection and buttoned neatly down his sternum. The sleeves had faint paintings of branches racing up his arms that crashed into gold shoulder plates. Pants made of the same material were tucked into shined black boots.

Kost didn't appear much different from his usual attire, but that didn't mean Fiora's work was any less stunning. In a high-necked tunic with turquoise leaf accents—Kost had openly sighed when I'd remarked on the color, insisting it was something called verditer—and shimmery metallic trousers, he was entirely at ease. The black cloak around his neck fluttered in the breeze, revealing an iridescent bottle-green lining.

But everything and everyone paled in comparison to Noc. He was a gods-damned king among men, and there wasn't a pair of wandering eyes that didn't snag on his presence. His black hair fell against the open high collar of his snow-white overcoat, a stark contrast to the ebony lining. Long-sleeved and tailored to his form, the garment fell to his booted feet. Black buckles and errant thick bands of charcoal leather stretched across his chest. Metal stars sewn into the fabric dripped down the right side of his rib cage, and an embroidered griffin clung to his right bicep. Heavy belts draped across his waist, holding up slim-cut black trousers.

He must have felt the weight of my stare because he shot me a curious glance before allowing a devilish smirk to claim his face. My heart ached. *Gods, how I miss that smile.* It'd felt like ages since we'd been together without the weight of the world pressing on our shoulders. I wanted—no, *needed*—him back.

"What are you looking at?"

There was no doubt in my mind that he heard my careening heart. "You, of course."

His glittering eyes roved the length of my body, paying extra attention to my curves. "Too bad you can't see what I do."

My cheeks burned, and want stirred low in my belly. Fiora had dressed me in a gown fit for a winter ceremony, with enough movement that running was still feasible. The gossamer white fabric was fringed in streaks of ice-blue like a glacier. A corset of platinum with aquamarine inlays was strapped in place over the gown, accentuating my waist and breasts. The silk skirt was so fluid it might have been made of water. Given the gown was sleeveless, Fiora had also handed over a thick winter cloak. The exterior was white and sparkled like fresh snow on a sunny morning.

I felt incredible in the outfit, and yet Noc's heated gaze had me itching to rip it from my body and steal away with him somewhere private.

"Two on either side of the gate. Countless more along the top of the wall," Kost muttered under his breath, gaze bouncing from Sentinel to Sentinel.

Lust died, and I inched closer to Noc. Every Sentinel looked identical: covered from head to toe in gleaming metal armor. Polished like swords and sharpened to kill with swiftness and surety. Noc had once told me they were a by-product of Mavis's blood, much like Zane had been to the assassins. I'd never had a personal run-in with the Sentinels, but I'd heard enough horror stories rambled over ales at Midnight Jester. Strong. Fast. Lethal. The recounts were always the same.

"Breathe," Noc whispered against my ear. "Act like we're out for a nice walk."

With a slow breath, I straightened and angled my chin high.

Noc slid his arm around my waist and put a lazy smile on display. Oz and Kost wore disinterested expressions, and as we approached the open ivory gates, not a single Sentinel glanced our direction. We joined the line of Wilheimians entering the city and kept our lips sealed. And then we were in. No warning flares or sudden shouts from the guards. Just happy laughter and mundane conversation from the locals. Oz stuck close to my open side, and Kost fell into step beside Noc.

Kost leaned close and offered a false grin. "We're in the clear."

Noc let out a quiet laugh as if Kost had just said something amusing. "For now. Follow my lead."

With Noc's warm hand on my hip and the security of Oz beside me, I took in Wilheim's splendor for the first time in my life. Glimmering bricks of salmon, daffodil, and tangerine made up the palette for the buildings. Roofs of all different shapes were covered in gardens, with vibrant greens spilling over windows and giving birds a place to nest. Waterways with crystal streams divided a maze of marble pathways, and slow-moving canoes leisurely paddled in the still waters. Trees with pink blossoms were planted at every intersection, and despite the winter chill, not a single petal dropped from the smooth white branches.

"Queen's Heart," Noc said. His gaze followed mine to the closest tree. "They say Adeline, Mavis's mother, planted the first one after her daughter's death. They've been growing steadily ever since with no signs of dying out."

"Gorgeous." My voice was barely a whisper.

Noc pinned me with his stare. "Yes." After a long moment, his gaze swept away, tripping over shops and people. A dark shadow flickered through his eyes, and his hand on my waist tightened a fraction.

"Noc." I placed my hand over his. "Do you miss this? Miss home?"

He let out a dismissive grunt, but there was a slight tightening of his jaw. "This isn't home. Home is Cruor. And right now, getting us through here safely and back is all I care about."

I couldn't bring myself to believe him. I knew how badly it had hurt to be cast away from Hireath, to lose the people and home I'd always known. Even if his family was gone, there were still memories here. Perhaps a childhood friend lingering on a street corner, or a battle-scarred brother from the royal army who he'd shared life-threatening moments with. Noc may have been hesitant to admit it, but I could see the masked longing. The way he shifted, the slight pain flickering in the dark depths of his gaze. How often he forced himself to swallow. The ever-increasing pressure from his fingers on my hip.

It was one thing to bury the past and walk away, but when the truth resurfaced, there was no denying every unraveling, unspoken feeling that came with it. Anyone would come undone.

We continued down the marble paths until they opened to a wide, circular courtyard with fresh-cut lawns. White rosebushes drenched in crystals tossed blinding light into the air, and an elegant tiered fountain showered the area in a fine spray of mist. On the highest layer, a man carved out of stone kneeled with his crowned head tucked to his chest. With one arm over his heart and the other pressed flat to the ground, he was the complete picture of reverence.

"The First King." Noc paused, and Kost and Oz stalled a few feet away. "Receiving his blessing from the gods."

I came up empty for words, and instead basked in the silence. Noc didn't seem to mind. Endless gaze locked on the hand over the man's heart, he didn't move. Didn't speak. An angry muscle feathered down his neck and spasmed through his shoulders. After a beat, he pulled himself away.

Squeezing his hand, I drew his attention. "Are you okay?"

"Zane's blood runs in my veins." His brow twitched. "That was his father. I...I don't know how to explain it. It's like I can feel his displeasure."

Alarm bells crashed in my head. On our way here, he'd recounted what happened at Oslo's Ruins. About the vision of a gleaming snake and the questions Oslo asked. Noc assured me that he didn't want to rule, that he had no intention of rewriting history like the gods seemed to want him to do. But I was beginning to wonder if the gods would take no for an answer.

I bit the inside of my cheek. "Should you really be going to Silvis's Ruins, then? We can go alone. We don't need—"

"Noc." Kost strolled toward us with Oz, feigning nonchalance, but the stiffness of his gait and rigid length of his spine set my nerves on fire. "We need to move. Now."

All traces of another man's anger disappeared from Noc's face. Calculating eyes swept through the crowd. "What is it?"

Oz minutely tilted his head to the left. "Darrien."

A brief flicker of shock, followed by ire, dominated Noc's face before he schooled it back to indifference. My heart plummeted to my feet. We'd guessed at Darrien's knowledge, but to see him here, lingering in the open mouth of one of the many walkways spilling into the courtyard, was more than jarring. Hope of getting through the city unnoticed took a nosedive, and I clenched Noc's hand tight.

Darrien leaned against a building with a cocky grin. With his brown hair oiled and slicked back, his curls caught on the lip of his high-necked tunic. He was dressed in Wilheimian clothing saturated in greens and gold. Errant hints of shadows drifted from the hems of his pants. A handful of men and women, including Quintus, appeared beside him. Their shadows dispersed, sending nearby locals skittering away with anxious glances over their shoulders.

"Dressed like a Wilheimian and blatantly displaying his powers." Kost's nostrils flared. "You know what this means."

Noc's jaw was tight. "It means he works fast. The king wouldn't let Darrien loiter here if he didn't have something to offer." Noc tilted his chin my direction, and worry fractured his stoic stare. "We must remain unseen. If Darrien's claims are validated and you're here with me..."

Death or a bargaining chip. He didn't need to say it for me to understand. There was also the matter of my newfound position as Council member, which could be seen as Noc striking an alliance with Hireath. Unease prickled along my skin. "What do we do?"

Grasping my hand, Noc turned his back on the traitor. "Walk away. Don't draw attention to ourselves."

The four of us crossed the courtyard as one, our pace toeing the gap between a brisk walk and an all-out sprint. The dull city sounds were suddenly too loud, each peal of laughter or vendor call a screeching alarm. Prying eyes lingered too long on our forms, and I was convinced that they knew. My heart slammed against my ribs. We'd never make it. The winding offshoot of a marble pathway grew closer, and the stacked buildings with hidden alleys promised reprieve from the open eyes of the square. Our feet ate the distance away, and Noc's hand slackened a fraction in mine.

He kept his voice low. "We're fine. We'll loop around and—"

An explosion of onyx shadows erupted before us. Thick tendrils shot outward like vines, crawling across the street and stretching toward our feet. Darrien stepped out of the plume with a wicked grin.

"Hello, Noc. Or should I call you Aleksander?"

Panic clawed at my throat. "What do we do?" Startled citizens yelped and backed away at the sight of Darrien's shadows. There

were offshoots and alleyways tucked between buildings, but they
all seemed so far away. Noc's tight gaze swept over the scene. His
jaw ticked. Finally, he squeezed my hand once, and then let me go.

"Run."

NINETEEN

NOC

There wasn't time to calculate or predict, simply to react. I pushed Leena toward Kost and bolted, running straight for Darrien. I had to trust that Kost and Ozias would protect her. That Darrien would focus his energy on me and not them. Shadows leaped around my body, and I delved into them, only to reappear behind Darrien. He turned on his heels spitting fire, but I kept running. I hoped he'd follow me and give the others a chance to escape the city.

"You can't outrun this, Noc!" Darrien shouted. I glanced over my shoulder to watch Kost wrap Leena in a hug and step backward into darkness, Ozias a breath behind him. They'd still be in for a fight if the city went on full alert, but at least they had a chance.

Darrien glanced between me and my fading family, letting out a wordless shout of frustration. "After them. Keep the woman alive—for now." The assassins waiting just out of sight, masked in shadows, took off after my brothers and Leena. Blood roared in my ears as panic took hold. This is what I'd feared. They'd get to me through her. I came to a screeching halt, weighing my options. Right now, it was just a handful of assassins tracking my family. If

I followed to try to help, soon the Sentinels would join the pursuit. And then there would be no keeping Leena from Varek's eyes.

As if reacting to my thoughts, a low, brassy grinding screeched through the air and shook the buildings. Blinding columns of light beamed upward into the sky throughout the city, and Sentinels stepped out of the blazing rays. A brute a good head taller than me manifested in the path of my escape. Shadows hissed as the unrelenting light lashed out and burned through weak points in the tendrils.

Fuck. I whirled back toward Darrien. With his bow already poised and an arrow nocked, he let the shadowed weapon fly. I ducked and slid, and the arrowhead whirred past to crash into the Sentinel's armor. A sharp whistling screamed through the air, and the onyx weapon disappeared in a cloud of wispy smoke. Shadows never could lessen their light. Leaping back to my feet, I sprinted past Darrien into the open courtyard.

Growing up in Wilheim meant I'd spent my fair share of time around Sentinels. Regular human armies for outside threats, assassins for deeds too dark to be mentioned, Sentinels for the crown. Their prized jewels. As a prince, I wasn't exempt from their constant presence.

Or blind to their abject power.

Shadows lunged toward me, and I careened into the world of darkness. People blurred into indecipherable swirls, and I blasted around them as I tore across the courtyard. It was faster that way, and my presence was nothing but a chill down their spine or a whisper of noise in their ear. Outside of the shadow realm, they were safe from harm, which is exactly the way I wanted it. Following my lead, Darrien bled into existence before me, very real and very tangible. Like called to like.

"Got you." His wicked grin preceded a punch, and I ducked to the side.

"Not quite." Cocking my arm back and letting it fly, I reveled in the crunch of his jaw beneath my knuckles. He stumbled, but righted himself quickly. With ease, he formed a glittering blade from the plethora of shadows and lunged. I raised my forearm just in time to protect my face. His weapon sliced through my skin, and blood swelled to the surface.

"Give up, Noc." He aimed his blade toward my throat. "Name me leader, relinquish your powers to me, and I'll let you live."

Blood dripped down my forearm, and power pulsed through me with every beat of my heart. Cruor was *mine*. One by one, the rivulets of blood falling to the earth shaped into fine needles. They hovered by my hand, waiting to do my bidding.

"You should have stayed away."

Without any further warning, I sent them flying through the abyss. He dodged, spinning on his heels and using his blade to knock away my weapons, but one found its way home in his neck. The connection between us surged just as Darrien's eyes went wide. It wasn't much, but it was enough to force him to my will until my blood cycled out of his system.

Pure triumph soared in me. "Stand down." It was so *easy* to bend him to my will. Why had I fought against this power for so long? I wanted to pull back and force myself to breathe. To remind myself what it meant to be in control.

Or maybe I didn't. This...this is what it meant to be the leader of Cruor. This is the power that I, and I alone, wielded. And Darrien didn't deserve my mercy.

I snapped the connection like a band and Darrien buckled. He stumbled backward, and the darkness abandoned him, thrusting him into the Wilheim daylight. A twisted thread of joy sparked in me, but I didn't have time to toy with him. Not in a city full of threats and far too much light.

Rushing past the fountain, I charged toward an open pathway just as a radiant beam detonated above and scorched my shadows from existence. Suffocating brightness pinned me, and I came to an abrupt halt.

"Stop." A Sentinel crashed to the ground before me. The earth thundered from his weight, and he stood slowly while extracting a polished sword from the sheath at his waist. His helm was made of the same gleaming metal, leaving only the slits of his green eyes visible. No mercy. No room for arguments.

I tensed, and my gaze shot over the stilled crowd. Four more Sentinels had fallen to the ground around us, each one a blazing shrine of light that made it impossible to call forth my shadows. A rivulet of blood slipped down my finger and beaded at the tip of my nail. Zane's blood. The black snake in my mind uncoiled and flared its hood wide. And then the droplet fell. When it splattered against the marble stones, an earthquake reverberated through my bones. This was my city. Zane's city. Our blood wouldn't be stopped.

With a quick swipe, I copied the wound Darrien had given me on my other arm. Blood swelled to the surface, and I reshaped it, forming long blades that coated my forearms and extended well past my fingers. "Give Varek my condolences."

I thrust my arm forward and the blade sank clean through one of the few chinks in the Sentinel's armor. One I'd learned about, thanks to years of training with them in the barracks at my father's orders. The man groaned and doubled over, clapping both hands over his side.

Kill.

A familiar red sheen tinged my vision and stoked the fire Zane's blood had started. The surrounding Sentinels surged forward, pushing past onlookers and encircling me with ease. Steady hands raised gleaming swords, each tip expertly poised at my chest. One wrong step, and I'd be skewered.

Bloodlust stirred low in my core and sped toward my fingers. An uncontrollable grin stole upon my expression, and I crouched low into my heels. Bulky armor clinked at the Sentinels' joints. They were fast, but I was faster.

Let the blood flow. A throaty laugh pushed through my lips. Dropping to the ground to avoid the swords, I lunged and swept the feet out from under the first Sentinel. Before he could react, I lodged my blade between a sliver of exposed space on the back of his calf. Blood spurted, and he howled as he blindly arced his sword through the air. His weapon connected with the soldier on his right, and I sprung forward. One quick swipe and his injury mirrored the first kidney shot I'd delivered earlier.

Their blood trickled down my forearm.

Swords came flying then, and I parried while backstepping toward the now-open getaway path. The tang of iron flooded my nostrils, and the red tendrils blurring my vision sharpened. Escape was possible. The path was open and within reach. All I had to do was break the next blow and bolt. The city's layout hadn't changed. I knew where to hide. Where to seek refuge when I didn't want to be found. I just needed to—

Kill.

My hand thrust in a deadly uppercut, and the Sentinel crashed into a nearby stall in an immobile heap. I didn't have to run. I could let this wondrous heat guide my hands. A rampant hunger worked its way through me. But their blood wasn't good enough. There was something else. *Someone* else I needed to eradicate.

A blistering mirage of competing reds took shape beside me. Bowen. He raised one brow and gave a flippant flick of his head toward the looming Sentinels. *"Killing them won't satisfy you."*

A resounding growl bellowed from somewhere deep inside of me just as another Sentinel sliced open the lower part of my cheek. Sticky heat coated my face. I reacted before I knew what had happened, kicking the soldier square the chest so he stumbled back. And with that opening, I brought my blade down on the soft space where neck and shoulder met.

His body crumpled before me, and Bowen sighed. Waving his hand over his shoulder, he stalked down the mouth of the alley. "*Better put a move on, love. There are more where that one came from.*"

Spires of raging light skewered the sky. More Sentinels. Darrien waited on the outskirts of it all, snarling and fighting against the command that kept his body motionless. It was only a small amount of blood, but my command would hold until it cycled out of his system days from now. Regardless, he was the least of my concerns for the time being.

The Sentinels were a different story.

Following Bowen's now-sprinting form, I took off down the alley. Beams of light crashed around me, shattering crates and stalls as Sentinels gave chase. The clashing of metal boots ricocheted off building walls, and adrenaline took control of my limbs. Veering left and right, I darted through the city, vaulting over rails and climbing walls to try to lose the soldiers at my back.

Bowen threw a glance over his shoulder and laughed. "*Brings back memories, don't it?*"

I chuckled. I'd first met him at a trading outpost while on a job. I'd watched from my seat at the back of the tavern as he'd strode in and moved from table to table, wide grin on display as sticky fingers deftly snuck into pockets. When he tried his routine on me, I chased him through the crumbling streets of worn stone until I cornered him at the docks. He didn't try to deny taking my bits. Even insinuated that I must have let him.

He hadn't been entirely wrong.

Bowen ducked between two crammed buildings, and I

followed him. Shadows cast from the walls devoured us, and I hid and watched as Sentinels raced by. The cramped space brought us close, and Bowen placed a hand on my chest. In the exact same spot where Leena had placed her hand as she'd ignited her power and brought me to my senses. For a moment, those disastrous red tendrils wavered. Bowen stilled, eyes wide.

"*Come with me.*" His voice dipped an octave and hinted at despair. Cardamom and orange flirted with my nose and left me groaning.

"You're not real." I needed Leena. I needed her to ground me. To remind me… Bowen ran his thumb along my jaw. Memories disappeared, and there was nothing except the feel of his touch.

"*Real enough. Let's get you fixed.*" He stepped away, and the space between us cut like ice. But I was helpless in this red sea, and I floated after him in a daze…wondering where his current would lead me.

TWENTY

LEENA

Dusk settled low over Luma Lake, and as each apricot ray of the setting sun softened to usher in a darkening sky, my pulse climbed higher. Noc was still missing. Still locked in that terrifying city with deadly Sentinels and Darrien on his tail. We had barely escaped with our lives. Assassins following Darrien's orders had chased after us. They'd fought against Kost and Oz in the shadows as I stood by, entirely useless and unable to access the beasts in my arsenal while stuck in their realm.

I didn't even have time to process what it meant to see my Charmer's symbol sucked dry of color. To find a locked door to the beast realm and no promise of opening. Despair had changed those beautiful shadows to dreadful, smothering smoke, and I barely kept control of my emotions long enough to escape with Kost and Oz.

Is that what I'd face if I were to accept Noc's proposal and rejoin him after death?

Screwing my eyes shut, I let out a breath. A question for another time. Death is all that would face him if he didn't make it out of that city. Slowly, I peeled my eyes open, hoping Noc would appear. Nothing.

We waited in a small cluster of willow trees, hidden in the

shadows of their trunks and the dripping strands of their leaves. Beside me, Oz leaned against the nearest one with his arms folded across his chest and his neck stiff. Dark eyes brewed something fierce, and his jaw ticked. Kost was a statue tethered to the hidden sewer gate we'd snuck through. I wasn't sure if Noc would emerge from the same path, but they had discussed some of the city's layout during the travel here.

If Wilheim hadn't gone on high alert, shining spotlights on every citizen, we would've exited through the gleaming back gates like every other local. For the most part, the rainbow cobblestone pathway leading away from the city was empty. A few patrolling Sentinels stalked along the walls and near the exit. With the lake as a natural barrier to outside attacks, there were fewer guards here, but that didn't mean they were any less vigilant.

All I could do was pace. I wore down a parallel path to the lake, the grass beneath my boots turned muddy. The placid, glassy waters reflected the sky and stretched from horizon to horizon, but there was a faint mist of white to the north. A billowing cloud that skimmed the surface of the water and hinted at a hidden world. Without a boat and with no bridge in sight, there were no obvious means for crossing. Not that we were ready to leave. Not without Noc.

Noc. I dropped my gaze to the pulverized grass before me. His shove had been a blade to my heart. I knew he'd sacrificed himself to give us a chance at escape, but what if that was the last touch I ever got?

Stop. I bit my lower lip. *Don't think like that.* The beams of light had ceased, and the awful grating intonation careening through the city had been silenced. Good or bad, I didn't know.

"The king will soon get word of our appearance, if he hasn't already. He'll assume we'll go to the ruins, even if his reasons are incorrect." With tense fingers, Kost clutched the strap of his satchel. "We need to put as much distance between us and the Sentinels as possible."

"We'll leave as soon as Noc appears." Oz's voice was thick, and he glanced past me toward the lake.

The gates groaned open and we all straightened, eyes laser-focused on the figures emerging. Hope disappeared with the sight of a young couple dressed in evening wear. They smiled and waved at someone behind the gates before hooking a left, following the narrow path lining the capital's walls toward a glistening cemetery a short distance away. I'd never been so frustrated with someone for simply going on a stroll.

Letting out a shaky exhale, I dropped my head into my hands. "Noc, where are you?"

Something icy teased the back of my neck before slipping around my throat. "I'm right here."

I yanked my head up and spun around.

Noc.

Tears flooded my eyes. Safe. He was safe. Noc stood perfectly still in a wreath of endless shadows, one of which was still locked in place around my neck. Chills seeped into my skin, and the tendril tightened a fraction. His cheek was smeared in blood, and blank eyes flitted about us. Dark. Endless. Unreachable.

"Thank the gods." Kost moved toward him and then froze by my side. "What's wrong?"

Noc blinked once. "Nothing."

Kost shifted closer to me. "Are you sure?"

"Yeah, you don't look so hot." Oz came up on my other side and placed a hand on my shoulder. Warmth ebbed into my skin from his touch, heightening the chill around my neck.

"Noc." I snuck a hand to my throat and stroked the shadow. The usual soothing feel was gone, and icy needles lodged themselves in my fingers. Steadying myself with a slow breath, I fought the urge to yank my hand away. "It's okay. Everyone is fine. Safe."

His eyes skipped from my fingers to the tendril of darkness swirling around me. A frown tugged at his brows. "What?"

When I swallowed, the noose tightened. "You're here now. Everything is okay."

His face contorted, and he held his hand out before him. Blood leaked around his fingers and fed monstrous red blades that grew right out of his forearms. They had ripped through the fabric of his coat and were shining with sickening wetness in the ocher light of the setting sun. A battle raged in his eyes. Something dark and foreign and beyond my reach. That damn oath on in his inner wrist practically pulsed with power, as if it were a reckoning of sorts that threatened to shatter Noc's control.

He's running out of time.

Before I could think, I stepped out of the safety of Oz's and Kost's reach and toward the mortal danger that was my lover. Shadows flared and wrapped us in an impenetrable cocoon. Kost and Oz shouted, but their cries were dim against the thick blanket of darkness. The snarling mess of tendrils lashed out, raising welts along my skin, but I didn't care. All I saw was Noc, lost and alone. But I would save him. I would bring him back.

Every. Damn. Time.

Wrapping him in my arms, I pressed my face into his neck and dug my nails into his back. Did whatever I could to anchor myself to his presence. A groan scraped through him, and I bit back tears as I waited for him to return my embrace. Limp arms hung by his sides, but his hands twitched.

"Come back to me." I swallowed twice and tasted salty tears on my lips. "Noc, please." Then, remembering that moment outside the abandoned house, I channeled my power to my emblem. Rosewood light battled against the swirling darkness around us.

His heart thudded against my chest. "Lee...na." Words

raspy and fighting for purchase, his voice was barely audible. But it was enough.

I latched on hard. "Yes. It's me. I'm here. I love you."

A fissure of light cracked through the maelstrom of shadows. Cautious hands hovered above my waist. "I can't remember."

"Don't say that." Red-hot tears rolled down my cheeks. Pulling back, I cupped his chilled face and trailed a thumb over his scar. "C'mon, Noc. Tell me you love me."

He stared at me without seeing me. "I can't... I can't remember who you are to me. Why am I so...conflicted?"

My heart splintered and cracked into pieces, and I swear he heard the sound. His puzzled eyes dropped to my heaving chest, and he placed one hand over my heart. I willed him to feel all those little broken shards. To know that he had the power to solder them back together. Everything I'd ever wanted was dissolving before me. And I couldn't stop it. Couldn't wrench the confusion and foreign rage from his eyes. All I could do was watch and lose myself because my heart was his. And if he couldn't remember what we were for each other...then why did any of it matter? Why did the gods bring us together just to rip us apart?

I would fight until my dying breath to keep us whole. No matter the cost.

"You listen to me, Noc." My lips quivered, and I placed both hands over his. Right over the top of my heart. The rosewood light from my symbol sharpened. "No matter what happens, even if you can't remember why you're fighting, I will always love you. I swear to you, I will bring you back. I will find a way."

A single tear raced toward his jaw. Heat bloomed beneath his touch and the shadows dropped, racing back to him in a flurry of motion. His blood blades dissipated in a pool of liquid at our feet as Kost and Oz leapt back into view. Their wild gazes tore over us, searching for injuries, and paused at the space where our hands rested.

My nails pricked the back of his hand. "Noc?"

The fog obscuring his eyes cleared, and his horrified gaze raked over my body before returning to my face. "Leena."

Relief crashed into me, and I slumped before him, cutting off my power. "Thank the gods." But when I went to pull his face to mine and envelop him in a kiss, he jerked away. Brushing me aside, he took several steps back.

"Noc."

He cringed at the sound. "Stay away. It's not safe. I'm not safe."

"It's all right. You didn't hurt me." I pushed forward, ignoring the way he flinched with every step I took. His wild eyes were full of uncertainty, full of doubt. A tremor swept through his shoulders when I finally placed my hand on his chest. "I promise, I'm okay. I *trust* you, Noc."

For a moment, neither of us moved. Slowly, I wrapped my arms around his neck. He stiffened, but didn't retreat. With a gentle brush of my lips, I kissed his cheek. Then his mouth. He finally cracked, a wordless sob coming from somewhere deep in his chest, and then his lips slanted over mine. Anxiety riddled his frame, and his hands traveled the length of my spine before securing themselves on my waist. Pressing my chest flush with his, he fused the shards of my heart back together. His love was all it took. That was all it'd ever take.

He broke away for a moment to rest his forehead against mine. "I heard you."

"You're my *anam-cara*. I will always find a way." Placing a gentle kiss on his now-tearstained lips, I swallowed his trembling breath and willed him to take solace in my words. "You wouldn't hurt me, Noc."

His grip on me tightened. "I'm sorry I made you worry." He rested his chin on top of my head and glanced at Oz and Kost. "All of you."

Kost kept his distance. "We don't have time to delay. We need to get the beast and get out."

Oz rubbed the back of his neck, but the tautness in his muscles remained. "Kost is right."

Noc let out a weary sigh. "Let's go." With one hand firmly grasping my waist and the other tucked into his coat pocket, he led us toward the edge of Luma Lake. Oz and Kost were barely a breath behind us, the heat of their bodies rolling off them in waves and crashing against my back. Touching my chin to my shoulder, I raised a brow at Oz.

Face set in a hard grimace, his gaze flickered from me to Noc and back again.

"Here." Noc stopped at the edge of the water. A set of smooth river stones flecked with opals were nestled between the blades of grass. With our boots inches from the sheetlike surface of the water, we stood between the rocks. "It's best if we use the shadows."

Kost's voice was edged. "Considering you just wrapped your pair bond in an unbreakable barrier, are you sure that's the best choice right now? Your control is nearly gone, Noc. Leena would be an easy target in the realm. At least out here she can run away."

Shock kept me from rebutting. There was a hint of protectiveness in his normally controlled tone. Glancing over my shoulder, I studied the quiet tremor racing through Kost's fisted hands. I hadn't spoken about my inability to summon a beast while we were running from Darrien's men, but maybe he'd noticed as much. They were my greatest strength against a threat like Noc, and without them... Oz shifted his weight beside him. Jaw set, his hard gaze targeted Noc's back.

Noc stiffened, but his voice was soft. "We move faster in the dark. Without the shadows, it would take us several hours to cross the lake, if not longer. And then there are the guard towers." He jerked a thumb over his shoulder. "We'll be exposed to three of them until we hit the fog."

I spied the glittering strongholds standing tall along the inside of the walls. Bodies moved in front of roaring fires, their frames bleeding into shadows and distorting their numbers. Just how many pairs of eyes would be on us? If a Sentinel discovered our whereabouts, they'd beam down to our location in an instant. Turning back to Noc, I leaned my head against his shoulder. I didn't fear his shadows.

He trailed my cheek with his knuckles. "You'll be safe."

"I know."

Taking a step forward, his foot connected with solid nothingness. Glinting water sparkled beneath his feet with the first stars of night, and he tugged at my hand to follow. My boots met something solid, but the water's surface remained untouched. An invisible bridge only a native Wilheimian would know to look for.

Gentle shadows lurched from his frame and blanketed my world in a beautiful mess of onyx. Unlike before, the familiar gentle kiss of smoke raced along my skin. A loving touch. I followed a fleeing tendril to Noc's hardened face, the ghost of desperation still etched into the somber depths of his eyes. Squeezing his hand, I placed a soft kiss on his knuckles.

His smile was tight. "Shall we?"

Kost and Oz emerged in the dark and added their own sets of shadows to our swirling expanse. Together, we walked away from Wilheim and across Luma Lake. The bridge was a shimmering fog of slate gray beneath our feet, somehow visible in the depths of the curling shadows. I'd never seen so many competing variations of obsidian. Sable tendrils snuck between blotches of ebony and charcoal streaks. Wisps of slate added texture and dimension to the inky world. Starless, and yet not without warmth. It was beautiful. And yet... As the minutes stretched by and the endless abyss pushed forward, a somber ache simmered in my soul. Beautiful and lonely.

When I glanced down at my hand, my fingers trembled. Once again my emblem had lost all semblance of color. No rosewood bark. No hint of light. Only sooty, graphite markings that appeared fragile enough to be brushed away. So enamored with the strange beauty of a world I'd never seen, I'd never thought to study my own marking before today. But now... It was all I could see.

I delved deep into my well of power and searched for the beast realm as panic escalated inside me. I could see the door in my mind's eye, but it still wouldn't open. It was as if the handle had been burned to ash and the cracks around the frame had been sealed shut. Barred from entry, just like before.

Twice now I'd tested out my ability to summon a beast in the shadows.

Twice now I'd been denied.

Everything I feared, everything I tried to get Noc to understand, unraveled before me.

My mind rewound to the conversation we'd had outside of the abandoned house. When the pouring rain had slammed into us while we waited for Kost and Oz to deem the decrepit manor safe. As cold as the night had been, the conversation had been worse. I'd told him to let me die if fate willed it so. Because I had feared exactly this: a world of darkness, beautiful as it may be, where my beloved beasts couldn't be reached. A horrid and painful reminder of what I could no longer have, a sealed door in the backdrop of my mind.

Inhaling deeply, I squeezed my eyes shut and forced the memory to fade. My death was a lifetime away. Another problem for another time. But Noc's? I peeled my eyes open and glanced upward at him. The dark veins framing his eyes throbbed beneath his pale skin. His cheeks were sallow, breaths ragged. My *anam-cara* was holding on, but just barely.

If we didn't find this beast, it wouldn't be me lost to the world. It'd be him.

TWENTY-ONE

THE FROZEN PRINCE
30 YEARS AGO

Rain hammered against the freshly laid soil at my feet. Dark splotches bloomed, and water turned dirt to mud. It was a simple grave, just as Bowen would have wanted. Though it was risky to bury him in Iero Sanctum, the hallowed grounds just outside of Wilheim's walls on the banks of Luma Lake, it was the right thing to do. Roughly the size of a small town, the cemetery housed the majority of deceased Wilheimians. The silver fencing enclosing the space gleamed in the rain, water droplets tracing the etchings of flowers climbing up the bars. Willow trees manned the corners, their branches heavy with strands that kissed the ground. A few rosebushes clambered against tombstones, but it was too cold for buds to bloom. In the spring, it would be almost beautiful.

If Bowen's family ever questioned his absence, perhaps they'd think to look here first. At least then they could find solace. My gaze flickered to the granite headstone, etched with nothing more than his name and the measly number of years that made up his life. He'd died too soon. I'd killed him, just like all the others.

My hands curled into fists. My curse had claimed so many. It wasn't just Amira. It was anyone, *everyone* I loved. Other brothers-in-arms during the war with Rhyne. A few other assassins I'd grown close to over the years. Now Bowen. Only my parents had been spared, likely out of obligation the High Priestess felt toward the royal family. It was her duty to protect and guide us. She'd turned her back on me but wouldn't condemn them to the same fate. They'd died anyway, some years after my death, and were buried in the crypt beneath the castle. Far out of my reach.

Behind me, a man cleared his throat. "We should be going."

I didn't bother to turn and face him. Kostya had been tasked with following me here, ensuring my identity remained intact. Not as if the ring had ever failed. Glancing at my hand, I stared at the scaled band and emerald stone that was imbued with magic. So long as it remained on my finger, my shock-white hair would stay inky black. My blue eyes, dark and unreadable. But more than that, its glamour prevented people from even questioning my appearance. If something caught their eye, if they felt my face matched too closely with that of their deceased prince, they'd suddenly find themselves distracted or thinking of something entirely different. Even so, I'd stayed out of the public eye to be safe. Until now.

The rain grew heavier, and I shook my head. "Just a few more minutes."

Kostya came up beside me and placed a gloved hand on my shoulder. Streams of water coursed down the angles of his face. Shadows bloomed between us, a small offering of comfort. I glanced at them before meeting his somber green gaze. We weren't exactly close. We'd worked a few jobs together, but he'd always been the one to distance himself, pulling away at every opportunity. He couldn't have known about the extent of my curse—I'd only just discovered it—but perhaps his detachment had been for the best. It had saved him from me.

With a sigh, I turned back to Bowen's grave. "You didn't have to come."

Kostya's grip softened. "Talmage insisted someone join you. We're so close to the capital." He nodded to the affronting walls a short distance away, luminous with magical brightness despite the gloomy weather. "It's been some time since your death, but we haven't tested your disguise with anyone who might have known you before you passed. Better to have someone along to help eliminate the problem, if one should arise."

Grimacing, I gripped the back of my neck. Talmage was always three steps ahead of everyone else. Killing someone who recognized me would've been necessary to keep me safe, but the thought still soured my tongue. I'd grown used to death over the years, even appreciated the clean lines bounties offered: no moral quandaries, no right or wrong. Just execution and payment. Simple.

But this... I toed a loose rock. "I'm cursed."

Kostya dropped his hand to his side. "I know." When he and Talmage had first raised me and given me my ring, I'd told them everything. They'd accepted it all and promised that it wouldn't matter in Cruor. That my past was simply that: my past. It never needed to be acknowledged again. I didn't need to worry about trying to explain a curse no one would believe. And I'd felt such relief knowing I'd be able to share meals with brethren without hearing whispered judgments. Build bonds with new friends. Family.

I just hadn't realized the full extent of my curse and what it would cost them.

"I didn't know..." My voice broke, and I tipped my head to the sky. Rain crashed against my face, and I steadied my shaky breaths with the cool feel of water pouring down my cheeks. Guilt sat heavy in my gut. Exactly how many people had died because of me?

"We'll find a cure." Kostya adjusted his glasses, and I caught a glimmer of something far warmer than I was used to seeing in his gaze.

"Why are you helping me?" I raised a careful brow as

conflicting emotions warred for control. I didn't want anyone else to die at my hands—not like this. If he got too close, if I allowed any feelings of warm friendship to grow on my part, I'd be putting him in harm's way. I took a careful step away, hoping the space would help. The biting cold from the wind and rain cut through the shadows between us.

Kostya didn't flinch at my sudden movement. If anything, he almost...relaxed. Patting his vest, he studied me over the tops of his glasses. "I'm partially responsible for this."

"No, you're not."

He lifted a shoulder. "I am. I convinced Talmage to raise you. Your curse would've died with you, had I let things progress as you originally intended."

"You're not to blame. I accepted this new life. The fault is all mine." I appreciated his sentiment, but there was nothing in the world that could alleviate the guilt for what I'd done, or the burden I would have to carry if I continued living. How *would* I continue living? Despair rooted through my gut and solidified my feet to the ground. I couldn't go back to Cruor.

"Noc?" Kostya edged closer.

"I can't go back." Turning, I gave him the full weight of my stare and prayed he'd understand. Prayed Talmage would understand. That, no matter how much I appreciated the gift of life they had given me, I couldn't put anyone else in danger. "No one is safe around me. I...I'll find a new place to live. Alone."

Kostya pursed his lips. "That won't be necessary."

"I'm serious. You have to let me go. Please, tell Talmage I'm sorry."

"Noc—"

"Gods dammit, Kost." I bristled, choking on my words and unintentionally shortening his name. Why was he fighting this? Why did he care now, after all these years? Running a hand down my face, I took several breaths before peering through my fingers. "Sorry. Kostya. Just... This is for the best."

Silence stretched between us, save the howling wind that continued to whip across the open plains and slam into our bodies. And yet, neither of us moved. We stood alone like the graveyard statues, unperturbed by the dead. And then Kostya offered the closest thing to a smile I'd ever seen on his face.

"Kost... I haven't been called that in ages."

"I'm sorry, it just slipped out."

He shook his head once. "It's...fine." With a staggering breath that seemed to loosen something in his chest—something intangible and full of unspoken emotion—he turned his unrelenting stare on me. "We will find a cure. You're not going anywhere."

The look he gave me brokered no argument. I swallowed hard. "And until then?"

He closed the distance between us and went to put his hands on my shoulders, hesitating only for a second before allowing his fingers to grip me tight. "You fight it. You fight every step of the way. You put distance between yourself and everyone else. Those who don't know you won't know the difference. And those who do..." He flashed a weak grin. "We'll understand. You just have to be...cold."

The laugh that escaped my chest was near-hysterical. *Cold.* That I could do. I'd been too aloof for my father's tastes, never fostering the right relationships with the right people in the castle. I hadn't earned the title the Frozen Prince for nothing. I just never thought I'd embrace it again.

"The only person I'm remotely close to anymore is Talmage... and now you."

"Yes, well..." He cleared his throat, and a faint pink touched his ears. "You'll have to lock your emotions away, if only to protect those around you. For now, anyway. Do you understand?" Kost's words were chilly and formal, but there was something almost warm to his gaze. It baffled me to no end that he chose now, while he was fully aware of my curse, to offer some semblance of friendship. Friendship that I *couldn't* accept or act upon. But to know it was there, to know someone was working with me to fight against the unthinkable... Emotions swelled in my chest, and I quickly locked them away in a cage of ice. I wouldn't lose anyone else to this curse. Slowly, I brushed his hands aside. Stepped out of his reach.

Rather than appear hurt, he nodded and adjusted his glasses. "Can you do it?"

"First the Frozen Prince, now the Frozen Assassin." With a shake of my head, I tossed one more look at Bowen's grave before stalking toward the exit. "I've had years of practice. It was foolish of me to think I could ever leave that part of me behind."

Kost fell into step beside me, eyes tight and gaze transfixed on something I couldn't see. "Don't fret. We'll find a way out of this. For now, we've got research to do."

After everything Talmage and Kost had done for me, I could at least give them a chance. I knew what it was like to live with regret, to hold myself accountable for consequences I never imagined would occur. If Kost really held himself responsible for me, for my current predicament... My gaze slid to him. I didn't want him to live with the same weight that I carried in my chest. Even if we never found a cure and I did end up leaving—for his safety and that of everyone else at Cruor—at least we tried.

As we pushed our way through the creaking gate of the graveyard, I left more than Bowen's body behind. I left my emotions with him and prayed no one in this world would ever have the ability to unbury them again.

Twenty-two

NOC
PRESENT DAY

We hit the northern banks of Luma Lake within a few hours. The bloated moon hung low in the ink-black night, and thousands of stars stretched across the crisp expanse. A snowcapped mountain range erupted in the north, and howling winds rushed through the canyons to race across the treeless plains. Ice-drenched fog clung to our ankles and crawled up our calves, ushering in a cold that couldn't be chased away with movement.

Shivering, Leena pulled her cloak tight around her. "Is it safe to make camp? I'll never survive if I can't switch to wool breeches."

"We can spare a few hours." I pulled her in close. "They wouldn't risk searching for us at night out here."

"I'll get our things. I don't think Tok would handle this cold well." She splayed out her hand and channeled her power. Skin obscured by her clothing, I couldn't see the spreading network of blooming branches and leaves as she prepared to enter the beast realm. I didn't know she was ready until flowers framed her temple and crept out of her hairline. She disappeared to retrieve our items, appearing moments later with more bags than arms and a flush to her cheeks.

We set to work without hesitation, erecting a single tent with thick, windproof canvas the same white as our surroundings.

Grabbing a nearby stone, Ozias hammered stakes deep into the permafrost of the earth. The four of us rushed in, and he tied off the open flaps to keep the howling winds at bay. Kost dove a hand into his pocket and extracted a small lighting orb the size of a river stone. Flickering warmth ignited in its center, casting the area in a warm marigold glow. There was barely enough room for four people to sleep side by side, but with this kind of chill, body heat was far from something to complain about.

"I knew it'd be cold, but holy gods, this is insane." Leena crouched and sorted the satchels until she found hers. Shaking fingers reached for the clasp at her neck, and her cloak pooled around her winter gown.

Kost kneeled and opened his own bag. "As soon as dawn hits, we should move."

Leena turned her back to us and began undressing. "The Azad comes out at night. As long as we're there when the moon rises tomorrow, we'll be fine."

Ozias whirled around to face the tent's opening with an apologetic glance in my direction. Kost kept his chin carefully tucked, a hint of pink skimming the tops of his ears. Despite everything, it was difficult not to laugh. A sliver of warmth melted the icy grip on my heart.

Bowen had led me straight to them. Once we were at the gates and out of sight, we'd delved into shadows, snuck through the sewer gate, and reappeared on the edge of Luma Lake. And standing there beside Leena was Amira. With her golden hair fanned out wide in a perpetual wind, she lingered close to Leena and ghosted her fingers along the expanse of my pair bond's neck.

I hadn't even told the shadows to act. They simply had. One dangerous tendril so wildly beyond my control had surged from my fingers and noosed my love. I couldn't fight it. I couldn't find the drive to remember or care why it was such a bad thing for it to be there. Everything else faded from existence, and I'd simply followed their leads.

And then Leena's words—and power—had burst through the sick mirage and brought me back. Guilt threaded through my gut as I watched her slip into thick cashmere tights, followed by a pair of wool-lined alabaster breeches. Pulling on a long-sleeved undergarment and a frost-blue tunic over the top, she then reached for her cloak.

"You're in the clear," I murmured to my brothers. Both Kost and Ozias relaxed, turning back around and slumping to the ground. We opted for fewer tents and supplies so as not to draw further attention to ourselves, which meant sharing blankets and an oversize hide with a down lining. Fortunately, for those who'd been touched by death, the icy nip of night air didn't hold the same sting it once did. Still a far stretch from comfortable, but the burn of snow wouldn't kill us. Shared heat would suffice.

Leena snuck her arms through her coat and pulled the hood over her head, protecting her ears. Then, she slid beneath the hide and wiggled her booted feet. Even with shoes, she insisted her toes be covered by blankets. "Much better."

"Here." Kost threw a white bundle through the air.

Leena snatched it. "Thanks." Peeling apart two thick gloves, she slipped them on with ease and then rubbed her hands together. Kost tossed a pair my direction and handed one to Ozias before placing his own black set on his hands.

Ozias arranged his bag in a mound and stretched out beside Leena, laying his head on his makeshift pillow. "Better get some shut-eye." He propped his back against the canvas and silently accepted the cold chill inevitably sinking through the tent.

Leena lay down next to him and plopped her head on her bag. "If I have to get up and pee during the middle of this, I'll cry."

Ozias grinned. "I hope the gods aren't that cruel."

She giggled, and the soft sound was unbelievably painful. I'd almost stolen that from her and she didn't even know. Lying down beside her, I wrapped my arm around her waist and pulled her close to my chest. A contented sigh slipped from her lips and she nuzzled against me, seeking warmth. Ozias's smile wavered, and a hint of apprehension lit his eyes when he met my gaze. It was gone in an instant, but I didn't miss his subtle shift toward Leena.

I couldn't blame him. I'd done something to keep him and Kost out. Created an unbreakable network of shadows they couldn't pierce. Ozias loved Leena like family. She was blood to him. And I'd jeopardized that.

Stiff and uncertain, Kost lay down on the other side of me. Tension roiled off his form. I didn't need to see his expression to know the battling emotions racing through him. The shadows told me. They whispered of torment and anger and concern and love. All conflicting and damning and unfair. With the snap of his fingers, the orb floated down to him and went out. Soon the steady rise and fall of Leena's chest called to my own tired mind. Sleep was a dangerous reprieve, but battling an army of Sentinels unrested was a far worse gamble than any nightmare Leena could eradicate.

At least one I hoped she could.

❖

We broke camp at dawn and trekked north. The sun, barely risen, offered only a hint of light. Weak rays painted the gray ground beneath our feet and caught on sturdy plants with leathery, faded-green leaves in the shape of tongues. Just a small dusting of snow coated the earth, but I knew the further up we climbed, the thicker it'd get. A trickling stream wound down from some place high in the mountains, flowing to the open mouth of Luma Lake at our backs. If we followed it, the crystal waters would lead us straight to Glacial Springs. Right into Silvis's Ruins.

It's as if the deceased mage knew I was coming. Despite the nearly vertical climb dotted with boulders, our progress was relatively smooth. Thick snow cushioned our footfalls and crunched beneath our boots. The constant wind had died down to a subtle breeze, and there was a silent beckoning in the air. Heat simmered from my ring. I tore my gloves off and tucked them in my pocket.

I should've stayed behind. But with Sentinels surely dispatched to find us, remaining at camp wasn't an option. More than that, the thought of leaving Leena's side was maddening. Ever since we'd landed on the north bank of the lake, I'd felt the presence of hungry eyes. A stare so profound and heavy that I couldn't help but constantly survey the blinding white expanse, only to turn up empty. But that presence urged me to continue. To follow Leena and make my way to the ruins. Another trick from the gods. Another reminder like Zane's memory slithering through my veins. It had to be.

But I wouldn't. I wouldn't become the king they so desperately wanted. I wasn't fit to wear a crown.

The climb demanded our full attention, so conversation gave way to heaving breaths and scrambling feet as we fought for purchase. When the air thinned and the sun descended over the highest peak of the mountain range, we hit a plateau and came to a collective halt. A statue carved out of mint-green stone with deep ivy veins stood on a small island at the center of Glacial Springs. Silvis. Armor covered her body, and thick shoulder plates with emerald jewels glinted with magic. Heavy gauntlets hid her hands, and her fingers wrapped around a thin staff that ended in a fist-sized diamond. A tattered cloak flared wide behind her. Long hair was caught in a frozen wind, almost hiding the gleam of garnet eyes.

Ozias whistled. "Wow."

"No kidding." Leena let out a hushed breath. "Where's the sarcophagus?"

Power throbbed from Silvis and slammed into me. "The statue is her tomb."

Kost tossed a quick glance behind him. "We shouldn't linger."

"Agreed." Leena's worried gaze caught on me. "I'll get set up."

The wind chill was magically nonexistent. Glaciers framed the gurgling hot spring, and an aura of teal, shimmering violet, and blazing gold hung like a thick haze above the water. Mountaintops clambered around the small opening, backing us into a stronghold of ice and rock. The only way out was back down. Not like we were ready to leave, and besides, Silvis didn't seem interested in letting me go. Her fiery eyes were alive with magic and studying me in earnest. Leena said something to me as she crouched, but her voice was lost in the urgent coos of incoherent whispers. Just like before with Oslo.

The third will realize.

A sudden pang bloomed in my chest. Distant memories resurfaced and took hold of my vision, thrusting me into the past and reminding me of a simpler time. One where I sat on the knee of my father, just as the summer sun was lazily peeking through mosaic windows of the grand hall of Wilheim's castle.

"Aleksander, listen closely." My father patted the mess of white hair on top of my head before sneaking a finger under my chin and forcing me to meet his blue-eyed stare. The same icy color of my own eyes.

"Yeah?" The toy sword in my hand demanded my attention.

"Answer me properly."

I folded my arms across my chest in a pout. *"Yes, sir."*

"Good." He smiled, and the corners of his eyes crinkled. *"One day, you will be king. It's important to listen."* Leaning back in his

throne, he placed his other hand on my knee. *"Now, tell me what you learned today from your tutor."*

Rolling my eyes to the ceiling, I recounted the singsong I'd learned only hours ago.

"The first Welcomes,
while the second Questions.
After the third Realizes,
the fourth Blesses,
and ascension is granted
when the fifth Bows."

My father smiled. *"Do you know what that means?"*

"No."

A baritone laugh rolled from his chest. *"You're nothing if not blunt. It means you will be tried and deemed worthy before ascending to king. Name and blood alone do not make you a prince. Only the gods can bestow that right, and one day, after you've been realized, you'll make your old man the proudest father around."*

My brows scrunched together. *"But what about blessing and bowing?"*

"That comes after. They're needed for ascension, but recognition comes from the third. Never scorn that mage."

The mage's chuckle rolled through my mind at the memory. Kost and Ozias were busy helping Leena. She'd placed the ruska fruit on a small stone slab and temporarily removed one of her gloves, readying a blade against her palm. Blood exploded from her heart line, and she dribbled a messy circle around the fruit. The red droplets burned against white frost. Kost handed her a bandage before she slipped the glove back on and began to arrange fire opals atop the sticky, red circle.

"Hello, Aleksander."

I dragged my gaze away from Leena and locked eyes with Silvis. *"Silvis. I'm not here to be realized. We only came for a beast."* I pushed my thoughts back to her, and I swore to the gods her statue grinned.

"Oslo told me you were stubborn." Her voice was sultry and rich, and the soft sigh that followed her words sent a wave of goose-flesh down my spine. *"No matter. You are the prince of Wilheim, and you've been both welcomed and questioned. Your worthiness is not something I'm convinced of, but I have no power over the gods' will."*

I rubbed my jaw, and the heat from my ring warmed my skin. *"We'll be gone soon, and you can return to your slumber."*

"I was not put here to sleep. I was..." The statue seemed to scowl. *"Why are you hiding?"*

My hand froze, and I frowned. *"I'm not hiding. I'm standing right here."*

"Don't patronize me. You've sought out one of my kind to help mask your identity. I can sense their magic all over you." A prickling sensation crawled over my skin, as if she were somehow assessing the strength of the ring's glamour. *"But it's fading. Let's speed things along, shall we?"*

Realization struck fast, and panic clawed up my throat. She meant to do away with my glamour completely. But before I could even think of defending myself—or even entertain the possibility of how—Silvis's statue burst to life.

There was a heady groan of stone on stone as she raised her arm. Leena, Ozias, and Kost whipped their heads up and stared with slack mouths at the gleaming face of the mage. The once-ivy veins racing across her body were now aglow with neon power. Motes of brilliant magic dripped off her in tiny spheres and floated about her form, gathering around the point of her diamond staff. She extended it my direction and aimed the tip at my face.

"You cannot deny who you are."

The magic gathering at the edge of her staff struck like a lightning bolt, streaking across the clearing to connect with the ring on my finger. A booming crack filled the canyon. Fissures raced across the silver scales of the ring until they met at the emerald. The stone seemed to shake in place, fighting against Silvis's will, but her magic was too much. It shattered in a fine spray of green fragments, and my ring fell in pieces to the snow.

My ring. My identity.

Leena launched to her feet. "Noc!"

And then it happened. Power crackled over me as thousands of magical fibers were forcibly ripped from my skin. Visible and sinewy, the threads were stripped from my body. One by one they dispersed in a shimmery glow around me. The glamour granted to me by the ring was being torn away. I curled my hands into fists, and the bite of my nails against my palm did nothing to distract me from the pain. The physical sensation was bearable, but the emotional agony… Each tear was a special kind of torment as I realized I could no longer pretend to be someone else. I could no longer keep Leena safe by denying my past. My identity as the Frozen Prince had finally been exposed.

As the last of the threads dissipated, my body shuddered. I didn't have a mirror to confirm what I was feeling, but I knew just by looking at my hands. At the way my skin was somehow…*different.* As if the magic had even been fooling me all these years, making me think I could lead a life where Aleksander was dead and Noc alone remained.

I'd believed it. Until now.

The scalding force of the Silvis's magic hissed over me, and something told me that if I tried to hide again, it wouldn't work. She'd never allow it.

She lowered her staff and smiled. *"Consider yourself realized. The gods have recognized you as the next true heir to the throne of Wilheim. You are worthy of being called prince and one day king."*

The magic in her garnet stare went out like a flame, leaving me cold and utterly raw.

"Noc?" Leena went to cup my face between her hands and paused. Slowly, she fingered a lock of my hair. One that was now undeniably shock-white instead of raven-black. Unease stirred in my chest. She'd always known me as Noc. What would she think of this frozen shell?

Swallowing the strange thickness in my throat, I met her probing stare. "It can't be that bad."

Leena blinked. And then she laughed. Real and honest and true. Reaching her arms around me, she locked her hands behind my neck and pressed a solid kiss against my cheek. "No. It's not bad at all. I like the real you."

And so did Zane. The image of a snake surfaced in my mind. It looked at me with knowing, gleaming eyes, and I shivered. I didn't *want* the throne. I didn't want to be the Frozen Prince of Wilheim. I wanted to be Noc, guild master of Cruor. Leena's *anam-cara*. I wanted a life entirely separate from the one I used to live. And yet, no matter how hard I fought against my blood, it seemed the gods and Zane couldn't be swayed.

Meeting Leena's gaze, I brushed my knuckles along her jaw. I'd always told her I was dangerous. But being Aleksander Nocsis Feyreigner was so much more than that. It wasn't just her life on the line, it was the Council's. All of Hireath. Cruor too. These allies of mine... They were in danger simply because they knew who I was, not because they agreed to support my claim. But none of that mattered to Varek, and the moment he laid eyes on me, identity revealed, he'd come after us with the force of a god.

And there'd be no stopping him.

Twenty-three

LEENA

Before, Noc had been a vision. But now... It was hard to focus when he stood so near. The coal of his former self had been shined down to the diamond inside, and he had the presence of a frozen god. White hair so bright it burned against the backdrop of the snow. Ice-blue stare jagged and sharp. The high angles of his face were the same, but there was something about him that was crisper. As if the glamour of the ring had sheathed not only his hair and eyes, but the true beauty of his appearance. The lithe muscles racing down his neck called to me. I wanted him strewn out beneath me so I could trace my fingers over his skin. Discover if all the grooves and contours were the same or heightened like the glass cut of his jaw.

"Leena." Oz nudged me with his shoulder. "I know it's a shock, but it's time." With a thick finger, he pointed to the swollen moon above.

"Right." My skin flushed as heat touched my cheeks. "Stand back. I'm not familiar with an Azad, so it's best if you leave this to me."

My assassins retreated to a boulder several paces away and waited, their gazes trained expertly on me. Settling into a crouch, I focused on becoming one with the environment. If Azads were as flighty as Gaige insinuated, no manner of offering would summon them if I couldn't keep my presence muffled. I'd save the rosewood glow until one went after the fruit, and then it was on with the charm and off with Noc's oath.

My symbol throbbed with anticipation beneath my glove. Hope. We were so close to ending this. So close to giving ourselves the first real chance at peace we'd glimpsed since our story began.

Time oozed by under the weight of the moon. White light reflected in tiny flecks across the snow, giving the ground a glimmering, diamond-like appearance. Unmoving, I waited, exhaling into the lip of my coat and obscuring the fog of my breath. Finally, when it was nearly too painful to continue to stare at the snowy expanse, my gaze caught on a porcelain form that lacked the same reflective sheen as the earth. I thought I was still before, but I turned to stone in that moment. The Azad had appeared.

Beady eyes the color and shape of pearls stared at me from behind a whiskered nose. Round ears wiggled in time with its swiveling head, and the small creature scampered up the stone. For a moment, it did nothing except sniff the ruska fruit. It sat on its hind legs, inspecting its prize with cautious paws. Then tilted its snout toward the circle of gems and nudged one.

My brow furrowed. Had I not arranged everything according to Yazmin's instructions? Mind reeling, I recounted the ingredients in my mind. Everything lined up. And yet, the beast seemed unconvinced by my display. A sliver of panic wormed through my gut. If I kicked on the charm now, before it tasted the fruit, would the taming work? Or would it fail? My fingers twitched. Finally, the Azad dug its large front teeth into the sticky hide of the ruska fruit.

Relief raced through me as rosewood light erupted from my hand. The Azad stilled, but didn't fight my charm. A connection started to form between us, and I nearly yelped for joy.

But right as his tail curled around his body, a strangled gasp pierced the air behind me.

Whirling in place, I barely managed to keep the charm intact. Oz and Kost had leaped a few feet away, and their panicked gazes were stuck on an immobilized Noc. Silky threads wrapped around his arms and legs, cocooning him in place. Unleashing a fury of shadows, Noc struggled against the trap and sent tendril after tendril lashing against the cage to no avail.

"Leena!" Oz cried, frantic. "Is this the Azad? What's happening?"

I shot a quick glance to the stupefied beast still hovering over the fruit. "No, I don't think so."

An enraged howl bellowed from Noc. Heavy skittering shook the ground as a beast crested over the closest mountaintop—a creature I'd never seen before in person but only heard rumors of from other Charmers. Silken threads dripped from her hands and leglike appendages at her waist. She shot them directly at Noc, enveloping him in sticky threads he wouldn't have the ability to cut. He writhed in her web, hands already immobilized, and tried to disappear into the shadows. But her cocoon held strong.

My mouth went dry. "A Fabric Spinner."

A woman's torso covered in errant webbing ended in the bulbous abdomen of a monstrous spider. Wild, matted black hair draped down her shoulders, and gray skin bled into an inky black carcass. Eight legs covered in wiggling hairs dug into the mountainside, and more webbing exploded from her hands.

But I was less concerned with the rapidly growing cocoon around Noc and more frightened by the dewy strand extending from the protruding spinner at her rear.

"Sever the back strand!" The charm beneath my hand wavered, and I cursed, diverting more power back to the beast at my feet. The one we needed to save Noc. Without an Azad, we'd be back to square one.

Oz and Kost lunged the instant I spoke. Shadows flung to their sides and carried them upward toward the beast. A throaty cackle much too high and entirely too grinding ruptured from the beast's throat, and she leapt into the air. The thread at her rear reacted, yanking her backward with breakneck speed into the dark expanse of the night. And Noc's suspended body went with her—a trailing, snarling mess that went limp after his head smacked against a boulder.

And then they were gone.

"Fuck!" Anger and panic collided in me, and the rosewood light sharpened at my fingertips.

"What just happened?" Kost rushed to my side, eyes wild.

Anxiety turned my voice shaky. "I don't know. None of this makes any sense."

Ozias crashed to the ground next to us, sending a billow of snow upward along our calves. "What was that?"

"A Fabric Spinner." My gut churned, and the charm wavered beneath my outstretched fingers. After a glance to ensure the Azad was still locked in place, I cast my gaze out toward the night in search of Noc. "They're not native to this area. They mostly live in caves where they construct massive webs to ensnare their prey. If they ever leave, they trail a string from their rear spinner so they can use it as a tether."

"What will happen to Noc?" Kost stared in vain into the night sky.

"She won't kill him until she gets back to her web. Fabric Spinners love fresh organs, so she'll want to harvest him from the inside out." With a steadying breath, I tried to strong-arm the fear making mincemeat of my gut. "But to do that, she'll have to cut the cocoon. I suspect Noc won't just let her dig into his stomach."

Oz's jaw hardened. "We have to go after him. Now."

"I agree. It's already gained a considerable distance on us. If we follow the same path—"

I cut Kost off before he could get ahead of himself. "It's not that simple. That tether I was talking about? It retracts when they're threatened, pulling them back to safety at incredible speeds."

"Which means?" He was still poised to run.

"That it's likely already down the mountain by now, if not already retreating across Luma Lake." I let out a shaky breath, ignoring the panic in my heart that begged me to abandon the Azad and simply *go*. "We'll go after him. I'm not letting him be taken from us, not when we're this close. Let me finish with the Azad, and we'll leave."

Kost's gaze darted between me and the beast. He nodded.

With a plan in place, Oz's shoulders loosened a fraction. "But what was that beast doing here?"

What *was* a Fabric Spinner doing in the remote peaks of Glacial Springs? Her body wouldn't be able to withstand this snowy landscape for more than a few hours, which meant the likelihood of a nearby den was beyond slim—it was impossible. Unease simmered somewhere deep inside me. If not a native beast, then...

I bit back a curse. "Charmer." We had to move. *Now.*

Kost tilted his chin my direction. "What?"

"She was tamed. There's no other explanation." A haughty Raven laughed behind a sheet of coppery-red hair in my mind. She *must* have overheard Gaige and me in the library. I hadn't noticed anyone else there, but I'd been so caught up in my excitement, in the possibility of a cure... She'd pay. I'd have her exiled for harming my *anam-cara*.

Oz palmed the back of his head. "But why?"

"I don't know." Anger simmered in my gut. Raven had Noc.

And I needed to get to her, get to *him*, and sort everything out once and for all. No more politics. No more dancing around the truth. She would confess her involvement and then remove the oath.

An unsettling crunch, like the scraping of bone on bone, sounded behind us, and my connection to the Azad vanished. As one, we turned back to the ruska fruit to find a decimated Azad trapped beneath the monstrous paws of a beast I never imagined I'd see.

Just barely smaller than Onyx, the legendary feline lorded over her snack with gleaming violet eyes. Shimmering snowy fur covered her muscled body, and dark spots of royal blue with indigo inlays dotted her entire coat. Glowing orchid light streamed from each spot and the depths of her unnerving gaze, as if she were an aurora that could dissipate into the colorful haze clinging to the surface of Glacial Springs. Twin horns burst from behind her ears and curled upward to the night, and elongated curved canines stretched past her jaw. A thick tail twice the length of her body swished behind her.

I struggled to find my breath. "Nix Ikari."

Apex of the legendary feline beasts. Her body went still, save the sudden sharpening of the glow emanating from her spots. The magic streaming from those circles masked these beasts' presence entirely and enabled them to teleport across both long and short distances. Their keen senses kept them away from humans and Charmers alike, but their preferred hunting grounds were scarce on game.

My gaze dropped to the Azad. We'd just served up dinner on a platter.

Orchid light emanated from the creature's claws, and her throat trembled with a rattling hiss. Raising my palms in a sign of peace, I took a careful step back. The crunch of snow beneath my boot sent the hackles along her neck shooting toward the sky.

"Easy now." I jerked my head to the side, signaling Oz and Kost to follow suit. "We're not here to hurt you."

Every muscle in her body tightened. Dread and despair made a mean cocktail in my stomach, sending my insides roiling. We didn't have time for this. Noc had been stolen from me right under my grasp, while a legendary beast ate the only creature with the power to save him. My gut churned at the thought, and I tried in vain to focus on the predicament at hand. My gaze flickered to the fruit squelched beneath her monstrous paw. Her scent would be all over what little morsels remained. No Azad would risk returning with her aroma hanging thick in the air.

And that meant my ability to save Noc, in case Raven had her own plans to disappear, had just vanished.

We needed to get to him immediately.

My hands shook. "Easy, girl."

Her eyes narrowed, and then she disappeared into the night in a smear of violet light.

"Thank the gods." Oz let out a heavy sigh as his shoulders slumped. "I for sure thought we were—"

The Nix Ikari reappeared behind him, bleeding into existence without even a hint of sound, and swiped the length of his back with razor-sharp claws. Oz hit the ground to dodge, but not fast enough. Tender, flayed flesh oozed blood that shone bright in the light of the moon. Kost moved before I could think. Wrapping his friend in a blanket of shadows, Kost dove with him into darkness.

Which left a confused and enraged Nix Ikari staring directly at me. Whiskers on end and nose twitching, she peeled back her maw to expose a massive collection of daggerlike teeth. Sinking low into her haunches, she prepared to pounce. And then she exploded in a spray of snow and yowling fury, her claws aimed directly at my chest.

Hiding my face behind my forearms, I braced for impact and forced all of my power to my Charmer's symbol. Rosewood light fractured in the space around me, and an echoing roar shook the mountainside. A white mass barreled through the air and slammed into the Nix Ikari. Followed closely by a snarling Onyx.

"Leena, are you all right?" Kost stepped out of the shadows with a wincing Oz at his side.

"Yeah." Lowering my arms, I peered at the tumbling beasts. They crashed into a snowbank, and a riotous explosion of white shimmered in the air. "Dominus and Onyx are here."

"Dominus?" Oz slumped to the ground and grit his teeth. Kost bent over his wounds and began murmuring to himself. With the flick of his wrist, he brandished a bronze key and called out Felicks. Without hesitating, Felicks bounded toward Oz and began licking the length of his back.

"He's got a mind of his own, though I'm grateful." Standing slowly, I studied the spitting beasts. The Nix Ikari had slipped out of Dominus's clutches and reappeared several feet away. He and Onyx circled her with cautious footing, and marrow-rattling yowls rumbled through their chests.

Sniffing Ozias's now-healing wounds, Felicks let out a quiet bark and promptly sat on the ground. The Nix Ikari's ears flicked to attention, and her gaze snapped to us. One moment she was there and the next she was gone, nothing more than a smudged violet afterimage burning against the night sky. Onyx and Dominus straightened and swiveled their heads in our direction.

My brows pulled tight together. "What's wrong?" Their hairs stood on end, and I braved a quick glance around. My eyes snagged on Felicks's orb, formerly crystal-clear and now churning with an ominous fog.

Shit. The huntress of the beast kingdom wasn't just agile, she was cunning. Lethal in her ability to assess her prey. The moment Felicks had appeared, future brewing in his orb, she'd sensed a threat. She could analyze her target and strike accordingly, but only

Felicks could predict what would happen two minutes down the line. And that would place her at a disadvantage. Panic sent a wave of icy water through my veins.

"Get out of the way!" I barely recognized the shriek that tore through my lungs as I crashed to the ground, hiding Felicks beneath the weight of my body just as the Nix Ikari appeared. Felicks yelped but I wrapped him tighter, unwilling to sacrifice him to the beast. Heated breath, moist and oddly reminiscent of peppermint, collided against my neck. A bead of saliva rolled off her canine and smashed against my skin. Turning my head slightly, I peered up at the monstrous feline poised over my body.

"Leena!" Oz and Kost shouted as one, but the Nix Ikari dominated my vision. Somewhere, I heard the ominous, heavy crunch of paws stalking toward us and the distinct battle roar of Onyx. Tension snapped through the air.

Throat tight, I forced out a whisper. "Don't move."

Shadows slunk along the snowy earth and wrapped through my fingers. The Nix Ikari noticed and howled, sinking her razor-sharp fangs directly into the tender flesh of my shoulder. Pain erupted from deep in my muscles, and I bit back the scream brewing in my lungs.

"Don't!" Shuddering, I fisted my hands. "She sees them. Don't. Move."

Oz's and Kost's shadows dispersed as Onyx and Dominus slipped into position on either side of me, their contrasting hides visible in my peripheral vision. Their muscles were tense enough to cut glass, and I prayed they understood. One move and she'd sever my head. One move and it'd all be over.

Tears rolled down my cheeks. It *couldn't* be over. We'd come so close only to have everything ripped right out of my hands. Noc. The Azad. And now... Felicks squirmed beneath me. If anything happened to him, Kost would never forgive me. I wasn't sure he'd ever look at me the way he looked at his brothers, but I couldn't live with myself if something else happened to my assassins. Calem. Noc. Now Kost.

An uncontrollable sob shook me, and I sank further into the earth. Hot tears slid over my cheeks, and I just let go. Let myself revel in the nightmare that this had been. I couldn't protect my *anam-cara*. Couldn't protect a beast. Couldn't protect my family. What good was I? No wonder Noc always wanted to keep me safe. I couldn't even protect myself.

But right here, right now, I'd do whatever it took to keep Felicks safe. *That* I could do.

The Nix Ikari paused. Time stretched for an eternity as she stared at me, her breath rolling over the fresh wound of my shoulder. Finally, she pulled back. Inhaling deeply, she took in my scent before shaking her head once. And then disappeared in a blur of violet light.

Gone. And judging by the way Onyx and Dominus relaxed into their haunches, she wasn't coming back. Focusing on my power, I opened the beast realm door and sent them home just as a light dusting of snow started to fall from the sky.

Adrenaline crashed through my limbs, and I suddenly felt too heavy and too light at the same time. My head swam as I blinked, slowly righting myself with Felicks still bundled in my arms. Standing, I turned to face Kost and Oz. They stared at me with open mouths and pale faces, gazes flickering from the now empty space behind me to the wound on my shoulder.

With a weak smile, I held Felicks out to Kost. "He's unharmed."

Kost cleared the distance in two strides, and I expected him to wrench his beast from my hands. Get his beloved creature out of my grasp and back to safety. Instead, he crashed into me and wrapped me in a hug. Chin angled down, he spoke into the crook of my neck not marred by the Nix Ikari's bite.

"Thank the gods you're safe."

All the emotions from earlier came rushing back, and I melted into him. I was a crying mess. The Azad. The Fabric Spinner. Noc. Too much. It was all too much, and I couldn't think, and I didn't know what was happening, and I was lost. So lost.

Kost's fingers pressed tight against my shoulder blades. "Leena."

The sobs tumbling from my lips wouldn't be appeased.

"Hey." Kost pulled back a fraction, giving me a glimpse of his face. "It's okay."

"But it's not. Noc is gone. The Azad is gone. Felicks was almost—"

"But he's not." Kost nodded to his beast, who wiggled in my arms. Turning to place his paws against my chest, Felicks aimed his face at my wound and began licking. Kost's smile was brilliant. The likes of which I'd never seen. "We'll find Noc. It's not too late."

Oz joined us, visibly torn between relief and worry. "What about the Azad?"

Weakly, I sighed. "If we can't find and force the Charmer responsible to release Noc, we'll have to come back. We don't have any more fruit, and it could take weeks, maybe months, for me to find one without a lure."

Kost released me, and his expression went dark. "Understood. Let's go after Noc first."

Settling my nerves with a steady breath, I gave him a sharp nod. We were already short on time. Now, we didn't have the ruska fruit or the Azad. But more than that, we didn't have Noc. And none of this mattered if we didn't have him by our side. Turning toward the cliff where Raven's Fabric Spinner had been, I sent out a silent prayer that he'd keep fighting until we got to him. Because we *would* get to him.

And then Raven would be sorry she'd ever laid a hand on my *anam-cara*.

TWENTY-FOUR

LEENA

We only made it a handful of steps away from Glacial Springs when our plan to track the Fabric Spinner went to hell. Just as we approached the ridge where the beast had been, a heavy thud ricocheted through the mountain pass. As one, we froze. Had the Nix Ikari returned? Several more thuds crashed in the distance. Closer. The snowfall had thickened, making it difficult to see anything. I couldn't *sense* a beast, but that hardly meant anything when it came to the legendary feline. She could appear without warning.

Panicked, I forced out a whisper. "What was that?"

Silver flashed momentarily several yards away and then disappeared.

Kost's eyes narrowed. Then widened. He snatched my wrist and yanked me the opposite direction. "*Sentinels.*"

Oz cursed, calling forth his own weapons. "We need to move. Now!"

We never got the chance. Columns of blinding light erupted around us, and Wilhelm's prized soldiers manifested with their swords unsheathed. Our run-in with the Nix Ikari must have alerted them to our presence. My breathing turned shallow.

My gaze bounced from Sentinel to Sentinel. Fifteen. I had beasts, but sending them against a brigade of soldiers? At least one would surely die. Not to mention, asking them to attack a human? It was too reminiscent of the First War. My gut churned as I thought of Celeste's watchful gaze. What would she do?

But Kost and Oz's shadows wouldn't work against these warriors of light. We'd nearly had our defenses burned to ash on a chance encounter with one after we'd outmaneuvered Darrien's assassins. Only Kost's wits had us escaping unscathed. But fifteen?

Out. We had to get *out.*

I tossed a quick glance at Kost and Oz. Their jaws were tight, fingers twitching. They leaned into their heels and were waiting, calculating. The last of the Sentinels had just fully emerged from his beam of light and raised the tip of his sword in our direction.

Kost whispered under his breath, "Leena, we'll hold them off. You need to run."

No. My heart jumped into my throat. I wouldn't let them sacrifice themselves for me. My mind raced for an option, tearing through the pages of my bestiary. Maybe I could create a diversion.

And I had just the beast to do it.

"Sorry, Kost. Not gonna happen." Thrusting my hand outward, I forced power into my symbol and opened the beast realm door. The groaning hinges howled like the winter wind, and Kost and Oz showed only the barest hints of recognition. I called on Iky, giving him the silent command to stay invisible. I felt rather than saw him appear beside me, his watery scent a welcome relief. His two-hour timetable clicked into place in my mind, and I gave the slimmest of nods.

It was all he needed.

He slipped through the night, footprints obscured by the ever-falling snow, and snuck behind the first Sentinel.

The solider glowered our direction. "Stand down. You're to return with us at once to the capital."

"For what reason? Visiting Glacial Springs isn't illegal." Kost held his ground, giving Iky time to slip into place.

The Sentinel grunted. "You're charged with treason. King Varek will—"

He fell face-first into the ground before he could finish, as if something had yanked his feet out from under him. Then, he was being dragged backward across the snow by his ankles. His shouts climbed higher as he kicked in vain against a foe he couldn't see, and I forced my expression to remain neutral. Kost and Oz glanced around at the distracted men. Took a few careful steps backward to see if they'd notice.

They were all too preoccupied with the mysterious force that was dragging their friend down the mountain slope. Two of the closest Sentinels turned to help him, dropping their swords in the snow and reaching for his hands. But as soon as they closed in, they too were bowled over by Iky's invisible limbs.

"It's Iky," I whispered once the Sentinels had all turned their attention downhill. "We should move. *Now*."

Shadows flared outward from Kost and Oz's frames, and I quickly sent Iky back to the beast realm before the shadows could swallow me too. The gods only knew what that would do to my beast. Our presence masked by darkness, we sprinted toward a nearby mountain pass. Frenzied shouts of soldiers met my ears, and I tossed a quick glance over my shoulder to see them advancing on the empty space where we used to be. Between Iky's tactics, the shadows, and the ghastly storm releasing a torrential onslaught of snow, we'd been able to slip away. If we put enough distance between us and them, maybe they'd give up. Or maybe they'd get lost.

My lungs burned as I pushed myself harder. The Sentinels'

angry shouts had dimmed, lost in the howling wind whipping through the pass. My heartbeat pounded in my ears, and I thought only of escape. Only of making it out of this alive so we could find a way to get to Noc. The outlines of the Sentinels grew smaller and smaller until they disappeared altogether. Finally, we slowed to catch our breath when we reached a small plateau dotted with smooth boulders.

We maybe had one minute of peace. And then several beams of light detonated to our right as three Sentinels manifested beside us. Their armor gleamed painfully against the snowy backdrop, and my pulse skyrocketed as they turned toward us. A sharp hissing cooked the air as their light permeated the shadow realm. And then the dark tendrils receded in a rush, leaving us exposed. No chance for safety in darkness.

"Found you." The leader unsheathed his sword.

"Run!" Oz pushed me, and we skidded down the mountain slope with Kost.

We tumbled over our feet, sliding down the face of a mountain until our bodies were battered and bruised. My breeches ripped over hidden brush, and the sting of snow and gravel against my knees sent curses flying from my mouth. Wincing, I rolled to my side and glanced back up. The Sentinels stared down at us from the small plateau and began to summon those blinding columns.

"Keep moving! They'll come after us." Kost yanked me to my feet, and the three of us ran. Icy wind whipped against my body and filled my lungs, making it hard to breathe. We had no idea how long it would take them to work their magic and reappear before us. All we could do was keep moving forward.

We raced over the icy plains, and my foot slipped on loose rock. My ankle rolled and killed my momentum as I slumped to the ground. Oz cringed and leaned down to scoop me into his arms.

"Ozias, here." Kost pointed toward a cluster of boulders and darted off, sequestering himself in their temporary shadows, then summoned more of his own to blanket the entrance of the cave in total darkness. Oz pressed me close to his chest and followed as the Sentinels' signature light began to bloom behind us. We slid into safety just before they appeared, the constant snowfall hiding our footprints.

Kost's wild eyes tracked the mountain range, searching for escape. "We have to keep running. Oz, no matter what, Leena makes it out of this." He added a few more shadows to the entrance, but a sweat was breaking out along his hairline. With the Sentinels' magic in full effect, it would be impossible to hold darkness in place for long.

"Understood." Oz gave me a subtle squeeze.

"Wait, what? No, absolutely not."

Sentinels shouted behind us, their brilliant light beaming like a sun over the frost-covered brush and rock. A few of Kost's shadows hissed and dissipated. We didn't have long.

Kost's gaze drifted to my quickly swelling ankle. "We'll go on together as long as we can. But if they catch up, Leena, you call Onyx and have him fly you out of here. Ozias and I will keep the Sentinels distracted."

Bile soured my tongue. They couldn't put their lives on the line for me. I couldn't have another assassin injured because of me. Another family member lost. "No. Absolutely not. Your shadows won't work against them. I'll stay and help, no matter what."

Oz set me on the ground to peer over the rocks. "They'll be on us in minutes. What do we do?"

Kost's smile was pained. "I understand how you feel. But how many beasts will it take to defeat one Sentinel? Let alone three?"

My mind whirled. My family or my beasts? To me, they were

one and the same. Condemning one to death to save the other hardly seemed like a valid solution. But I couldn't let the Sentinels get their hands on Oz and Kost. There was a chance I'd make it out of this alive—if King Varek truly was aware of my existence, he'd be better off keeping me prisoner to try to bend Noc into submission. But Oz and Kost? They were assassins who'd snuck into the capital and defied the king. Their deaths were guaranteed.

Wincing, I rolled my ankle and ignored the pain. I'd been through worse. "I'll face them. You two, find Noc. Save him. The Sentinels won't kill me. Varek will want me alive as a bargaining chip."

"You can't be serious." Oz snared my wrist as if he were afraid I'd bolt from the safety of the boulders before he could argue.

Kost glowered. "Leena, you can't—"

A column of light blasted to life before us, chasing away the shadows of the rock cluster and leaving us entirely exposed. A single Sentinel emerged. His head snapped to us. And while I couldn't see it, I swear I felt him smile.

We jumped to our feet, and I clenched my jaw against the pain from my ankle. Kost and Oz both moved to stand before me, but I shouldered my way past them.

"I'm the one you want. Let them go."

The sharp scrape of metal on metal sounded as the Sentinel pulled his sword from his sheath. With one easy movement, he leveled it at my neck. The tip barely nicked my skin, but my blood rolled toward the hilt just the same.

"You're all coming with me." His brassy voice echoed from the depths of his helmet, and he jerked his head in the direction of where the other Sentinels were still searching. He inhaled as if to bark an order, but it never came. Instead, a smearing of violet bloomed into existence behind him, and a heavy paw with gleaming claws punctured the armor around his neck. Blood shot outward with a wet gurgle. The Sentinel fell face-first. Blood pooled on the ground around him, turning the snow a vibrant red.

My eyes flew to the space behind him. The Nix Ikari watched me with pensive eyes, tail twitching back and forth. She retracted her claws and stood on the Sentinel's back, his body crunching beneath her weight. The world went still. Had she been following us all this time? Tracking our escape down the mountain and waiting to attack when we were most vulnerable?

No. My gaze slanted to the deceased Sentinel. If that were the case, she wouldn't have appeared now. Not with so many threats around. Slowly, I offered her the back of my hand. She sniffed it once, her whiskers just grazing my knuckles, then huffed.

Shouting erupted from the other two Sentinels, and her head snapped in their direction. Hackles standing on end, she let out a low, terrifying hiss. Something sharp and furious raced through her eyes.

"Leena. Are we in danger?" Kost asked, voice hushed.

"I don't think so." Still, I wasn't eager to make any sudden movements. "Just stay where you are."

The two men were closing in. Swords drawn, they cautiously moved toward us. The Nix Ikari let out a guttural yowl. Vibrant orchid light exploded from her spots, and she angled her head down, pointing her horns directly at the approaching men. Every muscle in her body went taut.

"I wouldn't come any closer if I were you," I said to the men. Everything about the Nix Ikari's stance screamed danger. Why she had chosen to protect us, I didn't know. But I did know that there was no need for more death. And death *would* happen if she decided to strike.

The first man shook his head. "You're coming with us, by order of King Varek."

And then he made the mistake of extending his sword outward in the direction of the Nix Ikari.

She winked out of existence before I could blink.

Reappearing behind him, she struck as she had with the first Sentinel. Except this time, only two of her nails tore through the armor, leaving the man wounded instead of dead. He tumbled to the ground and dragged himself a few feet away. His comrade leapt to his aid, striking the Nix Ikari's shoulder. Her hide split open, and she let out a yowl that threatened to start an avalanche. But the sweeping arc of the Sentinel's attack had left him open in other places, and the Nix Ikari didn't hesitate. She sank her massive canines into the soldier's side. The metal armor caved with ease beneath her bite, and the man went down in a spray of blood.

Before the first Sentinel could prepare himself, she turned back to him. And lunged. She snared the man's head between her teeth. It gave with a sickening crunch, and the body went limp in her maw. Shaking her head, as if in disgust, she backed away from the soldier and sauntered back toward us. She plopped on her haunches and began to meticulously clean her wound.

Relief rushed over me, and I sank to the ground as the last of my strength left me. "Thank goodness they didn't kill you."

She paused midlick to give me a bored look. I nearly laughed. Oz and Kost moved to join me, wary gazes locked on the beast before us. She tilted her head their direction for a moment before returning to her cleaning.

"Is it safe?" Oz asked.

"Yeah, I think so. We'd be dead already if it weren't." Maybe I was riding a high from escaping the Sentinels, but this time, I did chuckle. My nerves were fried. We still had so many problems, so many *urgent* problems, but I couldn't help myself. My body trembled as my adrenaline subsided.

Oz crouched beside me, brows raised. "Okay, then. Let's take a look at that ankle before the rest of them show up."

"Quickly," Kost said, voice tight. "We have no way of knowing when they'll appear." After a moment, his gaze slanted to the Nix Ikari. "Why is she still here?"

"I don't know." I glanced up at the beast. Her eyes were trained on Oz's hands as they assessed my ankle. I let out a groan when he stretched it to the left, and her ears stood at attention. Slowly, she leaned forward so her wet nose could kiss my cheek. Rosewood light fractured from my hand and showered us in a soft glow. Connected. The tether surged between us, and a soft purr started in the back of her throat.

My mouth fell open. "What? Why?"

She licked my neck. Right where the Sentinel's blade had nicked my skin. I didn't know anything about the taming process for a Nix Ikari. No other Council member had one, and they were so scarce that I'd only heard of the beast in passing. My brow furrowed. I'd provided her easy prey in a desolate landscape with the Azad. Had that been it? No. She would've bonded with me then. Other than that, all I did was stop her from attacking Felicks. She'd sunk her fangs into my shoulder and held steady, waiting to see what I'd do.

Something warm sparked in my core. The Sentinel had held his sword against my neck too, and threatened my life. My family's life. And I'd stood up for them. That was when the Nix Ikari had appeared and *chosen* to defend me. Just as I had defended Felicks.

"She's chosen me." I let out a weak smile.

At that moment, Kost's expression lit up. Bright eyes raced over the Nix Ikari, and then he turned his gaze to me. "Can she teleport us?"

I nearly kicked Oz from excitement as I jolted in place. "Maybe. I mean, I hope so. Let me send her back to the realm so she can heal and my bestiary will update." Flexing my hand, I channeled my power and opened the beast realm. She went willingly, and I quickly closed the door behind her. Touching my finger to my pendant, I opened my bestiary and immediately flipped to her entry.

My heart swelled as the script bled to life against the night sky. "Yes. Yes, she can." My eyes flew over the text. "Normally, she only teleports in short bursts, but it says here that she can travel great distances, though it expends all her energy. She'll have to recuperate for some time before she can travel more than a few yards again."

Oz braced his hands on his knees, finished with his work on my ankle. "This will be sore for a while. Once we get our things from Tok, I can wrap it."

"There's no need." Rolling it side to side, I winced. "I can manage. We have to get to Noc. The Fabric Spinner likes to take her time with her prey, but there's no telling exactly when she'll attempt to make a meal out of him."

"Not to mention the Sentinels still hanging around here somewhere." Oz stood and scoured the horizon. There were no signs of life, but that meant little when it came to Sentinels. Their blinding, magical columns of light could appear at a moment's notice.

"Where, though?" Uncertainty rolled through my gut. The Nix Ikari only had enough power to transport us once. Wasting it by traveling to the wrong location could jeopardize Noc. I rubbed my temples and tried in vain to piece together a plan. "We know the Fabric Spinner was tamed, so a Charmer *must* be involved... I think Raven somehow found out we were here and ambushed us."

"So Hireath?" Kost asked.

I let out quiet huff of frustration. "I'm not sure. If she is behind this, she'd want to keep him hidden. Which means he's probably not in Hireath—why risk the Council finding him? She'd keep him somewhere close, though. Within reach for whatever she's planning."

"We can check *Zane and the Fallen Leaders* to see if it's updated with any information pertaining to Noc's capture." Kost ran a stiff hand through his hair and then nodded. "It likely will not have specifics—that's not how the magic works—but it may give us an idea of where to go."

"And we can send out scouts." Oz said. "We'll be able to cover more ground quickly with our numbers."

"Cruor, then." Flexing my foot, I winced at the sharp pain shooting up my calf. Not enough to keep me from walking, but enough to slow me down. Standing, I ignored the flare of heat in my ankle.

Channeling power to my hand, I opened the beast realm and summoned the Nix Ikari. She returned mostly healed with just a slight pink tinge to her snowy fur. With a purr, she knocked her head into my arm.

"I'm going to call you Reine." My eyes trailed the length of her lithe body. I'd likely have to sit in Oz's lap, but we'd make do. It would only be for a moment, and I'd be sure to shower her with lots of love and handfuls of beast treats when this was all over.

"What now?" Oz eyed Reine with a furrowing brow.

"We climb on her back." I felt myself smile. *Zane and the Fallen Leaders* would have answers. This was all going to work out. It had to.

Standing before her, I cupped her maw in my hands and nuzzled her head. "Hey, sweet girl. Can you take us home, please?" She huffed into my chest, but didn't retreat when Oz and Kost approached her. I gave them a nod, and Oz hoisted himself onto her back first. Kost sidled in behind him. With one last loving pet down her muzzle, I moved to her side and reached for Oz's hand. He pulled me up, and I settled into his lap.

"You all set?" Oz asked, tightening his thighs against Reine's sides. She let out a disgruntled hiss.

I rubbed my hands along her neck. "Yes. Okay, Reine, whenever you're ready. Take us to Cruor."

Violet light bled from her spots and stretched before us like a mirage. The surroundings of Glacial Springs faded in an instant. A sudden pressure weighed down my limbs, and I struggled to breathe. Fingers tingling, I gripped my beast tighter for support. A dull ringing started in my ears, and just as I thought I would faint, Reine's spots glowed fiercely again. Light stretched before us, and then suddenly we were home. Cruor. My heart gave a hopeful thud, and I hugged my newly tamed beast tight.

Noc was within reach.

TWENTY-FIVE

NOC

A sickening rip broke through the silence in my brain as the spider tore sticky webs away from my head. Still wrapped tightly in a cocoon, my arms and legs were immobilized. I tried in vain to summon my shadows. To attack her or cut away at the cocoon. But it was as if the creature's web canceled out my powers, and nothing happened. She surveyed me with beady eyes. What did she want? Where had she taken me? A far-off grating howl rolled through the mouth of her cave, and she tossed a cautious look toward the opening.

My mind reeled. I knew that sound. Those bone-scraping calls were a constant backdrop in my world. Somewhere in Kitska Forest, then. How we'd managed to travel such a great distance in so little time baffled me. At least I hoped it hadn't been long. A dull ache still simmered from the impact of my head against that boulder, but I was alive and familiar with my surroundings. All I needed was to slip into the shadows. Race through the wretched woods to Cruor and find a way to get word to Leena.

Dank, wet, and reeking of dirt, the small cavern was a jagged maw full of stalagmites and stalactites. The beast clung to the ceiling and moved about them on dew-flecked threads. Muted-red lichen glowed faintly along portions of the rocky floor. She'd strung me up relatively close to the entrance, and I was just able to crane my neck enough to get a glimpse of the endless dark expanse behind me. A wheezing current skated through the air and churned the milky fog along the ground. Magic. Dark and alluring and damning. It surged around me and beckoned from somewhere deep in the cavern.

Devil's Hollow. A burial ground for dark mages who had sought to take down the Five—Nepheste, Silvis, Oslo, Tyrus, and Yuna—long ago. Their magic was so corrupt, so foul, that even in death it lingered in this gods-damned cave, pulsing around me. Red tendrils bloomed in my peripheral vision as though they'd finally been given the nourishment needed to grow. To spread like a weed and wrangle conscious thought from my mind.

The fog beneath me turned into a bloody mist, and Bowen appeared. The world blurred. Then steadied again. A hidden heartbeat pulsed from somewhere deep in the cavern. If I didn't lose my body to the putrid magic of this cave, my mind would surely go.

Bowen sighed. "*You had the chance to end this. Now, look at you.*"

"Get out of my head." My voice was more of a croak. The spider turned, her legs scampering against stone in a hair-raising scuffle. She lowered herself on a thick thread from her spinner and looked around. Bowen was invisible to her. It was no surprise the beast couldn't see him. If anything, it only proved how far I'd fallen to the oath. Or how strong the cave's magic was. It was suffocating. Endless. A constant weight pressing against my consciousness.

The ache in my head intensified. After several moments, the beast narrowed her eyes and ran sticky hands over my face. Once she deemed I was still thoroughly caught, she retreated up into the dark network of the ceiling and continued decorating the stalactites with webs.

The ghost of Bowen arched a careful brow. "*Cozy.*"

Not real. Not real. Not real. The mantra did nothing to lessen the oppressive magic.

A swirling wind churned the mist beside him, and Amira appeared. "*Oh, Aleksander. How did you end up here?*"

"Gods." Squeezing my eyes shut, I counted three breaths before opening them again. Deep, foreign laughs rumbled from the back of the cave, each one more grating and damning than the last. The oath was called to the dark mages' spirits. Pulling power from their cursed existence. The cave walls closed in around me.

Amira shook her head. "*Did you really think that would work?*"

"One can only hope."

Hurt flickered through her golden irises. "*I'm sorry it pains you to see us.*"

A brittle chuckle pushed through my lips. "You have no idea."

"*You don't think it's painful for us too?*" Bowen stalked forward with his hands fisted at his sides. "*Seeing you with her? Knowing you have the power to grant her, grant all of us, peace?*"

Silence. The sharp tang of magic spiked from the back of the cavern.

Amira gently rested a hand on his shoulder. "*Bowen is right, Noc. Give Leena what she truly wants. An eternal life by your side.*"

My mind spun. Their words sounded so *right*. But I knew they were wrong. They *had* to be wrong. "I can't do what you want. I can't kill the woman I love."

The red fog sharpened around Amira. "*Why? You killed us.*"

"I didn't have a choice!"

My exclamation echoed through the cave and crashed back into me. The weight of that truth was so *heavy*, magnified by their presence before me now. Amira inched closer. The spider had strung me up between two massive stalactites, so all I could do was look down at the mess I'd created. At the *lives* I'd stolen. They looked up at me, eyes wide and pleading, and the edges of my vision shook. I *hurt*. My head. My heart. *Everything*. The cave walls threatened to crumble around me.

Bowen's expression broke. *"But now you have a choice to save us all, and you'd still deny us?"*

Amira sighed. *"I thought we meant more to you than that."*

Agony arced through me. Somewhere in the back of my mind, I knew they weren't real. No matter that Bowen's deep chuckle was a sound my ears had forgotten they missed. No matter that Amira's smile was too genuine to be an illusion. They weren't real, and yet…

I couldn't fight them. Not when they were so clearly the people I used to love.

A silent tear tracked down Amira's cheek. *"This will all be over soon. Your pain, your despair—the choice will be taken from your grasp, and you'll be absolved of this torment."*

Every fiber in my being froze. For a moment, clarity pushed aside the dark call of the mages' magic. "What do you mean?"

Footsteps clacked against the rocky floor at the mouth of the cave. In a tawny, shapeless, floor-length cloak, a figure appeared. Hood pulled tight over their face, it was impossible to get a glimpse of who they were.

A coy feminine drawl sounded from the dark depths of the hood. "I wonder, Noc, who are you talking to?"

Unease stirred in my gut. I recognized that tone. That haughty chuckle. She'd been the one urging me to kill. This woman was responsible for my bounty. The fragile control I'd managed to find threatened to shatter.

Jaw clenched, I searched for any sign of who she was. Anything I could use to track her before I lost myself completely. "Who are you?"

She laughed. "I'm asking the questions. Tell me, what are you experiencing? Hallucinations? You've held on tremendously well. Not like I really have expertise in this area. I've never hired an assassin before."

"Leena has been pardoned. Remove the oath." Rumbling laughter started up again from the dark depths at my back, but the woman didn't notice. Or maybe she couldn't hear them.

"I don't think so." She folded her arms across her chest, and the billowing sleeves kept her hands from view.

A snarl escaped from me. "What has she done to you?"

The woman shrugged. "Nothing. At first, I simply needed her for a spell. But Wynn's remains were a better-suited ingredient, so she was no longer of use to me. The problem was, absolving the oath would've required me to out myself as the one who placed the bounty—an action I took without the Council's knowledge. It was easier to simply let things play out. That is, until Gaige told me of your true heritage, Aleksander."

Something hot and heady brewed in my gut. Leena was *not* expendable. Even with the pardon handed down by Yazmin, this person was willing to simply let things play out to protect her own hide. Cowardice. And she knew who I was, thanks to Gaige. What sort of game was she playing? What was she after? I strained against the sturdy webbing, only for the spider beast to descend from the ceiling and add more threads to my cocoon.

Cursing, I abandoned my struggles and stared her down with all the malice I could summon. Sickening red tendrils coursed through my vision, making it hard to focus. "What do you want from me?"

"You're just another ingredient. But before I could use you, I needed you to visit Oslo and Silvis's Ruins. That's why I sent Leena on that farce of a hunt."

Warning bells clashed in my head. Yazmin had given Leena the instructions for the Azad taming.

As if reacting to my thoughts, the woman reached up and pulled back her cloak. Her platinum hair fell out in waves around her face. There was nothing but malice in her cold eyes. She tilted her head toward my hand, and the oath seemed to pulse with recognition. The red tendrils in my peripheral vision multiplied. And still, the cave walls closed in. There was no escape. No way out.

My head throbbed. "Why?"

"I have my reasons." Strolling forward, she signaled to her beast. The spider descended from the ceiling and began tearing away at the webbing around my bicep. Yazmin snuck her hand into the deep pocket of her robe and extracted a small vial. A smile stole across her lips. "This shouldn't hurt. Much."

The creature sliced into my arm with one of her appendages, and blood welled along the cut. Yazmin caught it with the vial, all the while chanting something in a foreign language beneath her breath. The symbol on her hand started to change. The soft pink lines turned dark and ruddy—currant in color—as if the wrongness of this was tainting the very magic she possessed. We never would've thought to suspect her.

Now was my chance to act. I homed in on the blood dripping from my arm and willed it to take shape. To form into a deadly blade and stop Yazmin in her tracks, once and for all. My body tightened as I focused, and yet... Nothing. My breath left me in a rush, and Yazmin glanced up at me with a cocked brow.

If not blood, then shadows. Again, I tried to summon dark tendrils to do my bidding, only to come up empty-handed. This spider's magical web had doused my powers completely. Frustration reached a breaking point, and I let out a wordless groan.

"Not trying to escape, are we?" Yazmin asked, capping the

vial and then nodding to her beast. In an instant, sticky threads had recoated my arm, once again sealing my cocoon.

"What are you going to do with me?"

She shrugged. "Leave you here, for the time being. Your strength is already waning. How do you think I knew when to send the Fabric Spinner? I've been watching you, Noc. Apparently, the longer you deny the oath's call, the easier it is for me to try to sway you to answer it." Turning on her heels, she strolled to the lip of the cave before pausing. "And just in case Leena somehow survived her run in with the Nix Ikari, I could use you."

"I won't hurt Leena." I didn't even fully believe my own words. Not with Amira and Bowen standing so close. They'd been silent this entire time, but that didn't mean they'd gone unnoticed. Not by me. With every passing moment the red haze sharpened, and their looks became more damning. More *convincing*. As if I could save Leena from Yazmin by simply doing what they suggested.

Yazmin laughed. "I seriously doubt that. When I return, Devil's Hollow will have worked its dark magic on you. You won't have any fight left. You'll simply obey."

And then she left, the edges of her cloak flapping behind her. The faintest light pulsed from the mouth of the cave, but it couldn't chase away the brooding darkness swallowing me whole. Sickening power reverberated through my blood. I needed out. I needed to save Leena. To tell someone, to warn someone. Cruor was so close, and yet...

Amira floated beside me and placed a hand on my cheek. "*My love, don't fight it.*"

"*You've done enough.*" Bowen floated to my other side. Reaching through the unbreakable cage of silken thread, he twined his fingers with mine. "*It's time to let go.*"

I fought in vain to block out their words. The whispers of darkest magic.

"*Do you remember the day we met?*" Amira ran her fingers through my hair. "*I thought you were an insolent, arrogant prick. You were obviously annoyed you had to attend the treaty talks. You didn't even try to hide it. I thought, 'How could someone so beautiful be so cold?'*"

She smiled, and I lost all semblance of what was real. Bowen chuckled. "*Always aloof, this one.*"

"*You didn't even look at me. Didn't see me at all.*" Her wandering fingers paused.

"You're wrong." She was so unbelievably wrong. I still remembered that day. I still remembered the woman sitting in a pool of light as if she commanded the sun itself.

She angled her face my direction. "*I am?*"

Memories flooded my mind, and angry red tendrils strangled the lingering shadows in my brain. Nothing remained but shades of crimson. "I saw you. I saw only you."

Bowen sighed. "*And what about me?*" Pinning my chin between his fingers, he forced me to meet his gaze. Those eyes were a mirror into my past, and I couldn't deny him. Of course I remembered.

"You were striking. And bold. I can't believe you tried to rob me."

His crooked grin sealed my fate. And as the two of them traded stories of my past, my present faded away. Delicious red tendrils replaced my familiar dark shadows. They snaked through me, around me—around us—and Amira and Bowen were all that mattered.

The wet rattling of ragged breath from deep within the cave died, and the tittering, wordless calls of mages turned into a warm hum. There was nothing but my lovers. Each one so different and yet ultimately the same. I'd follow them anywhere. I was entirely devoted to them. I'd wronged them once before, and that betrayal would guide my retribution. I'd give them peace. I'd give Leena peace. And then finally, *finally*, we could enjoy our lives together. Forever.

TWENTY-SIX

LEENA

Cruor was mostly dark, thanks to the early morning hour. Hedges clambered against the masonry, and the slate-black rycrim core pulsed from the vibrant gems embedded in the stone. The vine-laden mansion was a wondrous reprieve, and though my heart soared at the idea of being home, my mind rebelled.

I slipped off Reine's back first, followed quickly by Oz. "C'mon. Emelia and the others should be up."

"Good. We need to hurry," I said.

"More importantly, we need to be careful." Kost dismounted and took the stairs to the front door with a glance over his shoulder. "If Raven is the culprit, then it's possible she's not acting alone."

Biting my tongue, I relented with a quick nod. Raven's legendary feline had decimated our forces. Her beast alone made a full-frontal attack the worst possible idea. Not to mention that if she were pulling the strings behind Noc's oath, then Eilan, her lover, was most certainly involved too.

Two council members with ferocious legendary beasts. We had to be strategic. With a quick glance at my own A-Class feline, I sent Reine back to the beast realm. Teleporting such a great distance had tired her, but she'd still be able to cover short spaces with her power.

And if Raven planned on fighting, my beast would need all the rest she could get.

Oz led the way inside, and warm light spilled over us as we stepped into the foyer. A fire on the verge of dying crackled from the hearth, and two assassins loitered around the flame. One of them was Astrid, and her face lit up at our entrance. Vaulting over the back of the couch, she practically ran across the tile floor to greet us. "Thank the gods you're back. Emelia just went out on rotation."

A familiar mess of black hair popped up from the armchair, and Iov smiled. "Hey, guys."

"Fetch Emelia immediately." Kost leveled Astrid with a stern look. "We have important things to discuss."

Astrid frowned, but didn't ignore the order of Cruor's second-in-command. Shadows claimed her in an instant, leaving an open path to the couch. Heading for the library, Oz left to retrieve *Zane and the Fallen Leaders*. I moved toward the sofa and sank into the cushions, pressing my fingers to my temples. I didn't even know where to begin in terms of preparing an attack against Raven and Eilan if the book indicated they had Noc.

Iov raised both his brows and asked, "You all right?"

"Yes. No." I wavered as a I stared at him. The new assassins were all so *young*. If not physically, then at least in the sense of being recently raised. Emelia and Iov we could count on, but how many others?

Iov crossed his ankles and leaned back in the armchair. Still wearing the signature black-on-black apparel the sentries donned to stay hidden in the night, he could've passed for a shadow. Kost dropped into the couch beside me and polished his spectacles. Tense hands worked the small cloth in meticulous circles until his lenses practically shined.

"Where's Noc?" Iov's voice was tight.

"Gone." Kost replaced his glasses. "We need to get him back."

Iov's gaze flickered between the two of us. "What happened?"

"He was taken." My lips flattened, and heat flushed through my body. Wrapping my fingers in the chain of my bestiary, I gave it a forceful tug. Information was traded freely among the Council members. Raven must have talked with Gaige. Hadn't he been reluctant to blame her? He was blinded by loyalty, and that fealty had resulted in Noc's abduction.

Maybe Gaige had told her about his true identity, and she'd seen an opportunity to strengthen the alliance between Charmers and Wilheimians.

Oz returned carrying the book, and my breath caught in my chest. He handed it over to Kost, who immediately flipped it open. Lightly, he dragged his fingers over the text as he read. My gaze snagged on Noc's name.

Kost's fingers trembled as he reached the end of the entry. "Vague, as I feared. It confirms he was abducted by a Charmer from Hireath, but that's it. There's no description of where he was taken."

I let out a wordless shriek and kicked the coffee table.

"Abducted? How?" Iov asked.

A low, angry rumble simmered from Oz's chest. "A beast took us by surprise."

Eyes bulging, Iov stared at his brethren. "Whose beast?"

"Raven," I said, voice shaking with thinly-veiled anger.

Iov's face paled. No doubt he remembered her and the way her legendary beast had cleaved through his stomach. Shaky hands clasped and unclasped before him, and he pressed his lips into a thin line. A rush of shadows blossomed in front of the mantel, and Astrid emerged with Emelia hot on her heels. Smile light, her gaze bounced from person to person. And then her grin faltered.

"Where's Noc?" Emelia asked.

"Gone." Kost stood and gestured to the couch. "Have a seat, we need to talk."

She sank into the cushions beside me, and Kost started to recount the events leading up to Noc's capture. My insides knotted. Hearing it repeated only made things worse. Each detail was a clue I didn't know how to decipher. How had Raven known when to send the Fabric Spinner? Why come after us at all? I threaded my fingers together and stared at the floor. Nothing added up.

Astrid braced her forearms along the back of the couch, fidgeting between Emelia and me. "So, what do we do?"

Oz flexed his hands. "*You* do nothing." Jaw set in a hard edge, he gave her a stern look. "You're freshly raised. You don't have enough control over your shadows to fight anyone just yet, let alone a Charmer."

Astrid stilled. "I don't need shadows to kick anyone's ass."

"Astrid." Emelia turned toward her, and her eyes went soft. "We know what you're capable of. But we only just got you back."

"You don't know what we'll be up against. We don't even know what we're walking into," Kost said.

My chest tightened. I didn't want to be responsible for Cruor's destruction. If we brought everyone with us, even the newly raised assassins, we'd be sending them to their graves. And this time, Noc wouldn't be able to raise them.

Standing, I began to pace in front of the stairs. I had to move. Had to do *something*. "They don't have to fight, but they can scout. Search for Noc and see—"

The front doors crashed open, and several injured people stumbled into the room. At once, everyone leapt to their feet, and shadows flanked my assassins as they fashioned blades from the dark. The intruders rushed forward without fear, one man shouting above the rest as his jerky movements caused his blond hair to skate around his shoulders. Muted-red eyes encircled in a mercury ring of magic met mine.

"Calem." His name was a breathy exhale as I took in the scene. An unmoving woman with sable hair was limp in his arms, and he gently laid her on the now-empty couch. Her face was sickly pale and near unrecognizable, but the sapphire emblem on her hand, though lacking in luster, clued me in: Kaori. Shallow cuts covered her body, and a sweaty sheen dampened her hairline. Her breaths were far too erratic for comfort.

After straightening himself, Calem rubbed his hand along a deep gash that ran the length of his bicep. For the most part, his lacerations were shallow. Nowhere near as severe as Kaori's, but they sent a wave of panic through me just the same.

Behind him, Gaige stumbled into view before slumping to the floor, hands clutching at his bloodied side. A circular wound oozed blood from his stomach, and he grimaced. It dribbled over his fingers and pooled in the grout lines.

The last person to snag my attention was a woman with infuriatingly familiar crushed-copper hair. She gripped the fabric of her breeches, as if needing to find something to hold onto, and the red symbol on her hand dominated my vision.

"Raven."

She looked up at me with hollow, sunken eyes, and I lost all rational thought. Lunging across the foyer, I crashed into her. Pinned her shoulders beneath my knees and snarled down at her. Rage took control of my limbs, and I wanted nothing more than for her to suffer. To pay for what she'd done.

"Leena!" Calem leaped to me and gripped my shoulders tight. "What are you doing? Get off her."

Raven hissed beneath me. "Go ahead. Fucking test me right now. See what happens."

I attempted to shrug off Calem's grip, but his arms wrapped around me in a tight cage, and he yanked me off. I pounded my fists against his grip, but he only tightened his hold.

"I'm not letting you go until you calm down."

"Leena, hold on," Gaige managed. His voice was shaky, but his gaze was steady. Calem tipped his chin down at me, a silent question, and I tightly leashed my desire to strangle the woman who had brought all this pain down on us. If only for a moment. Finally, he released me.

Oz dropped his battle stance. "What the hell happened?"

Frustration flickered through Calem's gaze. Mercury pools dominated most of his irises, but there was still a sliver of muted red at the edges. A hint of my Calem. He offered Raven his hand and pulled her to her feet. "We were attacked."

"Why are you helping her?" My whole body shook with betrayal.

Oz barred me from flying across the room with a firm arm. "Hold it. No one is fighting anyone. Calem, explain what's going on."

Everyone went silent. Astrid and Emelia gathered close to each other with Iov only a step away. Kost inched toward Gaige, finally kneeling beside him. They shared a quiet, weighted glance. Then, Kost fished his bronze key out of his breast pocket and summoned Felicks. His beast immediately turned his attention to Gaige. Calem stood in front of Raven, forehead scrunched in confusion.

Slowly, he raked a hand through his hair and fashioned a lopsided bun. "Like I said, we were attacked."

"And you brought the monster who did it into our home?" I seethed.

Gaige's head snapped up. "You've got it wrong." His words ended with a wheeze as he flinched away from Felicks's tongue. Despite his efforts, the wound simply wasn't healing. A peculiar, purple-tinted sheen coated the gash, and I swallowed. Yimlet poison. One bite from that beast's maw, and the skin would instantly start to deteriorate. Felicks's magic had stopped it from progressing, but he wouldn't be able to reverse the damage that it had already caused. Kost's expression turned grim.

"What the hell did I do to you?" Raven ground her teeth and glared my direction, pulling my attention away from Gaige's wound.

I nearly shrieked. "Everything!"

"Leena!" Gaige struggled to his feet, pressing one hand to his side. "It's not her."

Kost stood with him, gaze trained on Gaige's unsteady stance. "He's right."

"What?" I pushed around Oz, and he moved after me. "How do you know?"

"When the bounty was first placed, I met with the woman in charge. When she summoned a beast, there was a currant-colored glow around her hand. She wore gloves, but that means her symbol would be the same hue, right? Raven's is different." He frowned at Raven's exposed hand.

"Kost." Calem pinched the bridge of his nose. "What the fuck color is currant?"

A harsh sigh scraped through his teeth. "It's a distinct, ruddy shade of red."

"But—"

"I'm sorry. It's a very precise color, and she"—Kost nodded to Raven—"does not have it."

"Why would I place a bounty on you, anyway?" Raven asked.

Something in me snapped. Maybe Kost was wrong. Maybe he'd missed the true color of her mark. Maybe... I had to know for sure. Thrusting my hand forward, I opened the beast realm door and summoned Onyx. He came without hesitation and stood beside me, cautious eyes skipping from person to person, trying to assess who was the threat.

"Let Onyx judge you."

Raven glowered. "I have been through enough these past few hours."

"If you're innocent, it won't hurt." My words were harsh. Onyx glanced back and forth between the two of us, waiting.

Gaige took a shaky step in her direction, but she gently brushed him off. "Fine."

Onyx sauntered forward, neon-blue light streaming from his golden eyes as he stared directly into Raven's determined glare. The whole room fell silent. We couldn't see Onyx's mental flames, the ones that would burn away past transgressions and determine whether or not someone was worthy. But I remembered what they felt like as my own sins were forgiven. How they'd scalded my body as every memory, every action I'd ever committed, was played on repeat.

Minutes stretched on for an eternity until Onyx finally pulled back. He nudged Raven softly, offering comfort for whatever he saw, and then returned to me.

She was innocent.

Raven said nothing.

"Then, who?" Breathing turned difficult. The floor rushed at me, and I sank to my knees. I'd been so *sure*. I was going to force her to confess, to absolve the bounty. She was the person who could've saved Noc's life. But now... Now there was no hope. No direction. Nowhere left to turn. The room spun, and I cradled my head in my hands.

Oz looped his arms around my shoulders and guided me an open armchair. Onyx followed, worried yowls quietly escaping the back of his throat. The world quaked beneath my feet. This was too much. Too insurmountable. We didn't know where to start. Where to look.

A glimmer of relief touched Gaige's face. "There's no denying it, Leena. Raven is innocent."

"Gods dammit," I whispered, scrunching my eyes shut. Tears pressed against my lids. Wynn had insinuated his accomplice had been someone on the Council. If not Raven, then that left Kaori and Yazmin. But Kaori's symbol was blue and Yazmin's pink. Had I misinterpreted everything? Had Wynn had the foresight to lead me down the wrong path so his coconspirator could keep working?

Oz's gentle voice pulled me from my reverie. "We'll figure this out."

I peeled open my eyes. "I don't know where to start."

"Calem, give us a play-by-play." Oz glanced past me to Calem.

"Kaori and I had just returned from training yesterday morning, and we met up with Gaige, Tristan, Eilan, and Raven outside the dining hall for breakfast." His gaze dropped to the floor. "A whole mess of beasts appeared and just started attacking. Not just us, but other Charmers too."

"Other Charmers? Who?" What on earth was happening? Who was behind it? Unleashing beasts to attack Charmers... I couldn't fathom anyone ever doing such a thing. That act alone would turn the goddess's favor for good. Besides that, how had anyone gotten a jump on the Council? I reached out to run a shaky hand through Onyx's fur, steadying myself.

Gaige grimaced. "Mostly those who would've been potential Council members. They all could've easily been replacements for Wynn. Strong. Independent. Some already had legendary felines too."

"Eilan and Tristan didn't make it." Raven's voice was scraped raw. I tilted my head in her direction, catching the full weight of her glassy stare. She'd sunk back to the floor and curled in on herself, pulled her knees to her chest. She looked so small. Fragile. Nothing like the haughty fighter I'd encountered during the battle of Hireath. This woman was in pain.

And I'd attacked her. Subjected her to Onyx's scrutiny instead of believing Kost. Right after she'd lost someone she loved.

Guilt ravaged my stomach, and I swallowed several times before braving words. "Raven, I'm so sorry."

There wasn't an ounce of forgiveness in her gaze. I didn't blame her.

Calem cast his eyes to the floor. "We tried to stay and help as long as we could. But after they died and Kaori got hurt..." He looked up at me then, as if he were ashamed of what he was about to say and needed forgiveness. "We fled."

"The beasts had halted attacking the rest of the Charmers and were only targeting us," Raven said. "Escaping was the right thing to do to keep them out of harm's way. For now."

"She's right," I said, swallowing back tears, "You're alive. And Kaori...?"

"She'll live," Gaige said through a wince. "We escaped on the backs of our legendary felines and ran nonstop until we got here. They only just went back to the realm."

"I rode with Kaori. She passed out as we reached Cruor's border." Calem turned his somber stare to the unconscious woman on the couch. Tension rippled through his arms as he folded them across his chest.

Kost frowned. "Where was Yazmin during the attack?"

Gaige's shook his head. "She wasn't there."

"So there was this massive beast attack, and the Crown was simply missing?" Kost didn't bother to mask his apprehension.

"She wasn't missing. She just wasn't there." Gaige seemed to trip over his words. He shook his head. "Yazmin is always off attending to Council matters or on a beast hunt."

"That seems...odd," Oz said.

"Look, you're getting this all wrong." Gaige looked first at Raven and then me. He opened his mouth to speak, and then closed it. Frowned. He kept staring at me, sifting through some memory or bit of information that none of us were privy to, until he suddenly straightened. "What happened with the Azad?"

"What does that have to do with anything?"

His words were frantic. "Those ingredients you showed me... They weren't for taming an Azad. Yes, the ruska fruit acts as a lure, but the Azad itself was the bait. For something else, though my research didn't illuminate what that might be. I was on my way to confront Yazmin when we were attacked."

Extending my hand outward, I tapped into the power simmering through my veins. Rosewood light bloomed from the tree, and a heady purring preceded Reine's appearance. Shocked silence hung heavy in the air. Reine tilted her head and sauntered toward me, knocking over the coffee table to nuzzle me and rake a scratchy tongue along my hand. A curious Onyx leaned across my lap and sniffed her. With two legendary felines crowding around me, there was hardly any room left in the foyer.

"This is what we found. A Nix Ikari."

"She should have killed you," Gaige whispered.

"She tried." I scratched the space where her horns met her skull, and she plopped to the floor and rested her chin in my lap. Her wild, thick tail flicked back and forth like a broom across the tile. "She snatched up the Azad before I could tame it. I need to go back and find another before it's too late."

Raven scowled. "Why on earth would you need an Azad? Their only purpose is to sniff out buried treasure."

My throat went dry. "What?"

"How do you know that?" Gaige echoed a breath behind me.

"My grandmother was the last Charmer to tame an Azad. Why?"

My heart thundered in my ears. Raven *knew* all along that an Azad wouldn't work for Noc. But I'd been so preoccupied with blaming her that I hadn't thought to ask everyone on the Council. Gaige had mentioned that the last person to tame one had been a century ago. She had no reason to lie.

Which meant...

The air left my lungs. "But why?"

Gaige's mouth opened and closed until he finally squeezed his eyes shut. Yazmin had led us into a trap. She'd orchestrated a hunt that she thought would end in our deaths.

"What the hell is going on?" Tension roiled from Calem's frame, and the mercury surrounding his pupils sharpened.

"It's Yazmin." The words were acid against my tongue. "The Crown. *She* placed the bounty." Everything I knew, everything I believed in, came crashing down. Yazmin was our *leader*. She was supposed to protect us, guide us. Show us the way. Why would she send us on a hunt that would lead to certain death if she wasn't the one responsible? Pieces began falling into place. She must have arranged the bounty without anyone else's approval. If I died, the problem would simply disappear. The investigation would cease. But still...why?

Raven hissed. "Now you're accusing *her*? You're out of your mind."

"Yazmin's symbol is pink—I'm sure of it. I saw it when she offered us free passage after the battle," Kost said.

Gaige's voice was eerily quiet. "Perhaps she thought we would have stripped her of her title..." His trailing words did everything but instill confidence. I so desperately wanted to be wrong.

Raven turned on him, wild-eyed. "What are you saying? You believe her?"

"Look at the facts." Gaige dragged a shaky hand through his snarled hair. "Yazmin gave Leena specific instructions for a taming an Azad because she told her it would cure Noc. You just disproved that."

"This is the Crown we're talking about," Raven said. "What would she have to gain by lying about something like that?"

"I don't know, but…" He turned to me. "I have an idea. Leena, can you send the Nix Ikari back so we have a bit more space? But leave Onyx. We need him."

Gaige limped closer to the entrance of the manor and leaned against the stair railing for support. I sent Reine back just as he extended his hand, opening his own door to the beast realm and summoning the Zavalluna.

Her black coat shimmered with turquoise, fuchsia, and emerald auroras, as if she'd been born from the night. With a whinny, she tossed her head and shook out her mane. Her bladelike horn glowed a soft white. Gaige patted her on the neck before directing her attention toward Onyx.

"Amplify his power."

She nickered and then tilted her head in his direction, the glow about her horn intensifying. A dome of light bloomed outward around her until we were all encompassed beneath it, but only Onyx seemed affected. His eyes lit up, the electric blue streams snaking out like lightning instead of wisps. His hide turned lustrous, more magnificent. And even though I couldn't see it, I felt his power grow. The strength of his magic slammed into me, nearly knocking the air from my lungs.

Gaige swallowed thickly. "Have him judge Yazmin."

I blinked. "But she's not here."

"She doesn't have to be. Not with Valda's power." He nodded to his mare. "She can't hold it for long. Have him do it now."

As I ran my hand over Onyx's fur, a charge of static electricity crackled beneath my fingers. "Okay, Onyx. Go ahead. But if she's guilty, don't try and absolve her. Just stop." I didn't want her feeling the effects of his power in case she was responsible. Otherwise, she might flee with Noc before we ever got the chance to confront her.

Visible blue flames erupted around his body, and I retracted my hand with a jolt, expecting pain. But instead of searing heat, I felt nothing but a subtle warmth. The flames licked higher and higher, stretching toward the ceiling as Onyx turned his head in the direction of Hireath. Minutes stretched by. The flames crackled as if devouring brittle wood. Onyx pulled back his maw, revealing gleaming fangs, and snarled.

Guilty.

He recalled his power, and the flames receded in a whoosh. The chill of the room scraped along my skin, and I shivered. Glancing at everyone else, it was clear they felt his verdict just as I had. Raven had gone parchment-pale, and Gaige was shaking his head back and forth in disbelief. He sent Valda back to the realm, and I did the same with Onyx.

How could Yazmin do this? Why?

"But the color," Kost interjected, finding his voice first. "I know what I saw."

Gaige cleared his throat, pained words filling the room and suffocating whatever belief in our leader still remained. "Perhaps you were mistaken." He glanced at Kost. "Onyx's verdict can't be wrong."

Calem's rage was as plain as day in the shining mercury of his glare. "Maybe she convinced someone else to place the bounty. Either way, she's pulling the strings."

"Given this...revelation, it stands to reason that she was behind our ambush too." Gaige's voice was broken, soft. "She wasn't there. She didn't come to our aid. Think about the type of beasts that were summoned. Who else could call forth that many A-Class creatures at once?"

"But, Tristan… Eilan…" Raven's words cracked over his name. "If not for Calem's quick thinking, we could have been killed too."

A deep pang constricted my heart. The Crown. The woman I looked up to and trusted. The pinnacle of Charmer society. Tears spilled down my cheeks, and my body started to shake. Oz rubbed a gentle hand down my back, but nothing could chase away the burn in my chest. I'd been betrayed by my family before. Had my faith rattled by the Council.

I never thought it would hurt so bad a second time around.

A flicker of doubt toyed with Kost's expression, but he relented, turning to Astrid, Emelia, and Iov. Lingering in the corner of the room, they'd let us hash out the details without interjecting. But their wide eyes told me they understood. Emelia and Iov knew what the Crown meant to Charmers. It'd be the equivalent of Noc turning on them.

"Set up extra watches and get to work. If anyone followed them here or somehow learns of their escape, we need to be prepared. Notify me immediately if you sense anything. Understood?"

They nodded once and left. For a moment, no one spoke. And then Kaori moaned. Calem crouched beside her, brushing his fingers across her forehead.

Kost's voice softened. "Let's get her to the medical wing." Lifting his chin, he glanced at Gaige and then Raven, assessing their wounds. "You two, as well. Our healers and Felicks will do what they can."

Calem slipped his arms beneath Kaori and cradled her to his chest with heartbreaking gentleness. Slowly, he took the stairs to the medical wing with Gaige and Raven close behind. Kost hesitated only for a moment, glancing back at us just as his hand gripped the railing.

"Maybe there's more going on than we originally thought. We still need to fill in the blanks."

"Yeah." I stood, swaying as fatigue and despair turned my limbs to lead. Oz steadied me with a strong hand, enough concern in his heavy gaze for both of us.

I didn't know what to think. What to *feel*. Noc was missing. And Yazmin was...

My gut churned. I couldn't fight Yazmin. *We* couldn't fight her. She was the strongest Crown since Celeste herself. If she really was the one pulling the strings... Death felt closer than I ever imagined, and I gripped Oz's forearm and prayed to every god I could think of that I was wrong.

But somehow, deep down, I knew I wasn't.

TWENTY-SEVEN

OZ

The moment we walked through the medical wing's double doors, I sprung into action. Yes, we had an incredibly skilled healer with decades of knowledge. Uma could fix anyone and anything, given the right tools. But I couldn't stop myself. It'd been that way for as long as I could remember—the moment my family needed something, I was there. I just had to be.

And Uma didn't mind the extra help. Already dressed in a long-sleeve gown with gloves secured over her hands and a cloth mask covering her mouth, she was ready to face anything. She must have heard our conversation through the walls, used the shadows to help her decipher what was needed in order to care for our guests. Soft blue eyes met mine, and the wrinkles lining her forehead deepened.

We worked side by side, pulling back the cots' stark-white sheets. While she reached for silver trays with medical instruments and bandages, I helped Calem settle a slumbering Kaori onto the first bed and then turned my focus to Gaige. How he was still standing was beyond me. The weeping wound across his abdomen had started to emit a sour odor, and I frowned. Infection. And judging by Kost's worried look, he knew it too. He stood close by with Felicks cradled in his arms, the purple orb atop his head swirling every two minutes with a new predication for Kost to decipher. I hoped he'd give Kost some relief. Proof that Gaige would be okay, even though Felicks hadn't been able to seal the gash, and whatever was in that venom was wreaking havoc on Gaige's insides.

Uma took one look at his laceration and blanched. "On the cot. Now. Take off your shirt."

He stumbled as he made a move toward the bed, and I instinctively reached out and steadied him. With a wordless grunt, he allowed me to shoulder his weight and ease him onto the cot. Then, we peeled off his tunic. Even though he wasn't a member of Cruor, he needed help. He wouldn't be the first Charmer I'd gone out of my way to aid. Cutting a quick glance Leena's direction, I offered her what I hoped was a reassuring nod. She couldn't even muster a smile, and my heart tightened at the sight. She stood in the open doorway to the hall, face ashen and tears barely reined in. Beside her, Raven was a statue. Her once-fiery eyes had lost all light, and her faraway stare targeted nothing at all. Exhaustion. Despair. Loss. All emotions I recognized only too well.

The pang in my chest deepened, but I pushed away the thought of him and pulled my gaze back to Gaige, then to Uma. "What now?"

Deft fingers hovered above his wound, and Uma grimaced. "I've never seen this before."

"It's Yimlet poison." Gaige's voice wavered as a tremor claimed his body. With a shaky hand, he wiped beads of sweat away from his damp brow. "You'll need to douse it with mimko extract. That will stop the spread."

Without waiting for Uma's instruction, I turned to the cabinets lining the walls and pulled them open. Scoured the wooden shelves and read label after label until I came across a small, green vial. I snatched the concoction and hurried back to his side. Kost edged closer, and Felicks let out a worried bark.

Kost dipped his chin toward his beast. "Will Felicks be able to seal it up once the venom is stopped?"

"No." Gaige moaned weakly. "The Yimlet's poison permanently alters whatever it touches, making it immune to any other beast's magic."

"We'll stitch you up manually, then." Uma turned to the tray brimming with equipment and picked up an already-threaded needle, then reached for something I didn't recognized lying in a silver basin covered with a thin layer of water. Gently, she snared what appeared to be a leathery piece of parchment between her forefinger and thumb. "Burdyuk leaf. I'll graft it to your skin, and it'll dissolve once you've properly healed. First, the mimko extract. Be prepared for it to sting, but it will numb the area afterward."

She nodded toward me, and I uncorked the vial. I didn't know much about mimko extract—the herb in question was only ever used among healers—and the pungent, spiced scent that assaulted the air made almost everyone in the room gag, save myself and Uma. Even Leena and Raven, the farthest from the cot, sputtered. Kost visibly retracted, and Felicks buried his face into his chest to hide his snout.

Calem slapped his palm across his nose and mouth. "Get on with it."

"Best do as he says. Go ahead, Ozias." Uma gestured to the wound with her needle.

I gave Gaige a weak smile. "Sorry about this." And without any further warning, I splashed a heavy amount across the laceration, coating it as thick as I could to stop the spread of venom. Gaige cursed so loud, my ears rang, and he white-knuckled the sides of his cot. Steam formed where the extract met his flesh, and a hair-raising hiss punctured the air. Gaige jerked uncontrollably, and Kost pressed a firm hand against his chest to hold him in place. Finally, the sound subsided—along with Gaige's colorful language and thrashing—and he slackened against the bed. Slowly, Kost studied his face. His fingers lingered a moment too long...until he seemed to realize what he was doing. A blush touched his ears, and he took a definitive step back, giving Uma more room to work. She acted quickly, gently placing the burdyuk leaf over the wound and stitching so fast, I barely had time to register her actions.

Just seeing Gaige's somewhat-relaxed face lessened the tension, the fear, in the room. Kost sighed and placed Felicks on the floor by his feet. Calem let his hand fall away, only to press it gently against Kaori's forehead. She moved, ever so slightly, toward his touch, and his shoulders loosened. Satisfied with their well-being for the moment, I turned toward Raven.

A rock formed in my throat. Her physical wounds were minor—she pressed her right arm tight against her chest, a sign she'd likely broken something and was avoiding jostling it too much—and there were a few other minor gashes that Felicks could heal. But the emotional damage...the gaunt look in her eyes and the slight twitch she couldn't seem to control...

Slowly, I moved to her side and placed a gentle hand on her shoulder. To guide her toward the open cot so we could take a look at her injuries. I half-expected her to flinch. Or to scowl and shove me away. There was no telling exactly how grief would rear its ugly head. But instead, she blinked up at me, an expression of sheer confusion clouding her face. As if she'd forgotten where she was to begin with. And then all at once, she cracked. Tears welled along her lashes and she sucked in a sharp breath. Her lips quivered as she tried to keep herself together. To not completely fall apart in the presence of others.

I'd never been any good at talking. The right words always seemed to elude me. Besides, there wasn't anything I could say to alleviate her pain. That much I knew. And I wasn't about to belittle her feelings, her anguish, by telling her that it'd be okay. Because even if it would—and I hoped to the gods it would—hearing it would do nothing for her right now. So instead, I acted. Because that's what I always did. Because that's the only way I knew how to make things manageable. If I could do anything to ease her burden, then I would. After giving her shoulder a squeeze, I helped her to the open bed and then handed her a blanket. She rolled the lip of fabric between her fingers and then dotted her eyes. Said thank you without saying anything at all.

I heard her loud and clear. Wordlessly, I took her injured arm and assessed the damage. She never flinched. Only stared straight ahead, jaw set tight. Beneath all that pain was a world of anger. Of vengeance. Nothing would stop her from seeking justice in the name of her lost love. As I set her wrist and bandaged it tight, I knew that when we sorted through this mess, she'd demand to be part of the fight. Which meant it was on me to do everything I could to help her now.

That was a job I'd never shy away from.

TWENTY-EIGHT

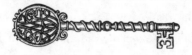

LEENA

Save the now steady rise and fall of her chest, Kaori didn't move. Stretched out on a cot beneath a layer of blankets, she looked unnaturally pale. A purplish bruise had swollen just beneath her eye, and her normally glossy hair was dull. But at least she was breathing. Gaige sat upright on a cot beside her, his shirt removed and bandages strapped tight over the wound in his side. He'd be left with a significant scar from the tip of his sternum to his waist.

Raven occupied the furthest cot. She sat without moving, her own wounds bandaged, thanks to Oz. Her wrist had been broken and was set with a splint, and while it must've hurt, the emotional pain she felt had to be worse. Now that everyone was healed, we had plans to form. A crown to dethrone.

We waited in deafening silence until the attendant left. The pungent lemon- and bleach-scented air stung my nose, and I fought to keep my breathing steady. Kost hovered close to Gaige, unable to hide the tremoring muscle near his temple. Calem leaned against Gaige's cot, crossing his ankles and giving me a worried stare.

"Where's Noc?"

"Gone." Slowly, I recounted the series of events that led to Noc's capture for Calem, Gaige, and Raven. From securing the

ruska fruit to the moment Noc had been whisked away by the
Fabric Spinner. His head cracking against stone played on repeat in
my mind, and I shivered.

Wincing, Gaige shifted on the cot. "A Fabric Spinner? Those
aren't native to that area."

"Yazmin has one." Raven didn't look at any of us as she spoke.
"It's possible she sent her beast to collect Noc."

"And left us for the Nix Ikari." I sighed. My head throbbed.
Nothing made sense. "Somehow, we survived her. And then she
came to our aid when we were fighting against Sentinels."

"Sentinels?" Calem's hands slipped off the edge of the cot, and
he nearly crashed to the floor. "Why were they after you?"

Something clicked in my mind. Gaige's report, dangling
from Yazmin's hands. He'd told her *something*. "Let's ask Gaige
that question." Eyes hard, I moved to stand in front of him. "Did
anything happen with Yazmin while I was gone?"

He went unnaturally still. "Possibly."

Kost's voice was edged. "What do you mean?"

Gaige gripped the back of his neck and averted his eyes. "I
discovered Noc was really Aleksander Nocsis Feyreigner, rightful
prince to the kingdom of Lendria, and I relayed that information to
Yazmin. In case we needed it as leverage during our continued peace
talks with the Wilheimians."

Calem turned in shock, his jaw going slack. Clearly Noc's
lineage had been a mystery to him too. And now to find that Gaige
had sold out Noc for a better bargaining chip with Wilheim? My
blood simmered.

"You mean in case you wanted to use Noc as leverage." I bit
back a snarl. "So much for trust."

Gaige winced. "I swear, that wasn't my intention."

Tension snapped in the space around Kost, as if he were his

own damn lightning rod. Gaze impossibly hard, he glared at Gaige so violently that it hardly seemed fair the look was magnified by his glasses. Rigid fists formed by his sides, and I reached out to place a hand against his heaving chest.

I'd already attacked one Charmer tonight. Taking down a second wouldn't do us any good.

"I didn't know. Information is shared freely among the Council. She is...was...our Crown. We trusted her implicitly." Steely eyes on the verge of cracking implored us to listen. To believe.

Kost had absolutely no interest in complying. Turning his back on Gaige, he stormed across the room and placed his palms flat on a desk littered with test tubes and stray parchment. And then he scattered them all with one wide sweep of his arm. Glass shattered against the tile, and papers dusted the floor beneath his feet. His rare display of raw emotion mimicked my own building frustration. Calem trembled, his fury showing in the widening mercury threads around his irises.

Only Oz was brave enough to reach over and place a gentle hand on Kost's back. "Easy."

"I didn't know..." Gaige stared after him.

"Gods, Gaige." I spoke through gritted teeth. "Do you tell her everything? Is anything sacred to you? Or is it all just a game to see how much information, how much *leverage*, you can collect?"

"That's not fair." He dropped his gaze to the floor. "You're telling me you wouldn't implicitly trust your family? Because up until now, that's what she was to me." Slowly, he lifted his chin. "She was my friend. My mentor."

I tried my best to ignore his pleading eyes. Of course I'd tell my family the truth, but he didn't even think of the consequences. About what this could mean for Noc. For *our* family. We'd been robbed of a chance at a normal life, one not attached to his title as prince, solely because of Gaige's probing.

Folding my arms across my chest, I gave him a hard stare. "What does she want?"

Gaige blinked. "I don't know. How could I know?"

"You just said she was your friend, your mentor. Or has it always been more of a one-sided relationship and you were just too naive to notice?"

"Leena," Oz said from Kost's side, still unwilling to leave him alone. "C'mon. Ease up a little."

"She does *not* need to ease up." Kost seethed. "We need to unearth his true intentions."

"I agree. This is Noc we're talking about, Oz." Calem's hands twitched, and for a moment, I panicked. If he lost control here, now, what would we do? But he collected himself, stealing a glance at Kaori's sleeping form, and forced out a slow, shaky breath.

Gaige blanched. "As I said, we pass information freely—"

"Don't." I held up my hand. "Just don't. You're either ignorant or loyal to Yazmin. Which one is it?"

Gaige bristled, but didn't fight back. Instead, he said, "Ignorant. I'm sorry." He let out a long breath, as if admitting that was more difficult than enduring our interrogation. I suppose for someone who prided himself on his intelligence, it was. Lines creased around his eyes as he stared at the floor. He was a thousand years old in that instant, and some of my frustration fled with his acknowledgment.

Rubbing my temples, I closed my eyes and took three steadying breaths. "I don't understand any of this. Why send us across Lendria on a beast hunt just to have a Fabric Spinner steal Noc away?"

"Not to mention the color conundrum. That's fun to say." Calem gave a tight smile at his word choice. "I say we just sit her down and ask her. There are ways of making someone talk." He cracked his knuckles, a dark glint in his eyes.

"We will *not* torture her." I gave him a firm look. "I just don't—"

"Where is she." There was no hint of a question in Kost's deadly calm voice. He was still lingering by the table, but his words carried an unspoken threat that rang loud and clear.

Gaige shook his head. "I don't know. I hadn't seen her all day." He glanced at Raven, who gave a weak shrug.

"Bullshit." Kost whirled on him, closing the space in a few easy strides. "I swear to the gods if I find out you're helping her, that you intentionally endangered the man I...*Noc*, I will end you. Slowly."

Something raced through Gaige's stare. Understanding. Disappointment. Hurt. And then he tucked it away. Emotion masked, he surveyed Kost with the cool detachment I'd seen Noc use. The same icy shield he employed to put distance between us when emotions were too dangerous to be recognized.

Gaige's tone was level. "I. Don't. Know."

Kost simmered, and I stepped between him and Gaige. "Let's take a breath." With a gentle shove, I pushed Kost toward Calem. Calem blanched, clearly not wanting to be close to an enraged Kost, but he didn't move. Gaige's control wasn't as practiced as Noc's, though, and I caught the crack in his gaze. The canyon of swirling emotion Kost had just created with his outburst.

"It's safe to assume Yazmin will still be at Hireath." I focused my attention on Gaige. "We need to go there immediately. If she attacked before, it's possible she'll attack the Charmers again. And Noc will likely be with her."

"Let's go, then." Skimming his fingers along his jaw, Calem straightened and tossed a furtive glance at Kaori. "Yazmin needs to pay for what she's done."

Gaige eased his way off the cot. "I'm coming too."

"You're staying. Your injury will only slow us down." Kost didn't look at him.

Gaige's nostrils flared. "My home is in upheaval, and the

Crown is allegedly behind it. Another member of the Council should be present to recount what happens to the others. I'm going." Reaching for a long-sleeved tunic left by the attendant, he painstakingly slipped it over his head.

"Me too," Raven said, slowly easing her way off the cot. "I can at least help the other Charmers escape if Yazmin starts attacking again."

Kost opened his mouth to argue, but I cut him off. "It's okay, Kost. Let's hope this doesn't come to a battle, but if it does, there's no need for Gaige to get in our way. And Raven can help us." I shot her an apologetic stare, hoping we'd have time to mend the rift I'd caused when this was all over. "And they can both bear witness. Yazmin's been manipulating us from the start. More eyes and ears will only help."

Not to mention Gaige should be the one to witness the chaos he'd caused. We didn't know for sure yet how we were all tied together, how Yazmin and the bounty and Noc's identity were intertwined, but I didn't believe they were coincidences. Everything was connected.

Silence stretched as Kost studied me with hard eyes. Finally, he gave a curt nod. "All right." Turning, he stalked toward the double doors leading out to the halls of Cruor. "I'll notify Emelia. The sentries need to remain on high alert until we return. Yazmin isn't our only enemy right now."

"Darrien," mumbled Oz. "I almost forgot about him."

Calem shot me an alarmed glance. "What? Did something else happen?"

I tried my best not to toss a frustrated look at Gaige and failed. "Thanks to the research this one left lying around, Darrien now knows of Noc's heritage too. He was at the capital helping the Sentinels."

If Gaige had been pale before, he was ghostly now. Apparently, his endless quest for knowledge had never been so disastrous before.

"That can wait." Kost stared at the door. "We need to save Noc before we can worry about how the king will invariably come after us too."

Without a second glance our direction, he left. The doors slammed behind him, and Gaige let out a shuddering breath.

Steeling myself against the frustration boiling inside me, I turned to face Gaige. I'd placed my faith in the wrong people before too. Wynn had been more than a friend and mentor—he'd been my lover. And he'd still betrayed me. The truth was, there was no telling just how far someone would go to get what they wanted. And since what Wynn wanted wasn't me, it had been easy for him to sacrifice our relationship.

There was no telling what Yazmin wanted or what she'd be willing to lose to make it happen.

I offered Gaige a strained smile. "Don't worry about Kost. Just stick around and prove that you're innocent...or rather, ignorant."

Gaige raised a single brow but didn't respond. Instead, he followed Oz out the doors with Raven by his side, leaving Calem and me to fall in step behind them. Calem's floppy bun bounced in time with his gait, and a few loose strands fell into his eyes when he glanced down at me. The mercury ring had crawled back toward his pupils, allowing the muted-red hue of his eyes to dominate his irises. Cracking a lopsided—if weak—grin, he nudged my side with his elbow.

"I missed you," I said. I hadn't realized how much that was true until now. He'd always been the stabilizing member of our troupe. The one who wasn't afraid to tease and lighten the mood while simultaneously lunging headfirst into conflict. Seeing him in control was the only salve that could possibly alleviate the despair spreading through my chest.

He stretched a lazy arm across my shoulders and winked. "I

missed you too. I knew you'd grow tired of that brooding guild master of ours one day."

I rolled my eyes but couldn't keep my own weak smile from my lips. "How are you doing?"

"Fine." He let out a long sigh. "I owe Kaori my life."

"Oh? And how do you plan on repaying her?"

His brows waggled. "I have some ideas."

A laugh bubbled up from deep inside me. "You're incorrigible."

"Yeah." His grin wavered, and he chanced a quick look behind him before we hit the stairs to the foyer. By the time we made it through the front door of Cruor, Kost was already waiting for us at the bottom of the porch. Early morning sun bathed the lawns in weak light. Bleached by winter air and frost, the normally plush green grass had turned a golden brown. Even the Kitska Forest clambering against the property's iron fencing a short walk away was dusted in crystallized flakes.

The first frost of the season.

My heart plummeted to my feet. Winters didn't last long in Lendria, and as such, Charmers celebrated the first frost with fervor. A feast would be orchestrated, candies and small tokens of love passed to family members and friends. Nights would be spent beneath the stars to chart out constellations and seek guidance from Celeste. Yet another thing I wouldn't get to share with Noc.

Don't forget Hireath. If Yazmin really was behind the attack, this day of beauty would now forever be tainted in the eyes of my people. Once-mesmerizing, glistening frost stained a sickly red. We had to save them.

Gaige and Raven stilled beside me, each one of their gazes locked on the ground. With a hard-set grimace, Gaige thrust his hand outward and opened the door to the beast realm. His Telesávra appeared by his feet. Without prompting, the beast unhinged its jaw, and a sparking, swirling portal appeared.

"Only Charmers and beasts can safely pass through the Telesávra's portal." He glanced at Oz and Kost, then extended his hand in invitation. "The only way for non-Charmers to do so is to be touching one of our kind or a beast."

Never in my life had Kost moved to my side so quickly. "Understood."

Gaige stiffened. Calem rolled his eyes before taking his hand, leaving Oz to pair up with Raven.

"Let's go," Kost said, looping his arm through mine.

In pairs, we stepped through the portal. Like most Charmers, Gaige had set his Telesávra's hearth point to Hireath. Meaning, we manifested on the outskirts of the Beast City in a matter of seconds. The portal was a one-way ride, but I couldn't have been more thankful for the quick transportation. Yet again another reminder that I needed to tame one for myself to make travel easier between Cruor and Hireath now that I was on the Council.

When we appeared beside the twin sentry towers marking the entrance to Hireath, Dreagles leaped from the stone platforms to inspect us. Oval eyes peered at us until they spied Gaige, Raven, and me. Once they did, they abandoned their pursuit and returned to their stations, folding their wings and ignoring us entirely. No need for their sharp bugle warning call when Charmers returned to Hireath.

"It's quiet," Gaige murmured as he sent his Telesávra back to the realm in a pool of citrine light.

"Very," I said.

The crashing water from the falls was the only sound, and it rushed over the open clearing with deafening authority. No bestial calls from happy creatures. No pleasant murmurings from milling Charmers or laughing children. Nothing. We took a few steps out into the frost-covered field, and our feet crunched against the sparkling grass.

"This can't be good." Oz rubbed a thick hand along the back of his neck. Wordlessly, Calem and Kost fell into step around me. Their protection was a soft blanket I wanted to wrap myself in forever, but the icy chill of the air couldn't be ignored. Something was wrong. And as much as my body ached to remain on the safe side of the unknown, my heart and soul urged me forward.

To Hireath. To the Charmers. To Noc.

TWENTY-NINE

NOC

The throne room in Hireath was quiet, despite being packed full of bodies. So many faces, and yet none of them belonged to the one I was searching for. The oath on my wrist simmered, and I cracked my neck. Soon. Yazmin had promised that if I protected her from potential danger, she'd give me what I wanted.

Lingering on the fringe of the congregation, hidden behind one of the thick columns and enough shadows to blanket an entire city, I waited and watched. Red tendrils threaded through the darkness, keeping my purpose clear. I would kill. I would end this horrible nightmare and bring peace to everyone I loved.

Yazmin stood on the dais with the Council's thrones at her back. "We've been betrayed, my fellow Charmers." Her voice was somber but clear, rolling through the room without an ounce of trepidation.

"What happened?" a voice called from the audience.

"The Council abandoned us. Our newest member, Leena Edenfrell, poisoned their minds and turned them against us. Tristan and Eilan are no more." She placed a trembling hand to her chest. "The rest are missing. They're responsible for the attack."

Leena. The red tendrils sharpened. Soon. *Soon.*

A hushed mumbling and shocked inhales sounded from the Charmers. Yazmin clasped her hands before her to quiet them. "It's true. I feel I'm to blame for this egregious turn of events. I was the one who recommended Leena take Wynn's seat."

"No!"

"It's not your fault!"

"Protect us!"

Yazmin waved her hand. "As the Crown, I will protect you. I will always defend our people." Stepping down from the dais, she approached a glowing circle etched with ruins from their ancient language. Pulsing, muddy-red symbols pushed faint light into the space around her. The same putrid shade of red as the red haze in my mind. As the color of her tainted Charmer's emblem.

At the very center of the circle sat an empty pewter basin. She stared at it as she retrieved a vial of blood from her cloak. My blood. A small price to pay to finally be able to deal with this oath.

Yazmin returned her gaze to the crowd. "I fear the worst is yet to come. The remaining Council members have fled. At Leena's behest, they've joined ranks with Wilheim. They intend to run us out of our home."

Angry shouts of confusion rose in a clamor.

Yazmin only raised her voice and spoke over them, ushering in more shocked silence. "I cannot pretend to understand why they would do such a thing; I only know it's coming. And so, we must stand up for ourselves. We must fight for our home."

A man in the front row frowned. "But we've never gone to war. Many of us don't even have beasts with that kind of power."

Yazmin's lips thinned. "We *must* go to war."

She was met with stifled silence. This was taking too long. The shadows flared around me, responding to my impatience. Their war meant nothing to me. I had a job to do, and the burn of the oath wouldn't subside until I took care of it. The people I loved wouldn't be at peace.

"War is inevitable," Yazmin said, voice level. "But the goddess is on our side. She has shown me a way to summon Ocnolog and use his cleansing fire to restore balance to our world."

She turned then, facing the beautiful statue of the goddess and her beast. "Charmers were once revered across Lendria. Powerful and kind beings who welcomed all life with a smile." Snapping back to face the crowd, she scowled. "And then the Wilheimians lied to us. They were greedy and wanted the power our goddess granted us. Ocnolog can right their wrong."

The same man from before dared to speak again. "Crown, that was centuries ago. We have no desire to relive the past for a war that could harm so many of our beasts. And Ocnolog..." His gaze slanted to the giant statue. "If there really is a way to awaken him... He was a danger to all. He cannot be controlled."

Her smile was tight. "You're wrong. I can revive him. I can *tame* him. He will be our protector." She gestured widely to include the entire congregation. "By channeling our collective power, I will bless this ingredient, making him amiable to our cause." A swell of energy followed her words. Invisible, yet tangible. Stunned Charmers looked to one another as the air thickened.

Uncapping the vial in her hand, Yazmin poured my blood into the waiting basin. It swirled down an invisible drain, until the last droplet disappeared, leaving the bowl clean. The energy in the room evaporated with it, and the Charmers went stock-still, eyes wide. Horrified. All the while, Yazmin's symbol continued to darken. The red haze dominating my vision throbbed.

"Wonderful." Yazmin beamed.

"That kind of dark magic *can't* be condoned by the goddess," the brave Charmer said.

"Drastic measures must be taken if we are to protect ourselves from the Wilheimians. They're already moving against us." She placed a heavy hand over her heart. "I've seen what they've done. What they're still doing in their bid to control us."

"That's enough, Yazmin. No more lies." A strong feminine voice rose from the back of the throne room. All eyes turned to the entrance, and a collective gasp rushed through the audience. They pressed against one another, creating an open path that ended with a woman flanked by three assassins and two Charmers.

A woman with rich brown hair like an oak tree. Hazel eyes fiery. Full lips pulled tight in a grimace. She was stunning in her fury, and the sharp rosewood glow around her hand pulsed with palpable energy.

Leena.

Leena. My lips peeled back in a snarl, and I crouched into my heels.

The time to answer the oath's call had come.

THIRTY

LEENA

Startled Charmers gaped at us with mixed expressions of fear and anger. We'd overheard most of Yazmin's speech as we rushed to intercede, and one thing was abundantly clear: she'd painted us as the villains. Unspoken accusations weighed down the room. Some Charmers were clearly injured. Others, crying. I didn't even want to think about how many were no longer with us. As I went to walk down the now-open path, Kost grabbed my wrist and brought me to a halt.

"Something's not right." His gaze scoured the room. "I can sense Noc's presence, but I can't see him anywhere. Be careful." Slowly, he released me and fell into line with Calem and Oz. They covered the entrance to the hall, tension rolling off them in waves. Gaige and Raven had moved to the sides of the room. Symbols glowing from the backs of their hands, they were poised to summon beasts in case Yazmin struck. In case we needed to protect the Charmers. We had already called forth our Asura, and they trailed behind us, arms extended in all directions to keep their shields activated. Quilla looked up at me, her ten white eyes wide and unblinking, and I prayed Yazmin would prove us wrong. That we wouldn't be attacked, and that there'd be no need for my beast's powers.

"Leena," Yazmin called from the head of the room. Her brow twitched. "How nice of you to join us. You as well, Gaige and Raven." She gestured to both of them lingering on the fringe of the crowd. "Back to survey the aftermath of your brutal attack?"

Gaige glowered. "We didn't do that."

"What you did to Kaori. To Tristan. To *Eilan*. How could you?" Hurt and fury made Raven's eyes blaze. "Explain yourself."

Yazmin ignored her, instead turning to the crowd of Charmers. "Do you see how they're trying to poison you against me? I'm the only one who's trying to protect you. I am your *Crown*."

Frenzied murmurs of support rose from the crowd. They had no reason to doubt her. No reason to believe she had lied to them. Memories of my own exile flooded my mind. How I'd begged the Council to listen to me, to see my side of things, but they'd been incapable of doing so. A beast had told them what I'd done, and that beast's words were proof enough.

And a beast would be the only thing that could convince the Charmers now.

Moving down the path toward Yazmin, I channeled my power and opened the beast realm door. Onyx barreled through the opening and landed before me, his hackles already standing on end. He hadn't forgotten what he'd seen in Yazmin's mind. A ferocious yowl ripped through his throat, and he targeted her with a fierce glare.

"Attacking me only proves what I've been saying." Yazmin shook her head, as if she were sorry I'd gone down such a terrible path. She might have been able to convince our people of her innocence with that act, but I knew better.

"No. I'm going to show everyone the truth." I nodded to Onyx, and he ignited his power. Blue wisps streamed from his eyes, and he let out a menacing hiss. Without Gaige's Zavalluna, his flames remained invisible, but his power was still palpable. Just as with Raven, his magic could be felt. It rushed over the room, angry and prickling, and a collective gasp sounded from the Charmers. We didn't have to wait as long this time to know Yazmin was guilty. Onyx had already deemed her unworthy, and now he was sharing that with everyone.

"You are responsible for this. Not us." I reached out and smoothed the hairs along Onyx's neck. He cut off his power, but didn't abandon his rigid stance. "Just tell us why."

For a moment, Yazmin didn't speak. She glanced from Charmer to Charmer, taking in their suspicious glares and whispered words. No one would challenge Onyx's ruling. And she knew it. Yazmin finally cracked. "Because they're killing us!" Hands shaking, she stormed forward a few feet before abruptly coming to a stop.

"Why do you think so many of us have been disappearing on beast hunts lately? We have been for decades, and no one is concerned." She whirled to the audience and pointed an accusatory finger at the crowd. "Your loved ones have gone missing, and you'd rather sit back and avoid conflict than confront the people responsible!"

My brows drew together. "What do you mean?"

"The royal family of Wilheim and their damned Sentinels have been capturing Charmers on beast hunts. Wynn unearthed their secret and told me. I'm sure you remember the trip that changed him."

A dull ringing started in my ears. She couldn't be telling the truth. She *couldn't*. "No."

Gaige echoed my disbelief from the side of the room. "If that's true, then why didn't you tell the Council?"

"We did." Yazmin bared her teeth. "You, all of you, denied our petition for an outright assault. You wanted proof, physical proof, before you would stir. You were always one for politics. Your lack of action sickens me."

"I don't remember any of this," he said.

"Don't believe me?" Yazmin laughed. "Check the logs in the library. It happened. And still you did *nothing*."

Gaige's spine straightened. "That can't be true."

"I will not let our people die out because you refused to act." She turned her sweeping gaze back to the Charmers standing in frozen shock. "Now we must band together to fight against those who would see us crumble. They must pay."

"You're lying." She had to be. I couldn't believe that the people of Wilheim would do such a thing. And yet, I remembered that trip. The one that had changed Wynn. He'd started his taming attempts on humans after that. Was that why? Did he think he could control them? Stop them? Bile soured my tongue. No, Yazmin *was* lying. It was just another ploy for her to gain support from the Charmers.

Yazmin shook her head. "I'm not. It must break your heart to know that Noc and his family are behind the death of your parents. I'll bet he never told you that."

Noc. My *anam-cara.* Capturing people, tormenting them, experimenting on them... It went against everything he stood for. "I don't believe you. Noc would *never* do that."

"We'll see. He's capable of terrible things, this frozen prince of yours."

I made a move to send Onyx after her when a blood-red blade crashed into the invisible shield protecting me and my beasts. Right between my eyes. Mouth open, I stared at it. It gleamed with unnatural power, and the dome around it cracked, splintering outward like fractured glass. Beside me, Quilla let out a strangled grunt. One eye closed. Then another. And another. I whipped my head back to the blade. It was inching closer, slipping through my beast's shield. She crouched low and pressed her hands flat against the floor, trying to pull more power from the earth.

My heart slammed into my throat. *Noc.* Where was he? My gaze roved over the room, scanning face after face, but I couldn't find him. A dark laugh carried through the air, and a chill swept up my spine.

"Noc!"

The laugh sharpened.

I looked over my shoulder and spied my assassins. Kost, Oz, and Calem had crouched low, ready to pounce, but they hadn't moved. If they couldn't see where Noc was hiding, couldn't tear apart his shadows, then maybe he was too far gone.

No.

I flexed my hand, contemplating what beast to call, when the blood dagger wormed further into Quilla's shield. Another eye closed. I backed as far away as I could while still staying safely within her shield.

"Leena!" Oz screamed. Or maybe it was Calem. Kost. All three of them were shouting and rushing toward me.

And then Noc appeared by Yazmin's side, and my heart stilled. He looked at me without seeing me, bloodshot eyes instead targeting the space where his blade met Quilla's protective dome. His fingers twitched, and the knife burrowed deeper.

All of Quilla's remaining eyes slammed shut. Her shield disappeared.

I barely had time to react. Crossing my arms in front of me, I braced for the hit. But it never came. Instead, a harsh scraping, like metal on stone, reverberated through the air. The blade had crashed into a rocky wall with fiery veins of lava. I tossed a quick glance behind me to see Oz frozen with his bronze key in hand. Beside him, Jax roared. His young Laharock wouldn't let anything happen to me. Calem and Kost were next to me seconds later, shadows streaming from their fingers and waiting to whisk me away into the shadow realm.

"I've had enough of this," Yazmin said. I peered around the wall just as she thrust her hand forward, and a ruddy-red light exploded from her symbol. A heady groaning rolled through the throne room. Mist hissed along the floor, covering the area and bringing with it a wet chill. It billowed upward, blanketing the entire throne room from floor to ceiling, and something massive thudded beside her. An outline of a paw with claws that clicked along the stone. A low, rattling growl shook the air. Something more monster than beast had emerged from the realm, and a chuckle sounded from Yazmin's direction.

Somewhere through the fog, Gaige's voice rose above the rest. "Run!"

At once, the Charmers scrambled for the exit in a fit of panic. Raven shouted above their screams, directing them to the open lawns and toward safety. She summoned a number of beasts to help guide them out, and then turned back to face us as the last of the stragglers escaped.

"Go!" I shouted. "Protect them, no matter what!"

She nodded and took off, calling to her beasts and pushing the Charmers as far away from the throne room as she could. And that was a good thing, because the creature looming behind us was more terrifying, more powerful, than all my legendary beasts combined. And with Yazmin commanding it, there was no chance we'd make it out of this alive.

Thirty-One

LEENA

Thrusting my hand outward, I opened the beast realm door and immediately sent Onyx and Quilla home. If I was right about the creature we were facing, they wouldn't stand a chance. None of us would. Burning white eyes targeted us from the thick of the fog. A faint outline began to form. Pinned-back ears and a fox-like head. A lithe, monstrous body. It was larger than a Laharock with the build of a wolf and three massive tails. Paws the size of boulders. Claws the length of our bodies.

"Holy gods." Calem stared slack-mouthed at the beast. Oz and Gaige rushed to join us, and Jax threw up more walls between us and the emerging beast.

Gaige swallowed. "That is an S-Class beast—a Vrees."

My stomach plummeted to the floor. Suspicions confirmed. Some of the fog thinned around its body, revealing the haunting reality of what we faced. Instead of a dense mass and solid form, negative space created cutouts within his white fur, and fog drifted through him like a sieve. That was what made him so difficult to defend against—weapons slid through without leaving a mark. Claws left him unscathed. Only the right kind of magic would work.

Sparking blue electrical currents snapped and crackled to life in his rib cage. They spiderwebbed outward through the fog in a dangerous electrical storm that sent the hairs on the back of my neck skyward.

My mind reeled. A-Class beasts were strong, and the ten legendary felines reigned over them with ease. But this? There were maybe five S-Class beasts in existence, and I knew nothing about them. How to approach them, how to fight them, how to tame them. They were nearly untouchable and existed in an echelon all their own. A tremor of acknowledgment raced through me. Yazmin was powerful. If she could tame a Vrees, then she just might have the power to tame Ocnolog like she claimed.

As we backed toward the courtyard, I refused to drop the creature's unnerving gaze. "What do we do?" My beasts ran through my mind.

Iky—not feasible.

Onyx—fast and powerful, but his fire was mental and not corporeal. Nothing that would scathe the Vrees.

Dominus—fast and also powerful, but again, claws couldn't damage this beast's hide.

"We have to take out Yazmin." Gaige's head swiveled to me. "My legendary feline's power is water, which will only act as a conduit. Maybe—"

Oz suddenly straightened. Inky blades formed between his knuckles, and he shoved me behind him. "Incoming."

Noc appeared on our left and lunged, blade already in hand. I wasn't sure who was more terrifying: him or the Vrees. He aimed right for my throat, but Oz parried him and cracked his fist into Noc's jaw. Blood coated the stone, and he laughed before lunging again. Calem leapt to Oz's aid. With blades of his own, he countered Noc's wild blows. Noc's grin faltered, and he snarled as he tried relentlessly to break through his brothers and get to me.

All thoughts of Yazmin faded. I needed to save him. I needed him to survive.

"Noc!" I reached for him.

Noc appeared before me and raised a long blade. Aiming for my neck, he drove down with a clean sweep, but not before Oz caught up and pushed me back, causing the blade to burry its tip into the stone so hard the floor fractured. "Stay away!"

Calem then crashed into Noc, momentarily pinning him to the ground.

Kost grabbed me before I could move. "Don't even think about it."

Before Oz returned to Calem's side, he glanced at his beast. "No matter what, protect yourself first, understand? Stay out of harm's way, in the clearing away from the Vrees. But if you can..." He indicated to us with a quick nod. "Shield them with your walls. But do *not* go inside. Okay?" Jax let out a throaty warble as he rushed toward the exit where the mist hadn't reached, and Oz took off to help Calem just as Noc threw him into a wall. I wasn't sure Jax's walls could really stop the Vrees's attacks, but at least they'd offer some reprieve in case Noc sent another blood blade flying in my direction.

Panic clawed at my throat. "What do we do?"

Yazmin sauntered forward through the fog. "Time's up."

The static charge that had been building in the room reached a breaking point. The Vrees had been charging up his attack, and now he was poised to strike. A bolt of lightning streaked through the air and cracked into the floor, right where we'd been standing. Kost had yanked me off my feet in record time, along with Gaige. We all landed a few feet away, wreathed in shadows.

Another one of Noc's terrifying blades soared toward me, but Jax was ready. A wall erupted in front of it, protecting me from the attack. Noc let out a wordless shriek before Calem and Oz pulled his focus again.

There were too many attacks to dodge. We barely had time to focus. "Gaige, what beast—"

Again, a swell of electrical energy began to fill the air, signaling the Vrees's attack. The charge surged through me, and Kost's eyes went wide. Snagging both Gaige and me, he yanked us into the world of shadows again just as a violent blue streak of lightning erupted where we'd been standing. We reemerged a few feet away with enough static hanging in the air around us to start a fire.

From the billowing fog at her beast's feet, Yazmin laughed. "What do you think of my Vrees, Leena? I only just acquired him. I'd been tracking him for years, and finally, he showed himself." Her smile turned feral. "Run all you want. Wherever his mist reaches, his lightning can strike."

And it was everywhere. The perfect conductor for the spark angrily brewing inside of his ribs. Swallowing hard, my gaze swiveled back to Noc. He parried left and right, all the while wearing a smile so unnerving that my blood ran cold. Oz's face was a bloodied mess covered in gashes and weeping wounds. Swollen flesh threatened to cover one of his eyes, but he placed a well-planted kick in the square of Noc's chest, and he went flying back.

Calem lunged forward, long gashes trailing his arms and chest, and took Noc's primary focus. Noc dodged Calem's assault and stole a murderous glance my direction. Had the oath finally claimed him? Was he beyond my reach?

No. I would always find a way to reach him. I'd promised.

Gritting my teeth, I turned back to Gaige. "We'll lose if we keep running. I need something to distract the Vrees while I take care of Yazmin."

Another crack of lightning, and we scattered. Gaige's knees

buckled, and he clutched his stomach. From the red blooming along his tunic, it appeared as though his stitches had split. Kost's torn gaze flickered between us and his brothers. Losing. We were losing.

The suffocating mist stretched further, and the wetness of it slicked against me and pressed damp clothing to my skin. If only we could blow it away or evaporate it with heat.

Heat. My eyes flew to Jax. He'd extended his neck fully and was constantly swiveling his head from left to right, searching for threats. He couldn't summon fires, but his mother could. Extending my hand, I channeled my power and the beast door groaned open. Brilliant rosewood light battled against the fog, and Lola emerged. Her gaze first targeted her son, then the Vrees. In the span of a breath, she'd determined him to be the threat and charged. Thick claws scraped against the stone floor, and she stood tall before him. Gleaming red scales rimmed in gold glistened beneath the mist. Pupilless white eyes burned with the intensity of the sun, and she let out a grating war cry that made her headdress of bone spikes tremble.

"Kost." I reached out my hand.

"On it." He gripped my wrist tight and looped Gaige's shoulder over his, and then enveloped us in shadows. Safely out of Lola's radius, we reappeared on the lip of the entrance to the throne room where grass met stone.

Our disappearance was the only signal Lola needed. The moment we were out of range, she kicked on her power and cooked the air. A heat wave rushed outward, and the mist began to evaporate. The stone beneath her feet glowed a fiery orange, and she inched forward. The Vrees shook its massive head and bared its teeth. Yazmin leapt back toward the dais, avoiding the skin-melting heat of the Laharock.

More mist sizzled, and the Vrees stepped back. Lightning sparked in his core, and he targeted Lola with terrifying certainty.

With him distracted, I could take out Yazmin. And I had just the hunter to do it. One Yazmin hadn't counted on me taming.

Thrusting my hand forward, rosewood light exploded from my symbol, and I summoned Reine. She bled into life in a smearing of nightly colors. Hackles already on end and endless eyes locked on the Vrees, she positioned herself in front of me.

"Not that." I pointed toward Yazmin. "Her. Go."

Part of me hated to do it. Hated to order a beast to kill like I'd done with Onyx. But this was so different from before. I'd been under Wynn's control, and in a sense, so had the Council. They had mowed down assassins under the false pretense of defending their home, thanks to him and Yazmin. My actions now would protect the lives of those I loved. Even of those I didn't know, like the Charmers hiding in their homes and the beasts they held dear.

I would fight for them. Just like Reine had fought for me against the Sentinels. She hadn't needed to—I'd yet to tame her. But she'd chosen me. Deemed me part of her family and acted to save my life.

Realization settled deep within me. Reine wasn't so different from us Charmers. She'd lived a life on her own, never confronting threats, only defending her territory. And yet... When something, *someone*, she cared for was jeopardized...she'd struck first. And Yazmin's decision to openly attack Charmers who might have threatened her plan? The people she was supposed to love? Protect? That was an egregious wrong I knew we had to right.

As if feeling my conviction, Reine heeded my command and slipped out of existence.

Behind us, Calem let out a gut-wrenching scream. The three of us turned in time to see Noc sink one of his blood blades beneath his collarbone.

He turned away, leaving his blade lodged in Calem. "Don't attack me anymore."

Calem's body strained in anger as he fought against Noc's blood command. His eyes flashed mercury, and scales raced over his skin, forming and disappearing, as if the beast inside him was fighting against Noc's compulsion. Fingers twitching, Calem reached after his brother. Talons formed and receded. His body shuddered, but he couldn't will himself any further. Oz howled and lunged forward, slamming his fist into Noc's temple so hard *I* almost saw stars. He stumbled forward and crashed to the ground. Blood leaked from his ears, but when he turned to look up at Oz, there was nothing but pure murder in his eyes.

"Go." I shoved Kost. "Go!"

He was gone in an instant, barely reaching the clearing in time to counter Noc's blood blade with a glittering black rapier. A moment later and that disastrous red blade would've found its home in Oz's heart.

A familiar swell of static energy brewed around Gaige and me. Bringing my gaze back to the Vrees, my heart dropped to the floor. Lola had evaporated most of the mist, but there were still two threads snaking from the beast's frame—one pooling directly before Lola and the other encircling Yazmin.

"No!"

My terror-filled warning wasn't fast enough.

Two things happened at once. Reine appeared and lunged toward Yazmin. And Lola took a small but significant step forward. And then the lightning god himself must have manifested, because a rain of bolts showered from the ceiling, right where the mist had formed. Reine crashed into a wall of electricity and let out a heart-wrenching yowl that ended in a soft gurgle as she staggered to the ground. Her chest rose and fell in erratic patterns, and her jaw cracked open wide. Wild eyes darted without focus.

Agony ripped through me. Channeling my power, I wrenched

open the beast realm door and sent her back to safety. The realm would provide, but there was no way of knowing if I'd sent her back in time. If her heart had already stopped for good.

My gaze snapped back to Lola. Her gleaming red scales had lost their luster, but they'd insulated her enough to keep her heart beating. Knees buckled to the earth, she wheezed in a heap and shuddered beneath the Vrees.

Yazmin's laugh was more horrifying than the Vrees's stare. "Nice try, Leena."

Behind me, a guttural cry escaped from Oz. I whipped my head around for a moment to find him crumpled on the floor, and Noc locked in battle with a wounded Kost. Calem's form still trembled, but he'd moved an inch. Somehow. His feral stare was locked on his brothers.

Calem. Oz. Kost. My beasts. The threats were too much. I snapped my attention back to Lola, and willed the door to the beast realm to remain open. "Lola, go back. Now!" Concern and pain and fear cleaved through me. But Lola refused to budge. She swiveled her head in my direction, eyes soft and fiery at the same time, and a soft call rattled from the back of her throat.

She would stay and fight. For me.

"No!" I'd already jeopardized Reine. If something were to happen to Lola too, I wouldn't be able to live with myself. Hadn't I promised Onyx that I would protect my beasts, *all* beasts, with everything I had? If I let Lola fall here, I'd be going back on my word.

I'd no longer be worthy. In his eyes, in all my beasts' eyes, in *my* eyes.

Mist surged from beneath the Vrees's feet and curled around Lola. This time, he would succeed. He'd blanketed her with enough fog to suffocate her, and she extended her neck so she could still meet my tear-streaked gaze. After a moment, she looked past me to her son. Jax had taken several steps forward, desperate wails echoing through the room. Lola responded with a soft groan that sounded too much like a goodbye.

The Vrees hesitated. Only for a fraction, but I caught it. A minute wince at the obvious display of love.

Yazmin bellowed from the dais. "End it!"

"I'll distract Yazmin. Save your Laharock!" Gaige took off, extending his hand outward and summoning a B-Class monkey-like beast called a Boxismus. Incredibly nimble and fast, it would be able to safely maneuver through the mist without being struck by lightning. For the most part it was covered in orange fur, but silver plates protruded from its shoulders and knees and along the backs of its hands and knuckles. They were volatile creatures that often fought for sport.

And while a punch would do little to a Vrees, it would certainly knock the wind out of Yazmin.

Gaige sent it after Yazmin, and the beast screeched at the top of its lungs as it barreled toward her. She shouted and tried to protect herself, but the creature landed on her chest and began wailing hits left and right.

I turned back to the Vrees. The air was swollen with static energy waiting to be ignited. But in that moment, all I could think of was the beast's hesitation. It reminded me of Wynn's Scorpex when it'd battled us on the sand dunes outside of Ortega Key. Doing the bidding of a master it didn't believe in.

And suddenly I was running. Right into the thick of the mist. A flurry of shouts erupted from my comrades. Gaige, Kost, Ozias, Calem. All of them. I charged right into the storm, and every hair on my body stood on end. Even my locks lifted upward as I came to a stop between Lola and the Vrees.

He stared down at me as blue sparks surged from his rib cage and flickered in the space around us. A sharp stinging prickled against my skin like I'd been caught in the tentacles of a jellyfish. I could take it. I would take it to save Lola. To save the Vrees.

My voice cracked. "You don't have to do this." A soft, rosewood glow pulsed from my body. The Vrees's maw peeled back to reveal rows of teeth. A guttural warning growl simmered from somewhere in his cutout form. More lighting flickered around us, and I winced.

From somewhere, I heard the groan of the beast realm door opening, followed by a vicious snarl. Yazmin's voice registered, commanding something to attack, and then Gaige was screaming at his beast to retreat.

Focus. Extending my hand forward, I offered the Vrees my palm. "You don't have to hurt anyone. Especially not Lola." I tilted my head toward my beast. The Vrees lowered his snout, dwarfing my body and showering my hand in a fine spray of heated mist from his nose. Blue currents raced down the space around my arm. Waiting. Testing. Ready to strike at a moment's notice.

A blip of doubt surfaced in my brain. I'd done this with a Scorpex. A *Scorpex.* A B-Class beast. This beast was S-Class. Why did I think this would work? Because he'd hesitated? He could've just been calculating. Shoring up power before making his next move. I knew nothing about this creature or what limitations and talents it had.

Slowly, I touched my chin to my shoulder and picked Noc out from the snarling mess of shadows that made up him and Kost.

"I'm so sorry. I promised I'd save you," I whispered aloud. Tears crashed down my cheeks. Noc's eyes were wild and lost, and he fought against his brother, his oldest friend, without an ounce of recognition in his gaze. I'd never get to see him again. I'd never get to truly experience a life with him like I'd always wanted.

And yet... I brought my gaze back to Lola. Back to my beast. Placing my hand against her chest, I channeled everything I had into my symbol. Rosewood light fractured from the place where her scales met my fingers, and I heard the door open. She tried to hunker down, to stand by my side through the end, but I wouldn't let her die for me. My muscles shook as my will battled against hers, and she let out a low whine.

Again, the Vrees targeted her with a curious stare. The swell of electricity receded a fraction.

Racked with fatigue and drowning in mist, I struggled to breathe. But Lola wouldn't budge. A lone tear dropped from my chin into the plume of fog surrounding me. A ripple of blue radiated outward, and the Vrees's ears flicked up. Lola lowered her head toward mine and rubbed her nose along my cheek.

The Vrees leaned forward and sniffed Lola, just behind her headdress. My whole body froze. If ever there was an opening to try to break his bond, it was now. Maybe his concern for Lola's life would be enough. The rosewood light around me radiated with renewed strength, and I brought my hand down and rested my palm on the Vrees's snout. White eyes locked with mine.

"You don't have to do this."

Somewhere behind me, Kost screamed, and then there was a loud thump, like that of a body falling to the floor. I didn't have the chance to turn and investigate. The Vrees held all my attention.

He huffed. Static built again until I could hear nothing but the crackle of electricity. I could just barely decipher my name shouted at the top of Kost's lungs. How he had the ability to break away long enough from Noc to search for me was a mystery I didn't have time to investigate. The Vrees studied me without moving, sending more waves of electricity racing down my arms. They singed my hair and left trailing welts, but I held strong. I waited. I believed.

Yazmin had only just tamed the Vrees. She was using dark magic and forcing him to kill another beast. A creature so powerful, so revered even by the goddess herself, wouldn't want to be in tamed by someone like our Crown.

Then the mist around us suddenly evaporated, and a gentle warmth rushed through me. All threats of electricity disappeared. A soft humming filled the Vrees's throat, and suddenly he began to diminish in size. He stopped when his back reached my midthigh, and the electric ball inside his rib cage pulsed like a heartbeat. When he glanced up at me, his tongue lolled out the side of his mouth. Bond broken.

And a new one forged in its place.

The beast realm groaned open, and the Vrees rubbed his head along the back of my knees before disappearing in a flux of rosewood light. Finally deeming it safe, Lola followed him into the realm to heal.

Yazmin's lips were parted, and she stared at me with unveiled rage. "How?" Behind her, Gaige lay motionless in a heap, beast gone—presumably back to the realm—and I stilled. I stared at him until I glimpsed the shaky rise and fall of his chest. Alive. I let out a tight breath.

Glowering, I turned on Yazmin. I didn't know exactly how I broke the Vrees's bond with her, but the reason shone clear. "Not all beasts want to kill."

She snarled, and her gaze flicked behind me before returning to my face. "No matter. Your time is up."

I made a move toward her, but Noc appeared before me in a vortex of shadows. He caught me by the throat and lifted me into the air. My hands jerked to his wrists, fingers digging into cold flesh. He stared without seeing me. The whites of his eyes had shifted to an enflamed red, heightening the ice-blue of his irises.

My *anam-cara* was gone.

Just like he had outside of Wilheim, he locked us away in an unbreakable, snarling mess of shadows. Somewhere in the distance, I could hear the muffled shouts of Calem, Oz, and Kost. They'd never be able to break through, but maybe I could. Channeling power into my hand, I tried to douse the space in rosewood light. To break the spell that held my love captive, just like before. But the man standing before me, the one with his fingers wrapped tight around my neck, wasn't my lover anymore. He was someone else entirely. And the air in my lungs was rapidly decreasing, and there wasn't enough time to try to bring Noc back.

I was going to break my promise after all.

My extremities started to tingle, and numbness tracked into my arms and legs. My rosewood light went out like a flame. I vaguely registered that I was kicking him, and that each swing was less and less effective. The heaviness of it all was suffocating. Darkness flared in my peripheral vision, and my hands went slack. Painful pressure around my neck squeezed the last bit of air from my lungs, and I sputtered.

This wasn't how it was supposed to end. Thick and absolute darkness, so unlike the shadows he commanded, burned around me until he was the only thing left in view. Until it was just his shock-white hair and then nothing but his eyes. My heart gave one last pitiful thud.

And then everything went silent.

THIRTY-TWO

NOC

The red haze that had dominated my senses for so long lifted just as a surge of heat stung my inner wrist. Gone. The oath was absolved in an instant. I glanced down at my wrist in time to see the black scythe burn away like a scrap of parchment over a flame. As I did that, something else came into focus: a lifeless body at my feet. Slowly, I blinked. And then realization slammed into me with so much force that I lost my breath.

Leena. *Leena.*

Her unmoving form dominated my vision, and the world around me blurred. I'd killed my *anam-cara*. Time slowed. Memories collided in a riotous mess. Amira and Bowen's twisted words. Yazmin's control. How I'd battled my brothers just for the chance to murder my love. And then succeeded. A splintering scream ruptured from my chest, and I went to cradle her head.

I never made it. Calem crashed into me, a snarling mess of scales and elongated fangs. His beast had broken through my compulsion. Half-feral, half-human, he tossed me to the side with otherworldly strength and then dropped on all fours defensively over Leena. In the flurry of movement, one of his paws had swiped her body. Blood flowed outward from the deep gashes, spreading across the stone floor and momentarily pulling his attention. Confusion raced through his pupil-less, mercury eyes. Then, horror. He recoiled, and the action forced his scales to recede.

"Oh gods," he croaked. He scooted away, eyes locked on the blood creeping across the floor. Ozias and Kost rushed over, their forms trembling.

"Give me some room," Kost commanded, dropping to his knees. A thick gash ran the length of his jaw. Disheveled hair was flecked with blood. He straddled Leena and began pressing his hands rhythmically against her chest. Her head jostled, and unseeing hazel eyes tore through my soul.

I scrambled toward them, but Ozias intervened, caging me in his arms. "Let him work!"

Rational thought escaped me. All I could do was scream and snarl and tear against Ozias's grip. He never wavered, and I was forced to simply look at what I'd done. At her lifeless face. Parted lips unmoving. Pink flush quickly fading from her cheeks. Limp hands. I'd murdered the love of my life. Again.

Raw pain scoured through me and set fire to everything I knew. She couldn't be dead. I couldn't live without her.

"If it's my time, then you have to let me go."

"No!" I yelled at the memory of her words. It wasn't her time. I wouldn't let her go. Not now. Not ever.

Calem was sobbing as Kost worked, each one of his compressions forcing more blood out of her wound. Kost tried to stop most of it by pressing his thigh against the laceration, but there was only so much he could do. His compressions were timed but forceful, as if he could barely restrain the raging emotions inside him. He paused to tilt her head back and open her airway. Pressing his lips to hers, he breathed life into her lungs. And I willed her body to accept it. To freely take what he was offering so she could breathe on her own again. But after two breaths her lungs still weren't moving on their own, and Kost was back to compressing.

"Noc." Kost spoke as he worked. "Will you raise her?"

Ozias grunted, and wet tears stung my shoulder from where his cheek rested. Goodbye wasn't an option. It shouldn't have been. And yet, that's what she would've wanted. She'd made that clear. To rob her of that choice... I broke free of Ozias's arms and slid to the floor by her head. My hands fluttered around her temples.

"Please," Calem begged from a few feet away. "Raise her. If she dies... I can't..." He choked back a sob. With shaky hands, he fished his bronze key out of his pocket and summoned Effie. "Can you help?"

She flew over Leena, dusting both her and Kost in a shimmery coat of magic, but nothing changed. Leena didn't move, and Kost kept working. Effie landed back beside Calem with a sorrowful coo, and he crumpled.

What do I do? All my life I'd been selfish. I'd been selfish as a prince, and it had cost Amira her life. I'd been selfish with Bowen, and I'd been selfish with my guild. With the Gyss's wish. And now...

Again, Kost breathed for her. One breath. Two. Nothing.

Oz stared at her, eyes glassy. "I say we raise her. Let her be mad at us. I'll take that over this."

"Noc." Kost's voice was pleading. He kept compressing, but his hands were starting to shake. "What do we do?"

Not we. Me. My fault. My decision.

Leena's somber voice echoed through my mind. *"It's not just my life, it's my beasts'. If those shadows permeate every facet of your life, what would they do to the realm?"* I didn't know. Couldn't possibly know. But if I condemned her beloved beasts to a world of darkness, if she couldn't see them anymore...she'd never forgive me.

When Kost went to breathe for her, I stopped him. "Let me." I wasn't ready to give up yet. Because once we stopped compressions, once we stopped breathing for her... It wasn't the way I wanted her to go, but I wouldn't strip her of her choice. No matter how much it'd hurt all of us.

"I'm so sorry," I whispered against her lips before forcing breath into her lungs. I prayed she had enough fight left in her to grab it tight, but if she didn't... Tears slid down my chin and dropped against her. I'd have to let her go.

Resting my forehead against hers, I closed my eyes and prayed the gods would forgive me, because I knew I'd never forgive myself. She was so *still*. She'd filled me—all of us—with so much life. And now...nothing. I so desperately wished I could feel her breath against me. Hear the beat of her heart. But the pained sobs of Oz and Calem drowned out everything.

And then a startled noise escaped the back of Kost's throat.

Shaky fingers traced the scar along my cheek. "Noc." My eyes flew open and there she was. Breathing ragged and uneven, but there was faint color to her cheeks. A sheen across her hazel gaze.

Pure, unfiltered joy surged through me as a primal shout ripped through my lungs. Alive. She was *alive*.

"Leena." I wrapped her fingers in my hands and pressed a shaking kiss to her knuckles. "Thank the gods. I thought I'd lost you."

"Not...yet." She coughed and then winced, a weak hand fluttering to her side. Kost had moved off her, leaving her wound exposed. He stripped his tattered shirt off in an instant and pressed it tight against her. A sharp hiss escaped her lips.

That sound made me recoil. I'd done so much damage. If not for me, she wouldn't have died. Calem wouldn't have gone half-feral, accidentally ripping into her flesh. He was still cringing just out of reach, his head in his hands.

So much damage.

"Hey." Her words were raspy. Damning. Still, I met her gaze. "Don't do that."

"Do what?"

She reached for me, and I hesitated. Her fingers twitched. "That." Slowly, strength came back to her voice, and she cleared her throat. "Don't pull away from me."

Something in me broke. "Leena, what I did—"

"Was out of your control." She gestured for Kost to help her sit, and he obliged. She winced, pressing her hand on top of his to hold the fabric against her wound. I moved to help and let her lean against me. A tired hum reverberated from her rib cage against my chest. Oz sidled in on her free side and held her hand. She gave him a tight squeeze and smile.

After a steady breath, she looked up at me. "It was the oath, Noc. You weren't in control, just as I wasn't when Wynn charmed me." She tilted her head to the side, rounding her gaze on Calem and Effie. He'd dropped his hands, but his eyes were locked on the bloody tunic covering her wound. "Calem? What's wrong?"

Calem swallowed thickly. "I did that to you."

Leena glanced between him and her wound. "Not on purpose."

"No, definitely not." He raked his hands through his hair. "I...I was trying to protect you. But I lost control."

Leena managed to roll her eyes. "So just like Noc. Like me. Calem, it's not your fault. I'll be okay."

"Are you sure?" His watery gaze mirrored everything I felt inside, and I snuck a hand around Leena's waist and held her tight.

"Yes. If you start blaming yourself for this, you're no better than I was after you died." Slowly, she rounded her gaze on me. "Same goes for you."

I nodded, unable to speak. She may have already forgiven me, but I hadn't forgotten what it felt like to hold her suspended above the earth. To see her crumbled at my feet because I'd squeezed the life from her lungs. Suppressing a shiver, I placed a chaste kiss against the crown of her head.

She let out a content sigh. "Now come here, Calem." Her voice was surprisingly stern, and he finally caved, inching toward us. "You're my family. All of you. I would go through all of this again just to make sure you were safe."

Kost grabbed Calem's hand and forced him to hold the tunic in place. "Don't move." Rooting through the fabric, he found his bronze key and opened the beast realm door, allowing Felicks to come rushing out. Effie followed her master to Leena's side as he peeled away the shirt, exposing three long gashes down her ribs. Without further prompting, Felicks went to work, licking her wounds. Slowly, Leena's skin began to reseal, and her eyes fluttered open. Her gaze was stronger. More vibrant.

Oz let out a weak chuckle before signaling to Jax, who'd been lingering on the edge of hall since Kost had started compressions. "He can't offer much in the way of healing, but he'll stand by you just the same."

Leena looked up at the young Laharock and smiled. "He did more than his share of protecting today."

My heart throbbed at the sight of my brothers and their beasts. Of my *family*. Still weak from blood loss, Leena continued to lean into me with her full weight. My fingers dug deeper into her hip. I'd nearly lost her. An unexpected groaning sounded, and the beast realm door opened. Winnow appeared beside me, her wild hair dotted with white flowers and yellow eyes full of emotion.

"Winnow? What are you doing here?" I asked, opening my hand to her.

She floated over my palm and looked up at me. *I'm here for you, Noc.*

I blinked, and then a sense of love, of belonging, bloomed in my chest. My beast had come without me calling to offer *me* comfort, in spite of everything I'd done. My throat tightened. Perhaps, with a family like this, I'd be able to find forgiveness sooner than I thought.

A weak cough sounded from somewhere behind me, and I jolted in place. My head snapped in the direction of the thrones. Gaige stood with his weight mostly on one foot and bearing wounds of his own, though they appeared shallow. Leena's face blanched, and she moved to stand but Kost beat her to his feet.

"Are you all right?" His stare roved over Gaige's frame, cataloging injuries.

Gaige weakly waved him off. "I'll survive. Yazmin is gone. She must have escaped during the commotion."

"We'll find her. I'm just glad you're okay. If not for you, I'm not sure I would've been able to tame the Vrees." Leena tried again to stand, so I placed Winnow on my shoulder and helped her to her feet. She braced herself against my arm. Calem and Oz stood, their worried stares bouncing between Leena and Gaige.

"Yeah." He looked around us at the wreckage that our battle had caused. Broken slabs of stone. Smeared streaks of blood. Singed spots where lightning had struck. The throne room had lost its luster. Gaige shook his head. "I can't believe she did this."

"We'll fix it." Leena's voice was strong. Confident. "Yazmin is fighting for the wrong reasons. But us? We'll defend our home, all our homes"—she gave a pointed look at each one of my brothers before ending with me—"with our dying breaths. And that's how we'll defeat her."

We. Us. My throat tightened. I'd done so much *wrong*. And yet she still wanted me by her side. My fingers tensed against her hip, and she raised a careful brow. Then, placed a soft kiss on my cheek.

"I don't know what you're thinking, but if it's anything bad or self-loathing, then quit it."

"Leena…"

"I'm serious." She shook her head once. "We're in this together. Always."

I wasn't sure I was ready to forgive myself for what I'd done, but looking into her eyes, feeling the depth of her love, it was enough to soothe my nerves for the time being. It was all I'd ever need.

"Before we start worrying about Yazmin's plans, you two need some rest." Kost moved to Gaige's side and placed a tentative hand on his shoulder. Shock raced through Gaige's expression, but he schooled it away and leaned into his touch.

Leena's smile was brilliant. "That sounds like a plan."

And as one, our family headed for one of the exits leading to the keep where healers could tend to our wounds and give Leena and Gaige the rest they deserved.

THIRTY-THREE

LEENA

After being attended to by a healer and given a draft of remcura, I'd been whisked away to a room in the keep. The healing potion worked wonders, but also thrust me into a deep and restful sleep. Now, several hours later, I awoke, body stiff and aching. A bandage had been strapped to my side with heavy amounts of salve to help reduce the appearance of scars. Rubbing my eyes with the backs of my hands, I peered over the room. Candles were lit, casting the ivory floor in a buttery glow. Windows took up the far wall, but the curtains were pulled close, blocking out the night. I was about to get up when the door opened and Noc stepped through the threshold.

I smiled at the sight of my *anam-cara*. "Hey."

"Hey." He ran a tired hand through his hair. "How are you feeling?"

"Better now that you're here." I patted the space beside me on the bed. "Come join me."

He crossed the room slowly, then sank onto the edge of the bed. I reached over and stole his hands, threading his fingers with mine. "How are things out there?"

"Gaige and Raven are picking up the pieces. Everyone is pretty shaken up by Yazmin's actions. No one suspected their Crown could do something like this. The remaining Council members will meet tomorrow in front of all Charmers, but for now, they said to rest." Noc stared off into nothing for a moment before turning back to me. "Any permanent damage to your side?"

"Nope. Between Felicks's saliva and the salve, I should be good to go. Maybe a faint scar." I shrugged. At this point, a blemish along my ribs was the least of my worries.

He dropped his gaze. "Ah."

"Noc, don't start with that again." I squeezed his hands tight. "Please, don't pull away."

"Twice now, Leena."

"What?"

He looked up at me, pain riddling his gaze. "Twice we've been used as weapons against each other. First you, then me."

A rock formed in my throat. "Yeah." I didn't know what to say. How to respond. I remembered what it had been like to command Onyx to kill him. I couldn't imagine what it would've been like to actually see him do it. Noc, on the other hand... A cool shiver raced over my skin.

Noc shook his head. "If I lose you again..."

"You won't." I scooted closer to him.

"But I could." He turned, cupping the side of my face with his hand. "People are after us, Leena. And they'll use whatever they can to break us. I'd do anything to keep you safe."

"Me too." My voice was hushed.

"And that's my point." His fingers trailed over my jaw. "We're each other's greatest weakness. I'm the Frozen Prince of Wilheim. You openly defied Yazmin. Between her and Varek, we're facing some powerful enemies."

"Then we'll fight them together, just like we always have." I placed my hands on Noc's chest and gripped his tunic. "Not just you and me, but Cruor and Hireath." The truth of that statement settled deep in me. I didn't know if I could convince the Charmers to go along with it, but I'd try. Both of these places were my home, and they both needed protecting. If we joined forces and stood together as one, then maybe we had a chance.

Noc stilled. "That's a dangerous thing to say. I don't know what Varek is planning, and I won't jeopardize your people like that."

"They're not just my people, Noc. They're *our* people." I pressed my forehead to his and willed him to understand. "Our family is full of both Charmers and assassins. And they all need protecting. The Charmers know what Yazmin is capable of now, and we've always known about the threat Wilheim possessed. Joining forces, making a stand—it's the right thing to do. It's the only way we'll survive. Together."

For a moment, neither of us spoke. My words hung in the air around us. As much as I believed them to be true, if Noc didn't agree, if half of my family refused to stand beside me... Finally, he pinned my chin between his fingers and forced me to meet his gaze. I saw nothing but love in his ice-blue eyes.

"Okay, Leena. I can't promise it will be easy. There might be a war, and I know what that means to Charmers."

"Beasts protect their own. It's high time we did too." I pressed my lips to his and wrapped my arms around his neck. He groaned, parting his lips for me. Our tongues met and my heart skipped a beat. His hand roamed down my side, pausing when he traced over the bandage across my ribs.

Gently, he pulled back. "Let's get some sleep. Tomorrow, we can talk to the others about this."

"Okay." I shimmied beneath the sheets and waited as he stood, tossing his shirt and pants to the floor. He joined me in bed and wrapped me in his arms. I scooted my butt against him, and he chuckled.

"Leena?" he asked, breath skating over my ear.

"Yeah?"

"I love you."

My whole body warmed. "I love you too. I'm so glad to have you back. Promise me you won't disappear again."

Angling his head down, he planted a gentle kiss on my shoulder. "I promise, Leena Edenfrell, I will never leave you again."

And that was an oath I'd always hold him to.

———◆———

Early morning light streamed through the windows and gently nudged me from sleep. If I had moved in the night, my body didn't show it. Noc's arm was still draped over me, and his other stretched beneath my head even though his fingers must've been pins and needles.

Rotating slowly so as not to disturb him, I faced him. My breathing slowed. I still hadn't gotten the opportunity to appreciate his new appearance. With a light finger, I toyed with a lock of white hair. He opened his eyes, revealing those ice-blue irises that made my heart skip a beat. Magnificent.

"Morning." The sleepy rasp of his voice stirred want low in my belly.

I scooted closer and brushed my nose against his. "How did you sleep?"

With a sigh, he wrapped his arms tighter around me. "Not great. I can barely feel my hand."

"You should've moved me."

He chuckled. "You looked so peaceful. I didn't want to wake you."

"Silly." I traced the length of his jaw before allowing my hand to wander down his chest. Hard grooves and ridges met my fingers, and a delicious shiver rippled through me.

Noc caught my hand with his. "You've only just recovered—"

"I'm *fine*." I sat up in bed and pulled off the formless shirt I'd been sleeping in. Then, I wrenched the bandage from my side and tossed it to the floor. Noc eyed the yellowing spread of a bruise across my skin. One that should've been violet, but thanks to the salve was already close to healing. He pushed away from me, as if the sight wrecked him.

"I don't want to hurt you."

I rolled my eyes. "Since when has sex ever hurt me?"

He shook his head. "You don't understand, Leena. I *killed* you. I can't jeopardize your health. No matter how badly I want you."

"Stop blaming yourself." Placing my hands over his, I willed him to hear the truth in my words. "You are not going to hurt me. I am safe, I am healthy, and I love you. I will always love you. And just like you put me back together after Wynn, I will put you back together now."

Uncertain eyes met mine, and a single tear threatened to spill over onto his cheek. I brushed it away before it could dare mar his expression. He sighed and turned his face so he could kiss my fingers. "You're too good for me."

"Not in the slightest." I entrenched both hands in his hair and tugged. "We almost lost each other yesterday, but we can be together now."

For the first time since I'd gotten him back, a slight smile pulled at his lips. Still tense, but not as pained. "Promise me you'll tell me to stop if I hurt you."

"I will. Now, would you kiss me already?"

Hunger devoured my other senses as he finally slanted his

lips across mine. His hands traveled the length of my back, and his fingers teased the curves of my waist. I tilted my head back in a heady moan.

"Gods." I mumbled. Raking my nails down his back, I remembered what I wanted when I'd first seen his new identity revealed. Bare and spread out beneath me. He nipped at my neck, and I sucked in a breath before pulling him back. "Lie back. Now."

He complied with nothing more than a raised brow. Yanking the sheets back, I reveled in the sight of him. Hungry to touch, to reaffirm our connection, I dragged my fingers down his body. Memorized every groove and the hard muscles of his stomach. I wanted nothing more than to be with him completely, but I took my time. Stroking the length of his thighs. Appreciating the strenuous muscles of his legs.

His fingers dug into my hips. "You'll be my undoing."

"I can live with that." I stopped teasing then, allowing us to come together and relish in the feel of each other. We traded moans and breaths, a secret language all our own. We'd been through so much, and yet we were still here. Together.

He sat up and caged me in his arms, kissing me so thoroughly my lips bruised. And we tumbled back to the sheets together, a mess of quiet giggles and wanton sighs.

His lips laved my neck. Peppered sweet fire along my collarbone. Wrenched pure ecstasy from my skin. He had the ability to make me feel everything and nothing but him all at once, and it was a pure state of euphoria I never wanted to leave. Our joined bodies, moving together in perfect unison, was the only connection I needed.

"I love you." His whispered words were full of raw emotion, and my eyes burned.

"I love you too."

He smiled—a devilish, masculine thing—and then kissed me with enough ferocity that I felt every emotion. Every lingering tendril of doubt and fear and guilt. They eked out of him and I chased them down. Showered them with love. Praised us both for going through such hardships just so we could find ourselves together again.

A flicker of pain, of uncertainty, raced through his eyes. Cupping his face with one hand, I guided his lips to mine in a tender kiss. We would make it through this. Together.

We came undone, foreheads pressed together and eyes conveying emotions too strong for words. All we did was stare at each other. At the beauty we always found in this undeniable connection. Whatever tore us apart, we'd always find a way to put each other back together. It was an unspoken promise between us, but stronger than any vow I'd ever taken in my life.

Finally, he pulled away and the rush of icy air nipped at my skin. He covered me in blankets and then snuggled close, draping a gentle hand over my stomach.

Warmth bloomed at his touch, and I sighed. "See? I'm fine."

"Good." His voice was low, but his fingers moved against my skin in a soothing, circular fashion. "I don't know what I would've done had I truly lost you." Noc wrapped me tight against him and nuzzled the top of my head.

"But you didn't, so there's no need to think of that."

"Yeah." He didn't seem entirely convinced. And if needed, I was willing to spend all day in bed convincing him otherwise. But my stomach growled, and the thought of food had me pulling the covers back. Noc laughed, slipping out of bed to dress. "C'mon. Let's eat."

I grinned. "Sounds good to me."

———◆———

Located on the ground floor of the castle, the dining hall was large enough to house all of the Council and attendants who worked in the keep. Wooden plank tables with heavy pedestal benches were centered beneath dangling chandeliers. Polished rafters held up a gabled roof, and large marble archways made it easy for Charmers to spill out onto the surrounding lawns. A table weighted with food stretched along the back wall, and we stopped there first to fill our plates.

Hushed whispers and heavy glances followed us through the line. Noc inched closer to me and rested a protective hand on my waist.

"They're just frightened." I gave his hand a squeeze and turned to the hall. Heads immediately dropped down, and they returned to their own private conversations. My gaze found a table at the back with a familiar group of people I was eager to see. "Over here."

Gaige had an array of books spread out before him, as well as loose scraps of parchment with ancient script etched in ink that resembled blood. Kost sat across from him with a book of his own and a steaming cup of coffee. Beside him, Oz and Calem were in a heated debate about pancakes versus waffles, and Calem was waving a fork around with a flaky, syrup-drenched square for effect.

Setting my plate next to Gaige, I eased onto the bench. "Hey, guys."

"How are you feeling?" Ozias asked.

Calem spoke over him through a mouthful of food. "Should you be moving yet?"

"Easy." Noc silenced them with a look as he sidled in beside me. "She'll never be able to answer you all at once."

"It's all right. I'm fine, guys. I promise."

Calem studied me with remorseful eyes. "Are you sure?"

"Calem, you stop right there." I picked up my fork and wielded it his direction. "Don't you dare do what I did. Don't blame yourself for this." How long had it taken me to forgive myself for ordering

Onyx to attack? For taking his life? I couldn't let himself carry that same guilt when he'd been the one who'd worked tirelessly to save me.

He grimaced, but didn't back down. "I hurt you."

"And Onyx killed you," I exclaimed, exasperated. "We've got a funny way of showing how much we care for each other, don't we?" Oz pressed his lips into a thin line to bite back a smile, and even Kost snorted into his coffee.

Noc only sighed. "You won't win this one, Calem. I didn't, and we all know I did far worse than you."

"Hey, we've been over this." I rounded on him, and he held up his hands in defeat before placing one on my thigh and giving me a tender squeeze.

"Fine." Calem relaxed a fraction, not totally convinced. "I'm glad you're okay."

"Me too." I forked a massive amount of eggs into my mouth. And moaned. Partially because it was that damn good, and partially because I knew it would get a rise out of Calem. I was right.

He raised a careful brow. "You need to eat more often. I only sound like that after...you know. Noc, are you sure you're doing your job right?"

I choked on my food and Noc rolled his eyes. Handing me a glass of water, he stroked a loving hand down my back. "Positive."

"I'll second that." I set the glass down and went back to my food, stealing a bite of buttered sourdough toast.

Calem laughed, drawing a few eyes from eavesdropping Charmers throughout the dining hall. Oz shook his head and went back to his pancakes, but his grin was light. Easy. Even Kost seemed relieved, and he offered me a timid smile. Just the faintest acknowledgments.

It warmed my heart entirely.

Gaige set his book down and turned toward me. "Not to bombard you with information so quickly..." His voice trailed off when his gaze darted over my head. Turning, I spied Noc's frigid stare. I batted him in the chest.

"Don't scowl. Let him tell me."

His gaze flickered down and back up again. "Fine."

I shoved another round of eggs into my mouth and turned back to Gaige. He gripped the back of his neck, but relented. "I found some disturbing tomes and spells in Yazmin's room."

My back straightened. "Go on."

"They're coded, but not beyond deciphering." He toyed with a piece of parchment that was full of scratched-out words and numerals, as if he'd already been hard at work. "It will take time, but I have a feeling these hold the answers we're looking for."

Noc's brow furrowed, and he nudged away his plate of untouched food. "Like?"

"Like why she went to all the trouble of sending you to Oslo's Ruins and Silvis's Ruins only to hope you'd fall prey to a Nix Ikari when she could've easily killed you both with a beast in her arsenal." He gave a sheepish shrug. "No offense."

"None taken," Noc said.

"That, and..." He hesitated, glancing up for a moment at Kost before dropping his eyes to the texts before him. "This is blood magic. She needed your blood for *something*. I can only imagine it has to do with the old Charmers' prophecy. She had notes on that too."

"Prophecy?" Kost asked.

Gaige nodded. "There's an old hymn sung to Charmers when they're kids. It's really just a lullaby nowadays, but... It's all about Ocnolog's return and the destruction he'll cause."

Ice settled across my skin, and I dropped my fork. Noc glared at Gaige and then at me, but I ignored him. "The lyrics are also etched beside Celeste's statue in the throne room. There's something about someone helping Ocnolog find peace too. Right?"

"Yes." Gaige picked up one of Yazmin's notes and grimaced. "Yazmin clearly sees herself as this person. All these spells were her attempts to make it happen. I think, anyway."

"What do the spells entail?" I asked.

"I've only managed to get a few words out of this." He lifted a leathery piece of parchment. My stomach churned. "Ocnolog's name is in here. From what I can tell, it seems convoluted and impossible to accomplish. I'll have to keep digging."

Gaige's somber voice hammered a nail into my heart and served memories up fresh in my mind. Hadn't Wynn said something of the sort when he'd tried to tame me? Something about a spell and the things she needed not existing? A dull ringing sounded in my ears. This had to be what he was referring to.

"There are a few books back in Cruor that might help." Kost's voice was low, but he gave Gaige a meaningful nod. "We'll find the answers."

"I just don't understand why she felt the need to go to such lengths. To turn on her own kind." Heat simmered through my veins. Was she so blinded by the desire to tame Ocnolog that she'd sacrifice her own people to make it happen? I'd seen Celeste's tears. Whatever plans Yazmin had, they weren't right.

Gaige stared into nothingness. "I'm at a loss myself."

I slammed my hand against the table. "Gods dammit."

"Leena," Noc said as he rubbed my shoulder. "We'll get her."

Gaige tucked the leathery parchment carefully in a tome. "She was right, by the way. Our meeting records were here all along. I just never thought to look. I never realized she'd altered our memories."

"She did what? How?" I stared at the books before him, recognizing one of the thick tomes that Actarius had penned with his magic. The one with meeting records dating back fifty years.

"It's all here." His fingers listlessly moved across the text.

"After we denied her petition for an outright attack, she conceded. But only on the surface. We close every meeting with a ceremonious sharing of wine. She must have come prepared for us to deny her, because she slipped a potent, memory-altering potion made from Quolint secretion into our drinks." He stared at his goblet for a long moment before clearing his throat.

I struggled to find words. Quolint secretion. The smallest amount would certainly cause memory loss. Not many Charmers owned such a creature, but it wasn't surprising that Yazmin had one. Or that she knew how to brew this disastrous concoction. Nothing about her surprised me anymore.

Gaige cupped his chin in his hands. "That whole day is wiped from my memory. Even now, reading what we discussed, it feels completely foreign. Almost as if it were a lie—that's how strong Quolints are. I never would've thought to check for it."

"You couldn't have known." Kost's voice was soft, forgiving. Gaige looked up at him and paused. A faint blush touched his cheeks.

"We stopped her yesterday. We can stop her again." Calem chased the last piece of his waffle around his plate.

Oz grunted. "She put our family in danger. She has to answer for that. And if that means going to war... Then count me in."

"Your support is appreciated." Gaige let out a long sigh that seemed to age him ten years. "Hireath is in disarray. Raven left last night to escort Kaori back here. They're on their way now. An emergency meeting will be held in front of the people to name Leena as Crown of the Council."

My throat went dry. "What? No. Gaige it should be you. Or Kaori. Or Raven."

He smiled, the first genuine sign of relief he'd shown all morning. "The people have already spoken. Some saw what you did with the Vrees. And, well, you know how rumors spread. You're the only one they can trust. The one who would lay down her life for a beast—and for all of them."

Astonishment swelled inside of me, and I looked out over the Charmers with new eyes. Their whispers weren't exclamations of terror, but muted mumblings of awe. Of devotion. They *trusted* me to fix this, to right all the horrible wrongs that had happened in Hireath. It'd become a place of abject horrors for both me and my family, but we had the power to cleanse it. To start over.

"If that's what's best…" I glanced at Noc, and he offered me a warm smile. Pulling me against his side, he placed a soft kiss atop my head.

"I would follow you anywhere."

And I knew he would, just as I would follow him. We weren't done fighting yet. We needed to sort through Yazmin's records. Strategize and build alliances so we could stand against her. And then there was the claim she'd made about Charmers falling prey to Wilheimians on beast hunts. I needed to verify her words. If that's what drove her over the edge… Well, then maybe our war was just beginning.

And I had no idea how Noc would feel about me wanting to find justice for my people if it meant taking a stand against his homeland.

My parents. My heart fluttered, and I reached for Noc's hand. I knew in the depths of my heart that Noc had no idea whether my family had fallen prey to his kingdom. And as much as he didn't want to, maybe he *needed* to take the throne again. Maybe together, we could stop all these horrors and unify our country.

I tilted my chin up and stole a kiss from my *anam-cara*. Together, we'd get through this. Just like we always did.

EPILOGUE

YAZMIN

The throne room in Wilheim was empty, save a handful of guards stationed at the entrance. I could feel the weight of their lethal stares digging between my shoulder blades as I strolled forward. The pale, ocean-blue runner edged in gold ran the considerable length of the room, right up the stairs of the raised dais. A single throne waited, unoccupied. Gold leaves formed a shiny highback, and the smooth seat reflected light from the circular windows in the ceiling. Potted plants, lush and vibrant, surrounded the dais, giving the throne an earthy appeal. Between that and the stories-tall mosaic windows at its back, the whole place almost seemed magical.

I hated every square inch of it.

Slowly, I climbed the steps and stopped before the throne. Trailing my fingers along the gilded arms, I only halted when muffled footsteps sounded behind me. My body tensed, but I forced myself to relax. To smile. To set my plan in motion. Turning, I faced the man who'd help me accomplish my dreams, knowingly or otherwise.

"King Varek. It's an honor to finally meet you."

He was hardly anything remarkable. Brown hair peppered at

his temples. Hawkish features and sunken eyes. His beard was oiled and gleaming in the light from the windows, and while I'm sure he did that to look presentable, it only made him look greasy. His jeweled platinum crown was heavy and covered in diamonds. A silver griffin was embroidered across the chest of his navy tunic. My fingers itched to tear it off and set it on fire.

Not now. Now was the time for games. For strategy.

The man eyed the space where my fingers rested on his throne. Well, his throne for *now*. "Yazmin, is it? Crown of the Charmers Council?"

"That's correct." I removed my hand and walked down the steps to meet him at the base of the dais. "I'm humbled you agreed to see me."

He was right to look wary. But I knew he wouldn't deny me. Not now. Not with the offer I'd present. He had the audacity to circle me—as if searching for weapons, as if his Sentinels hadn't already done so—but I allowed it. I was amiable. Weak. In need of his assistance.

That's what he needed to believe.

Clasping his hands together, he came to stand before me. "What can I do for you? I spoke with your envoy already this month."

"You'll no longer be dealing with him." I tempered my anger and put on a gentle smile. "From now on, I will be your point of contact with the Charmers."

He turned his back to me and climbed the steps to his throne, reclining into it and regarding me with distrust. "My Sentinels tell me that you have something to offer me. Quite different than any previous visit I've had from your kind."

The way he elongated the word *kind* made my skin crawl. For the cause. For Ocnolog. For my people, I would endure. No, I would *prevail*. Even if it meant dealing with this monster for the time being.

"It's true. Tell me, King Varek, what would you say if I could offer you a way to unify all of Lendria, Charmers and Wilheimians alike, while simultaneously serving Aleksander Nocsis Feyreigner's head to you on a silver platter?"

The king stilled in his throne. "Then I'd say that you and my *dear friend* have much in common." He waved his hand to one of his guards, who slipped through a hidden door and returned with a man I didn't recognize.

For a moment, my heart stilled. This was *my* plan. Who could put forth a more seductive offer than me? No one would take this throne, this world, from me. Certainly no pawn with dreams of placing a crown on his head.

The newcomer stood before us and gave a half-assed bow that reeked of arrogance. His curled brown hair skated just above his shoulders, and amber eyes full of deceit moved from King Varek to me. Shadows drifted from his frame and skated along the floor. An obvious display of power.

"This is Darrien, a former member of Cruor. He too, would like to bring me Aleksander's head." King Varek reclined in his chair and steepled his fingers.

I tried to keep my voice level. "The beasts in my arsenal are far more dangerous than a single assassin."

Darrien raised a brow. "Is that so? I believe Noc has already gone to Hireath once and returned with his life. Unless that was his ghost I saw stumbling around the capital a few days ago."

"And judging by the fact that this offer is still on the table," I seethed, "I'm guessing you also failed to kill him when you saw him last."

Darrien's shoulders stiffened, but he said nothing.

King Varek only smirked. "As you can see, he's not so easy to kill." With a drawn-out sigh, he waved his hand absently. "Which is why I'll be needing both of you if we're to eradicate this heretic and protect the sanctity of my throne."

Schooling my rage into place, I nodded and played at reverence. "Of course."

"Whatever gets Noc dead." Darrien cracked his knuckles. "He's been lording over that guild for far too long."

"Tell me, Yazmin, exactly how many beasts do you have at your disposal?" King Varek leaned forward and pressed his elbows to his thighs.

A smile touched my lips. "More than you could possibly imagine. And the king of all beasts is within my reach. I just need protection until I can acquire him, and then it will be easy to keep Noc—Aleksander—from trying to take your throne."

Eyes wide, his gaze dipped to the darkened symbol on my hand. It throbbed with power, and a familiar hunger claimed his gaze. He wanted what I could offer. All the kings and queens of Wilheim were prone to paranoia, thanks to Mavis's unjust sacrifice. Such was the price for killing her and using her blood to create Sentinels. If Varek saw a chance to strengthen his forces, he'd take it. Even if the threat wasn't real. Or better yet, even if the threat was standing right in front of him and he was just too blind to see it.

His malicious smile split his face in half. "I certainly believe we can work something out, my lady."

My lady. I curtsied nonetheless, hiding my triumph beneath the sheet of blond hair that fell across my face.

He wouldn't know what to do with a *lady* like me. And neither would the rest of Lendria when I used his armies to crush any opposition from atop the scaled back of Ocnolog. His crown, and all of Lendria, would be mine.

Just as Celeste had intended.

BESTIARY

Asura

Pronunciation: *ah-sur-ah*

Rank: B-Class

Description: An Asura is the size of a small child, with an upright humanlike torso, cow legs, and a cow head. Its body is covered in tan hide, and it sports six humanlike arms. It also has ten milky-white eyes, which correspond to the number of hits that can be absorbed by its shield. When activating its impenetrable defensive shield, the Asura holds two hands palm up toward the heavens, two flat and parallel to the earth, and two pressed firmly against the ground. The invisible, bubble-like dome this creates can withstand any attack for up to ten hits. The number of closed eyes indicates the number of hits sustained at any point during the battle. Asura are slow to move and incapable of physical attacks. Their shields will remain intact if they travel with their Charmer, but since movement requires them to remove their lower two hands from the earth, this weakens the shield.

Taming: Taming an Asura takes considerable time. The Charmer must sit cross-legged before the beast, with arms extended outward, and activate charm. This position must be held for several hours while the Asura chews on wheatgrass and evaluates the Charmer's power. If it finds the Charmer unsuitable, the Asura will walk away and become untamable for seven days.

Azad

Pronunciation: *a-zad*

Rank: C-Class

Description: Azad are small, mouse-like beasts with porcelain-colored fur and pearl-like eyes. They primarily reside in frozen landscapes, where food is scarce, and they will use their treasure-tracking powers to find their prize—grubs and grass. Their claws are incredibly sharp, and they can dig easily into frozen earth in search of food and to hibernate between feeds. Once tamed, Charmers can use their power to seek treasure of other types by communicating their desires to the beast.

Taming: Azads are incredibly hard to find, and only surface under the light of a full moon. While they're used to eating grubs and grass, they're particularly fond of fruit. Due to the frozen landscape in which they live, they rarely get to enjoy this treat. As such, if a Charmer wishes to tame an Azad, the easiest way to do so is to lure one out with fruit and wait under a full moon. Eventually, the scent will attract the beast. Initiate charm once it has started in on its meal.

Bone Katua

Pronunciation: *bone cat-ew-ah*

Rank: A-Class

Description: The Bone Katua is one of the ten legendary feline beasts and is russet-brown in color with bone spikes protruding along its spine. Its devil-red eyes have the potential to cause paralysis in prey, making it a supreme hunter. Since the Bone Katua can heal itself by rubbing its fur against trees, it's difficult to kill. Its yellow fangs stretch past its maw and can pierce thick hides with ease.

Taming: Bone Katua are difficult to locate, often living reclusive lives in mountains populated by dense forests. The Charmer must discover the Bone Katua's den and take up residence near it, demonstrating a willingness to live fully with nature by eating and drinking only enough to survive and maintaining no contact with the outside world. After several months, the Bone Katua will approach and paralyze the Charmer with its stare. It will then sniff and lick them from head to toe, determining whether they've truly dedicated themselves to nature. If it believes the Charmer has, it will sit before them until the paralysis wears off and then allow them to tame it. If it feels the Charmer does not value nature, or has contacted another human or indulged beyond what's necessary during those few months, it will kill them.

Boxismus

Pronunciation: *box-is-mus*

Rank: B-Class

Description: Nimble and fast, Boxismus swiftly move through jungle trees with ease. They're covered in orange fur with silver plates protruding from their shoulders and knees and along the backs of their hands and knuckles. They live in large groups together and are known to be extremely territorial, with the strongest Boxismus becoming the leader of the family and responsible for all members' safety. If a Boxismus considers a Charmer part of their family, it will go to any length to protect them.

Taming: To charm this beast, the Charmer must locate a family and challenge a Boxismus to fight in physical combat. However, entering directly into a fighting match with this beast will always result in serious injury or death, as the Boxismus has incredible power and stamina. To counteract this, set up a series of heavy sandbags and lure the Boxismus to them with fruit. The Boxismus will punch each one until they split. After five or so bags, they will have spent enough stamina for the Charmer to safely enter a fighting match without risking loss of life. Injuries will likely still happen, but once the Boxismus tires, initiate charm.

Canepine

Pronunciation: *cane-pine*

Rank: C-Class

Description: Canepine are wolf-like beasts with ivy-green fur and powder-blue eyes. Male Canepine have small white flowers that grow naturally along the undersides of their bellies, neck, and around their faces, while females have indigo flowers. They live in packs deep within the woods and are peaceful in nature. They have excellent tracking abilities, making them sought after by Charmers who frequent beast hunts. In addition, they can purify any water source, making it safe for consumption.

Taming: Taming a Canepine largely depends on whether or not the beast is attached to its pack. It is impossible to convince a Canepine to leave if it has already mated or birthed pups. Therefore, it's easier to tame youngsters than adults. Once a Charmer has caught the attention of a Canepine, they must play fetch for as long as the beast desires. Once the Canepine is satisfied, it will take an item off the Charmer and run away, returning sometime later. At that point, the Charmer must find the missing item. If they're able to track it down, the Canepine will allow itself to be tamed. If not, the Canepine will leave.

Dosha

Pronunciation: *doh-sha*

Rank: D-Class

Description: Dosha are no bigger than teacups and have

exceptionally long tails and large hands. They're generally tawny-colored, with slight coat variations between males and females. While all Dosha have three eyes, female eye color is blue and male eye color is green. The adhesive secreted from their palms is so strong that a single finger attached to a branch could keep them from falling. When they wish to unstick themselves, a secondary dissolvent secretion is released from their hands, granting just enough movement for them to dislodge themselves. They live high in the treetops to avoid predators and eat a variety of leaves and fruit to sustain themselves. Thanks to a special lining in their digestive system, they're immune to any poison they might consume. As such, they're useful for detecting whether or not food is safe for human consumption.

Taming: Dosha never leave their treetop homes. To tame one, the Charmer must climb as high as the tree will allow and present the beast with a ripe coconut. If the Dosha accepts, it will glue itself to the Charmer's body while consuming the fruit. Once the Dosha is finished eating, the Charmer should initiate charm.

Dreagle

Pronunciation: *dree-gul*

Rank: B-Class

Description: Dreagles live in flocks atop mountain peaks and form deep bonds with their family. As the seasons change, the coats of their deer-like bodies adapt to match the environment—dirt brown and black during the warmer months and snow-white during the winter. With powerful, eagle-like wings, they can fly for hours without tiring. They use their antlers and sharp talons to catch small game or unearth grubs. Their incredible eyesight cannot be fooled by magic, and they're able to detect threats from great distances.

Taming: Dreagles have a unique relationship with Charmers. So long as high peaks are provided for them to stand guard—as well as more secluded mountaintop perches to nest and birth young—they'll watch over a designated area without needing to be tamed. They can be tamed with standard charm, but it's generally not recommended to separate a Dreagle from its flock, due to their highly social natures.

Drevtok

Pronunciation: *drev-tock*

Rank: B-Class

Description: Drevtoks are no bigger than a toddler with two spheres that make up their body. The bottom, larger sphere is hollow with branch-like bars that display an empty cage if the beast has not recently gathered food. The smaller, bulbous sphere is its head. Endless vines erupt from its center mass to snare its fruit and protect itself from potential threats. Drevtoks can open and close their lower sphere, and once tamed, store both people and belongings safely within their bodies.

Taming: Drevtoks are solitary creatures that live near orchards or locations with a large amount of fruit, which is their preferred food source. They only eat when hungry and the rest of the time protect their fruit from other threats by ensnaring them with vines. To tame a Drevtok, a Charmer has to successfully steal a piece of fruit. When the Drevtok attacks, the Charmer must bypass the endless vines without harming the beast in order to make it amicable to taming. If the beast is harmed, it will immediately flee.

Effreft

Pronunciation: *eff-reft*

Rank: B-Class

Description: Effrefts are roughly the size of small dogs, with falcon heads, long, feathered tails, and wings. Their mint-green coloring and pink eyes make them easy to spot during the day, so they typically hunt at night. They can shower the space beneath their wingspan with magic, encouraging plants to reach maturity in seconds, and the soil left behind is regarded as the most fertile in the world.

Taming: The Charmer should find an open field on a moonlit night and prepare a cornucopia. After overflowing it with a

variety of food, they must initiate charm and wait. A successful taming may take several days, because Effrefts have unknown migratory patterns and might not be present. More sightings have occurred in the south, as they seem to prefer warmer wind currents.

Fabric Spinner

Pronunciation: *fabric spinner*

Rank: B-Class

Description: Fabric Spinners are reclusive beasts that live deep in caves far from civilization. While they're skittish in nature, they've been known to attack anything that strays into their territory. The wrap their prey in a web and slowly devour its organs over a period of time. They have humanoid heads with insect features, and human torsos that end in bulbous abdomens reminiscent of arachnids. With eight hairy legs, two pincers at the space where the torso transitions to abdomen, and two spiny, human-like arms, they're exceptionally talented at snaring prey. The ducts on their inner wrists shoot an endless supply of near-unbreakable silken thread. Their fingers are coated in tiny, retractable barbs that allow them to slit their webs if need be. The spinner that protrudes from the beast's rear produces a single thread that tethers the Fabric Spinner to its lair. If it senses danger or wants to return after a successful hunt, it will retract that thread and be pulled at immense speed back to safety. Given they're solitary creatures and rarely mate—females often attempt to eat males after copulation—not many Charmers own this beast. Those who do own the beast are often tailors, using the silk threads to craft immensely sturdy clothing or other sought-after materials, such as fishing line.

Taming: After finding the lair of a Fabric Spinner, the Charmer must bring several buckets of fresh organs to present to the beast. It will examine each offering one by one, and if it finds the organ appealing, it will wrap them in webbing for later consumption. If one of the organs has gone foul, the Fabric Spinner will become enraged and attack. Assuming all organs are satisfactory, the beast will then weave an intricate web. The Charmer must willingly ensnare themselves and wait patiently while the Fabric Spinner eats the provided organs, symbolizing the patience the beast exudes while hunting. The Charmer must remain completely still for the entire duration of the meal, otherwise the Fabric Spinner will attack. Once the beast has finished eating, it will cut the Charmer down from the web and allow itself to be tamed.

Femsy

Pronunciation: *fem-zee*

Rank: D-Class

Description: Like the sparrow, the Femsy are small and flighty. They travel in flocks and rarely hold still, making it difficult to snag one's attention long enough to charm it. They're steel gray in color with violet breasts. When one is tamed, a yellow film slides over its three black eyes, marking it as owned. After a successful taming, the Charmer can tap into the bird's eyesight for short intervals by concentrating on the bond. Because there are no distance limitations to shared sight, the Femsy is often used for reconnaissance. However, the act is quite draining on the bird and can only be used three times before it must be sent back to the beast realm to recover.

Taming: No additional taming requirements are needed aside from standard charm.

Graveltot

Pronunciation: *grah-vul-tot*

Rank: D-Class

Description: The Graveltot is a small, spherical beast covered in slate and rocks. It moves by rolling across the ground, only popping out its head and feet when prompted to activate its power. When its hooves meet the earth, it manipulates the force of gravity in a perfect circle around it, making it impossible for anyone caught in its trap to move. It only lasts for fifteen minutes, and the Graveltot must rest for several hours before it can use its power again.

Taming: No additional taming requirements are needed aside from standard charm.

Groober

Pronunciation: *groo-ber*

Rank: E-Class

Description: Groobers are round, fluffy beasts with white fur softer than a rabbit's fluff. They have stubby arms and legs and circular eyes. When squeezed tightly, Groobers emit a mixture of lavender and valerian to aid with sleep.

Taming: No additional taming requirements are needed aside from standard charm.

Gyss

Pronunciation: *giss*

Rank: C-Class

Description: Gyss are the size of coffee mugs, with human torsos and misty, wisp-like tails for the lower half of their bodies. They can only be found in sacred sites and often adorn their hair with flowers or leaves. Their sharp, pointed teeth are used to crack nuts, one of their preferred food

sources. Exceptionally cunning and mischievous, they like to talk in riddles and are the only known beast with an active relationship with the gods. Male Gyss have been spotted but not tamed. Gyss have the ability to grant one wish every six months. There are no limitations, so long as payment is met. However, the breadth of their ability is dependent on the master's power and intelligence. While Gyss can use their relationship with the gods to argue for less severe payments, they often don't, as they take joy in using their power to the fullest extent of their abilities. As such, they are rarely, if ever, called upon. Many Charmers feel Gyss should be ranked higher, but their restricted conditions for wish-granting caused the Council to rank them as C-Class beasts.

Taming: Gyss can only be found at sacred sites and require utter stillness to tame. Otherwise, standard charm is all that's needed.

Havra

Pronunciation: *Hav-rah*

Rank: E-Class

Description: Havra are small and slender in stature with gangly limbs and knobby fingers. They have long faces with four deer-like eyes. They are solitary creatures who live in forests and survive off berries. While holding their breath, they are able to materialize through objects. Because of this and their bark-like skin, they were initially thought to be tree spirits.

Taming: Havra can only be found in dense wood. The Charmer should place a basket of fresh berries at the base of a tree and wait. Once a Havra is spotted, the Charmer must hold their breath and initiate charm.

Iksass

Pronunciation: *ik-sass*

Rank: B-Class

Description: The Iksass alters its constitution to suit its master's needs. Generally, though, they appear to be tall and slender and take human shape, but are faceless. Despite that, they have excellent senses. Limbs appear and disappear on a whim, and they prefer invisibility, making them difficult to locate. They lurk unseen and hunt small game or steal food from wandering travelers. Needing vast amounts of sleep to power their ability, they can only be called upon for one two-hour stint during a day once tamed. Many Charmers use Iksass for protection, as their shape-shifting abilities make them formidable opponents.

Taming: The key to taming an Iksass is locating it. Without a known preferred habitat, the only way to tame one is for the Charmer to catch it picking their pocket in search of food. When this happens, immediately activate charm to keep the beast from fleeing, and maintain it for two hours or until the beast tires.

Kaiku

Pronunciation: *keye-kew*

Rank: C-Class

Description: Kaiku are small, pale-blue beasts with jelly-like bodies and four stubby tentacles. They're found in shallow ocean waters (not on any Lendrian coast). Females have an aquamarine gem embedded in their centers, whereas males have a ruby. When its power is activated, the Kaiku can, without fault, guide the Charmer to any location they desire. Their gem glows as they determine the location, and then they direct accordingly with their limbs.

Taming: After discovering the Kaiku's habitat and noting its sex, the Charmer must acquire at least twenty matching gemstones and offer them to the beast. If the beast finds a stone that is shinier than the one embedded in its body, it will shed the old gem and replace it with the new one. Then, charm can be initiated. If the Kaiku does not find a suitable replacement, it will flee and taming will be unsuccessful.

Kestral

Pronunciation: *kes-tral*

Rank: Unknown

Description: The Kestral is an untamable beast that magically appeared when Wilheimians forced Charmers to flee after the First War. The Kestral emerged and created an unbreakable border around Hireath to keep the dark magic of the Kitska Forest out. The beast maintains the threshold at all times, only allowing Charmers and those it deems fit to cross. It has incredibly long tail feathers, a large wingspan, and a slender, paper-white body with blue eyes.

Taming: Not possible. Trying results in the beast casting the Charmer across the threshold, only allowing them to return after an undetermined length of time.

Krik

Pronunciation: *crick*

Rank: D-Class

Description: Krik are pear-shaped birds with tiny green feathers. They have small, trumpet-like beaks that emit a staticky, dissonant sound known to steadily drive those who hear it insane. The Krik's lungs operate independently of each other, allowing the bird to inhale fresh air while still exhaling to maintain its call.

Taming: No additional taming requirements are needed aside from standard charm.

Laharock

Pronunciation: *la-ha-rock*

Rank: A-Class

Description: Larger than an elephant and built like a wingless dragon, the Laharock is one of the largest beasts in Lendria. It uses its thick claws to traverse the rough volcanic terrain of its preferred habitat and is surprisingly nimble. The bone mane around its crown acts as an extra layer of protection for the head, and large, pupil-less white eyes glow with the intensity of fire. Red scales rimmed in gold cover the Laharock's spine, neck, and legs, making the underbelly the only unprotected portion of its hide. These scales are easily corroded by salt water, which can cause damage to the Laharock. If

the Laharock grows up in the wild without threat or human interference, it will develop magic that allows it to summon scalding fires and intense heat. Offspring, on the other hand, are empathic metamorphs, susceptible to an outside trigger that could alter their power. Once the trigger event occurs, the power solidifies.

Taming: Laharock absorb minerals from the volcanoes on which they live. Charmers will need to seek out an active volcano and bring a freshly caught marlin. Once the Laharock spots the Charmer, they should leave the fish on a slab and take several steps back. While the Laharock is eating, the Charmer should insert ear plugs, then summon a Songbloom and use its lullaby to put the Laharock in a stupor. The Charmer must remember to approach slowly and find sure footing along the mountain, because one loose rock or loud noise can break the trance and enrage the Laharock. Regardless, the Laharock will produce an intense aura of heat as a means of protection. Being burned is unavoidable. To avoid severe damage, Charmers should immediately summon a Poi afterward to tend to their skin. Once upon the Laharock, Charmers must place a hand on its snout and initiate charm.

Alternative method (discovered by Leena Edenfrell): Find a Laharock with her recently birthed young. Separate the mother from the child. Carefully approach the offspring and tame it first (no additional requirements outside of standard charm). Be careful not to spook it, as that might cause a flood of unstable powers to occur. Once the offspring is tamed, the mother will call off her pursuit and willingly allow herself to be charmed in order to stay with her young.

Mistari

Pronunciation: *mis-tar-ee*
Rank: A-Class

Description: The Mistari is one of the ten legendary feline beasts and has a white coat and scaled crystal plates over its chest. Four wings sprout from each of its ankles, resembling jagged pieces of precious gems. They enable the Mistari to propel itself forward, even gliding over short distances. The crystal feathers are highly valuable and, when dropped, can be broken and embedded in the skin of two people, granting them the ability to share thoughts. Mistari live in small prides scattered throughout the plains. Due to their wings and speed, they are difficult to track.

Taming: Charmers should approach with caution and begin the following sequence: first, encircle the Mistari with a mixture of highly valuable gems and stones while half crouched and chuffing to symbolize deference. Then, lie facedown on the ground and remain completely still. If the Mistari does not approve of the Charmer's offering, they should run. Taming will not be successful and could result in death. If the beast does approve, it will pick the Charmer up by the scruff (Charmers should wear thick clothing to prevent injury) and bring them into the circle. Charmers should stay limp until the beast begins to lick them, then initiate charm.

Myad

Pronunciation: *my-ad*

Rank: A-Class

Description: The Myad is the largest of the ten legendary feline beasts, with a panther-like build, black fur, and a mane comprised of peacock feathers. The same vibrant teal and emerald feathers travel the length of its spine and tail, as well as onto its wings. Gold casings protect the weak points of its ankles and appear around the crown of its head. When the Myad is about to take flight, blue magic streams from its feet and eyes. The Myad has the unique ability to place its prey in a stupor while prying into their deepest memories. The person in question is then forced to face the horrors of their past, which often results in insanity. If the Myad finds them unworthy, the person's mind is burned to ash, leaving them in a comatose state for the rest of their lives. Because Myads are carnivorous, they are likely to consume their helpless and unfeeling prey.

Taming: Taming a Myad is a dangerous three-step process. First, the Charmer must acquire the blood of a murderer, freely given, and present it to the beast. Second, they must offer a token of loyalty with high personal value. And finally, they must allow the beast to bite them, thus spurring a connection that enables the Myad to review memories and determine worth. Throughout the entire process, the Charmer must not scream, because that will break the Myad's concentration, causing it to either flee or attack. If the Charmer can survive the evaluation of their past, the Myad will grant permission to tame.

Nagakori

Pronunciation: *na-ga-kor-ee*

Rank: B-Class

Description: Nagakori mate for life at a young age and, as such, are always found in pairs. They are twin serpents that float in the air with dragon-like heads and whiskers that trail the length of their bodies. Females are electric-blue in coloring and can spew water from their unhinged jaws, while males are snow-white and shoot frost. When tamed, they must both be summoned at the same time, as they refuse to be separated.

Taming: Pairs can be found in cold areas near bodies of water. They're attracted to pleasant sounds, so Charmers should lure them out with a musical instrument or by singing. While maintaining the music, the Charmer must then perform a ribbon dance. The Nagakori will begin to mimic the flourishes of the ribbons, eventually surrounding the Charmer and allowing charm to be initiated. The Charmer cannot falter with the music, as this will cause the Nagakori to freeze them and flee.

Naughtbird

Pronunciation: *nawt-bird*

Rank: C-Class

Description: These small, sparrow-like creatures have hundreds of tiny iridescent feathers. When they're in flight, their wings move so fast they're hard to pinpoint, and their tail feathers resemble that of a boat's rudder, angling from left to right to help steer. They have long, needle-shaped beaks that can pierce nearly any hide. When that happens, their saliva infiltrates the target's system and places them in deep slumber.

Taming: Naughtbirds live in hives. To lure one out, create a trail of flower petals that lead to a small bowl of nectar. If interested, the Naughtbird will follow the trail and drink from the bowl. Once the nectar is gone, initiate charm.

Nezbit

Pronunciation: *nez-bit*

Rank: C-Class

Description: Nezbits are small, have rabbit-like builds with brown fur, and are coated with teal feathers. Exceptionally rare, they're near impossible to find because of their low numbers and their preference for living underground. They form small colonies and create large networks beneath the soil, only poking their wing-like ears up once every few days to absorb nutrients from the sun. Their ears can hear sounds from miles away, and they track reverberations in the earth to avoid danger. When tamed, they're used to listen to people's hearts and determine lies from truth. Their opal eyes flash green for truth and red for lies.

Taming: As they live underground, the Nezbits have no known preferred environment. Finding a colony involves luck and careful examination of the earth, because Nezbits leave behind small mounds after sticking their ears up from the ground. Once a possible mound has been sighted, the Charmer should remain still for several days until the ears appear. The Charmer should then quickly

yank the beast up from the dirt and immediately initiate charm. It's important to note that the mounds in question are extremely similar to those left by prairie dogs, and because of that, reports of colonies are often inaccurate.

Nix Ikari

Pronunciation: *nix ih-car-ee*

Rank: A-Class

Description: One of the large legendary feline beasts, Nix Ikari are known as supreme hunters given their ability to completely mask their presence and teleport. They have snow-colored fur covered with dark, royal-blue spots with indigo inlays. When their power activates, glowing orchid light streams from their eyes and the spots, indicating they're about to teleport. They have elongated canines, twin curling horns behind their ears, and a thick, bushy tail twice the length of their bodies. They can travel great distances, though they normally only teleport in short bursts when hunting. The greater the distance required for teleporting, the longer it takes the Nix Ikari to recover.

Taming: Nix Ikari are fierce predators and will not be tamed without first deciding whether or not the Charmer in question is willing to fight. As such, very few Charmers have ever tamed this beast. After a Nix Ikari has marked a Charmer for a potential master, it will follow them unseen, judging their actions for an undetermined period of time. Once the decision has been made, the beast will appear and either kill the Charmer or allow itself to be tamed. Nix Ikari live in cold, near-inhospitable climates, and to start the taming process, the Charmer must provide prey, encircle it in the Charmer's blood, and decorate the area with fire opals.

Ossilix

Pronunciation: *oss-eh-lix*

Rank: A-Class

Description: While Ossilix are the smallest of the legendary feline beasts, they exude a calm fury and are lethal, using size to their advantage to outmaneuver prey. Slightly larger than an ocelot, they have lithe bodies coated in metal, giving the appearance of silver and making their hide near impenetrable. They're known to be incredibly intelligent, displaying exceptional tactical thinking and striking only when they see the possibility of a killing blow. Ossilix saliva is a potent healing balm with the capability of bringing someone back from the brink of death. However, accepting this gift requires the recipient to sacrifice a sliver of humanity in exchange. The effects vary from person to person, but largely involve a physical transformation to that of a beast.

Taming: After finding an Ossilix, the Charmer must allow it to inflict a life-threatening injury and then accept its healing balm. If the Charmer does not accept, it will kill them quickly. If they do accept, the Ossilix will retreat and watch from a distance as their humanity slips away and they transform into a beast. This transformation represents the constant fury the Ossilix feels and, as such, is incredibly difficult to control. The Ossilix will study the Charmer's behavior, killing them if they're unable to withstand the burning rage, or accepting them as its master if they're able to revert back to human form.

Poi

Pronunciation: *poy*

Rank: B-Class

Description: Poi are solitary creatures that often establish territories over small clearings in the woods. They have fox-like bodies with white fur and a single black stripe running the length of their spines. Their most identifiable feature is the jewel-like amethyst orb nestled between their ears, which turns cloudy when a prediction is brewing and clears once the future has been set. Poi bites are venomous and will slowly kill, but the poison can be removed by the beast if tamed. Their saliva can close minor wounds and alleviate burns, though their true power lies in their ability to predict outcomes two minutes into the future. When tamed, the Poi can share its visions with its master.

Taming: No additional requirements are needed outside of standard charm, but the Charmer must hold their charm for several minutes while making no sudden movements, allowing the Poi to perform a series of predictions and determine the outcome of being tamed.

Quolint

Pronunciation: *qoh-lint*

Rank: D-Class

Description: These small, frog-like beasts are the size of one's finger, with bright-green skin and red spots. They have tiny, see-through wings, allowing them to glide short distances while hunting for flies. Their skin secretes a viscous poison that has memory-altering powers. In the wild, this acts as a defense mechanism, causing a predator to pause and forget its actions if the poison touches its mouth. When tamed, Charmers can wear gloves to safely siphon some of the secretion and brew memory-altering concoctions that are tasteless.

Taming: No additional requirements are needed for taming other

than to initiate charm, but it's important to note that the
Charmer must not touch the Quolint during the process. While
ingesting the poison will cause more lasting memory loss, touch
can still cause temporary amnesia. Thus, if the Charmer grazes
the Quolint while taming, they will forget why they're there,
and the beast will escape.

Scorpex

Pronunciation: *scor-pex*

Rank: B-Class

Description: The Scorpex is a dangerous beast that can grow to
roughly thirty feet in length. Its wormlike body is plated in
thick orange scales and coated with a shimmery mucus. It has
four legs, each ending in hooked fingers, and a barbed tail with
a stinger like that of a scorpion. Its poison is painful but not
incurable. With six eyes, three on either side of its mandibles,
the Scorpex is difficult to catch off guard. It is carnivorous and
uses its eight tongues to strip carcasses down to the bones in a
matter of minutes.

Taming: Scorpex are rarely owned, because taming one requires
collecting carcasses for weeks to accumulate enough food to
entice the beast. The smell alone dissuades most Charmers, not
to mention the danger of the Scorpex itself. After presenting
the pile of carcasses, the Charmer should wait until the beast
has finished eating to initiate charm. If the Charmer has not
provided enough to satiate the Scorpex's hunger, it will strike.
A relatively "safe" number of carcasses to present is somewhere
in the high twenties.

Songbloom

Pronunciation: *song-bloom*

Rank: D-Class

Description: The Songbloom is a relatively harmless beast found in rosebushes in remote parts of Lendria. The lower half of their bodies mimic the petals of a flower, and their human-like torsos bloom out of the center of the bulb. They can detach and float from plant to plant, reattaching via miniscule roots at the base of the petals that allow them to pull nutrients from the plant. Male Songbloom are ivy-colored and camouflage with the leaves, whereas females take after the actual roses. Both male and female Songbloom spend their days singing in an unknown language. There are a variety of tunes, and each one has a unique effect on the listener, ranging from feelings of elation to causing temporary slumber. Charmers frequently use Songbloom to elicit feelings of joy and love during ceremonies between mates.

Taming: Find a Songbloom colony by listening for their voices while searching through rosebushes. Once found, the Charmer must seat themselves before the beast and listen to a song of the Songbloom's choosing. Once the tune is complete, they should offer applause and then initiate charm. If the Songbloom elects to perform a sleeping tune, the Charmer will fall into slumber and be unable to offer applause, and the taming will fail. As the effects should only last a few minutes, the Charmer is free to try again once waking, assuming the Songbloom has not fled.

Telesávra

Description: *tell-eh-sav-rah*

Rank: D-Class

Description: The Telesávra is a lizard the size of a small boulder and has a rocky hide. It can detach its jaw to suck in air and summon a flickering white portal that will transport any beast or person with Charmer's blood to a designated location, referred to as a hearth point. The Telesávra can only remember one hearth point at a time. Many Charmers set Hireath as their hearth point for efficient and safe travel home.

Taming: No additional taming requirements are needed aside from standard charm.

Uloox

Description: *oo-locks*

Rank: C-Class

Description: The Uloox is a black snake found in caves with yellow eyes and three fangs. It can eat prey up to five times larger than its body size, thanks to its unhinging jaw and fast-acting digestive system. Tiny ducts are found along the roof of its mouth, just behind its fangs. Uloox venom is dangerous, and is known to cloud the mind and cause hallucinations, as well as weaken the body. Muscles will seize and become nearly immobile until the venom fades. Very few Charmers own one, as they're known to be temperamental and find little joy in being summoned from the beast realm.

Taming: To tame an Uloox, a Charmer must allow themselves to be bitten as many times as the beast deems fit. This is highly dangerous, as multiple bites can result in death. Once the Uloox is satisfied that the Charmer has become immobile, it will wait until its venom has cycled out of the Charmer's system. Only then will it allow itself to be tamed. However, if the beast becomes hungry during the taming process, it will slowly devour parts of the Charmer, such as fingers or toes, until it is either full or the Charmer is able to move. It's recommend that several field mice are brought along to the taming to prevent this.

Vissirena

Pronunciation: *vis-sy-reen-ah*

Rank: B-Class

Description: Vissirena have human torsos and fishlike lower bodies that end in long, colorful tails. Iridescent scales varying in color cover the entirety of their figure, and their hair is a mixture of seaweed and tentacles. Their faces also share similar structures to those of fish, and additional fins often develop along the forearms. Vissirena live in schools in the waters to the west of Hireath. The fleshy voids on their palms can open and close, altering currents to bring prey in their direction. When tamed, they can channel powerful streams of water with immense force. Vissirena can only be summoned in bodies of water.

Taming: Do not attempt to charm a Vissirena underwater. At the first hint of danger, they will send the threat to the bottom of the ocean via an unforgiving current until drowning has occurred. Likewise, do not attempt to catch from a boat, as they'll simply destroy the ship. Instead, a Charmer should fish for one from the shore. Only a magically reinforced pole, coupled with fishing line made from Fabric Spinner silk, will hold the Vissirena's weight. Preferred bait is tuna wrapped in orange peel. Once the Vissirena is hooked, the Charmer should prepare for a fight that could last several days. After the Charmer has reeled one in, they should initiate charm.

Vrees

Pronunciation: *vrees*

Rank: S-Class

Description: As one of the five known S-Class beasts, the Vrees's power exceeds that of all A-Class beasts. Normally, the beast is massive in size with burning, white eyes. It has a fox-like head with the body of a wolf and three foxtails. Its form is more like a sieve with cutouts and negative space that mist passes through. In its center, a ball of blue electricity sparks and summons lightning. Weapons cannot scathe its hide, and only the right type of magic can harm this beast. When summoning a bolt of lightning, it takes a few minutes to charge prior to striking. When there are no threats around, the Vrees will shrink in size, reaching about midthigh in height.

Taming: The exact number of Vrees in the wild and their breeding habits are entirely unknown, as they are thought to live in storm clouds. Tracking this creature takes years and can span many continents, as they have no set home. To start, the Charmer must first find a lightning storm and look for a storm cloud in the shape of a wolf. Then, they must follow the storm until the clouds reach a sandy area. If it strikes, the lightning will petrify, creating an object that looks similar to a tree branch. Once cooled, collect the petrified lightning. If the bolt came from a cloud other than the wolf-shaped one, it won't work. If the Charmer is lucky enough to collect petrified lightning from the wolf-shaped cloud, they must then wait again for the

storm to reappear, sometimes years later in an entirely different location. When this happens, the Charmer must present the
petrified lightning. The Vrees will sense the offering and strike
it, shattering the object and manifesting before the Charmer. It
will then strike the Charmer with a bolt of lightning, and if they
survive, allow itself to be tamed.

Whet

Pronunciation: *wet*

Rank: B-Class

Description: Whets are owl beasts that lead solitary lives and can
only be found in high treetops at night. They have three gleaming ocher eyes, bark-colored feathers, and twin branch-like
horns that stretch outward on either side of their head. In the
wild, these horns embed themselves into trees and telegraph
information to the Whet about where their prey are, making
them expert hunters. Once tamed, they can be used to record
information into tomes based off what they hear.

Taming: Whets are extremely difficult to locate, as they can sense
when another being is in their territory and will flee. However,
if they have recently eaten and are sated, they're less likely to
fly away and will instead survey the approaching Charmer.
The Charmer must then sit on the forest floor and read to
the Whet for hours. As the Whet will likely get hungry during
this process, it's necessary to bring small game to keep them
in place. Once the Charmer has finished reading at least a
minimum of three hundred pages, the Whet will be open to
taming. Initiate charm.

Xifos

Pronunciation: *zy-fos*

Rank: A-Class

Description: Because of its replication magic, the Xifos is regarded as one of the most difficult legendary feline beasts to tame. It has a slender, slate-gray body with twin tails that form sharp arrowheads. When the Xifos is activating its power, all the hair on its body stands on end, solidifying into fine needles, and then it shudders, creating an exact replica of itself. The number of copies one Xifos can maintain varies, though the recorded high is two hundred and three. Each copy can attack with the full strength and force of the original. If a copy is injured or otherwise incapacitated, it will dissolve into smoke. Xifos are solitary, yet they usually have a pack of copies flanking them for protection.

Taming: A Xifos will only bond with a master cunning enough to separate the original from the copies. Simply approaching the beast and initiating charm will cause the beast to activate its power, surrounding the Charmer with copies. After the copies have shuffled, the Xifos will wait until the Charmer touches the one they believe is real. If they're wrong, the copy disappears, and all remaining forms attack. No one has ever guessed correctly via this method. Instead, after locating a Xifos, the Charmer should study it for several months to ensure they have the original version pegged. Charmers should find a cavern that can be used as a den, and construct an elaborate display of mirrors. They should then lure the Xifos to the cavern with the mating call of a pheasant, their preferred prey. If arranged correctly, the mirrors will trick the Xifos into thinking it has already summoned copies of itself. While it's searching for the pheasant, the Charmer should slowly approach. Thinking the Charmer is already surrounded by copies, the beast will sit and wait for them to choose. Touch the original Xifos, and initiate charm.

Yimlet

Pronunciation: *yim-lit*

Rank: B-Class

Description: Yimlets are beetle beasts with iridescent orange hides, barbed horns, and pincers larger than their heads. The size of a small dog, these beasts are surprisingly fast and can fly short distances, making it easy to snare their prey. When they bite their target, a toxin secretes from their mouths, deteriorating the skin of their prey immediately upon impact. The toxin will spread, eventually killing the target and allowing for the Yimlet to eat in peace. They can ingest up to five times their body weight in one sitting.

Taming: The only way to tame a Yimlet is to capture it with a net made of Fabric Spinner thread. Any other material will dissolve with the Yimlet's venom, and they will attack the Charmer in a rage. Because Yimlets eat so frequently, they will soon become hungry after capture and allow for the Charmer to tame them, simply so they can be sent to the beast realm to hunt.

Zavalluna

Pronunciation: *zah-val-loo-nah*

Rank: A-Class

Description: Zavallunas are incredibly rare horse-like beasts found only in foreign lands near places of highly concentrated magic. Auroras of varying colors, ranging from emerald to fuchsia to turquoise appear across their ink-black hides as they move.

They have large feathered wings and a single blade-like horn that glows white. When their power is activated, they produce a dome of magic in a small radius that amplifies the abilities of any beast. This can only be done for a short amount of time, though, as extended use may cause permanent damage to the Zavallunas' horns.

Taming: Zavallunas are extremely selective when it comes to choosing a Charmer. As such, many become family beasts that are passed down from one generation to the next. To tame a wild Zavalluna, the Charmer must first travel to mage lands and partner with a mage in order to summon the beast. Once the beast has appeared, the mage must make a case on behalf of the Charmer, attesting to their magical prowess and kindness. Zavallunas will only agree to a taming if the mage and Charmer have been true friends for several years. The stronger their relationship, the more likely the taming will be a success.

Zystream

Pronunciation: *zy-stream*

Rank: A-Class

Description: The Zystream is the only legendary feline beast that prefers water to land, though it's capable of breathing in both environments. Liquid-blue, its coat is a mixture of water-resistant fur and scales. It has a long tail that ends in fins, as well as finned whiskers lining its jaw and throat. Fluid in nature, it's nearly impossible to pin and can shoot immensely powerful jet streams from its mouth. It's stronger in water and can summon small rain clouds to follow it when on land.

Taming: The Zystream can be found in fresh or salt water during the warmest month of summer. A Charmer must approach while the beast is swimming, where it will assess the Charmer by circling them several times. At some point, it will dive beneath the surface and snare the Charmer's foot, dragging them into deep water. It's imperative that a Charmer does not resist. If they do, the beast will become irritated and either kill them or release them and flee. If the Charmer remains calm, it will continue to swim until it senses the Charmer's lungs giving out. At that point, it will leap out of the water and place the Charmer on the bank. Then, it will press its snout to their chest and use magic to coax any water from their lungs and encourage them to breathe. Now that the Charmer has become one with the water in its eyes, the Zystream is ready to be tamed.

CHARMER
COLOR QUIZ

There's a superstition that the rainbow of colors associated with a Charmer's magic can shed secret light on their personality. If that's true, what color would your Charmer's symbol be?

1. **What traits best describe you?**
   a. Eccentric and charismatic
   b. Family/friend-oriented and empathetic
   c. Curious and intelligent
   d. Free-spirited and intuitive
   e. Fair and adventurous
   f. Passionate and independent
   g. Down-to-earth and observant
   h. Detail-oriented and reliable
   i. Confident and loyal
   j. Open-minded and driven
   k. Hardworking and bold
   l. Self-reliant and dominant

2. **What weakness best describes you?**
   a. I've been known to be aloof and cold.
   b. I can be clingy, and it's hard for me to move on.
   c. I've been known to manipulate others to get my way.
   d. Moodiness is common for me.
   e. I avoid conflict and don't always stand up for myself.
   f. I'm impatient and can be impulsive.
   g. Jealousy has been known to get the best of me.
   h. I'm closed-off and overly critical.
   i. I can be dramatic and short-tempered.
   j. Sometimes, I'm blunt and insensitive.
   k. My stubbornness gets the best of me a lot.
   l. I'm unforgiving and mistrustful.

3. What is your favorite activity?

a. Visiting museums and learning new things

b. Hanging out with friends

c. Reading and writing

d. Taking naps or daydreaming

e. Playing an instrument

f. Playing with animals

g. Arts and crafts

h. Board games and cards

i. Sports or physical activities

j. Traveling and outdoor activities

k. Movies and video games

l. Spending time at home

4. What is your astrological sign?

a. Aquarius

b. Cancer

c. Gemini

d. Pisces

e. Libra

f. Aries

g. Taurus

h. Virgo

i. Leo

j. Sagittarius

k. Capricorn

l. Scorpio

5. What mythical creature calls to you?

a. Sphinx

b. Minotaur

  c. Griffin

  d. Unicorn

  e. Kitsune

  f. Chimera

  g. Phoenix

  h. Sea Serpent

  i. Dragon

  j. Mermaid

  k. Kraken

  l. Cerberus

6. **Pick a stone.**

  a. Citrine

  b. Amber

  c. Diamond

  d. Quartz

  e. Topaz

  f. Morganite

  g. Carnelian

  h. Emerald

  i. Ruby

  j. Sapphire

  k. Amethyst

  l. Obsidian

7. **What habit are you secretly guilty of?**

  a. I can be a bit of a flirt.

  b. I *love* matchmaking games.

  c. I'm not jittery, I'm just dancing. In place. With no music.

  d. I talk to myself out loud a *lot*.

  e. Superstitious? You mean well-prepared?!

f.   That's not clutter, just a pile of super-important mementos.

g.   I MUST TOUCH EVERYTHING.

h.   I have a system for literally everything. And *no one* can mess it up.

i.   Humiliating? Please. I love it when the whole restaurant sings me "Happy Birthday."

j.   I place a lot of faith in astrology.

k.   I'm so sarcastic that I don't know how *not* to be sarcastic.

l.   I enjoy people-watching and learning what makes others tick.

8. What job appeals to you most?

a.   Actor

b.   Teacher

c.   Architect

d.   Artist

e.   Diplomat

f.   Wildlife Biologist

g.   Chef

h.   Doctor

i.   Athlete

j.   Astronomer

k.   Engineer

l.   Lawyer

Results

If you answered mostly a…

Your Charmer's color is **yellow**! You have a vibrant personality and aren't afraid to be yourself. You're a people person who loves to learn, and you tend to be the life of the party. People love you!

If you answered mostly b...

Your Charmer's color is **brown**! You're a caring person with a heart of gold. Family and friends are incredibly important to you, and you're loyal to your core. You might also secretly be a fan of rom-coms, because you love a happy ending!

If you answered mostly c...

Your Charmer's color is **white**! You have a sharp mind and prefer quiet activities like reading and writing. You're great at planning ahead and prioritizing, and you consider all angles before rushing into a project.

If you answered mostly d...

Your Charmer's color is **silver**! You prefer your dreams to reality, and often find yourself picturing fantasy worlds different than your life. You're guided by your intuition and have a keen, artistic eye.

If you answered mostly e...

Your Charmer's color is **gold**! Ever the diplomat, you always listen to both sides of a story before weighing in. Your sense of adventure keeps you on the move, and you're not likely to put down roots anytime soon.

If you answered mostly f...

Your Charmer's color is **pink**! You're incredibly passionate and always stand up for what you believe in, even if you're the odd one out. You don't mind people, but prefer the unconditional love of animals and would do anything for them.

If you answered mostly g...

Your Charmer's color is **orange**! You're down-to-earth and practical, preferring to focus on the here and now. You're good with your hands, and love activities like crafting.

If you answered mostly h...

Your Charmer's color is **green**! You're extremely detail-oriented, to the point where plans aren't just preferred, they're vital. You value intelligence and love a good board game, especially if it involves strategy.

If you answered mostly i...

Your Charmer's color is **red**! You're not afraid of the spotlight—in fact, you welcome it! Your confidence is admirable, and you put your heart and soul into everything you do, which is why you often excel at sports.

If you answered mostly j...

Your Charmer's color is **blue**! You're open-minded and willing to entertain multiple perspectives, which makes you a great listener. When you set a goal, you see it through, no matter what.

If you answered mostly k...

Your Charmer's color is **purple**! Dedicated and hardworking, you're the type of person who will burn the candle at both ends to finish a project. You're smart, analytical, and likely to tear something apart just to see how it works.

If you answered mostly l...

Your Charmer's color is **black**! You're extremely self-reliant and tend to lead rather than follow along with the herd. While you prefer working alone, you love learning about what makes people tick.

ACKNOWLEDGMENTS

Tackling book two in this series was both exhilarating and difficult, but it would've been so much tougher if not for all the amazing support I received from friends and family. A big thanks to Lindsay Hess, Alexa Martin, Katie Golding, and Tricia Lynne for pushing my work to new heights, listening to my endless ramblings, and being general badasses.

Thank you to all the readers who fell in love with *Kingdom of Exiles*—I hope *The Frozen Prince* is everything you wanted it to be and more. Your reviews and kind words kept me going whenever I hit a bump in my draft or edits. You all rock.

And of course, a special thanks to my amazing agent, Cate Hart, my über-talented editor, Mary Altman, and the entire team at Sourcebooks. Because of you, my publishing journey has been incredible, and every day I'm humbled that you picked my book to share with the masses.

Finally, a big thank-you to my family. For supporting me no matter what, for babysitting my darling daughter so I could squeeze in a few words, for believing in me when I struggled to do that on my own. Mom, Dad, Chaz—you're the best relatives I could ever ask for. And to my husband, Jacob, thank you. Thank you for soothing my stressed-out nerves, for believing in me as a writer, and for being the best father to our newborn daughter. And to you, my sweet Remmy, I owe the biggest thanks. You've taught me so much in the short amount of time you've been here, and I can't wait to see you grow into an amazing person. Mommy loves you.

ABOUT THE AUTHOR

Maxym M. Martineau is an article and social media writer by day and a fantasy author by night. When she's not getting heated over broken hearts, she enjoys playing video games, sipping a well-made margarita, competing in just about any sport, and, of course, reading. She earned her bachelor's degree in English literature from Arizona State University and lives with her family in Arizona. Connect with her at MaxymMartineau.com or through Twitter and Instagram @maxymmckay.